Elaine
Enjoy the Story

Shameless

Book 2 in The Orphan Train Saga

Written by Sherry A. Burton

Shameless, The Orphan Train Saga Book 2 © Copyright 2019 by Sherry A. Burton

ISBN: 978-0-9983796-5-4

Published by Dorry Press

Edited and Formatted by BZHercules.com

Cover by Laura J. Prevost
www.laurajprevostbookcovers.myportfolio.com

For more information on the author and her works, please see www.SherryABurton.com

To the more than two hundred fifty thousand children who rode the orphan trains and their families who would not exist if not for their rider's inherent determination to survive.

Table of Contents

Chapter One

Magnifying glass in one hand and flashlight in the other, Cindy inched her way across the attic floor. While the attic had overhead lighting, the beam of the flashlight helped to illuminate smaller search areas.

Linda was on the opposite side of the room, mirroring her actions. "We've covered every inch of the floor at least a dozen times. Maybe they're not here."

Cindy had a sinking feeling her mother might be right. The X that marked the spot where they'd found her grandmother's journals was the only one they'd found. "Then why send us on a wild goose chase? You read the letter. It said the other journals are hidden in the attic."

Linda switched off her light and rubbed at her knees. "Maybe she dreamt it. She was getting on in years."

Cindy laughed. "Not likely. That woman had the mind of an owl. I don't think she ever forgot anything."

"Well, if it's all the same to you, I'm going to go down and start a load of laundry and figure out something for lunch," Linda said as she stood.

"Go ahead. I want to finish this section before I give up. The guys are coming to move the contents of the storage unit back up here on Friday. I just need to make sure I'm not missing anything before we cover the floors."

Linda shook her head. "I don't know why the woman didn't leave everything up here in the first place. Why go to the bother of having everything put in the unit if she knew you would bring it all back?"

"I don't think she knew. Besides, if she would have left it up here, I might not have found the clues that led me to her journals. Look how long it took me to decide to go through the storage unit. And we both know I only did that so I could stop paying rent on the thing. Where would the incentive have come from to go up in the attic and sort through things, especially at this time of the year? And you know I don't have time during the winter months with school and all."

"You have a point there. Let me know if you find anything."

Cindy continued to army crawl across the floor, shining her light and looking for the elusive Xs. Grandma Mildred was adamant that strangers not read the journals. She held the magnifying glass closer to the floor, thinking maybe Grandpa Howard had purposely made them smaller so that no one would stumble upon them by mistake. Her heart skipped a beat as the beam of light caught a mar in the wood. She sighed. Not an X but a small half-moon nick. An obvious flaw in the wood that she'd seen at least a dozen times before.

Cindy reached the wall and sighed her frustration. Linda was right; there were no Xs, no clues, and certainly no journals to be found. While she knew she should be happy with the sheer fact of finding her grandmother's journals, now that she'd gotten to know the other children, she was genuinely interested in how things had turned out for each of them. With one final glance over her shoulder, she descended the attic stairs and lifted them back into their resting place within the rafters of the ceiling.

"You look like a kid who struck out at home plate and lost the game," Linda said when Cindy entered the kitchen.

"Yeah, well, I kind of feel like a kid who went looking for hidden Christmas presents only to find a lump of coal. Only,

I didn't even find that."

"I think you need to find a bar of soap," Linda said when Cindy reached into the cabinet to get a glass.

Cindy sniffed at her armpits and grimaced. "Sorry. It's hot as Hades up there."

"Tell me about it. Who needs a gym membership? Just spend time in the attic and save a few dollars."

"Not doing either; reading is my cardio. I just wish we would have found something to read."

"Are you going back up?" Linda asked, filling Cindy's glass with fresh lemonade.

"No, I've had enough fun crawling around in the heat for today. I'm going to jump in the shower."

"Speaking of shower, that window seems to be leaking again. Why Howard insisted on having that little crescent window installed in that shower right after they moved in is beyond me. It doesn't even serve a purpose."

"I don't know. I guess it looks good from the street. I'll make some calls after I get out of the shower."

"It's not like it lets in much light," Linda said as she was leaving the room.

Cindy reached into the shower and turned on the water, eyeing the window as she did. Linda was right; the window didn't make sense. Why put in a half-moon window when a full moon would have added so much more light? It was the same as the north-facing window in the garden shed. What was it with Grandpa Howard and half-moons? Cindy reached to turn the water off, a flicker of hope rising over her like a child who'd just found the answer to a long-dwelled-upon math problem.

"Mom, could you please come in here?!" she called, trying unsuccessfully to keep her voice even.

Linda was there in an instant. "What is it?"

Cindy pointed at the window. "Maybe we were looking

for the wrong clue."

***

The little half-moon marks in the wood looked more intentional once they knew what to look for. Using the new clues, they'd uncovered sixteen wooden cases hidden in the recesses of both walls and floor, each mirroring the one that held Mildred's journals, including those from Grandpa (Paddy) Howard and Uncle Frank. Each box had both a number and name burned into the polished wood on the top, and all securely locked. The names coincided with the children Grandma Mildred had mentioned in her journal burned into the polished wood. All but one, which simply had the number eighteen. They'd tried the key belonging to Mildred's case to no avail. They were still looking for both the keys and the box with Tobias' name since Mildred had specifically mentioned it in her journal.

Linda patted the stack of wooden boxes that protected each set of journals. "Given the animosity between Tobias and Howard, I wouldn't be surprised if your grandfather didn't toss his in the trash."

"I have to admit to having the same thought, but I'm not ready to give up just yet," Cindy said, moving to the other side of the room.

"What are you looking over there for? We found all the others over here," Linda said, wiping the sweat from her brow.

"That's precisely why I'm looking over here. You said it yourself. Grandpa didn't like Tobias. Plus, think about it. Grandma has mentioned more than once that Tobias was not part of Mary's little gang. He was an outsider, so maybe Grandpa wanted to treat him like one."

"I never knew Howard to be one to hold a grudge, but it

4

makes sense that he would want to keep Tobias away from Mildred, even in death," Linda said, joining her.

"Can you blame him? I mean, the man drained the love right out of the woman. Took everything she had and left her with nothing to give to Grandpa," Cindy said sourly.

Linda turned from the wall she was searching. "Or you."

Cindy shrugged. "He led her into a life few could recover from."

"True, but what if what he said were true? If they had sent Mildred back on the trains, you would not be here. Tobias' death created the domino effect that followed."

Cindy wiped the sweat from her face. "You see what is happening here, don't you?"

Linda's brow wrinkled. "See what?"

"The total role reversal. You standing up for Mildred. I never saw that coming."

Linda's frown increased. "Huh. Imagine that. The old girl is probably turning over in her grave right now."

Cindy laughed. "You're probably right."

Linda looked up at the ceiling. "Yo, Millie, since we seem to have found some common ground, how about giving us a hand finding that last journal? Oh, and while you are at it, how about some keys so we don't have to trash Howard's handiwork by sawing open the boxes?"

Both women looked around as if they actually expected something to happen.

"Witch," Linda said when nothing did.

Cindy laughed and lowered to the floor. She got onto her knees, flashlight, and magnifying glass in hand. "Keep looking for anything out of the ordinary."

Linda turned her attention back to the wall she'd been searching. "Like?"

"Anything. Grandma Mildred's box was under an X.

Everyone else's was covered by a sliver of moon. If Howard wanted Tobias to be left out, he would have marked his spot by something different. Anything out of the ordinary. Like…"

"Like a mouse paw?!" Linda said, cutting her off. "This has to be it."

Cindy pushed to her feet, hurried to where her mother stood, and peered through the magnifying glass. Sure enough, a tiny rodent footprint was carved into the wood just below where the wall met the ceiling.

Cindy traced a finger over the tiny print. "He sure didn't want that one found, did he?"

"If Mildred hadn't mentioned it, I don't think we would have thought to look."

Cindy retrieved the cordless screwdriver and loosened the screws that held the planks in place.

"It makes sense now," Linda muttered with a flourish of the hands.

"What does?"

"The way this attic is pieced together. Howard never asked for help when he was doing the planking up here. Given Howard was a master carpenter, your father was appalled when he first saw how his father had spliced the room together. Nothing, including the flooring, lined up. Howard had used every piece of scrap wood he could find, insisting he was too cheap to buy new boards for a room no one would ever see. Your father actually lost sleep over it, thinking his dad was suffering some kind of dementia or something. It turns out the man had more forethought than any of us put together. Look at how he was able to hide all the journals so that none of us had a clue."

"I've got it," Cindy said, removing the final board. She dislodged the box, carefully pulling it from its hiding place. There was no name on the box. However, when she turned it over, she saw the wood was etched with a small, perfectly carved mouse. Above the mouse was the number two.

"At least Howard didn't carve out a rat," Linda said, peering over her shoulder.

"This is true," Cindy agreed. She handed the box to Linda, picked up a plank, and returned it to the wall as she had done with each board they had removed thus far, marking each hiding spot with an X in white chalk. It was Cindy's idea, adding that she planned to take photos so she could share with her classroom during a history project she was forming in her head. It would be a fun way to tell the children about the orphan trains. She'd returned all the planks but one when she sighed. "I think I am going to be sick."

"Heat stroke?" Linda's voice was full of concern.

"Worse." Cindy turned the board so that her mother could see the key mounted to the back of the plank. "We are going to have to unscrew every board we have returned today just to find the rest of the keys."

Linda's face went white. "I don't think I have it in me today."

Cindy studied her mom for a moment. Over the last week since finding the initial journals, Linda's color had returned, and there was a sparkle in her eyes Cindy had not seen since her father died. While Cindy herself had not yet experienced the kind of love her parents shared, she had felt an enormous loss as she watched the lights slowly dim in her mother's eyes. For the first time since her father's passing, her mother had found something that excited her. And that something pulled her from the darkness Cindy was unable to reach. That in itself was the answer to a long-awaited prayer.

"That's okay, Mom. Now that I know where to look, it shouldn't take long."

Linda smiled. "That Howard was a real card, wasn't

he?"

Cindy closed her eyes briefly. "I can think of other things to call him right about now."

Linda shot her a look. "What would Uncle Frank have to say about that?"

Cindy sighed once more. "He would warn me not to speak ill of the dead."

"Yes, but I think he'd also agree with you on this one." Linda picked up the box with the mouse, added a couple more to the pile, and started for the stairs. "I'll take these down and come back for more."

"Hang on. I have a better idea," Cindy said, taking the stack from her mother. "You go down to the bottom, and I'll hand them down to you. That way, neither of us has to carry them down the steep steps."

Linda nodded. "You always were the smart one in the family."

"I get it from my mother," Cindy replied. She waited for Linda to reach the bottom of the stairs and passed the journal boxes down one at a time.

"This should be the last one if I counted correctly," Linda said, reaching for the box.

"It is," Cindy said softly.

Her mother's eyes went wide. "You sound disappointed. Aren't you tired?"

Cindy laughed. "Of course I am. This is the most I've exercised in years. It's just that, in the scheme of things, this all seems so insignificant. From what I've read, there were over two hundred and fifty thousand children sent out on the orphan trains. Most schools don't even cover this. We've got eighteen journals. What happened to the other children? Who's going to tell their stories?"

Linda was quiet for a moment. "What was that saying

your Uncle Frank used to tell you when you got all stressed out about something?"

Cindy pictured Uncle Frank kneeling to her level, pushing the hair from her eyes and, when necessary, handing her a tissue to wipe the tears. "He would ask me how do you eat an elephant."

Linda smiled. "And what was the answer?"

Cindy returned her smile. "One bite at a time."

"That's right. He always said not to get ahead of yourself, that things always have a way of working themselves out. You're the teacher in the family. Start with the journals we have and see where they take you. Sound like a plan?"

"No what?" Linda asked when Cindy shook her head.

"No, you are the smart one in the family. Leave those there, and I'll move them when I'm finished."

"Well, I am definitely smart enough not to argue with that. Hang on a sec," Linda said and disappeared from sight. She returned a few seconds later, reaching up to deliver a cold bottle of water. "I'm going to drum up something for dinner. If you need anything, stomp on the floor."

"Mom?"

"Yes?"

"It's nice to have you back."

Linda's eyes moistened. "It's good to be back."

Chapter Two

Freshly showered, Cindy sat on the couch in the front room, pushing ribbons through the ends of the keys she'd found.

"Mission accomplished," she said, tying the final ribbon to the ornate skeleton key. While she'd managed to find all seventeen keys, her task was made harder than necessary when she hadn't found the keys at the same time as the box each opened. Once found, she and her mother had set about the arduous task of matching each key to the appropriate box. This task was hindered by the fact that Linda had opened a bottle of blackberry wine to celebrate finding the journals. At long last, each key now had a numbered ribbon that coincided with a number on the box showing which order the journals should be read. The locked cases were now stacked in three piles on the cedar chest. They'd placed towels between each wooden case to ensure against scratches.

"At least she took the time to number the journals in the order of which she thought they should be read," Linda said, watching as Cindy threaded the keys onto a large brass ring.

"True. It just surprises me that Grandma Mildred picked Tobias to be next and not Grandpa. Seriously, look where she placed the man. It makes me wonder if she ever even felt anything for Grandpa."

"Well, Tobias was Mildred's first husband. And according to your grandmother's letters, it was your grandfather who made the boxes. I would think he knew what was inside.

Surely he'd have said something if he had a problem with the order the journals were to be read. Besides, look at the trouble they both went to, to see they were preserved."

Cindy groaned. "Trouble is an understatement."

Linda took a sip of wine. "Are you sure it's necessary to read the journals in order? It's not like she would know if you didn't."

Cindy sighed. "I'm not sure of anything anymore. At this point, I'm not even sure you're my real mother."

Linda laughed. "Have you looked in the mirror lately?"

"Not enough proof. Grandpa Howard had the same red hair as Dad, and they are not related."

Linda pulled up her top to expose a thick scar that traveled the length of her stomach. "What do you think came out of this, a space alien? I can show you my stretch marks if that would help convince you."

Cindy put up her hand to stop her. "Okay, I accept you as my mother."

Linda lowered her shirt. "Why, that's mighty nice of you."

"Is Paul really my father?"

A sly grin crossed her mother's face. "Yes. Would you like to hear the details of your conception?"

"Eww no. I just want to know where I came from. Then again, I won't, will I? Because we don't even know where Paul came from. I can't believe Dad lied to me."

Linda's smile faded. "Is it really considered a lie if it's never spoken?"

"I can't believe you're not upset about this."

"Is getting upset going to change anything? So your father had a past he didn't want to talk about. Does that make him a bad person? Is he any less your father just because he was adopted? Come on, Cindy, tell your mom what is really

11

troubling you."

Leave it to her mom to get her off her high horse. "It's just that I find this all so fascinating. I would have loved for them to tell me their stories. Not just in the journals, but in person. I have so many questions…"

"And we have more journals. Maybe our questions will be answered when we read them."

Cindy raised her eyebrows. "Our questions."

"Sure. I have questions too, a lot of them. But not knowing the answers will never take away the love I have for your father. He was a good man. And a very good father to you. Promise me you won't let your anger destroy your memories of him."

Her mother was right. No matter what she found or didn't find, Paul was a great father. "I promise."

Linda sat her wine glass on the end table and leaned forward, fingers caressing the wooden box containing Tobias' journals. "So, are you ready to see what that Tobias fellow was really up to?"

Cindy shook her head. "No can do. We haven't copied the journal pages yet."

Linda sat back in her chair. "Oh poo. I knew you were going to say that."

Cindy's phone chimed, advising of a new e-mail. She noticed the sender, *Gravedigger59@yahoo.com,* and smiled.

"What is it?"

"It's from Gravedigger."

Linda arched an eyebrow. "Who?"

"Remember Becky from school? Her brother is into genealogy. I asked her to see if he could find any information on that couple that almost took Grandma from the train."

Linda leaned forward once more. "The Shivelys? What did he say?"

"Hang on; I haven't opened it." Cindy clicked on the e-mail and waited for it to open, then read it aloud. "Cindy, it took some doing, but I'm ninety-nine percent sure I found the couple in question. I found a Stewart and Sonia Shively living in Chicago, Illinois during the time you mentioned. Sonia Griffin was born 1886 to well-known architects with ties to Frank Lloyd Wright. A member of Chicago's high society, Sonia married Stewart Shively in 1904. I am not sure if this is important, but I have not been able to find this Stewart guy prior to their wedding. It is like he was dropped off by aliens or something. (Let me know if his beginnings are important and I will dig deeper.) In searching through Newspapers.com, I see mentions of the couple at galas, charity events, and Christmas parties, both as hosts and guests over the years. Lucky for us, the world was starved for news, and everything was well-documented in the society column of the *Chicago Tribune*. Give me enough time, and I will tell you what they had for breakfast on their wedding day.

"Anyway, the exciting thing is I actually found mention of the couple returning from a trip to New York in October of 1924. So if there were any question of this being the right couple, I think that pretty much sews things up. The article quoted the wife as having been on some kind of shopping trip and complaining they'd had to return so quickly, they had to ride with the lower class. She goes on to say that her husband Stewart's wallet was stolen on the train and blamed it on one of the street urchins, saying they should stone the kid. Try publishing that in the newspaper these days and see what kind of reaction you'd get.

"After the trip, I found more meet and greets, and it looks like things slowed down after 1929. That makes sense, as that was the beginning of the Great Depression.

"Now Sonia falls off the planet in 1931. I mean, she's

gone. No obituary. No notice the woman had gone missing. Nothing. I was able to follow Stewart when I picked him up again in 1932 for failure to pay a debt. A hotel filed a lawsuit saying he'd run up a huge debt and were suing him for $2623. The paper quoted Stewart as denying ever staying at the hotel. There were no other mentions until I found his obituary in 1933. There was a short article a few days later saying he died of 'mysterious circumstances.' But I couldn't find any follow-up information. I know you didn't ask for all the backstory into their lives, but, hey, it's what I do. I didn't see any mention of any children in any of the articles. I hope this helps. Let me know if you need anything else. Bruce," Cindy said, finishing the e-mail. She closed out the email and let out a disappointed sigh. "It seems as though the more we find out, the more we do not know."

"Well, at least we know they didn't have any children," Linda offered.

"It doesn't mean they didn't have servants he could have … bothered."

Linda took in a breath. "Well, that's putting it mildly."

"Yes, well, I didn't want to offend you."

Linda chuckled. "Thank you for protecting my delicate ears. Who do you think killed him?"

"What makes you think someone killed him? He could have had a heart attack." Cindy regretted her words as soon as she said them.

Linda shook her head. "No, the email said he died under mysterious circumstances."

Cindy slid a glance towards her mother, surprised her slip hadn't reduced the woman to tears. She wanted to say as much but decided to leave well enough alone. "Maybe Sonia didn't disappear. Maybe she was hiding. Maybe she had something to do with his death. Unfortunately, it looks like we'll never find out."

Linda pulled Tobias' journal into her lap. "Do you know what we can find out? We can know the secrets this little mouse was keeping from Mildred. Tell me you aren't the least bit curious."

Cindy laughed. "Curious is an understatement."

"Then we can read some of it before bed?" Linda splayed her fingers and brushed them across the smooth wooden box as if she were a model showing the next prize to bid on.

Cindy held her ground. "Not until we Xerox it so we're not reading over each other's shoulder."

"Pretty please," Linda said and stuck out her bottom lip to form a pout.

Cindy gave her mom a look normally reserved for her students. "I'm a third-grade teacher, Mom. I've seen it all before. Your begging is lost on me."

Linda pulled in her lip.

"Yes, but have any of your students ever offered to buy you a steak dinner at The Vault? Or elk sliders at the Brewery? What about a quesadilla from Benchwarmers? You know they have the good ranch," her mother said, playing on Cindy's weakness for food.

"Betrayed by my own body," Cindy replied when her stomach answered for her. She picked up the brass ring and found the key marked by a number two and handed it to her mother. She watched as Linda took the key and slid it into the lock, smiling when it turned. Her eyes twinkled when the key opened the box. Cindy's heart swelled at seeing her mother's joy. That reaction was even more gratifying than the previous offer of food. She thought about expressing that thought, but the lure of said food kept her silent.

Linda lifted the lid to expose the same white cloth that

lined Mildred's case. A thin strip of leather held it securely in place. Linda's fingers trembled as she fiddled with the knot. "I'm so excited, I can't even get a grip on it."

"Need some help?" Cindy asked, knowing the offer would be rejected.

"No, I almost got it. There it goes," Linda said after three more tries. She lifted the fabric, exposing a stack of what they knew to be journals, each individually wrapped in white tissue paper. On top of the stack lay a soft pink envelope. Cindy's name was printed on front in her grandmother's handwriting.

"Too bad your grandmother didn't have this much to say to you when she was alive," Linda said, handing her the envelope.

"I was just thinking the same thing." Cindy opened the envelope and pulled out a loose paper. Unfolding it, she confirmed it to be written in her grandmother's hand. "Grandma Mildred had such lovely handwriting. Look at that scroll; penmanship is such a lost art."

"Save the lecture for your classroom and tell me what it says," Linda scolded.

"Which is precisely why we will not open the journals until we are ready to copy them," Cindy said, lowering the sheet of paper.

"I'm sorry," Linda said, pretending to zip her lips shut.

"Mother, you would fit right in with the kids I teach." Before Linda could respond, Cindy started reading.

"*Dear Cynthia,*

These notebooks contain my Tobias' story. While he technically was not a member of Mary's little gang, he did come over on the orphan trains, and so I asked him to document what he could remember from his life. I do not know why I felt this so important; maybe I felt his story needed to be told. Or just maybe it was merely because I knew he kept secrets from me and I wanted to know what they were. I smirk as I write this because I never actually finished reading them myself. I made it partway through before the pain of his untruths took their toll. After reading his words, my life was never the same. My trust never again earned.

I considered destroying these notebooks—it would have been easier just to move on and forget—but if you are reading this now, you must know that never happened.

My Tobias was not a book-learned man, but you will see in his writings he was not only smart but also a brilliantly resourceful man. It takes a smart man to stay alive on the streets for as long as he did. Especially considering the company he kept. I've heard the term 'dog eat dog world' all my life. After reading Tobias' words, I am sure you will agree that phrase pretty much sums up the world Tobias lived in. I guess this note is my way of apologizing for the man who stole my love, but God help me, I did love that man. Promise me you will keep an open mind and realize this was not the world you live in. This was the place preachers warn of during Sunday congregation. A place where sinners lurk and demons prey upon the innocent.

M."

"Your grandmother seems to have had a flair for the dramatics," Linda said, rubbing her arms.

"Yes, who'd have thought? Too bad she was too damaged to let me in. I think I would have liked the woman," Cindy said, returning the letter to the envelope. "You know, while the promise of food sounds intriguing, I think I'd prefer to wait until we copy these before we start reading."

"I think maybe you're right," Linda agreed.

"Wow, I must admit I didn't think you would give in so easily."

Linda laughed. "Sometimes I even manage to surprise

myself. Now let's go get something to eat. We can be more productive on a full stomach."

"Do I need my purse?"

"Of course."

"I thought you said you were buying."

"I'm buying; you're paying," Linda replied with a snort.

It was a saying she'd heard many times over the years, but the words had always been those of her father. It was said with humor then and sounded funny coming from the woman who'd spent the last few years in tears with even a mention of Paul's name. Cindy lifted her gaze to the ceiling and said a silent thank you to Grandma Mildred. All the love the woman couldn't give while alive was radiating from the letters she'd left, and in turn, slowly helping to heal the hearts of those left behind.

Chapter Three

Cindy woke early, hoping to get a start on copying the journals while her mother slept.

Linda's bedroom door was open. Cindy peeked inside the empty room and shook her head. So much for letting the woman sleep in. The house was quiet except for the birdsong that drifted in through the open windows. The kitchen was empty, but the smell of coffee greeted her like a warm hug the second she entered the room. She poured a cup, added some vanilla creamer, and took a sip, moaning with delight as the sugary blend slid down her throat. She was nearly halfway through the cup when Linda breezed through the door.

"I picked up some cinnamon rolls from Sugartown Sweets."

Cindy marveled at her mother's cheerfulness. "Do you ever sleep?"

"Not since I hit menopause," Linda quipped, setting the box down.

Cindy plucked a cinnamon roll from the box, took a bite, and emitted another moan. "What about the sleeping pills the doctor gave you?"

"Oh, I stopped taking them a few days ago. They were making me put on weight."

"You don't think the weight could have been from poor eating choices?" Cindy said, eyeing the bakery box.

Linda frowned at the box. "Of course, but I'd rather give up sleeping pills than food."

"Yeah, maybe we should revisit our diets and look for some healthier choices on Pinterest," Cindy suggested.

Linda pulled out a cinnamon roll, scraped some icing off with her finger, and deposited it into the box. "There, see, I'm making smarter choices already. I'm going to grab Tobias' journals so we can get to work copying them."

Cindy waited for her mother to round the corner, added the discarded icing to her own roll, and took a bite. Smart eating choices had never been her strong suit. If temptation was near, temptation won out. She made a mental note to show her mother how to use Pinterest before the day was over.

Linda was already busy feeding the journal pages through the copier when Cindy joined her. She smiled and nodded at the stack of papers lying beside the printer.

"Just what time did you get up this morning?" Cindy asked, noticing that most of the journals had already been copied.

"My eyes popped open at four forty-five," Linda said, nodding toward the wooden box on the table beside the printer. "There was a letter lying loose just inside the first journal. It's in the box. I promised I would wait for you, so I didn't read it."

Cindy picked up the letter and began reading aloud.

"Dear Mileta,

I know you don't like to be called that, but that is the name your mother gave you, and I call you that now to honor her. You asked me to write this since I too came over on the trains. We never really spoke of the trains so I am not sure what their importance is here, but since you seem to think it means something, I will tell you my story. I've asked you not to read this until after I am gone. I pray you honored my wishes. If not, you will see how truly ugly my soul is. But while my soul is black, my love for you has been nothing but pure. Before I go any further, I will now apologize for the things I kept from you.

I pray you will find it in yourself to understand my motives and forgive me for my untolds. Is that even a word? If not, it should be, because I do not think of them as untruths. I think of them as untolds. I always tried to tell you the truth, even if the rest of the story remained untold.

Some people call themselves Italian, Irish, English, or Polish. Or they may identify more with their religion: Catholic, Protestant, or Jewish. While being Polish and Jewish is what has gotten me to where I am, it is not truly who I am. My life, as well as my name, is an illusion, one created out of desperation to ensure my survival and one I shared with you to offer the same protection. My true, or birth name is Tobias Alphers Millett. While some people refer to us street kids as street urchins or street Arabs, I prefer street rat.

With a few exceptions, I've been on the street for as long as I can remember, so my voice is that of the street. And, My Love, since I know that one day you will see me for who I really am, I will try and remember that in my writing. While you may know the tale, I will attempt to shield your eyes from the blood and gore and the language used by my kind. So without further apologies, here is my story. " Cindy peered over the letter to gauge her mother's reaction.

"No wonder Mildred didn't get far in her reading."

Cindy swallowed. "The only two things he ever gave her in life were lies. The spoon was stolen, and his name, the one they gave to their daughter, was a lie."

"I'm sure he had a good reason." Though Linda said the words, her tone didn't seem to agree. She shoved the last of the paper into the copier and waited for the machine to spit out copies. Once finished, she handed one pile to Cindy. "Where do you want to do this?"

"Living room?" Cindy said, realizing her mother did not intend to read alone.

"Lead the way," Linda said, hugging the journals to her chest.

Settled onto the sofa, each took a small stack of papers and began to read, the story coming to life at once.

***

Late September, 1914

The sound of breaking glass shattered the silence. Seconds later, Tobias cringed as his father's voice boomed his displeasure, chastising Tobias' mother for her clumsiness. He scurried behind a tattered chair in an attempt to put as much distance between himself and his father as possible, knowing any movement would subject him to his father's wrath. It wouldn't be long before his sister Anastasia came for him, shuffling him and his brother Ezra out of the house as she'd done so many times before. The shouting intensified, and Tobias whimpered as a shadow crossed in front of his hiding spot. He looked past the shadow, saw his mother kneeling to pick up the pieces of broken glass, and whimpered as his father raised his arm, moving closer to his mother.

Anastasia replaced the shadow. She grasped Tobias' hand, motioning for Ezra to follow. The three of them crept across the room as she led the way to the front door.

Once in the hallway, Tobias watched as Anastasia paused, her thin fingers lingering on the doorknob. She sucked in air as their mother screamed, then slowly pulled the door closed. She pulled her hand free of his and placed a finger to her lips, warning them to be quiet. Tobias nodded, knowing full well the danger that lurked behind that closed door.

Anastasia reached for his hand, which he willingly gave, sighing as she wrapped her fingers tightly around his. She moved quickly, and he struggled to keep up as she led the way down the stairs and out the front of their building. He wanted to ask where they were going, but in truth, he didn't care. Anything was better than staying inside listening to his mother's screams.

Anastasia released their hands only after they'd exited the building. He and Ezra followed as she led them through the alley, down two side streets, and onto the bustling street where the food carts lined both sides, vendors shouting for people to come and buy what they were selling.

"What shall we have for breakfast?" Anastasia asked, kneeling in front of them.

"Apples," both brothers shouted at once.

She smiled and touched the side of each boy's face. She pulled the ribbon from her hair, ran her fingers through the long, dark strands, and then replaced the fringed ribbon. "Apples it is. But I need you both to do something for me."

"What kind of something?" Ezra didn't seem pleased.

"What kind of something?" Tobias parroted.

Anastasia stood, searching from side to side. Finding what she was looking for, she smiled. "See those steps over there?"

"Yes." The boys nodded.

"I want both of you to go sit on the top step and wait for me to come for you."

"But what about our breakfast?" Tobias groaned.

"I'm going to get you the apples, but you need to wait here. Don't move until I come for you, promise?"

"Promise," Tobias said, nodding his head.

"You too," Anastasia said, looking at Ezra.

Ezra sighed. "Yes, I will stay."

Anastasia kissed them each on the cheek before leaving.

Tobias moved to the top of the stairs and watched as Anastasia crossed the street, made her way to the apple cart, and stood looking at the red, green, and yellow bounty in front of her. When the apple man was busy bagging apples for a lady standing next to Anastasia, his sister turned to chat with the woman. When Anastasia pointed down the street, the lady shook her head and pointed in the opposite direction. Tobias' stomach rumbled as Anastasia moved closer to the woman, pointing in the same direction. As she did so, she reached out with her free hand and pocketed three bright red apples, one at a time. She smiled at the lady then moved in the direction they had pointed. Moments later, he saw his sister hurrying down the dirt sidewalk towards where they sat. As she approached, she handed each boy an apple, and sitting beside them, pulled one out for herself.

"You forgot to pay for the apples," Tobias chided.

"I couldn't pay. I had no money," Anastasia said between bites.

Tobias frowned. "Father will be mad."

Anastasia turned towards him and narrowed her dark eyes. "If you tell Father, I will never bring you with me again, do you understand?"

"But what if the apple man would've caught you?" Tobias asked.

Anastasia took another bite. "I know how to be careful. The man won't catch me."

Tobias didn't like her answer. "But what if he did catch you?"

Anastasia sighed. "Then I would give him something to keep him from being mad."

"What kind of something would you give?"

His sister sighed once more. "I would give him something only girls have to give."

"What kind of something?" Tobias pestered.

"She would kiss him," Ezra said with a snicker.

Tobias wiped the juice from his chin and licked it from his grubby hand. "A kiss is better than money?"

"Sometimes it is." Anastasia took another bite of apple and tossed the core onto the street. "What shall we do today?"

"You'll teach us how to steal apples," Ezra said, dropping his core off the side of the porch.

"I will do no such thing." Anastasia rose and started to leave the stoop.

Ezra caught hold of the hem of her dress to stop her. "But you will."

She slapped his hand. "And why would I do that?"

Ezra rubbed at his hand. "Because if you don't, I will tell Father what you did, and he will beat you with the belt again."

Tobias watched as his siblings bickered. He had felt his father's belt many times and couldn't understand why Ezra would purposely do anything to make his father use it on their sister. Apparently, Anastasia was as terrified of being hit by the belt as he, because she quickly consented to show them how to steal apples.

"Okay, I'll show you, but you'll need to do as I say. Understand?"

The boys nodded their agreement. At ten years old, Anastasia was older and presumed smarter.

"First, you need to wait until there is someone else at the cart. That will keep the apple man busy. Then you step up as quietly as possible, so the apple man does not notice you. You will take the apple and be gone before he even knows you are there."

Tobias thought of the little mouse that frequented their apartment, sneaking in and stealing scraps of bread and cheese before anyone could stop him.

"Quiet like a mouse?" he asked.

Anastasia smiled. "That's right, Tobias; I want you to be quiet as a mouse. Just remember, no squeaking. You're going to walk very softly, take the apple, and hurry along before anyone sees you. That goes for you too," she said, looking at his brother. "After you get the apple, hurry down the street that way. Circle behind the food carts and hurry back to this spot. Wait for me and then we'll all go home together. Understand?"

Ezra nodded, and Tobias did the same.

"I will go first and talk to the apple man to distract him. Once he is talking to me, take your apples and do as I told you."

Fear crept over him. "What if the apple man sees me?"

"You're four years old. He will not see you unless you forget to be quiet as a mouse. Remember, Tobias; you're a mouse and mice are very quiet."

"I'm a mouse," Tobias repeated.

"Okay, we will all start walking together, and then I will move ahead. Once I'm talking to the apple man, you do what I said. Ezra, you're older, and I expect you to watch over your brother."

"I will." His brother promised.

"Do not let him out of your sight. If he gets in trouble, you come back and get him." Anastasia's voice was firm.

Doubt crossed Ezra's face. "Where will you be?"

"I'll be talking to the apple man. But if I'm delayed, I want you two to go back home. Do you remember how to get there?"

Tobias thought that to be a strange question, as they all knew how to get to the market. It was something they did on a daily basis during outings with their mother.

"Don't be stupid I'm not a baby," Ezra bristled.

Anastasia smiled. She stooped to look Ezra in the eye. "I didn't say you were a baby. You are six years old and are a smart fellow. I want you to promise me that you'll see to it that your brother makes it home if I'm delayed. Can you do that for me, Ezra? Can you watch over your little brother when I'm not around to do it?"

Ezra shrugged and nodded his head. "Sure I can."

Anastasia stood and patted Ezra on the head. "Good. Now follow me and do not take your apple until you see that I have the apple man's attention."

Anastasia held Tobias' hand until they neared the apple cart. Tobias felt a gentle squeeze before she released his hand, and without looking backward, walked towards the apple cart. For a brief moment, he wanted to yell at her and tell her to stop, but she was older and probably wouldn't listen if he had. The apple man frowned as she approached. Anastasia whispered something they could not hear, and the man's lips turned upward. Anastasia moved to the other side of the cart, and the man moved closer to where she was standing. With his attention focused on their sister, the boys made their move.

"Come on, Tobias," Ezra said, tugging at his shirt.

"I'm not Tobias. I'm a mouse," Tobias said, following.

"Okay, Mouse, come on. You'll get caught if you don't hurry," his bother scolded. Ezra reached the cart first. He had a bright green apple in his hand and was putting it in his pocket just as Tobias reached for an apple of his own.

"Not that one," Ezra whispered as Tobias pulled one from the bottom of the pile.

Too late, Tobias pulled his prize free, and the pile began to shift, several toppling from the cart in quick succession, landing on the hard dirt in four quick thuds. Ezra caught hold of Tobias' arm and pulled him in the opposite direction. As they were racing off, Tobias heard his sister yell for them to keep running. The boys ran for several moments before Ezra looked over his shoulder and slowed.

"Ya goof, you nearly got us caught," Ezra scoffed.

"What were you thinking taking the apple from the bottom anyhow?"

Tobias felt his lips tremble. "I couldn't reach any higher. Where's Anastasia?"

Ezra looked past him. "Let's go find out. Stand behind me and don't do anything stupid."

He didn't know what kind of stupid thing Ezra didn't want him to do, but he followed anyway.

Ezra crossed to the opposite side of the road and kept behind the carts that lined that side of the street. When they reached the stoop where they had sat earlier, Ezra pointed. "You go up there and wait. I'll go check on Sister."

Tobias wanted to object to being left alone but decided against it. Taking his apple, he climbed to the top of the stairs and watched as Ezra pocketed his apple and casually walked towards the apple cart. A few moments passed before Ezra came running in his direction, motioning for him to follow. Tobias scampered from his resting place and raced to where his brother stood.

Ezra's face seemed to have lost its color. But what concerned Tobias the most was that his brother's eyes were brimmed with tears. Wiping away the moisture, Ezra choked back a sob. "Anastasia, she's gone."

Chapter Four

Cindy looked up from her reading to see Linda staring at her. "Yes?"

"I knew that Anastasia girl was trouble. Kissing men at ten years old. And just look what she did to that poor innocent brother of hers. If not for her bad influence, he probably would have been a good kid," Linda speculated.

Cindy nodded to the next stack of papers. "Do you want to debate things or read?"

Linda pulled the next stack from her pile. "Read now, discuss later."

Following her mother's lead, Cindy picked up the next set of journals and began reading until she was there watching the events unfold.

Early May, 1915

While I do not recall my parents, I do recall their anger: the screaming, fighting, and physical abuse that was the norm in that early life. After Anastasia disappeared, my brother, Ezra, took the brunt of my parents' wrath. It was he who woke me from my sleep one dark, foggy night and set the wheels in motion for the path I now find myself on. I resisted at first. There had been such chaos in the house that day, and I had not fallen asleep until late. I was tired and wanted to stay in bed. Ezra insisted I wake and whispered the four words I've never forgotten even after all these years.

"Papa has killed Momma."

Those words got me moving, that's for certain. I was up and dressed in seconds. I remember Ezra shaking the pillow from my pillowcase and stuffing the case with clothes from our dresser. He'd already packed for himself before waking me. He told me to be quiet, and I followed as he tiptoed through the front room towards the main door. Ezra opened the door and pushed me into the hallway. He told me to wait there, and when I resisted, he said he would keep the door open so that I could see. He said that he was going back to get a hunk of cheese for our morning breakfast. I watched as he unwrapped the cloth and used the knife to saw off a hunk of cheese. Then, before he had a chance to put the knife down, Papa appeared, drunk as always and screaming at Ezra for stealing food. He had Ezra by the arm and Ezra was fighting to get loose. Papa punched Ezra in the face and Ezra stabbed him in the stomach with the knife. It all happened so fast. Ezra screamed for me to run and never look back. That time, I did as I was told. I was but five years old, and it was the last time I saw my papa or Ezra. I'm sorry to say that I do not know whatever happened to my brother Ezra. I'm not sorry to say I do not know, or care, whether my dad lived or died that day.

***

Tobias ran from the building and was instantly met with darkness. However, it wasn't the darkness that frightened him, but the thick blanket of fog that hovered in the air. A damp netting surrounded him as he rushed out into the night. In his haste, he forgot to turn and veered just before running into the tall brick building he'd not been able to see only seconds before. He slowed his pace but continued to move forward, frightened not only of the fog but of inhabitants that could be heard but not seen. The fog reminded him of the steam that rose from the many vents in the city. Only the fog was everywhere, and he could not run through it to get to the other side. He heard voices drifting about the fog and trembled. He'd seen fog before, but he'd never had to face it alone. Still, he was more afraid of what his papa would do to him if he caught up with him, so he kept moving forward. He thought he was lost but then realized instinct had taken him to where he often traveled with his mother and his brother. As he remembered his brother's words, a tear slid down his cheek. He didn't want to believe that his momma was dead, but if Ezra said it was true, he believed him. Ezra didn't lie. An image of his brother came to mind, replaying the way the knife Ezra had slid into his papa's belly easier than it had torn through the hardened hunk of cheese. Without warning, his stomach lurched, sending its contents flying. The single tear was replaced by a steady stream.

He spit to clear the vile taste from his mouth, wiped at his nose with the end of the pillowcase, and cursed at the tears that continued to fall. He half-expected to feel a hand strike a blow as the words slipped past his trembling lips. When nothing happened, he repeated the words and added a few more for good measure. The tears ebbed as he felt empowered by the toxicity of the forbidden words.

Somehow he made his way to where the vendor carts were supposed to be, but the street was mostly empty. Behind him, a man's voice bellowed in the distance. Fear propelled him forward. He saw a shadowy shape and squinted to see past the fog. He caught sight of a wagon and sighed. There were no horses attached, but as he neared, he saw the wagon was surrounded by bales of hay. He pulled at a bale until he had an opening large enough to squeeze through then ducked under, intending to hide until the fog lifted. The moment he stopped, he knew he was not alone. The smell of sweat and unwashed bodies invaded his nostrils. He tried to stay quiet, but fear won out as he felt fingers grasp hold of his leg. He screamed, and the hand let go of the leg, covering his mouth instead.

"Silence that yap of yours before you get us all tossed in jail with the murderers and rapists." The voice was firm but seemed more concerned than angry.

Tobias squelched his fear and nodded his agreement. He breathed a sigh of relief when the hand lifted.

"You are welcome to stay under here if you can remain quiet. The night is much too dangerous to roam the streets. With fog this thick, we wouldn't be able to see anyone until they were right upon us. What is your name, boy? You are a boy, right?"

Of course he was a boy, but then the voice would not know that, as it was too dark to see. "Yes, I'm a boy."

"Your name, then?" the voice said when Tobias hesitated.

"Mouse." Of course it was not his real name, but he didn't know who was asking and was afraid if he told his real name, they would take him back to his papa.

"Better a mouse than a rat," the voice said in reply.

Tobias waited for further conversation, but there was none. As he sat there, he felt his eyes grow heavy until exhaustion won and he drifted into an uneasy sleep. Sometime later, the dreams began. *He ran through the fog calling for his sister. "Anastasia! Where are you? I know you are out here somewhere. I don't know what has happened to the family. Papa is mad, and I can't go home." A muffled voice called his name. Not the one his parents bestowed upon him, but the one given to him by his sister. Mouse.*

"Yo, Mouse, time to get moving," the voice called more urgently.

Tobias opened his eyes, blinking to orient himself. Daylight drifted in through the cracks between the hay bales as the mixture of damp hay and unwashed bodies pulled at his senses. Suddenly, the events of the previous evening came flooding back. Instantly, he was fully awake, crouched on his heels and ready to bolt.

"Didn't I tell you the boy has some grit?"

Tobias recognized the voice from the previous evening. Turning, he could just make out the face that went with it. The boy looked to be several years older than he. Although his hair was neatly cut, that was the only thing neat about him. Shadows surrounded the boy's eyes, his clothes hung from his body in tattered shreds, and he emitted a smell bad enough to make a five-year-old take notice. He was just about to mention the odor when a second voice drew his attention. He turned to his left and saw another boy he hadn't realized was there.

"He's quick on his feet, but that doesn't mean we should let him in. He's just a kid," the second boy sneered.

The first boy laughed. "So were you when I brought you in."

The second boy snorted. "We're the same age."

"Yes, but we're older now and wiser. Besides, the kid would be a great distraction."

Tobias wasn't sure what was going on, but something told him to remain quiet until things were settled.

The boy to his left was just as grubby as the first, and when he spoke, Tobias could see he was missing several teeth. The boy tilted his head in his direction and Tobias was shocked to see he was also missing a good chunk of his left ear. Tobias gasped and the boy lifted a hand to his ear.

"What happened to your ear?" Tobias whispered.

The first boy laughed. "Chunk got into a fight with one of the Gas House Gang. Chunk belted him a good one, so the boy got mad and bit off a chunk of his ear. That's how he got the name Chunk."

Tobias blinked and stared at Chunk in wide-eyed

wonder. "Can he still hear?"

"Why are you asking him? Of course I can hear. People don't hear with their ears; they hear with the hole in their ears."

The first boy rocked back on his heels. "Go easy on the kid, Chunk. A thing like that takes a bit of getting used to. Why, I nearly pissed myself the first time I saw ya."

"Oh yeah, well, why don't you tell him how you got *your* name, Lucky."

Tobias turned towards the boy who had allowed him to stay.

Lucky held up his hand to show the first two fingers were missing all the way down to the palm. Nary so much as a stub remained to show if they'd even ever been there. The hand appeared to be long healed, as Lucky smiled and tapped his two remaining fingers to his thumb.

Tobias studied the hand with a mixture of fear and awe. He'd seen men with missing legs and arms standing on the street and asking for money. His momma told him they got injured in the war and that the doctors had to cut off their limbs. He didn't know what a war was, but he remembered being scared he would end up in one. He'd been afraid to go to sleep that night. When his momma asked him why, he said that without a leg, he wouldn't be able to run away when his papa was mad. Without arms, he wouldn't be able to hug her before he went to bed at night. She'd pulled him close and told him she hoped he would never have to go to war either. He shook off the memory and pointed at Lucky's hand. "Did the doctors cut your fingers off?"

Lucky shook his head. "No, the law took my fingers for stealing."

Tobias swallowed. "How come you call yourself Lucky if they cut your fingers off?"

"Because they wanted to cut off my whole hand.

Instead, they cut these two off to teach me a lesson."

"Did it work? Did it teach you not to steal?"

"No, but it did teach me not to get caught," Lucky said, and both he and Chunk burst out laughing.

There was a rustling sound as one of the hay bales slid from beneath the wagon, allowing light to flood in. The shadow of a man appeared in the opening. "You boys come on out of there."

Lucky and Chunk scrambled through the opening. Tobias hesitated before grabbing hold of his pillowcase and following. As he crawled through the opening, he noticed the street once more filled with wagons. Some had slipped into their spots for the day; others waited in line, ready to park and sell their offerings. He was relieved to see the thick fog had mostly lifted, the damp streets quickly growing dry via the bright rays of morning sun. Men laughed and joked as they greeted one another, a scene he'd seen so many times when he visited Market Street with his mother. While she was not with him, the scene was momentarily comforting.

The second he breached the opening, rough hands latched on to his collar, lifting him so that his toes barely touched the ground.

"Who do we have here?" The words came out in a growl flowing past in a haze of cigar smoke.

"The kid's name is Mouse. He rolled in with the fog last night. The poor sap was scared out of his wits, so we let him stay," Lucky offered.

The man scowled at the boy. "You know the rules, Lucky. It's five cents a night to sleep under the wagon. What do you say, kid? Got any dough?"

Tobias shook his head in reply.

"What about you, Lucky? You allowed him to stay. Are you going to cough up the nickel?"

Lucky pulled out his pockets to show his lack of funds and shrugged.

The man snatched the pillowcase from Tobias' hand and released his hold on his collar, causing him to land in a heap at his feet. "What's in the sack, boy?"

Before he could reply, the man dumped the contents onto the dirt. The scowl on the man's face must have matched his own, as the man laughed and placed a heavy foot onto the pile of clothes, twisting them further into the dirt. Tobias pictured his mother standing in front of the kitchen sink, rubbing the family's laundry across the rough washboard until the knuckles of her fingers bled. As he pictured his momma, he remembered Ezra's words, *Papa killed Momma,* and something inside him snapped. He lunged forward, wrapping his arms around the man's leg. Opening his mouth, he latched on to his thigh, biting for all he was worth. The man yelled, sputtering vile words and shaking his leg. Tobias tightened his grip, burying his teeth deeper. The man's voice pitched higher, screaming for someone to kill the varmint. He felt the blood seep into his mouth as two sets of hands managed to separate him, tossing him backward. He scrambled to his feet, wiped the blood from his face, and glared at the man.

"That boy is an animal," the man screamed, pointing a shaky finger at Tobias. "I'll have him thrown in the jail with the rest of the crazies. The two of you too!" he shouted at both Lucky and Chunk.

The boys rushed to where Tobias stood. Each hooked an arm through his and kept running, dragging him backwards. Tobias wanted to shout at them to stop so that he could return and retrieve his discarded clothing but decided against it. Now that he was calm, the clothing didn't seem worth the trouble. Instead, he lifted his legs and waited to see where the boys were taking him. He didn't have to wait long as they veered into an alley and released him.

"I saw a dog act like that once, and the farmer had to stab him with a pitchfork," Chunk said breathlessly. "Are you mad, Mouse?"

"I'm not mad at anyone," Tobias said, shaking his head. "I think that man might be mad, though. He sure sounded mad."

Chunk blinked, staring at him open-mouthed.

Lucky bent and peered into his eyes. "Are you okay, kid? What came over you? Why did you bite that guy like that?"

Tobias shrugged. "He reminded me of my dad."

Lucky studied him for a good minute without saying a word. Finally, he stood and nodded his head. "I get that, Mouse. I really do. I've wanted to tear into my pops a time or two."

Tobias felt his stomach rumble. "I'm kinda hungry. Ezra cut a hunk of cheese, but Papa caught him."

"Ezra?"

"My brother," Tobias said and felt his eyes grow misty as he told the boys of the events that led him to the streets.

"Not to worry, kid," Lucky said when he finished. "Chunk and I are your brothers now. Ain't that right, Chunk?"

"Brothers," Chunk agreed. "But I think you need a better name than Mouse."

"We could call you Chomps or Chops," Lucky agreed.

"If it's all the same, I prefer Mouse," Tobias said. He wanted to add that his sister gave him the name, but he was feeling rather emotional. He'd already shed a few tears, and the last thing he wanted was to have his new friends think he was a crybaby. A reputation like that would be hard to live down.

"Mouse it is, then," Lucky said, clapping him on the back. "Have you ever dipped pockets before?"

Tobias shrugged. "I don't know what that means."

"Then you probably haven't done it. Have you ever taken anything that didn't belong to you?"

Tobias felt his face flush. He'd been stealing apples the day Anastasia disappeared. He couldn't help but think he was responsible for her disappearance.

The boys burst out laughing.

"Ha, from the look on your face I would say that you have. You don't have to be embarrassed around us. You just have to be good at what you do. That's where we come in. Stick with us, and we'll show you how it's done. Just make sure you do exactly as I say so you don't end up like me," Lucky said and waved his defective hand in front of Tobias.

Chapter Five

Tobias and Lucky stood in an alleyway near the Five Points Mission, where they hoped to spend the night. The area reeked of human waste, and the boys stood on wooden planks, which did little to keep their feet dry from the sewage that seeped into the dirt beneath the boards. It was an ongoing issue in the city, where the population continued to grow with each rising tide. So common, that those who lived there took little notice. Why fret over something beyond their control when it was a struggle just to find a safe place to spend the night and food enough to keep stomachs from rumbling? Tobias listened intently as Lucky schooled him in the fine art of dipping, which turned out to be another term for pickpocketing.

"Chunk is a leather worker. That means he prefers wallets and purses. If the man is wearing a coat or jacket, it's highly likely the wallet will be in the inside coat pocket. Those are pretty easy to dip. It's merely a matter of bumping and snatching. Now if the guy has the wallet in the back pocket of his pants, that's a prat. Prat-digging is a bit more tricky because then you have to top and poke, meaning you have to get close enough to push the wallet up from the bottom of the prat until it's visible, then use your fingers to retrieve the wallet. If the open end of the wallet is exposed, then it's best to use the pinch technique using your thumb and index finger. If it's the folded end that shows, then it's best to fork the wallet free using your index and middle finger. If you get enough of the wallet to show, you can easily spear it using a single finger without the mark being the wiser. Going it alone is pretty risky. That's why we work in teams." As Lucky spoke, he demonstrated each maneuver with his left hand. He looked past Tobias and smiled. "Just in time."

"I found some stuff at the garbage heap," Chunk said as he approached.

"Perfect," Lucky replied, retrieving a tattered jacket from him. He sniffed the jacket and wrinkled his nose. Shaking it several times, he motioned for Tobias to join them. "Step over here, and we will show you a few tricks."

Tobias did as told and Lucky slipped the ragged suitcoat through his arms. Once it was on, Lucky straightened the jacket and pushed what looked to be a new wallet into the front pocket of the coat. He then slid another wallet into the rear of Tobias' pants. Tobias recognized that particular wallet from a pinch the boys had done earlier in that morning. It had belonged to an elderly man who was leaving a pastry shop with his arms full of white boxes. The boys offered to help the man carry his load, and in return, the man had gifted them each with a still warm donut. Tobias had been thrilled to eat the gooey delight until Chunk showed him the wallet he'd lifted from the kind man. When Tobias had voiced his concern, Chunk laughed and pulled out several bills, telling him they needed the dough to find a place to bed down for the night, since it was his fault they had lost their spot under the wagon.

"Okay, are you ready?" Lucky asked, moving to the other side of the alleyway.

Tobias wasn't sure what was about to happen but nodded anyway. The second he did, both Chunk and Lucky moved towards him. Lucky bumped into his shoulder and instantly stopped to apologize, clamping him on the shoulder as he did. Chunk passed on the other side and kept walking.

"You okay there, Mouse?" Lucky asked, clamping him on the shoulder once more.

"Sure, I'm okay," Tobias answered, wondering what the fuss was about.

Lucky stepped away, and Chunk returned to his side, flashing the wallet that Lucky had previously stashed in his back pocket.

Tobias put a hand to his backside. Sure enough, the wallet was gone. He reached for the one Lucky had placed inside his jacket, surprised to find that one missing as well.

"Looking for this?" Lucky asked, producing the wallet.

Tobias was impressed. "How did you do that? I didn't even feel you take it. Will you show me how to do that?"

"In due time. First I want to try it again, now that you know what to expect," Lucky said and handed him both wallets.

Tobias returned both to their original positions and then nodded his readiness. Once again, both boys moved towards him, only this time, it was Lucky who passed without comment. As Chunk moved towards him, he wrinkled his nose.

Tobias looked to see what Chunk was looking at and saw what looked to be bird droppings on the shoulder of the jacket.

"Not to worry," Chunk said and took out a rag to help clean the mess. Seconds later, the droppings were removed, and Chunk smiled when Lucky took his place next to him.

"Thanks," Tobias said. "Now are you going to show me how it's done?"

Lucky and Chunk smiled as each boy once again produced the wallets that Tobias had secured only a moment before.

"It's called a distraction," Lucky said when Tobias felt his pockets. Lucky bent to retrieve a purse Chunk had brought. He pulled out a smaller coin purse, added three gleaming pieces of silver, and showed it to Tobias. Lucky closed the purse and smiled at the clang the coins made when he dropped it inside the larger purse. "Here, take this and put it on your arm like you see the ladies do."

"You want to learn or not?" Lucky asked when he objected.

Tobias took the purse and placed the strap on the crook of his arm. Seconds later, Lucky moved past, lingering ever so briefly before moving on. The boy circled behind him then returned to his spot beside Chunk. Opening his hand, he showed Tobias the three pieces of silver.

"I was standing right there, but I didn't hear or feel you take them," Tobias said in awe.

Chunk laughed. "And using his left hand too. Lucky is a master nipper."

"You mean dipper?" Tobias corrected.

"No, we are all dippers, knucklers, finger smiths, but it takes skill to be a nipper. Lucky is one of the best around. He can remove silver coins from the deepest pockets or bags without a sound," Chunk said with a flourish of the hand.

"I want to learn to do that!" Tobias said, lowering the purse. "Will you teach me? Will you teach me everything?"

Lucky opened the first wallet and removed the cash. Next, he tossed Tobias the empty wallet and a handed him a single coin. "Place those in the pockets of the jacket I gave you. Anytime we're not working, I want you to practice removing both the coin and the wallet without touching the fabric of the pocket. When you can do that, I will teach you more. For now, you can be our apprentice."

That didn't sound very important. "What does an apprentice do?"

Lucky moved closer and draped an arm around his neck. Pulling him close, he whispered, "Being an apprentice is the most important job there is. To start, you will distract the marks so that me and Chunk can do our job."

Tobias thought of Anastasia and grimaced. "I'm not kissing anyone."

Lucky lowered his arm. "Who said anything about kissing anyone?"

Tobias sighed. "My sister."

Chunk moved closer. "This sister of yours, is she pretty?"

Tobias nodded.

Chunk smiled, showing several holes where teeth should have been. "Well then, I would like to meet her."

Lucky gave Chunk a shove. "Now why would a nice girl want to meet a grubby, half-eared ruffian like you? If the boy's going to introduce anyone to his sister, it's going to be yours truly."

Chunk turned his smile to Lucky. "As if the girl would prefer a thief with two missing fingers. Why don't you tell Mouse the truth about how you lost them? If the boy's going to be one of us, he should know the truth."

Tobias turned toward Lucky, waiting for a reply. Lucky studied him for a moment before spitting in the dirt and walking away without comment. Tobias turned to Chunk, who was no longer smiling. While he wanted to ignore what had just happened, curiosity got the better of him. "The police didn't cut off Lucky's fingers, did they?"

"Not in the way he tells it. No, the coppers threw him into jail. Have you ever been in jail before, Mouse?"

Tobias shook his head.

"Yeah, well don't get yourself caught because it's not a place you want to be. It happened before we teamed up. Lucky was working alone picking marks near Ellis Island as they came off the boats. Dang law likes to welcome the newcomers, so they tried to make an example out of him. Most people know to stay away from there, but Lucky was looking for an easy mark. He found one too, but the coppers—they were watching. So they tossed him in with the murderers and rapists. Well, people like that are not nice to kids. Some guy—a man, not a boy—stole Lucky's food. Lucky was starving to death, so he decided to get even with the louse. Lucky is normally the best there is, but he was weak from being hungry, so the guy caught him stealing. The thing was, it was his own bread he'd been stealing. The guy grabbed him by the hand that was still holding the bread and bit two of Lucky's fingers plumb off."

Tobias swallowed. "What did he do with the fingers?"

Chunk shrugged. "I suppose he ate them. Then again, Lucky never did say."

Tobias was incredulous. "Lucky said he'd gotten his name when he lost his fingers. How can he call himself lucky if he got his fingers bit off?"

"That's the best part," Chunk replied. "The police saw what happened and decided he'd learnt a lesson and set him free. Not many kids get out of that place without something bad happening to them. So Lucky was lucky."

Tobias was even more confused. "But he lost his fingers, so something bad did happen."

Chunk sighed. "You have a lot to learn, Mouse. Just do as Lucky and me say and don't ever ask questions when we are working the streets. If you got questions, you hang on to them until we get back to our meet-up place. Never ask when we are making the frame."

Tobias thought about that for a moment. "Chunk?"

"Yeah, Mouse?"

"What's making the frame?"

Chunk laughed. "You sure got a lot to learn, Mouse. It means getting into position."

"Chunk?"

"Yeah, Mouse?"

"I don't know where my sister is."

The older boy sighed. "No matter. She wouldn't want someone like me, no how."

"Yo Chunk, Mouse, we got us a bed for the night," Lucky called from the corner. "Hurry, and we can get some soup as well."

"I thought he was mad," Tobias whispered as he followed Chunk.

"He was. Probably still is, but he hides it pretty good. That's another thing you have to learn, Mouse. You can't let people see when you're flustered. The streets can eat a fellow alive if you show your emotions. You have to learn to be invisible. Take that rat over there; see how calm he is sniffing the garbage. He sees us coming, and you know he wants to run off 'cause he's scared we're going to catch him and cook him for our supper. But instead of running off, he's standing his ground. Make no mistake, that rat is watching us and will run if you even veer in his direction, but for now, he's just watching. You going to survive on the streets, you going to be like that rat. Got it, Mouse?"

"Got it, Chunk."

They reached the corner; Lucky was nowhere to be found. "Come on; Lucky will be inside. Got to get the beds early or someone else will get your spot, and you'll be left with nothing but a blanket on the floor."

As Tobias followed Chunk inside the mission, he remembered a conversation he'd had with Anastasia. Only then it had been a mouse, not a rat. He wondered where his sister was and what she would think of his current predicament. Somehow he thought she would approve. "Chunk?"

Chunk turned to look at him.

"I don't know where my sister is, but I think she would like you just fine."

Chapter Six

October 23rd, 1915

Tobias followed Lucky and Chunk through the throng of people crammed along Fifth Avenue watching the National American Women's Suffrage Association Parade. He'd been following the boys around for weeks, watching and learning. Now, as he trailed along behind, he knew what to watch for. An innocent bump was never innocent. A stall to look at something was never without a prize. In the life of a dipper, every movement, no matter how random, was planned and more than often rewarded.

Lucky moved in close to a man who was shouting and waving his fist above his head. He stumbled, bumped into the man, then apologized as Chunk passed on the other side, lifting the man's wallet before casually walking away. Now it was his turn. He moved up beside Chunk, who casually handed him the wallet, then moved on to the next mark. Tobias placed the wallet into the bag he was carrying and continued to follow. While he could not see what was going on beyond the boundaries of the crowd, he could hear the chants as the women marched through the streets carrying signs he could not read and shouting something about equal rights and freedom to vote.

"Get back in the kitchen where you belong," a man bellowed. This brought a lot of cheers from the crowd.

A murmur sifted through the crowd like a swarm of angry hornets. Tobias stopped and turned to see what was happening. A woman pushed her way into the crowd. He froze in place when he noticed the woman's face red with anger and sucked in a breath when the lady stopped and spat in the man's face. Seconds later, a police officer appeared, took hold of the woman, and escorted her away. Several men cheered, much to the dismay of the women in the crowd. He took a step backward. He'd watched his parents fight on numerous occasions, and this looked like the beginning of one of their fights.

Lucky stepped up beside him and elbowed him in the ribs. "See, I told you the police would be too busy with the adults to worry about us kids."

"Why is everyone so angry?" Tobias asked.

"I hear women are mad they can't wear pants," Chunk said, joining them.

Tobias frowned. "Aprons would look silly over pants."

As soon as the words left his lips, several men snorted with laughter.

"You got that right, kid," one of the men shouted. "Hey, Mario, did you hear what this kid said?"

"No, what'd he say?" another man asked.

The first man grabbed Tobias and lifted him onto his shoulders. "Go ahead, kid, tell Mario what you said."

Several men gathered around him, waiting to hear what the man thought so funny. Tobias could smell alcohol on their breath as they encouraged him to repeat what he'd said. He searched for Lucky and Chunk to get their approval, but both boys had disappeared into the crowd.

"Come on, kid, don't be shy. Tell the guys here what you said," the man said and jostled him up and down. As he did, the bag slipped from Tobias' grasp, and several wallets spilled out from the opening. "What the heck? The little varmint is nothing but a filthy pickpocket."

In his surprise, the man had loosened his grip on his

legs. He stretched his arms wide and brought them together as hard as he could, clapping each of the man's ears. The man screamed in pain, buckling at the knees. Tobias took that opportunity to shove off from the man's shoulders and took off running the second his feet hit the ground. Being small, he was able to push his way through the crowd and into the street where the ladies were marching. He moved through the group of ladies, intending to make it to the other side of the street and disappear into the crowd. As he moved forward, he caught the attention of a middle-aged woman with brilliant red hair. She wore a long deep green velvet dress with a matching jacket that stopped at the waist and held a white sign with lettering that nearly matched the red in her hair. Standing on the curb, she looked past him, saw the reason for his hurry, and waved him forward. As he dodged between the women marching in the parade, others moved in to create a cocoon to keep the men from entering. To his surprise, the woman with the sign lifted her skirt and motioned him underneath her long petticoat. Fearing the angry men more than what lay beneath the woman's dress, he clamored under the skirts, pulling his limbs in to make himself as small as possible. It was dark, but there was still enough light to see the woman's stockings. He brushed a hand along the inside of her leg. The woman stamped her foot, landing the heel of her shoe right beside his bare foot. He removed his hand and wrapped them around his knees. A few moments later, the skirts lifted and he cautiously crawled from beneath.

"They're gone," the woman said, bending to his level. "Why were they chasing you?"

"I heard a man on the other side of the road tell a woman she would never be allowed to wear pants. This seemed to make her sad, so I offered to let her wear mine. I knew they wouldn't fit, and as ragged as they are, knew she wouldn't wish to have them, even if they did. I didn't want to see her sad, so I offered all the same," he answered as innocently as he could.

The woman's green eyes grew misty. "Well now, aren't you the sweetest boy."

Tobias listened as the women in the streets yelled for equal rights. He wasn't certain what equal rights meant but was fairly sure that was what the lady holding the sign wanted as well. "Yes, ma'am. My mother is marching in the parade today. She told me to watch out, as there are some very bad men in the crowd who do not want women to have equal rights."

The woman laughed. "And just what do you know about equal rights?"

"Just what my mother told me. She and my daddy fight about it all the time. She would never do anything to upset my papa because he is a mean man. But this subject, she dares to fight with him. I guess I don't really know what it means, but I figure they must be really important to her," Tobias said smoothly.

"That they are, boy. That they are. Now you better go before those men come back looking for you. And, since you are such a smart boy, I suggest you let us women fight this fight. We wouldn't want you to get hurt fighting our battles. All the same, when you grow up, you remember how important equal rights were to your sweet momma."

"Yes, ma'am," Tobias said. And picturing his mom, he felt his bottom lip quiver.

The smile faded from the woman's lips. "What is it, boy?"

"Nothing, ma'am," Tobias said as single tear trickled from his right eye.

"Don't you nothing me. I can see you are upset," the woman said, producing a hanky from her purse.

"I guess those awful men kind of scared me," Tobias

said, and tears began to stream down his cheek.

The woman pulled him close and hugged him as he sobbed. As she whispered words of comfort into his ear, he reached into her pocketbook and relieved her of her coin purse, silently slipping it into his own pocket.

"I'm feeling better," Tobias said, pushing away. "I must go now; my momma will be expecting me to meet her when she's finished marching."

The woman stood and dabbed at her own tears. "Do be careful and mindful of saying things that will make the men angry."

"Yes, ma'am. I will," Tobias said and disappeared into the crowd. He kept his hand in his pocket as he pushed past the bystanders. With crowds this thick, there was no telling who he could trust. Fighting against the urge to turn around, he pushed forward until at last he'd cleared the crowd. Once unencumbered, he walked in long strides, feeling rather empowered with his first successful pinch. It had shocked him that he'd been able to produce tears so easily. Something like that could come in handy in his line of work. He made his way to the rendezvous spot well ahead of Lucky and Chunk. Leaning against the side of the building, he looked to make sure he was alone before pulling the coin purse from his pocket. His fingers trembled as he pushed the clasp that held it shut and nearly dropped it altogether when at last he saw the contents. His mother's coin purse had held just that, coins. But not this one; this purse was crammed full of both coins and bills. He transferred the money to his pocket, walked to the far end of the building, and tossed the empty coin purse into a trash barrel. He went back to where he'd been standing and wondered what was keeping Lucky and Chunk. As the moments passed, he began to worry. What if they never returned? What would he do? He had no clue what time it was, but the sun had dipped behind the buildings, so it wouldn't be long before darkness set upon him. His stomach rumbled, reminding him he hadn't eaten anything since morning. He wished his friends would hurry so they could all go find something to eat.

But what if they don't come back?

He moved to stretch his legs, and when he did, he heard the jingle of the coins within his pocket. Surely Lucky would understand if he spent a few on something to eat. He walked down the street and slipped inside the first store he found. It was a general store with clothing on one side and a counter where one could grab a quick bite on the other. He headed towards the counter. As he approached, a man dressed entirely in white turned, appraised his appearance, and scowled. Ignoring the man's scowl, Tobias took a seat at the counter.

The scowl deepened. "Yo, kid. You come in here, you better have money to spend. We don't give out handouts. Understand?"

"Course I got money," Tobias said, slapping down the bills he'd lifted.

The man gave him a once over then nodded. "Just doing my job, kid. We get our share of street urchins. Can't blame me for thinking the worst of you, seeing the way you look and smell. Maybe you should take some of that money you got and buy yourself a new set of clothes."

Tobias looked over his shoulder. He'd never worn anything that hadn't belonged to Ezra first. *Did he really have enough money to buy a new set of clothes?* "I'll take a bowl of soup if you please, sir."

"Soup it is. The name's Marv. You got dough, you can call me by my name," the guy said, eyeing the bills. "Do you want a soda pop to go with it?"

He'd heard of soda pop but never tried one. "I guess I would like one."

Marv pushed off the counter and walked the short distance to the soda machine. "What's your pleasure?"

Tobias blinked his confusion.

The man placed his hands on his hips. "You mean to tell me you have never had a soda pop?"

"No, sir," he said with a shake of his head.

"Well, then you are in for a surprise. We have Coca Cola, Dr. Pepper, and root beer. Personally, I prefer Dr. Pepper, but most boys your age seem to prefer the root beer," Marv said, gathering a glass.

"Then I think I would like to try the root beer," Tobias replied.

"Aw, root beer it is." Marv pulled a lever, and seconds later, a glass filled with deep amber liquid capped with a beige foam sat in front of him.

Tobias lifted the glass and took a sip of the foam. "It doesn't taste like much."

Marv laughed.

"You are just tasting the froth from the machine. You have to taste the soda to get your whistle wet." He shoved a paper straw through the foam. "There. Now take a nice long pull from that."

Tobias did as told, coughing as the liquid slid down his throat. It burned but in a good way. He smiled and took another drink.

Marv placed a bowl of vegetable soup on the counter and Tobias dug in without another word. As he ate, Marv lifted a bill, replaced it with several coins, then busied himself at the counter. Tobias took his time eating, enjoying the occasional clang as his spoon hit the white china.

"You want a piece of pie?" Marv asked when Tobias finished.

Tobias felt his mouth water but declined. He'd been

extravagant enough ordering the soda. "No, sir."

"Suit yourself," he said, removing the empty dishes.

"Sir?" Tobias asked before Marv moved away.

"What is it, kid? Change your mind about the pie, did you?"

"No, sir. It is just, I was wondering, do I really have enough money for a new set of clothes?"

Marv eyed the remaining bills and laughed. "Son, you could buy yourself an outfit, new shoes, get yourself a real bath down at one of the bathhouses, and still have some coins left. How does that sound?"

It sounded amazing, considering rain was the only water he'd felt on his skin since he'd left home. He'd not changed his clothing in the same length of time either. "I think I would like that, sir."

Marv raised his hand, and a salesman hurried over from the other side of the store. Dressed in a suit, the salesman was eager to help until he saw his client. The man looked at him the way his momma looked at the roaches climbing the wall in their apartment.

"Mr. Kramer, the young lad here would like to buy a new set of clothes. He doesn't need anything fancy, just something that will keep him warm as the weather cools and make him look a little more acceptable."

Kramer gave Tobias a once over and wrinkled his nose. "That would take some doing."

"Now none of that, Kramer. The boy has money. I've seen it," Marv chided.

Kramer sighed his acceptance and turned his attention to Tobias. "Very well then, son. If you will follow me, I think we can find you something with less… aroma."

He followed to where the trousers were and waited as Kramer took out a length of cloth and wrapped it around his waist. Kramer kneeled and placed the tape near the upper portion of his inner thigh.

Tobias took a step backward. "Hey, none of that funny business."

The man closed his eyes, pinched at the bridge of his slender nose, and exhaled slowly. Opening his eyes, he spoke. "I assure you I am not in the habit of funny business, especially with the likes of you. If a young man wants a pair of trousers to fit then, he must do one of two things. Either he allows himself to be properly measured or he tries them on. To put things frankly, you sir, stink. One can smell you from across the room. No decent person will have anything to do with you in your present state. And I assure you, no one wants you in their trousers."

Tobias considered telling the man he was under a fine lady's petticoat not more than a few hours ago but decided against it. So far, no one had questioned where someone like him had acquired so much money. Most likely, they knew if they made a fuss over it, he might decide not to spend it in their store. He nodded his acceptance, knowing if Kramer did try any funny business, he was in the correct position to kick him in the teeth. When Kramer finished, he told him to stretch out his arms. Tobias did as told, and Kramer stepped behind him and took another measurement. He turned in time to watch the man throw the length of tape in the trash. He wondered if the man did that with every customer and knew the answer to be no. It was at that moment Tobias pledged that one day he would be able to shop in a store such as this with no one questioning if he belonged.

Chapter Seven

Freshly showered and sporting new store-bought clothing, Tobias strutted down Park Avenue like he belonged, smiling and nodding his head at everyone he met. For the first time in his life, his greetings were returned. Some merely met with a quick nod or grunt, but each acknowledgment was a long way from the grimace of disgust that was normally cast his way. His chest swelled; yes, he could get used to this. His outward cockiness did little to ease his inner turmoil. He'd returned to the rendezvous spot, hoping to find Lucky and Chunk, but found no one. Finally, he'd given up and taken the trolley to the free bathhouse on West 41st Street that Marv had told him about. Unfamiliar with the area, he was now hoping to find a place to bed down for the night. A door opened, and a tall man in a suit and overcoat exited a building wielding two large suitcases. He took a step and waited as a woman joined him. The man fumbled with the door as the woman placed a hand on her hat to secure it from the breeze that threatened to blow it free. She tucked a small travel bag under her arm and stepped from the curb as he neared. The woman smiled, and Tobias tipped his hat the way he'd seen done on many occasions. The man pulled his heavy load from the steps, sizing him up as he walked past.

"I hope we'll make our train on time. I have the key. You did lock the front door, didn't you?" the woman asked before he was out of earshot.

Tobias smiled. A train meant a train station. Surely no one would pay any notice to a small boy sleeping on a bench.

Especially one so neatly dressed. He turned on his heels and addressed the couple. "Did I hear you mention the train?"

The man hesitated. "What business is it of yours?"

Tobias removed his hat. "Oh, it is no business of mine to be sure. It's just I heard you say you're late and your load looks so heavy. I'm on my way to the train station this very moment, and I'd be most happy to help you carry your bags."

The man narrowed his eyes. "If that's true, then you are heading in the wrong direction."

"Oh dear, my papa will be most disappointed with me. He told me I was much too young to find my way in the dark by myself, but I insisted. I'm supposed to fetch my grandmamma. My poor mother is deathly ill, and grandmamma is coming all the way from Boston to help look after her. My papa was going to go fetch her, but being my mother is ill, I thought it would be best if he stayed with her. It's the first time I've been out on my own and I wanted to show I could be of some use." As he finished, he choked away a sob. To his delight, he even managed to squeeze out a few tears.

"Oh now, Adam, look what you've done. The poor boy was merely trying to help his mother."

Adam didn't look as convinced, so Tobias willed a few more tears to flow.

"Since we're all going to the same place, which by the way is in the opposite direction, I guess we may as well allow the lad to help us with the bags," Adam said tersely. He shoved the smaller of the two in his direction.

Tobias lifted it with both hands and followed closely behind.

"What train is your grandmother coming in on?" Adam asked over his shoulder.

"The one from Boston," Tobias said, sticking with his earlier story.

"Yes, well, trains have schedules. Surely if you are to find the right train, you have to know where in the terminal you are going. Do you know the number?"

Tobias felt like a mouse suddenly caught in a trap. "No, sir. I have it written down in my pocket, but this case is so heavy, I must use both hands. I could stop and tell you the number, but then you'd miss your train."

The woman glanced over her shoulder. "He's right, Adam; we don't want to be late. Maybe we should have taken a taxi as I suggested."

"We are spending enough money on this trip of yours. There is no need to fork over more, especially now that we have help carrying the bags. Isn't that right, lad?"

Meaning you are too cheap to pay the fare, Tobias thought but didn't articulate. He'd heard of people going places just for the pleasure of going, but he'd never met anyone who had actually gone. "Are you two going on vacation, then?"

"We are." The woman's voice was full of excitement. "Adam has promised to take me to Philadelphia. It is in Pennsylvania."

"What's in Philadelphia?" Tobias asked, hoping to distract them from further prying.

The woman's enthusiasm continued. "My family. I haven't seen them since Adam and I married three years ago. My mother keeps begging us to come for a visit, but Adam couldn't find the time. Until now. We're going to stay for three whole months. Aren't you just thrilled, Adam?"

"Couldn't be more so, Felisha," Adam replied, sounding much less thrilled about their impending journey than his wife.

Though he couldn't see the man's face, Tobias knew him to be lying, though he couldn't understand why. While he had to steal just to eat, this man had enough money he could go on a trip just for the pleasure of doing so.

Felisha laughed. "Cheer up, husband. You sound as if I am taking you to the gallows."

"I'm to spend the winter holed up with a house full of women. The cackling alone should be enough to drive a man mad," Adam replied dryly.

"It is not the whole winter; we shall be home late January. And for the record, we don't cackle."

"You most assuredly do. When you get with your sisters, a man can't get a word in edgewise. I won't get a sip of brandy without someone raising a stink about it. Do you have sisters, lad?" Adam asked.

Tobias sucked in his breath at the mention of his sister. Tears welled in his eyes once more, but this time, they were real. "I have one, sir."

"Ah well, consider yourself lucky, then. A boy can live with one sister, but you get any more than that, and the house is all aflutter like a hen house. And her mother is the biggest mother hen of them all. Won't let a man have a drink or enjoy a good cigar without flapping her wings and saying how the smoke burns her eyes."

"Adam, you stop with that talk right now, or I will send you back home the second we arrive," Felisha scolded.

"If only I could get so lucky," Adam said sourly.

The trio walked the rest of the way in silence. Once they were inside Union Station, Adam stopped to get his bearings as Tobias took in the massive building. Just as he'd thought, the station was large enough a small boy dressed such as himself could blend in without anyone being the wiser.

Felisha turned to Tobias. "Could you watch the baggage for just a moment while we retrieve our tickets? Oh, Adam, stop being so distrusting," Felisha said when Adam hesitated. "We've sent the valuables ahead in the trunk. Besides, look at the boy. Does he look like a street urchin to you?"

Adam studied him momentarily. "Well, the lad is in desperate need of a haircut."

Tobias held his breath. He hadn't even considered getting a haircut.

Felisha smiled. "Yes, there is that. I'll tell you what, boy…wait, we are practically friends. I can't keep calling you boy or lad. What's your given name?"

He considered telling them his name was Mouse but felt neither would look at him the same way if he divulged his street name. He let out a sigh. It was doubtful anyone on this side of town traveled in the same circles as his family. Deciding it would be best to keep things simple, he opted not to divulge his full name. "Tobias."

That produced another smile from Felisha. This time, the woman showed a mouth full of the whitest teeth he'd ever seen. He ran his tongue over his teeth, some of which had fallen out recently.

The smile disappeared. "What is it, Tobias?"

"Your teeth are so nice."

The smile returned. "Thank you for saying so, but why does that make you sad?"

"Because mine are all rotten. See, they're falling out." He parted his lips for her to see.

"Oh, Tobias, your teeth aren't rotten. You're just losing your baby teeth. Tell him, Adam."

The tall man stooped and took a long look inside Tobias' mouth. "It's true; I don't see any rot at all."

"Adam is a dentist. It's his job to look at people's teeth."

Tobias rocked back on his heels and chuckled. "You mean to tell me people pay you to stand there and look in their mouths?"

"I assure you there is much more to it than just standing there looking. Speaking of standing here," he said, glancing at his wife. "If we don't retrieve our tickets, we're not going to make our train."

Felisha sat her small bag on top of the larger suitcase and followed behind her husband. Tobias waited for them to reach the ticket window and moved so that his body blocked their view. He moved quickly to unclasp the small bag. Lifting the lid, he retrieved a few bills and stuffed them into his pocket. Moving aside a small mirror and things he did not recognize, he found exactly what he was looking for, a brass key he felt certain would unlock the residence on Park Avenue where he had first met his new friends. He placed the key in his front pocket and hurriedly resealed the bag just as the couple turned from the counter.

"I'm afraid we must be on our way. Our train is to depart in thirty minutes. We'll have just enough time to make it to our cabin if we hurry."

Felisha looked as if she would cry. She retrieved a peppermint stick from her coat pocket and handed it to Tobias. "I feel so bad not helping you find your grandmother."

"Don't worry. I have everything I need in my pocket," he said, patting the pocket where the money and key rested.

"If you are sure, then," Adam said, hoisting the bags. "You're a good lad, there, Tobias. Keep your nose clean and don't let anyone take advantage of you."

"Yes, sir," Tobias said sweetly.

The man turned to leave then hesitated. Resting his bag, he dipped into his pocket and retrieved a quarter, which he tossed to Tobias. "Keeping a sharp appearance will go a long way to earning someone's trust. Take this coin and get yourself a haircut."

Tobias slid the coin into his pocket with the rest of his score and tasted the peppermint. "Thank you, sir. You and your wife have been most generous."

***

Cindy stared at the journal in disbelief. The brazenness of the child was unmatched by the children she taught, and her children were much older than Tobias.

"That boy needs a good old-fashioned kick in the pants," Linda said, reading her mind.

"Or a hug. It's hard to imagine being thrust into the streets at five years old," Cindy replied. "He's just doing what it takes to survive."

"Your expression says you don't entirely believe that," Linda observed.

"No, I do. It's just that after reading this, I find myself questioning my abilities as a teacher. I wonder if I'd been born in that era if I would've been an effective teacher. How do you reach children that are that far gone?"

Linda placed her hand on Cindy's. "You've had your share of challenges in the classroom. To my knowledge, you haven't failed a child yet. Have you?"

Cindy sighed. "Not that I know of."

"I have to say one thing, though. These journals show why Reverend Brace was determined to get those children off the streets and to a better life. Can you imagine seeing a child his age walking down the street and being like, 'Here, kid, carry our suitcase'?"

Cindy laughed. "Yeah, nowadays, it would be more 'Oh you poor thing. Honey, call DHHS."

Linda turned serious. "You know he's going to be living in that apartment for the next three months. I bet he drinks all that man's bourbon and smokes his cigars."

Cindy sighed. "Sadly, I think you're right. From what I've read, there were no laws on things like that back in the day.

I read that the newsboys spent the better part of their night in alehouses. Opium dens were big during that time as well."

"Do you want me to make something to eat?" Linda asked when her stomach rumbled loud enough to hear.

Cindy rolled her neck to relieve the tension. "Why don't we order something instead? We can have the taxi deliver it."

Linda reached for the phone and hesitated. "Define irony."

"Using language that normally means the opposite," Cindy replied.

"Spoken like a true school teacher," Linda said, shaking her head. "What I meant was, Tobias was able to steal keys to the house and more cash than it would have cost to hire a taxi, all because the man was too tight-fisted to pay the fare. And here we are calling the cab because we are too lazy to go pick up our own food."

"And because the taxi and Pizza Hut are the only ones in town that delivers. Hey, how about we learn from Adam's mistake? Let's take a break and go get our own food."

"Alright, but let's go to Pizza Hut. I have a hankering for one of those little peppermints they give you when you pay for your food."

Cindy pushed off the couch and reached a hand to help her mother. "You had me at pizza."

Chapter Eight

Cindy and her mother sat curled up on opposite ends of the couch, each fed, freshly showered, and ready for another marathon reading session. They'd taken to reading the manuscripts together so they would finish near the same time. It was easier that way so neither woman could spoil the read for the other. It was easy to get caught up in the story and forget they were reading about actual children and not just some fictional farce someone had penned.

"Ready to do this?" Cindy asked, picking up her copy of the journal.

"Just try to stop me," Linda replied.

***

Tobias woke with the feeling of being watched. He opened his eyes to find a station policeman standing over him. Instantly awake, he pulled himself upright, wondering if his identity had finally been discovered. He further chastised himself for opting to spend the night in the train station instead of trying to find his way back to the apartment under cover of darkness.

"Didn't think I'd catch you, did you, son?" the man said, sounding pleased with himself. "I've been looking for you for nearly an hour. They thought you'd left, but I have a nose for these things."

Tobias sighed. Apparently, he hadn't been as clever as

he'd thought. The couple from the previous evening must have noticed their belongings missing and ratted him out.

"It's not the first time one of you kids tried to escape."

Escape? What on earth was the man yapping about? "Excuse me? I have no idea what you're talking about."

"Still playing the part, huh, kid?" the man scoffed. "They parade you through the station in all your new fine clothing, but I can smell one of you urchins from a mile away."

Tobias glared at the man. "I had a shower just yesterday."

The man prodded him with a long black stick. "Don't play smart with me. Get yourself up off that bench so I can return you to where you belong."

Tobias felt his stomach flip. If the policeman was sent to take him home, that meant his father was still alive. No doubt his father would be furious that Tobias had run away. He thought about running but did not know his way around the train station. He decided to wait until they got outside, where he would have a better chance to escape. He got up without further argument, hoping to get the man to let his guard down. The second he stood, the man gripped him by the collar and began pulling him further into the terminal. He thought about asking where the man was taking him, but something told him to remain quiet. They approached a large group of kids and the policeman let go of his collar and pushed him into the group. To his surprise, due to his recent shopping spree, he fit right in with the group, with the boys anyway, wearing black pants that stopped at the knee and a black jacket over a crisp white shirt. Even his black shoes and knee high socks were the same schoolboy garb. Not for the first time, he wished he'd taken the time to get a haircut.

Leaning in, the policeman addressed Tobias. "These people are trying to help you, and all you can think is to run away. And to do what? Die on the streets? You have a chance that not many have, to go out to the country where the air is clean and food grows fresh in the fields. So much food, you'll never be hungry again. Crap, kid, I wish I could get on that train and go with you. You think about it long and hard before you run away again. Because if you do and I catch you, I'll have no choice but to take you to jail. Do you know what happens to little boys like you when they are in jail?"

Tobias remembered the conversation with Chunk and nodded his head. "Yes, sir, I do."

"Do you want that to happen to you?" the man said sternly.

Tobias tucked his fingers into his fist. "No, sir."

The man pulled himself straight. "Good. I'll be watching you. All of you. Let this be the end of the foolishness."

He watched as the policeman walked to the front of the line. He turned to the other children, who were looking at him with a mixture of distrust and awe.

"You don't belong here," one of the boys finally said.

"Tell me something I don't know," Tobias retorted. "You heard the man. If I try to run away, he's going to take me to jail. I don't know where you're going, but it has to be a heap better than jail. People in jail cut your fingers off. I've seen it with my own eyes."

There was a collective gasp from the group of children.

"You saw them cut someone's fingers off?" one of the girls asked.

"Sure did," Tobias lied. "My friend Lucky. A man caught him stealing bread and wanted it back. The man was so mad at Lucky, he ate two of his fingers along with the chunk of bread. He swallowed them whole."

"You're lying," one of the older boys ventured. "Couldn't no one eat two fingers without choking."

66

Tobias narrowed his eyes at the kid. "They were small fingers."

The boy nodded towards the front of the line. "He's not looking, so you might want to run."

Tobias thought about what the policeman had said about the food. "Is what he said about the food true?"

"That's what the agents told us," one of the children said.

Tobias was intrigued. "What agents?"

"At the Children's Aid Society. That's where we all came from."

He was confused. "And they're taking you on vacation just to get food?"

A couple of the children laughed.

The girl who had spoken previously shushed the others. "No, they're taking us to find new mothers and fathers."

"So if I get on that train, I can go and find a new mother and father, and I will never be hungry again?" Tobias asked in disbelief. An image of his father came to mind. "What if I don't like my new father and mother?"

"Then they send you back," the girl replied.

Tobias looked to the front of the line and saw that the policeman was still there. If he took off now, the man would never be able to catch him. He dipped his hand into his pocket, pushed past the money, and fingered the key. If he could find the right apartment, he'd have shelter for three months. *What then? Where would he stay after that?* If he stayed in line, he had a chance at finding a whole new family, and if he were lucky, they would be nice to him. If not, he would insist they send him back.

The policeman started in his direction. The man he'd been talking to followed close behind. If he was going to run, he had to go now. The desire to be normal again won out, and he was still standing there when they approached.

The policeman nodded at Tobias. "This is the lad I was telling you about."

The agent frowned. "I'm afraid he's not one of ours."

A red blush crept up the officer's neck. "You should have said so before. Off we go, lad. We have a place for street urchins."

Tobias took a step backward when the policeman started to remove him. He looked at the agent. "Don't make me leave. I have no place else to go."

"I've got a place for you," the policeman growled.

"He'll take me to jail. He said so himself. All I did was sleep on the bench. I have no mother or father to care for me. They died weeks ago of the pneumonia. I had a wee sister, but another family took her away. I asked to go with them, but they told me they had enough boys. I tried to take care of myself. I stayed in our apartment until last night when the landlord made me leave as I could not afford to pay. I walked all day and took the trolley, hoping to find a place to stay. It got dark, and there were people coming and going from this building, so I thought no one would mind if I rested my eyes for a while. Look at me. Do I look like I have been living on the streets? I didn't mean no harm. Really, I didn't." When he finished pleading his case, he pushed out some tears to help win the man over.

The agent sighed. "Well, we did have a boy run away just this morning, leaving us with an extra ticket. It's not our usual way, but it has been done before. What's your name, boy?"

He thought about giving a false name but didn't see the need for another lie. "My name is Tobias, sir."

The agent nodded to the policeman.

"Well, Tobias. It looks as though you have yourself a chance at a new life," the officer said, releasing him. "I'm glad they'll be taking you with them. The jails are no place for innocent lads such as yourself. Good luck to you then, the lot of you."

The agent checked his pocket watch. "Okay, children, we're ready to move to the trains."

Tobias felt strangely giddy as he fell in line with the others. Could he really escape life on the streets as easily as being in the wrong place at the right time? His breath caught when he rounded the corner and saw the trains. Growing up within the city, he'd seen trolleys but they didn't compare to the enormous black engine that idled before him. He followed the children into the train car and took a seat next to a boy with a face full of freckles.

"Want to trade seats?" Tobias asked.

"What for?"

"I would like to sit so I can look out the window."

The boy grinned. "What will you trade me for it?"

Tobias pulled out the last of his peppermint stick he'd been saving for breakfast and showed it to the boy, who immediately snatched it from his hand then moved to allow him access to the window.

The boy removed a piece of lint from the peppermint. "I'm Simon. Where'd you get the candy?"

Tobias shrugged. "My father gave it to me."

The boy's eyes grew wide. "I thought you told the agent your father died."

"Maybe he did maybe he didn't."

Simon tasted the peppermint. "I've got parents. But they told me to go when they found out Momma was going to have another baby. Told me since I was ten, it was time for me to make my own way. I have three brothers who are younger. I suppose they'll be told to leave as others come along. You got any brothers?"

"I got one. His name's Ezra. I had a sister, but she's gone."

"Did she die?"

"I don't think so."

"Where'd she go?"

Tobias shrugged once more. "I don't know."

The train whistle blared. A few seconds later, the train jerked and began a slow crawl out of the station. Moments later, the train breached the tunnel and sunlight spilled into the train car. After a few moments of silence, the boy began to speak once more.

"The agent at the asylum said some of us might get adopted. Others will just live with the family and help them on the farm. You ever see a farm?"

Tobias wasn't even sure what a farm was. "Don't think so."

"Me neither. But I saw some pigs and chickens in a book. You know how to read?"

Tobias shook his head.

"The agent said the folks who pick us have to send us to school so we can learn."

This got his attention. He'd never been to school before, but Anastasia had, and she could read. She read to him and Ezra all the time. At least she used to. Ezra had started school, but he couldn't read just yet. "Will they teach me to read at school?"

"School will teach you all kinds of things," the boy replied. "They're supposed to send us four months a year. Least that's what the agent said."

Tobias was intrigued. He'd been living on the streets for five months and had learned a great deal during that time. If he got to go to school for four months, he should be able to learn all there was to know. "What else did the agents tell you?"

Simon grinned. "Said that there are fields full of food.

And we will never have to be hungry again."

The policeman had said that very thing and policemen didn't lie. Tobias' stomach rumbled. He wondered how it would feel not to go to sleep hungry every night. The train picked up steam, leaving the city and life as he knew it behind. He looked toward the window, watching as the landscape gave way to large pastures of green grass and trees as tall as buildings, whose leaves were just beginning to change. He saw something that resembled a horse, which was quickly determined by other children to be a cow. *How could they put a saddle on such a thing?* Before he could ask the question, another child beat him to it, and the whole train car burst into laughter.

"Well, how do you ride it if it ain't got a saddle?" the same boy asked.

"Ya dope, you don't ride cows," another boy scoffed.

"What do ya do with 'em, then?" The boy wasn't giving up.

"Ya milk 'em and drink the milk. Where do you think milk comes from anyway?"

"I guess I never thunk of that before," the first boy replied.

Tobias thought about telling the boy he hadn't thought of it either but didn't want the others laughing at him. Something orange caught his eye.

"LOOK AT ALL THOSE PUMPKINS!" several children yelled at once.

"There must be hundreds of them," someone said. "What do people do with all those pumpkins?"

"They make pumpkin pie." This time, it was a girl's voice, her statement filled with longing. "I haven't had pumpkin pie in so very long. Do you think if I asked, they would stop the train and just let me stay here? I wouldn't mind living in a place where pumpkins grow so big and free."

"Maybe we should all jump out the window." This time, it was a boy who spoke.

As the train continued to head west, trees replaced the fields. The pumpkins disappeared from sight, but not from the minds of the children. Each child had been told of fields of food fresh for the taking. Though they'd barely left the city, they'd now witnessed such miracles of abundance with their very eyes. Tobias felt his stomach clench but not from hunger. This time, the ache he felt was hope.

Chapter Nine

The train swayed under him as Tobias made his way down the aisle. He'd purposely waited until he knew the privy designated for the children's use to become occupied before claiming he could not possibly wait a moment longer. With one agent supervising the child in the privy and the other supervising the children in their car, Tobias was now on his own to do some quick exploring. Cool air blasted as he slid the door open. He stood on the open porch between the trains for several seconds watching the landscape scroll by at an alarming rate. The train jiggled on the track, and for a moment, he expected the cars to break apart. Unnerved, he quickly moved into the other train car and the one beyond that. He half expected someone to stop him, but when they didn't, he continued. The next car was different, as it merely had a walkway with doors on either side. One of the doors opened, and an elderly man in a suit stepped in front of him. Leaning heavily on a walking stick, the man seemed surprised to see him.

"Sorry, lad, didn't see you there." The man stepped back inside what looked to be a tiny apartment.

"Do you live on this train?" he asked, straining to see inside.

The man laughed. "Only for the next few days."

He wondered what it would be like to live on a train, even if only for a few days. "Are you going on vacation?"

"To be certain. I am long retired, so every day is a vacation."

"Are you going to Philadelphia?" Tobias asked, giving the name of the only place he knew outside of New York.

"No, no, not at all. I hope that's not where you are going, for if you are, you have made your way onto the wrong train." The man looked past him. "Where are your parents, lad?"

He thought about telling him how he came to find himself on the train but reconsidered. In his experience, people did not take too kindly to orphans. "My parents are two cars back and my mother is feeling ill."

A frown creased the man's brow. "Ill, is she? Why, I am a physician. Mayhap I should grab my bag and tend to her."

Tobias hadn't been expecting this and quickly came up with another lie. He'd once watched a pregnant woman lose the contents of her stomach when the trolley they were riding on started moving. Surely a moving train would produce a similar reaction. "Oh no, it is nothing, to be sure. My mother is with child, and the movement of the train is spoiling her stomach."

The man tilted his head, his smile touching the creases of his eyes. He leaned in and whispered, even though they were alone in the passageway. "Ah well, a good thing too. I am no more a doctor than you have parents who let you run the train at will. I saw you with that group of orphans they brought onboard."

Tobias narrowed his eyes. "What would you have done if you were mistaken and I insisted you go take a look at my dear mother?"

"I would have looked upon your mother and told her to take quinine and see a doctor as soon as she departed the train. To be a good storyteller, a man always has to have a backup story. Insurance, if you will. Never let them catch you in the lie, and if they do, then you are going to need some insurance. Now, if you would like to follow me to the dining car, we shall find you something to eat. Unless, that is, you have something more devious in mind?"

Tobias looked at the man in awe. Before this day, he never knew grown people to lie. He followed the man through two additional cars until at last they entered a car fixed with tables complete with white linen tablecloths. The man took a seat at an empty table and motioned for him to join him. He sat and looked to the man for direction.

After a few moments of silence, the man began to speak. "I will see to your supper, and you will indulge me in polite conversation. You need not lie to me, young man. I have traveled with the master of the silver tongue and listened as he told tales that made grown men blush and women swoon. He had a story for all occasions and a backup story in case someone questioned the first. He was my dearest friend and closest confidante; God rest his soul. We were friends for so long, I can spot a storyteller before they so much as open their mouth."

A man dressed in white stopped at the table and deposited two glasses of water. He eyed Tobias then turned back to the man. "The usual, Mr. Twichell?"

The man sitting across from him nodded, and the waiter placed a glass on the table, filling it from a decanter.

"Will you be in need of anything else, sir?" the waiter asked, replacing the stopper.

"Bring a cup of hot cocoa for the boy." Twichell looked Tobias over. "And a ham sandwich."

"Very well, sir," the waiter said and walked away.

Twichell took a sip from the glass and closed his eyes as he swallowed. Opening his eyes once more, he began to speak. "Do you drink, son?"

"Yes, sir," Tobias said and lifted his water glass.

The man's eyes twinkled. "Have you seen what alcohol can do to a man?"

Tobias thought of his father and swallowed. "I have,

sir."

The twinkle left as the man's face turned serious. "Then you must heed my warning when I tell you to never let a drop of alcohol pass through your lips. Not even one. It is the devil's nectar. One sip and the devil will have you. Your friends will insist you try it. They will shun you and call you names, telling you drinking makes you a man. Don't you listen to them. Because it is not your friends talking, it is the devil doing the talking. Do you understand?"

No, but he found himself nodding anyway.

Twichell looked at his glass with disgust and took another drink. "Do you like your daddy, son?"

"No, sir," Tobias said without hesitating.

Twichell sat his glass down and slapped the table hard enough to make those sitting near jump. "See, that right there. Saying you don't like your daddy is the work of the devil. Your daddy was not always bad. He was once a little boy just like you. But the devil, he got him to take that first drink. And if your daddy hadn't listened, your life would be drastically different. Do you know where you'd be right now?"

Tobias shook his head.

"Why you'd be home sitting at the table with him right now. Does that make sense, son?"

Not really. "Sir?"

"What is it, boy?" Twichell said and took another sip from his glass.

"If you know it's that bad, why don't you stop drinking it?"

Twichell sighed. "Because the devil caught hold of me a long time ago. That's not easy for me to say, given I'm a reverend. Besides, I'm an old man. I got kids that are old. Eleven in total. You got any kids, son?"

Tobias giggled. "I'm not even married. How could I

have kids?"

Twichell chuckled. "Yes, well, what are you are looking for in a wife, then?"

Before Tobias could answer, the waiter returned and set a covered plate in front of him. He removed the silver dome covering the plate, exposing not only a ham sandwich but two oatmeal cookies, complete with raisins.

"They were left over from the evening meal," the waiter said by way of explanation. He left briefly then returned with a steaming cup of cocoa. Setting it next to Tobias' plate, he looked to Twichell, who smiled and waved him off with a flick of the hand.

Tobias took several bites of his sandwich before speaking. "I want a wife who is pretty."

"That's an admirable quality to be sure, but what else are you looking for?"

"What should I be looking for?" Tobias asked between bites.

"You and your wife should make beautiful music together. Do you know why my wife and I get along, boy? Wait, do you have a name?"

"They call me Mouse," Tobias replied, giving his new friend his street name.

"The name fits you. You are quiet. I like a good listener. Harmony."

"What?"

Twichell rolled the liquid around in the glass. "My wife, her name is Harmony."

"I like that name."

Twichell smiled. "So do I, son. I liked it so much, I bestowed it on one of my daughters. And now she is making beautiful music with her husband. You know why?"

"No, sir," Tobias said, finishing his sandwich.

"Because she married a composer. Do you know what that is?"

"No, sir." Tobias thought about telling him he had no idea what anything the man said meant but decided against it.

"Ives—that's my daughter's husband—takes notes and turns them into the most beautiful music. He gets paid handsomely too. I've never seen my daughter so happy. Not because of the money, mind you, because of the music. He is working on this piece now that makes her eyes light up whenever he plays it. Concord something or other is what he calls it. Anyhow, that is what you need to look for in a wife. Find a woman who makes beautiful music and don't let her out of your sight. Because if you don't marry her, some other man will, and that man will steal your happiness. Does that make sense, son?"

It didn't, but Tobias nodded anyway. He didn't have to understand the man's words to enjoy his company. The fact that he had a full belly and was sitting at a table with a real tablecloth drinking hot cocoa didn't hurt either. They sat in silence for a bit, each lost in their own thoughts.

"Walk me to my room, will you, Mouse?" Twichell said when they finished.

"Yes, sir." Tobias hastily wrapped both cookies in a napkin and followed him out of the dining car.

The man staggered a bit as he walked but didn't have any trouble finding his way to his cabin. "I thought I would have to endure this evening alone. I am most grateful for the company."

"I thank you for the meal, sir," Tobias offered in return.

"Wait here for a moment. I want to give you something." Twichell disappeared inside the cabin and returned moments later handing him a cream-colored book.

Tobias looked at the cover and saw a boy standing by a

fence. "I can't read, sir."

"That's okay, son; you will be able to read it someday. My best friend gave it to me. I think you should find it a most enjoyable read one day."

"Won't your friend be mad if you give it away?"

The smile left Twichell's face. "My friend is long dead, so he won't mind. He and I had some grand adventures in our day, one of them on a train much like this. I think he would be pleased that I gave it to you."

Tobias opened the cover and frowned. "Someone went and wrote inside the pages."

The smile returned. "My friend wrote me a message in there before he gave it to me. Would you like me to read you the message?"

Tobias nodded and handed him the book.

"It says: *To Joe, the only man who never believed my lies. Sam.*" Twichell patted him on top the head. "If you do nothing else in life, learn to read. A good book will take you to places you might not see otherwise. Now you best be heading back. They'll be missing you and wondering where you have made off to and none too happy you've been gone so long."

"Sir," Tobias said, accepting the book once more.

"Yes, Mouse?"

"I don't think the devil has you like you think he has."

"What makes you so certain?"

"Because I've seen what it is the devil can do, and I don't think you could do those things." Without waiting for a response, Tobias tucked the book securely into the waistband of his trousers and headed back to the orphans' car. He slid the door open, expecting the agent in charge to tear into him for taking so long. As it turned out, the agent was busy with another child at the rear of the car and Tobias slipped into his seat unnoticed.

"What took you so long?" Simon asked as soon as he was seated. "The agent told me to tell him as soon as you came back."

"Why, I haven't been gone long at all. When the agent comes by, you can tell him you forgot to tell him I'd come back."

"And get myself into trouble? Now why would I want to do a fool thing like that?"

Tobias unwrapped the napkin, pulled out one of the cookies, and waved it in front of Simon's face.

Simon licked his lips. "Well, I may have dozed off for a while, and in doing such, I could have failed to notice that you'd returned."

"That's what I thought," Tobias said. He handed Simon the cookie and broke the second cookie in half. He placed one half on his lap and wrapped the other in the napkin.

Simon's gaze drifted to the linen. "Why are you saving the other half?"

"A man's got to have insurance," he replied and slid the cloth into his coat pocket.

Chapter Ten

Bellies full and faces washed, the children sat in a semicircle on the stage at the Wild Opera House in Noblesville, Indiana, staring out at the faces of strangers who'd come to view the children. The kids fidgeted in their seats as Agent Smith enlightened the onlookers on the Placing Out Program. As he spoke, thunder from a late-season storm boomed, echoing in the expansive building.

A chill raced down Tobias' arms as if the storm was warning of impending doom. He looked toward the door, wondering if he could escape without being noticed. Not likely, since every eye in the building was focused on the very stage on which he sat.

Standing rail straight, Smith crossed the platform and turned his attention towards the children. "And these are the fine children of which I am speaking. They are each of good health and well-disciplined. Homeless through no fault of their own, each child merely looking for a place to call home. The girls will help you in the household and the boys, well, see for yourself, what fine, strong lads they are. Each eager and willing to help you with your day-to-day work. And all they want in return is to feel welcomed and, if you have it in your heart, loved."

A clap of thunder rattled the roof, and the crowd started murmuring.

The agent pointed to a tall boy in the front row, motioning for him to stand. "Tell the fine folks in attendance your name and a little something about yourself."

The boy stood, took a step forward, and addressed the crowd. "My name is Hans, and I'm twelve years old. I can't read, but I can work and would be much obliged if one of you would like to take me home."

Two hands went up at once.

"Good. Very good indeed." The agent nodded. "Give your papers to the committee, and they will give their decision after the noon meal."

It went on like that for some time with the agent pointing, the children speaking, and members of the audience vying to be allowed to give that child a home. Finally, the attention turned to Tobias. He rose and stood staring into the sea of faces, unsure what to say. He'd never spoken to so many people at one time. He searched his mind, wondering what story best suited for the occasion. He'd not had a choice in the beginning and look at how well that turned out. He thought about his father, silently praying this time would be different. But what could he say to help him get what he wanted?

"Go on, son," the agent encouraged. "Tell us your name and a bit about yourself."

He swallowed and took a step forward. "My name is Tobias, but they call me Mouse. I don't look like much, but I can outrun most boys my age. I guess that comes from years of outrunning my papa when he'd had too much of the drink. If you are thinking to hit me, I will tell you now don't pick me. I won't stay in a place where people hit me for no good reason. If I deserve it, I'll take it, but I've lived a life of being slapped around for no good reason, and I'll not abide that again."

The agent moved towards Tobias and motioned for him to be seated.

"Let him speak," a woman's voice called out. "I want to hear what the boy has to say."

The agent stepped aside and frowned as he continued.

"I'll not have you hit your woman either. I've seen enough of that in my day. I guess as long as you feed me and let me go to school, I'll be happy." Tobias moved to sit then thought of something else. "Oh, and my teeth are not rotten; they are just missing. A man told me so, and I guess since he gets money just for looking at teeth, he'd know."

The last was met with snickers from the crowd. Tobias returned to his seat, and much to his disappointment, there were no hands raised.

So much for telling the truth.

***

It was well into the evening when the knock came upon the door to the church. Tobias was the only child who'd not been placed. The other agent had left on the evening train. He and Agent Smith had settled for the night, stretched out on the pews, which were converted into makeshift beds. Agent Smith told him they would try again tomorrow in a nearby town. He'd cautioned him to be less forthcoming about what he was asking for in a home, saying folks were not likely to pick a rabble-rouser.

Tobias lifted his head, peeking above the bench to see who'd entered. He could only make out a shadow in the candlelight. A woman, it seemed, rather large, wearing a skirt that skimmed the floor as she moved. The woman spoke in urgent whispers, arms flailing and giving way to monstrous images that danced along the walls of the hallowed room. The agent looked in his direction, and Tobias ducked. More whispers floated through the air, only this time, the whispers mentioned him by name.

Tobias raised his head once more. Smith motioned for

him to join them. He scurried to his feet, anxious to see what the fuss was about. As he thought, the shadow was indeed a woman, a rather robust one at that. In truth, she was as large as she was old.

Smith smiled at Tobias and placed a hand on his shoulder. "Mrs. Fannie is offering to take you home with her. She does not have a husband, but the committee has approved her credentials."

Tobias blinked his surprise. The woman in front of him was decidedly different from what he'd expected.

"Close your mouth there, boy; you'll catch a fly. Gather your belongings, and we'll be on our way. That is, unless you want to wait and see if you get any better offers," the woman scoffed.

Tobias looked the woman over for several moments before finally nodding his acceptance.

"We shall bid you farewell, Mr. Smith. And if for some reason it does not work, we will send you a letter." She smiled at him. "I doubt that will be necessary, but we will post you a letter just the same, just to let you know how he's getting along."

Tobias left the same way he'd arrived, with the clothes on his back and the gifted book stuffed into the waistband of his pants. The hope he'd had upon arrival only slightly diminished. The rain had given way to a star-filled sky with moonlight illuminating the street.

Mrs. Fannie gathered her skirts and stepped off into the muddy street. "We'll just be around the corner and down the street a bit. As Mr. Smith said, I don't have a man in the house. You won't get a father, but then again, neither of us will have a man to slap us around. I wasn't really looking for a young'un. I had two. They died umpteen years back of the whooping cough. Husband too. He went first. Can't say I miss him. Miss the boys, though. Maybe that's why I went to the Opera House. Anyhow, I wasn't expecting to bring any of you home, so I didn't have the paperwork filled out. It took me all day to get that settled. Not that there was any rush. Do you know why no one spoke up for you, boy?"

The woman was surprisingly fast on her feet and he nearly had to run to keep up. "Mr. Smith said it was because people don't like rabble-rousers."

"Yes, well, at my age, I find it best to know where you stand with a person. Do you know why I picked you, Tobias?"

"Because I was the only one left?" he replied.

"Because you spoke the truth. Like I said, I like knowing where I stand with people. Too many people these days like to stretch the truth, but not you. No siree. I can see you are honest as the day is long. When you've been around as long as I have, you learn how to judge people. We're over here," she said, cutting through a yard to get to a small house with a covered front porch. "It's not much, but it stays cool in the summertime and warm in the wintertime. Can't ask for anything more than that, can you, boy?"

"No, ma'am," Tobias said, following her inside.

The front room appeared cozy and delightfully warm. Multiple chairs filled the room, each facing the hearth, which took up an entire wall of the small room. The room glowed its welcome from the low fire burning in the fireplace.

Mrs. Fannie stooped, added a log from a pile in the corner, and soon the fire was blazing higher. She pointed at a rocking chair that appeared to match her in age. "That's my chair; you are free to sit anywhere else. My daddy made that chair for me and gave it to me on my wedding day. He made things to last, which I guess is the reason it outlasted the man I married. He was a fair one until we got hitched, then his true colors started showin'. Sometimes a man's soul is so black, there's no help for it. I was young then and didn't see it coming. He was so ornery, he took my boys when he left. Haven't seen them in years."

Tobias sat on the floor and pulled off his shoes. He looked up. "I thought you said they died of the whopping cough."

A puzzled look crossed the woman's face. "Did I say that? I must have been mistaken. Why are you sitting on the floor?"

He shrugged. "I was taking my shoes off."

"Yes, well, pull yourself up from there. People will think I don't have what it takes to care for a boy."

He wondered what people she was speaking of but obliged her anyway.

Mrs. Fannie looked toward the kitchen. "I made a coconut pie yesterday. Would you like a piece?"

"I've not had pie in a long time," he said, following her into the kitchen.

"Didn't your momma fix pie?" she asked, reaching into the cabinet.

"No, ma'am. We didn't have money for extras such as that." He watched as she cut two slices of what looked to be cherry pie. She lifted a slice and placed it on a small plate in front of him. *Hadn't she said coconut?* Maybe he was mistaken. "That looks like cherry pie."

She sat opposite him. "Of course it's cherry. What were you expecting?"

Coconut. He took a bite. "It's good."

"You say that as if you are surprised."

"No, ma'am. Just happy to be eating is all."

"Tell me about yourself, boy," the woman said, taking a bite.

Tobias dipped his fork into the pie. "What do you want

to know?"

This evoked a chuckle from the woman. "If I knew what I wanted to know, there would be no need for you to tell me now, would there?"

"I guess not." He took another bite and thought of what to tell her. Finally, he decided on the truth since that was why she picked him in the first place. "My name is Tobias. But my friends on the street call me Mouse. I had a papa and momma, but I think they are dead."

"What makes you think that?"

"Well, Ezra, he's my brother. He told me that my momma was dead and I saw him stick my papa with a knife, so I think my papa might be dead as well."

Mrs. Fannie cocked her head. "Did Ezra kill your mother too?"

"Oh no, ma'am. It was my papa who killed my momma. At least, that was what Ezra said."

She pointed towards him with her fork. "And you believe what your brother told you?"

"Oh, yes, ma'am. I've never known Ezra to lie," he said between bites.

"When did all of this happen?"

"I guess I don't know the exact date. I've been living on the street for some time now."

Her eyes grew wide. "Why, you are no more than a baby. How could you survive on the streets of a big city?"

He bristled. "I'm not a baby. I'm nearly six."

"Nearly six is still awfully young for a boy to be running the streets alone," she countered.

"Not in New York City. There are lots of us kids living on the streets there. Some are even younger than me. Besides, I wasn't alone. Not until the end anyway."

Mrs. Fannie sliced another piece of pie and slid it onto

his plate. "No?"

"No, my friends Lucky and Chunk were with me. They're the ones who taught me how to dip pockets." He went on to tell her about learning the trade and the events that led to him being sent out on the trains.

Mrs. Fannie sat back in her chair. "Do you do it very well?"

"Do what?"

"Pick pockets?"

Tobias frowned. "Not as good as Lucky and he's missing some fingers. He said I have to learn to be invisible, but I ain't learned that yet."

A slow smile spread across her face. "That's because he didn't teach you properly."

Tobias stared at her in disbelief. "What do you know about dipping pockets?"

The smile spread. "Wait here."

He finished the second piece of pie, lifted the plate, and licked it clean. In his world, nothing was left to waste. He'd just set the plate down when Mrs. Fannie returned.

She had a coat draped over a wooden hanger, which she hung over a cabinet door. There was a handkerchief in the right front pocket. She reached a gnarled finger toward him then pointed to the kerchief. "Let me see how good you are. Pretend as if I am wearing the coat and remove that from my pocket."

"You are treating me like a child, asking me to take something I can easily see."

"Well, Mr. Smarty Pants, show me you can take it," she teased.

Begrudgingly, Tobias stood. He made small talk about the pie as he crossed the room. As he neared, he pointed to a painting on the wall to draw her attention. As soon as her eyes lifted to the painting, he slid his hand in, intending to retrieve his prize. To his surprise, as he lifted the handkerchief, he heard a bell. He tugged the cloth free and found it had a string sewn to the end. Pulling the string, he found it attached to two small jingle bells.

He narrowed his eyes. "You tricked me!"

"If we were on the streets, you would have been caught and thrown into jail," she said, reaching for the cloth. Tucking it in, she made a show of placing it and the bells back into the pocket. Then she tucked it firmly out of sight. "If you are finished with your plate, you can place the dishes in the sink."

He stood and retrieved both plates. As he was placing them in the sink, he heard the bell. He turned and pointed at the coat. "Ah ha!"

To his surprise, Mrs. Fannie was not standing by the coat as he'd thought but sitting at the table, dangling the handkerchief for him to see. He had to give her credit; the woman could move. He hurried and took a seat at the table. "How'd you learn to do that?"

The woman's eyes twinkled with delight. "I learned a long time ago on the streets of London. My family was dirt poor, and my father became ill. We were in danger of starving to death, so I went out on the street to find us food. I met a boy, and he showed me how to dip pockets. He told me I would be no good until I could pull the handkerchief from the pocket without ringing the bells. It took me months of practicing every day to learn. I would often grow impatient. But as you know, hunger is a great motivator. Each time my belly would rumble, I would pull out that hanky. And soon, I learned so well that my belly was not often without food."

Suddenly, it all made sense. "So that's why you are so fat?!"

The woman started laughing, her girth shaking as tears welled in her eyes. "You are without a doubt the most straightforward child I have ever met."

Tobias wasn't sure what that meant, but her reaction told him it was a good thing. "Does that mean you will teach me how to pull the handkerchief without ringing the bells?"

Calmer now, Fannie wiped the tears from her eyes. "Boy, I am an old woman with nothing but time on my hands. I will teach you everything I know."

"Lucky said I have to be invisible. Can you teach me how to do that?"

She studied him for several moments then asked him to move closer. She closed her eyes and placed her hands together just in front of him. "You're a ghost."

"Is that like being invisible?"

"It's better than being invisible, just you wait and see," she said, lowering her arms.

Chapter Eleven

March 17ᵗʰ, 1916

The sun was high in the sky when Tobias woke. He hurried to make his bed then went to the closet to retrieve the old coat. Climbing onto the stool, he placed the hanger on a high nail. Stepping to the floor, he reached inside the pocket, removing the handkerchief without as much as a jingle from the bells. He'd been doing the same routine for months, being careful to hang the coat at different heights to represent various heights of those he might encounter. Not that he'd had the opportunity to truly test his skills. Mrs. Fannie hadn't allowed him outside the house other than to use the outhouse since the day he arrived. Each time he'd asked, she'd say it was too cold and tell him she was afraid he'd catch his death of cold. He replaced the hanky, returned the coat to his closet, and went in search of Mrs. Fannie.

She was not hard to find; he could smell breakfast cooking the second he opened his bedroom door. He followed his nose down the short hallway to the kitchen.

"So you're still here," she said when he entered. "I suppose you'll be wanting breakfast, then."

"It would be nice to have something to eat if you don't mind," Tobias answered, taking his usual seat at the table. It was not the first time she appeared surprised to see him. The first time it happened, he'd thought her to be teasing him. They had the same conversation often, as if she expected him to leave during the night.

Mrs. Fannie turned from the stove. "What will it be today, boy?"

"I'll have some of that ham and eggs," he said, nodding to the stove.

"You're in luck. I just happen to have enough."

Her comment didn't surprise him. It seemed that even though she appeared surprised to see him, she made enough to share.

A sadness crossed over her face, as if wondering why she'd made so much.

If he didn't act quickly, tears would soon follow and he wasn't good with tears. "Tell me some more about when you lived on the streets of London."

Sure enough, her mood lifted. "Ah, those were the days. I can remember one time my friend Phillip and I went down to the boats. We made sure to stay with boats that would be leaving soon. That way, if we were caught, it was rather unlikely they would do anything but run us from the boat. You see, if they decided to pursue us, they would have to go to the station and file a report. If they did that, then they might miss the boat. There were some that would steal everything in sight. But not us. Phillip and I never acted out of greed. Most folks were not likely to bother a constable over a few shillings or any of the other stuff we lifted. We wore our Sunday best, although our best wasn't very good. Even so, it was better than the rags we wore most days. I had a lovely red basket full of beautiful combs for the ladies' hair. Of course, none of the ladies knew we'd stolen them from other ladies such as themselves. My job was to distract the lady, or gentleman, as they often purchased things for their wives, while Phillip took whatever he could find to sell."

Tobias leaned back as Mrs. Fannie sat two loaded breakfast plates on the table. The woman sure knew how to cook. He waited for her to sit, as she'd instructed on one occasion, before digging in.

She chuckled, then continued. "I recall one occasion of us being led into a spacious cabin where a woman was rooting through her suitcase in search of a particular comb for her hair. Her husband was trying to tell her she'd forgotten the thing, but the woman was certain she'd packed it. To her surprise, we had one exactly like the one she was searching for. Her dear husband was happy to fork over several shillings just to find some peace."

"How was it you happened to have the exact one she was searching for?" he asked.

This produced yet another chuckle. "Because Phillip had stolen it from her pocket as we followed them up the gangway."

Tobias stopped chewing. "And she did not recognize it as her own?"

She pointed a ham-loaded fork at him. "Of course not. She was just happy to have the comb that matched the outfit she wanted to wear. I figure the ship was halfway to America by the time she realized it had been hers all along. If she ever realized at all."

Tobias inhaled just as he took a bite of egg. The egg went down the wrong way, throwing him into a coughing fit.

Mrs. Fannie's face went pale. She stood, sending her chair crashing to the floor, and hurried to where he was sitting. Without so much as a word, she gathered him in her arms and hurried from the house in a panic. The more she jostled him, the worse he coughed. It didn't help that she carried him facing her and his face was pressed firmly into her bosom.

Mrs. Fannie, put me down. I can't breathe.

Unable to articulate his thoughts between coughs and her suffocating bosom, his words went unheard, his pleas unheeded as she continued to run. Where they were going, he hadn't a clue, as all he could see was the calico print on the day dress she wore.

"What's the matter, Mrs. Lisowski?" a voice called.

"My boy, he has the whooping cough." The words came out in a great sob.

Tobias' mouth went dry. *I have the whooping cough?* He'd seen plenty of instances of what that could do to a body. He remembered hearing his neighbor's racking cough through the walls of their tenement building and hearing the sadness in his mother's voice as she declared him not long for this world. Was that the fate which awaited him? He didn't want to believe it, but he was coughing.

A door opened, and he could hear Mrs. Fannie's bare feet slapping heavily on the wood floor.

"Doctor Sid? You have to do something," she wailed. "It's my boy, he's dying. He's done gone and caught the coughing disease."

It was true, then.

As rough hands peeled him from his new mother's arms, Tobias began to cry, and this time, there was nothing insincere about the wetness that poured from his eyes.

***

It didn't take the doctor long to figure out Tobias was not ill. Unfortunately, Mrs. Fannie was still in an agitated state and Dr. Sid was busy trying to calm her.

Against his wishes, which he made firmly known, he'd not been allowed to stay with her. Instead, he'd been taken to a house across town and pelted with questions by a short man in a dark suit, who identified himself as Mr. Cole, the town banker. The door opened and several men joined them in the large room.

"Gentlemen, come in. I'm glad you're all able to join us. Please be seated," Cole said, pointing to the dining room chairs a second man, who had been introduced as Mr. Johnston, had carried in and placed in the center of the room.

The men each took a chair and looked expectantly at Tobias.

"Tell us again how you came to be in Mrs. Lisowski's care," the man sitting across from him said.

Tobias narrowed his eyes. "I told you two times. Where is Mrs. Fannie?"

The man looked to the others. "Now, son, there's no need to be impertinent. I know you told me and Mr. Johnston here, but now I need to you tell the other members of the committee."

Tobias looked to the other men. "And then you'll let me go see Mrs. Fannie?"

"First things first," Cole said with a glance toward the others. "Now tell the others what you told us about how you came to be living with Mrs. Lisowski."

Tobias wanted to tell them to get lost but knew the only way he was going to be allowed to return home was to answer their questions. "I was in the church when Mrs. Fannie came and got me."

"What were you doing in the church?" one of the men asked.

"I was in the church because no one in this town wanted a boy who dared tell the truth," he said heatedly. To his satisfaction, the man turned a deep shade of red.

"He was with Agent Smith; the church knew they were there," the man called Johnston explained. "Go on with your story, son."

"Mrs. Fannie wasn't looking for a kid. She decided too late and had to rush around to get the paperwork signed. You men are on the committee, so you should know," he fumed.

"And you have been living with Mrs. Fannie since that first day?" the red-faced man asked.

Tobias nodded. "I have."

His face scrunched in thought. "Why, that was five months ago. How come no one has seen you?"

Tobias kicked at the floor. "Because Mrs. Fannie was scared I'd take up a cold."

"So you haven't left the house in five months?" he repeated.

"Of course I have."

The man leaned forward. "Well, where'd you go?"

Tobias leaned in close, and all the men leaned forward to hear what he was about to say. "I went to the privy."

For some reason, the men found his answer humorous, as they all laughed.

"Well, I can't see that I had any other choice, since Mrs. Fannie's house is not fitted with a water closet," Tobias added.

"In all your time going to the outhouse, you didn't see anyone?" This time, it was Cole who asked.

Tobias shook his head. "No, not a single person."

Another man spoke up. "And you didn't think it strange that Mrs. Lisowski didn't let you out of the house?"

"Mister, when you've lived on the streets as long as I have and find yourself in a warm house with plenty of food, you don't ask too many questions."

The man nodded in agreement. "What did you do in the house?"

Tobias scrunched his brows. "What do you mean?"

"Five months is a long time for a boy such as yourself to be holed up inside. What did you do to pass the time?"

"I learned things."

"Mrs. Lisowski used to be a teacher. Before..." a man

with a large mole on his cheek added then turned back to Tobias. "What did she teach you?"

Tobias considered this for a moment. So far, he'd told the truth, but men like these would not be happy if they knew him to be capable of stealing from them, so he opted to leave out the part of dipping pockets. "She taught me my letters and my numbers. I cannot read just yet, but I can count really high. Want to hear?"

Cole waved him off. "No, that won't be necessary. Did she teach you anything else, son?"

"She just told me stories about when she was young and living in London." There, that wasn't a lie.

"I didn't know Fannie lived in London," one of the men commented.

"Probably another of her tall tales," the man with the mole offered and several of the others snickered.

Cole raised a hand to quiet them. "Did Mrs. Lisowski ever seem off to you, son?"

"Did she ever say things that were not true, son?" another man asked when Tobias didn't answer.

Of course she had, but he wasn't about to tell the men this. He glared at the men before him. "Mrs. Fannie doesn't lie."

A man who hadn't spoken before smiled. "Mrs. Fannie told the whole town you had the whooping cough. 'Bout scared the women folk out of their minds. My Florence had to take a drink of tonic just to calm herself. You don't think that was stretching the truth?"

"I was coughing. She was scared," Tobias replied.

"And why do you think a little cough would scare the woman, son?"

"Because cough is what killed her husband and little boys."

"That's an out and out lie," the man with the mole said.

"Mrs. Lisowski's husband left her years ago. Told the court she was crazy and took the boys with him when he moved back to live near his mother in Indianapolis."

Tobias stood and yelled at the men, "She is not crazy. She just...sometimes she don't remember too well."

Cole stood. "Now calm down, son."

Tobias doubled his fist. "I'm not going to calm down, and I'm not your son. I am not any of your sons. My name is Tobias. You had the chance to adopt me, and you didn't do it. Only Mrs. Fannie came for me. She may forget things, but she is nice to me and I've never gone to bed hungry. She cooks real swell and since I've never given her cause, she's never laid a hand on me. Now if you would please take me to her, I would be much obliged."

Cole placed a hand on Tobias' shoulder.

"Keep your hands off of me and take me to my mother!" The last comment surprised everyone, including him.

"She's not your mother, Tobias, and we cannot in good conscience allow you to stay with the woman. It just wouldn't be proper," Cole said softly.

"Then who's going to take him in?" the man with the mole asked, looking for direction from the other men.

"Nobody," another man said firmly. "The contracts all state that if a placement doesn't work out, the child is to be sent back."

"But there was not actually a contract. The papers must have been fabricated. Maybe we should check with the townsfolk again, just to be sure."

"Earl, if you're not willing to take the boy in, then I must insist we send him back. If we put him in another home and it doesn't work out, it will make us look bad. They'll wonder why we didn't follow the rules," the man with the mole added.

Earl lowered his head.

"Is it settled, then?"

It took several moments, but in the end, each man nodded his agreement.

Cole sighed. "I shall purchase him a ticket on the evening train. After the train departs, I'll send a telegram letting them know to expect him. It's better that way."

***

True to his word, Cole escorted him to the train station just as the evening train arrived. While he had been taken to the house to retrieve his coat and shoes, Cole had not allowed him to say goodbye to Mrs. Fannie.

"It's for your own good, son," the man said softly.

"I told you not to call me son." Tobias swallowed, trying to maintain his composure. "You could have at least let me say goodbye."

"The doctor had a difficult time calming her and didn't think that a good idea."

Tobias scowled at the man who hadn't let him out of his sight. "I didn't see you talking to no doctor."

Cole shifted from side to side. "Now, Tobias, this is the attitude that got you into this predicament in the first place. You have an edge to you that makes folks uncomfortable. I'd swear if I didn't know better, you have red hair under all that darkness."

His father had red hair, but Tobias decided not to mention that. He preferred not to think of the man, much less talk about him. The train conductor shouted for people to board, drawing their attention. "Will you at least tell Mrs. Fannie I didn't wish to go? And that I'll remember everything she taught me."

Cole considered him for a moment. "I'll tell her of your

reluctances. Now you must climb onboard before the train closes its doors."

He sniffed and turned towards the conductor.

"Tobias?"

He turned back towards Cole.

"The committees were formed to see that things like this don't happen. You should never have been in that home in the first place. I know you don't believe it now, but this really is for your own good."

Tobias wanted to shout ugly words at the man. Words so vile, they would make him turn as red as the man in the living room. Instead, he turned and walked towards the train without further comment, tears sliding down his face with each step. He handed the conductor his ticket and took an empty seat on the far side of the train. He would not give Cole the satisfaction of seeing him cry. As the train jerked to a start, Tobias reached into his pocket for the hanky he'd taken from Mrs. Fannie's house to remember her by. He smiled through his tears as the cloth slipped free without as much as a jingle.

Chapter Twelve

Cindy opened her eyes, wondering if she'd actually heard a noise or if it had been just another part of the unsettling dream. She lay there fogging in and out, trying to determine the time without actually turning to look at the clock. The sun was up, but given the low lighting in the room, it had to be early.

"I was wondering if you were ever going to wake up."

Cindy's heart skipped a beat. "Mom? What are you doing in here? You about scared the crap out of me."

"I was waiting for you to wake up so we could see what happens next," Linda replied.

"Mom, we need to have a discussion on boundaries. What time is it anyway?"

"Just after five."

Cindy took a calming breath. "Five? It's my summer break. I'm supposed to sleep in."

"How can you sleep in when there are journals to read? Aren't you worried about Tobias?"

That was precisely the problem. She'd been so worried about the boy, she'd barely slept. When she did finally drift off, her dreams were filled with images of the child alone on the train heading back to the monster she knew to be New York City. "Of course I am, but it's not as if we both don't know what will become of him."

Linda's face darkened. "It didn't have to be, you know. He obviously cared enough about the woman to name his daughter after her. If they'd have let him stay, things might have been different."

Cindy sat up and maneuvered to the side of the bed. "Maybe, maybe not. Clearly something's up with Mrs. Fannie."

"Probably dementia, or something like that. You remember how Uncle Frank started," Linda mused.

Cindy did remember, and her mother was right; it did have a similar ring. Rambling about things that didn't make sense, forgetting things he should have known. "Maybe, but if the journals are correct, these things had been going on for a long time."

"What makes you think that?"

"One of the men referred to the husband having left because Fannie was crazy. Tobias referred to her as being old. The guy said he took the boys, so it had to have been years prior."

"The boy is young, so I wouldn't put too much stock in him thinking Fannie is old. I'm sure some of your students think the same thing about you." Linda tapped her fingers on the arm of the chair like she tended to do when thinking. "One of the guys mentioned she used to be a school teacher. Would they have hired her if she were crazy?"

"Who knows? It was the early nineteen hundreds. I'm not sure what kind of vetting process they had in those days. Besides, Tobias seemed to think she was fine, other than being forgetful."

Linda laughed. "The boy was what, six? Do you really think he was capable of determining if someone were sane or not?"

Cindy raised her eyebrows. "We are talking about Tobias, right? That boy is more astute than I am. Can you imagine being savvy enough to steal a key from strangers so that you had a place to live for the better part of winter?"

The smile left Linda's face. "Up until we discovered

these journals, I couldn't even figure out how to live past the death of my husband, and I'm seventy-two."

Cindy was well aware of the effect the journals had had on her mother's mental health. She'd tried everything she could think of to get her mother out of her funk, but each day, the woman sank deeper. It wasn't until they'd discovered the journals and started reading them together that the light returned to her mother's eyes. She reached over and touched her mother's hand. "Finding the journals was what we both needed."

"How so?"

"You found something that makes you feel alive, and I got my mother back."

Linda laughed. "Now don't we sound like a sappy pair?"

"Sappy is okay." *I'll take sappy over depressed any day.* "Let me get some coffee and check my e-mail, and I'll meet you in the living room."

Linda pulled herself from the recliner beside Cindy's bed. "You see to your e-mail, and I'll get you the coffee."

"Deal." Cindy walked to her office and opened her laptop. As her computer came to life, her phone chimed, letting her know she had mail. She looked at her phone and saw she had an e-mail from Gravedigger59. She hurried to log in to her account, struggling not to get her hopes up. She'd sent her latest request for information before she went to bed. Most likely this was just an e-mail letting her know he'd received it. Even so, she held her breath as she hit the button to open the email.

Good morning, Cindy,

I saw your e-mail when I woke this morning. Since this old body don't let me sleep more than a few hours at a time, and the internet is smoking fast at 3 am, I had plenty of time to poke through the weeds. Good news, I was able to locate Fannie

Lisowski. She was rather easy to find, since you provided so much information. I wish all my searches were this easy. Anyway, since you mentioned a possible London connection, I decided to dig a bit further. This posed a bit more of a challenge, but hey, I like to test my skills now and then. So this is what I found.

Fannie Marie Collins was born to Rita and Brian Collins on September 10th, 1859 In Liverpool, England.

According to records, Rita boarded the steamer ship, City of Limerick *on July 5th, 1871. My calculations will have your girl at about eleven years old. According to the ship's manifest, Rita was listed as a spinster. We already know she was married, so that was simply a term for a woman traveling alone. Since the husband was not with her, and she was not classified as a wife, I did some more digging. I found that Rita's husband, Brian, and two sons, Patrick and Phillip, died from whooping cough a year prior. I picked up your girl again in 1878 when she married Ralph Lisowski in Indianapolis, Indiana. I found a land deed from the house they purchased in Noblesville, Indiana the same year. They were listed as married and living together on the 1880 census, but then I found court records from July 23rd, 1885, which shows Fannie was granted a divorce on the grounds of abandonment. Just an FYI, no children are mentioned anywhere. It doesn't mean Fannie did not have any; it just means none survived. Women in those days gave birth at home, and the birth was not documented until such time when the family made it to the courthouse to do so. It was common practice not to put a name on the original birth ledger for upwards of a month. Infant mortality was high, and if a child died early, it was not recorded. I found a death certificate for her from November, 1934.*

Thanks for helping keep this old brain active, I hope this information is of help to you.

Let me know if I can be of further help. I live for this kind of stuff.

Bruce

Cindy's hands shook as she hit print and waited impatiently for the printer to spool up. She snatched the paper from the printer just as Linda arrived with a steaming cup of coffee.

"Well, something's got you in a state. If I didn't know better, I'd say you got a letter from a secret lover," Linda said, handing over the cup.

"Better," Cindy said, taking a sip.

Linda's eyes took on a faraway look, and a smile played at the corners of her mouth. "Nothing's as good as a secret lover."

"Mom, whatever you are getting ready to say, don't," Cindy said, shoving the paper at her. Cindy watched as the smile disappeared and Linda's mouth fell open as she read.

"The man is a regular Sherlock Holmes." She lowered the paper and looked at Cindy. "It says she had a brother named Phillip. Do you think that could be the same Phillip she referred to as her friend?"

"That's what I was thinking. It also mentions whooping cough; maybe she wasn't crazy. Well, not in the same way as we think of it. Maybe she had some kind of post-traumatic stress disorder. It would explain why she got so upset when Tobias coughed. If that was the trigger, it could be the reason she lost her teaching job as well. Kids get sick all the time. If she had students coughing in class, it could have been a vicious cycle that kept tormenting her over and over."

Linda nodded her agreement. "The fact that she refers to her brother as her friend instead of her brother tells us they were probably very close. It must have been very hard on the poor thing when he died."

Sherry A. Burton

"So instead of getting the help she needed to work through her pain, she was simply declared crazy. Poor woman, I wonder how she fared after they took Tobias away."

"We'll probably never get the answer to that one," Linda said softly.

"Agreed. But we can read the rest of the boy's journals." While Cindy loved that her mother's face brightened at the mere mention of the journals, a small piece of her wondered what would happen when the journals had all been read. Would she continue to move forward with her life or would she sink back into despair? Cindy took a deep breath. There were plenty of journals left; they'd cross that bridge if and when they reached it.

Cindy followed as Linda led the way down the hall and into the living room, and laughed when she saw a basket with packages of cookies and several bags of chips. Her gaze shifted to a cooler sitting in the middle of the floor. "What's in the cooler, Mom?"

Linda slid onto her usual spot on the couch. "A couple sandwiches, some snacks, and a few bottles of water."

Cindy bit her lip. "As opposed to walking twenty steps to the kitchen."

"Yes, but this way, if we are hungry, we can just reach in and grab something without having to stop reading."

It suddenly occurred to her that her mother was becoming obsessed with the journals. "What's next? A catheter, so we don't have to get up to go to the bathroom?"

Linda grinned. "Want a Depend? I have a box in my bedroom."

Cindy sighed. "Mom, I hate to say it, but I think you may need an intervention."

Linda patted the couch beside her. "Aren't you always saying we need to do more things together?"

"You've got me there." Taking a seat on the couch, Cindy reached in the basket and snatched a bag of cookies. Breakfast at its finest. She took a drink of cool coffee, wishing she'd topped off her mug before sitting. "I'm surprised you didn't bring the coffee pot in."

Linda smiled and pointed to a thermos on the side table. "You just let me know when you need a refill."

***

Tobias had plenty of time to brood over the next three days. The more he thought of Mrs. Fannie, the worse his disposition. He'd made several attempts to get off the train during the frequent stops, but Cole had paid extra for him to have a constant attendant to see to his wellbeing. The attendant, a young man named Robert Clarke, had transferred trains twice along with Tobias, and to his credit, Clarke took his job seriously. On occasions during which the man had gone to the privy, he'd called for a train agent, who didn't let Tobias out of his sight.

The train jerked to a stop in Grand Central Station, and Clarke stepped beside his seat, turning on occasion to allow someone to pass. "We'll be the last ones off, so you don't get lost in the crowd."

Tobias let out a sigh. Hopefully, he would have better luck once he was handed off to the agent. He decided to pretend to cooperate in hopes of lessening the man's defenses. "Where are we supposed to meet the agent?"

Clarke pulled out his wallet, revealing several bills as he drew out the paper that held the agent's name. Tobias watched closely as Clarke returned the wallet to his front coat pocket. "We are to meet Agent Houser at the clock tower in thirty minutes."

Tobias followed Clarke into the station. As they entered, they were greeted with rich smells of baked goods and other offerings. The place was full of people, and several times, he was pushed into Clarke as people made their way to and from the trains.

Tobias' stomach rumbled. He hesitated and tugged at Clarke's jacket to get the man's attention. "Best keep an eye on your wallet. This is the kind of place where thieves rob ya blind."

Clarke reached for his wallet, and his face went pale. "It's gone!"

Tobias surveyed the room and pointed. "There's a policeman. You should tell him at once."

In his panic, Clarke raced to the officer, leaving him alone for the first time since he'd taken him in his charge. Tobias waited for a crowd to near then maneuvered between them, heading up the white marble ramp towards the main floor. Reaching the top, he got his bearings and headed for the nearest exit. The sun was past the buildings, and the air held a chill. He smelled food and followed his nose to a street cart selling hot pretzels.

"What'll it be, kid?" The man asked when he approached.

"I'll have a pretzel with mustard."

The man leaned over the cart. "You got money, kid?"

Tobias reached into his coat pocket and pulled out Clarke's wallet. "Of course I got money. What do I look like, a bum?"

Chapter Thirteen

Monday, April 22, 1918

Tobias jumped from the second stair of the trolley and began his daily stroll down Park Avenue. He was dressed in his finest outfit, and so accustomed were people to seeing him, most nodded in greeting when they neared.

He saw her coming and stooped to tie his shoe. He watched out the corner of his eye until she passed before rising and hurrying to the apartment she'd just vacated. He used the key he'd pilfered to enter the apartment, just as he'd done nearly every day since arriving back in the city. It had taken him a few days to locate the right apartment and two weeks of shadowing the couple before he felt confident enough actually to enter. Adam was easy; he went to work each day, preferred to have lunch at a café nearby his office, and did not return to the apartment until after five. Felisha was a bit more difficult. She went to the market on Mondays and Fridays, so he had to be cautious of how much time he spent in the apartment. Tuesdays and Thursdays were a bit better, as she went to a morning tea several streets over, where she and her friends would discuss what books they were reading and talk about girl things. They even talked about their husbands and laughed. That bit of information had come as a big surprise, as he'd never heard his mother talk badly about his father. Still, he knew this to be true as he'd made his way up the back stairs and crawled through the open window of the apartment on more than one occasion. He stopped that practice when nearly caught by the woman serving the ladies tea and cookies. On Wednesdays, Felisha remained in her apartment until ten, then she would walk to the end of the street and climb on the trolley to go have lunch with Adam. He liked Wednesdays, as it gave him plenty of time to sneak into the apartment, find something to eat, and take a hot bath without having to pay. Saturday evenings, the couple always met friends for dinner and danced well into the night, giving Tobias a safe place to catch a few hours' sleep. Sundays allowed him to wash out his second set of clothes as the couple always enjoyed a lengthy lunch after attending church.

He entered the apartment and went straight to the kitchen to see what kind of goodies she'd left for him today. Oh, to be sure, she didn't know she was leaving him anything, but sometimes he'd pretend that she had. He went to the small icebox and smiled when he saw the roast. Felisha was a creature of habit; there was always leftover roast on Monday. He carved off a slice with his pocketknife then returned the roast to the icebox. He lifted a cloth on the counter and used the same knife to carve a small slice of bread. Replacing the cloth exactly as he'd found it, he moved to the cabinet and removed a plate. Taking a cup from the same cabinet, he drew some water from the sink. He would have preferred to have a bit of milk, but there was never milk in the apartment on Monday. He sat at the table and ate his breakfast in silence. Sometimes he'd pretend Felisha and Adam were there with him. Today was not one of those times. He finished his meal and took his plate to the opposite counter, where he knew there would be something sweet to finish the meal. This is the one area where Felisha was not a creature of habit; there was always something different. Sometimes so different, he didn't know what it was called, but that did not lessen the taste. He lifted the cover, exposing a white cake with pink frosting. He wiped the blade of his knife across his shirt before cutting a thin slice and taking it to the table to enjoy.

When he finished, he rinsed his plate and glass in the sink then removed his shirt, drying each dish before returning them to the cabinet. He'd made the mistake of using the kitchen towel once, but the wrinkles left in the cloth scared him. The last thing he wanted was for anyone to know he'd been there. He returned to the icebox, pulled out the drip tray, and emptied the contents into the sink. Doing so had been his job for the short time he'd lived with Mrs. Fannie, and somehow it made him feel close to the woman.

Tobias looked to the clock on the wall and did a quick search of the kitchen to make sure he hadn't forgotten anything. Crossing the room, he placed his ear to the door for several seconds before leaving the same way he came in.

Racing down the street, he rounded the corner just as Felisha stepped off the trolley. He reached for her bags, which she gladly relinquished. "Good morning, Mrs. Wilson. How was the market today?"

"Good, thank you. How is your mother this fine day?"

He fell in beside her. "She says she is good. But my grandmother still does all the cooking and cleaning."

"Your family is lucky to have your grandmother."

"To be sure. I don't know what Father and I would do without her. It is just they are all so busy taking care of my mother…"

"Yes, well, sick people require a great deal of care. Tell me, Tobias, do you have time for another lesson today or do you need to go home to help tend to your mother?"

He flashed a smile in her direction. "Oh, I have time. My mother is quite pleased to hear you are teaching me to read."

She returned his smile. "Yes, well, it was such a lucky coincidence you saw me reading my book on the trolley that day. If not, I wouldn't have known you were unable to go to school because you were helping to care for your mother."

"Yes, ma'am, a lucky coincidence indeed," Tobias agreed.

In truth, Felisha had seen him because he'd been careless when shadowing her. The instant he'd been caught, he'd motioned to the book she was reading and made up the story to keep from being outed. It worked to his favor, as she took pity on him and offered to give him lessons on Mondays and Fridays after she returned from the market. In return, Tobias met her at the trolley stop and carried her bags.

"I've got some leftover roast beef if you would like some," Felisha said, opening the front door.

"No, ma'am, I've already had my breakfast," he replied, following her into the apartment.

"Well, the least you can do is to have a slice of cake. A boy simply cannot say no to cake."

He lowered the bags to the counter and watched as she pulled the same plate he'd used only moments before. "Oh, I guess I have room for a small piece."

***

Friday, May 10, 1918

Tobias stayed in the shadow of the building, waiting. It was well after five when the mark strolled by, oblivious to the boy hidden in the shadows. He fell in behind the man, keeping his distance as he made his way home. There was no hurry to rid the mark of his hard-earned money; he knew where the man lived, as he'd been following him for weeks. The man, one Mr. Livingston, always had cash on hand, but on Fridays, the wad he carried was significantly larger, and Tobias was intent on relieving him of his heavy load.

Today was the day he would make his move. The man

stopped to purchase a paper and looked over his shoulder as he pulled out some coins. This scenario had played out the same each day, and Tobias was ready for it, sinking into the shadows so as not to be seen. It was this very action that had piqued his curiosity in the first place. Experience told him only a man with something worthy of stealing would be so cautious. So he'd followed and learned. To the naked eye, Livingston owned a cigar store and did all right. But in reality, the store was a front. On more than one occasion, he'd watched as, just before closing time, a handful of men would enter, handing Livingston a stack of bills. Livingston would smile then casually walk to the front of the store and turn the sign around to show the shop closed. Moments later, Livingston would exit, repeatedly looking over his shoulder as he made his way home. After watching the same course of events play out on multiple occasions, Tobias' curiosity had gotten the better of him. Making his way to the back of the shop, he'd waited for Livingston to exit the rear entrance to toss the day's trash, and had entered the shop unnoticed.

Hiding in a closet in the large storeroom, he waited. His curiosity paid off when the door opened and the men entered. Tobias watched through the partially opened door as the men sat around a small table, playing cards, smoking cigars, and using language that would make a lady blush. The amount of money on the table nearly caused him to hyperventilate. Surely he could buy half of the city if he had that kind of money. If not for the pistols lying among the cash, he would have dared dashing to the table, grabbing a fistful of loot, and scurrying from the room before they knew he was there.

As it was, he'd lowered his sights to Livingston, knowing he could rid him of his wallet without the man being the wiser. Livingston paid for the paper, skimmed the headlines, and frowned. Shoving the paper under his left arm, he continued on his way. Tobias silently fell in behind him, intent on the big score, not a few pieces of silver. As they made their way down the tree-lined street, piano music drifted out through an open window of a large brownstone. A small girl sat on the porch, elbows on knees. Chin resting on her hands, her long hair hid the features of her face as she swayed to the tune. Something about the music tugged at him, insisting he investigate further. He sighed, watching as his mark turned the corner and disappeared from view.

Resigning himself to going to bed hungry, he approached the house and peeked through the open window. A woman with long curly black hair sat on the bench in front of a shiny black grand piano. Back straight and fingers gliding along the keyboard, the woman sat on the bench as if she belonged. The only thing out of place: she was dressed in clothing that belonged on the other side of town — his side.

A girl a few years older than he sat next to the woman, watching as the lady showed her which keys to press. When the woman finished playing, the girl took up where she'd left off. It was easy to see the girl needed more practice, as she kept hitting notes that made him cringe. Even still, he enjoyed the sound and decided since he'd already missed his window of opportunity with Livingston, he could find worse ways to pass the time.

He lowered to the ground and sat under the open window, eyes closed, listening to the music. It was easy to hear whether it was the woman who played or the student she was teaching. He pictured himself sitting on the bench and wondered if his fingers would ever be able to move so delicately. He could easily remove a wallet or coin purse without anyone noticing; would that talent translate to the keys of the shiny piano? Minutes raced past. Tobias knew he should be on his way, but the music continued to call to him, keeping him glued in place. He remembered the conversation with Mr. Twichell on the train and wondered if this was the kind of music of which the man had been speaking.

The music ended, replaced by muffled voices. The front door opened and the little girl disappeared inside the house. Tobias was just about to leave when the music started anew. This song was different, compellingly more dramatic than the first. The player must have had more practice with this tune, as the notes floated out the window so seamlessly, it left little doubt that it must be the woman with the raven black hair. Taking a chance, he pulled himself up and stared brazenly in through the window. The woman was still in place, but sitting at her side was the young girl who'd been sitting on the porch. With her hair now pulled from her face, it was easy to see she was several years younger than himself. It took him a second to realize it was the child whose fingers danced effortlessly along the keys, not the woman beside her. He wondered how long it had taken the girl to learn to play. He watched the tune through its entirety, mesmerized at the beauty of the melody, disappointed when at last it ended. It was then he noticed his eyes were moist and hurried to wipe them before he or the tears were discovered. It would be bad enough to be caught listening to music, much less to be labeled a sissy baby.

The woman stood and held out a hand to help the girl from the bench. A stern-looking lady came into the room, and the child hid behind the woman.

"I pay you to give my daughter lessons. Not waste my time with Mileta, who obviously does not need the practice. If you want to continue teaching here, you will not abuse my good graces again."

"I not cheat you. Your daughter's time was finished," the curly hair woman responded.

"Yes, well, Mileta is much younger than my Sarah and

plays exceptionally well. We would not wish for Sarah to feel inadequate. Especially to someone like that," the woman said, pointing at the child she'd called Mileta. "Now would we?"

The curly-haired woman shook her head. "I do not know this word, inquat?"

The stern-faced woman smiled a fake smile. "Let's just say children like your daughter do not belong on this side of town. You are welcome to bring her with you, but she must remain outside. If the weather is too dreadful, she may come in, but she is not allowed in the parlor. I am paying you, and as such, it is your job to make sure my daughter gets your full attention."

The woman handed the curly-haired woman several coins. The curly-haired woman counted the coins and frowned.

"I deducted the time that Mileta played. I am doing this for your own good, Melina. It is best you learn your place from me and not someone who would be…less forgiving."

The curly-haired woman gave a thin smile and tucked the coins into the front pocket of her dress. She took the young girl's hand, and they headed for the door. Tobias hid in the bushes until both woman and child passed before him, following at a distance and growing angrier with each step. While he was well aware of the social ranking of the city, it was obvious the woman, Melina, didn't understand enough English to fully realize what had just happened. Someone like her could easily become prey for someone who wished to do them harm, and then what would happen to the child? She'd most likely end up on the streets. Watching them walk down the street hand in hand reminded him of a simpler time when he used to walk to the market with his mother. The woman even reminded him of her, though his mother's hair had not been curly. The girl wasn't much younger than he when he'd been cast out onto the streets, and he'd survived. Still, she was a girl, and girls needed protecting. He thought about his sister and wondered for the hundredth time what had happened to her. Had there been anyone there to protect her? As Tobias followed, keeping his distance so as not to be seen, he made a vow to watch over this girl and do everything within his power to see that she remained safe. Why he felt so strongly, he wasn't quite certain; maybe it was just because it gave him a purpose when previously he'd had none.

Chapter Fourteen

Tobias was correct in his assumption of where mother and daughter lived. He followed them to Ludlow Street, just a couple streets over from St. Paul's Chapel on Broadway, both of which were located on what was known as the Lower East Side. He kept his distance as they walked into a tenement building at 49 Ludlow Street. The door closed behind them. He rushed to the entrance and peeked inside. Several people were milling about the hallway, but mother and daughter were nowhere in sight. He let himself inside and started up the stairs. His steps were hurried at first, but then he heard the little girl's voice and knew they were still in the stairwell above him. One flight above him, a door opened, the happy chattering replaced with heavy footsteps. He heard a man cough and slowed his pace. The man, a bucket in hand, narrowed his eyes at Tobias as he passed. It was then Tobias realized he was still wearing what he referred to as his uptown clothes. Uptown clothes were stylish, free from stains or holes, and rarely seen on the Lower East Side, most certainly not in a tenement building such as this.

Funny, the way clothes made a person. If Mileta and her mother had been wearing the proper clothing, the woman of the house probably would have welcomed them instead of turning up her nose and withholding her pay. Now it was he who was considered an outsider and he would have to hurry before someone questioned his presence. He stopped at the next landing, listening at the door. Not hearing anything, he pushed open the door to the fourth floor and eased it closed behind him.

The stark hallway was empty, except for a few children playing at the far end. He wrinkled his nose at the rancid smell of filth and disease, a norm for tenement buildings where multiple families squeezed within the walls of the adjoining apartments. He made his way along the long hallway, stopping to listen at each door. When he reached the end of the hall, he repeated the process in the opposite direction. While he heard voices, it was difficult to tell if they were the ones belonging to the people he sought. He thought about asking the children at the end of the hall, but children on this side of town didn't trust outsiders any more than adults on the other side of town trusted his kind. The poor kind. He repeated the process, listening at the doors, when suddenly, he heard the click of a door behind him. He turned just as Melina stepped into the hallway. She had a bucket in hand and headed for the stairs without looking in his direction. She reached the stairway door just as the man that had glared at him returned. They exchanged words in a language he did not know, but it seemed to have something to do with the buckets they each carried.

"I must not speak Polish," Milena said. "People look at me like I am no smart when I do."

"It is a different country we live in, to be sure," the man said, switching to the language of his new country. "What part of Poland are you from?"

"Karkonosze." Though Tobias could not see her face, he could hear the longing in her voice.

"Aye, yes, the mountains. So much different here, aye?"

"Very different, indeed."

The man's glance traced the length of her. "Your husband?"

Milena stiffened. "I must get the water. My daughter, she is waiting."

The man moved to let her pass and continued to watch

until the door closed behind her before continuing on his way. Tobias made note of which apartment she'd exited and decided to leave before anyone decided to question his appearance. He cast a glance to the bucket as the man passed. Water. If there was an issue, it might mean a lot of foot traffic in the building this evening, not good, as he'd already decided to stay the night. First, he would have to go home and change into something less memorable.

***

It only took a few moments for Tobias to get to St. Paul's Chapel. The chapel lights welcomed him home as they did most evenings. He walked in through the front gate and turned left, heading into the graveyard. Walking with nary a sound, he was nearly on top of the boys before they realized he was there.

"Sheesh, Mouse, you nearly scared me to death," a voice called from behind one of the headstones. "No one ever hears you coming, even when we're expecting you. I don't know how you do it, especially with the leaves and all."

"That's the reason they call him Mouse," a voice whispered.

"No one asked you, Tommy," the first boy replied.

At that, a small group of boys slinked from their hiding spots amongst the tombstones. While each boy was different in regard to height and age, they all had one thing in common. They were all dressed in rags, with a few being barefoot despite the cold.

The boy who'd first spoken jabbed a finger at him. "You're late. I was afraid they were going to close the gate before you made it home. Thought me and the boys would have to help you over the fence to keep you from getting your guts pierced by the spikes."

The boy, who went by the street name Slim, was a couple years older and stood a good foot taller than him. Slim tended to fidget and move around a lot, and could throw a punch better than anyone he knew. So good that Tobias had paid him to show him how to throw a punch, something that had come in handy on more than one occasion. Kids like him were easy targets for some of the local gangs that liked to hassle kids they found alone on the street. Sometimes throwing an unexpected punch was all it took to break free.

Stepping around him, Tobias hurried to the tall tombstone he'd claimed as his home and reached under the base of the stone to retrieve his bag. Pulling out his street clothes, he hurried to change and carefully folded his uptown clothes and placed them in the tattered pillowcase he'd swiped from an unattended laundry line.

"Yo, Mouse, what's your hurry?" Slim asked, stepping from one foot to the other.

"I gotta get out a'for the gates close," Tobias replied, reverting to the street talk he often used when around his pals.

Slim's eyes grew wide. "Out? Ya just got here. You know the gangs come out at night. Nothin' but trouble past those gates after dark."

Tobias had lived on the streets for four years, plenty long enough to know how bad they could be after dark. "Can't be helped, Slim. Got something I gotta do."

"When you get back, the boys and I'll put our coats over the fence and help you over," Slim replied.

"Don't wait up; I won't be coming back tonight. Like I said, I got something I gotta do," Tobias said, placing the pillowcase under his arm.

Slim focused on the sack, and his fidgeting grew worse. "You're taking your stuff. You coming back tomorrow?"

Probably not. Honestly, he didn't have a clue. All he knew at this point was he needed to be near the girl who played the piano. "Sure I am. I just need my fancy clothes in case I have to go uptown. Can't get in if the gates are locked. Right?"

This seemed to pacify Slim, and the fidgeting eased.

"Can I have your spot tonight?" one of the younger boys asked, causing a great debate between all the boys, each vying for the spot he'd claimed for his own. "I called it first; it's not like the dead guy cares. He was probably nothing but a bum no how," the younger boy said and pushed one of the other kids to the ground.

Tobias cuffed the kid on the side of the head, sending his cap flying. "I'll not have anyone speaking ill of the dead. Quiet now, before you are heard. All this ruckus for a spot on the damp ground. The gatekeeper only lets us stay the night 'cause we don't cause no trouble. Each of you has lived on the other side of those gates and has struggled to find a safe place to spend the night. You know how things are. Do you each want to have to find a new place to live?"

Most of the small group lowered their eyes to the ground, shaking their heads in response. The kid placed a hand to his head and glared at Tobias.

Slim stepped in between the two boys. "Don't pay no mind to Paddy. He didn't mean nothin' by it. None of us did. We all know it's your spot."

Tobias wasn't so certain. The kid in question had red hair, and everyone knew red hair meant defiance, even though the boy was younger. He'd been pushing back ever since he'd arrived. While the other boys looked to Tobias for direction, Paddy often tried to sway things his way. Tobias had a manner about him that made people trust him. But he trusted no one, and inside the graveyard, his word was the one that mattered — only fitting since Tobias had lived in the cemetery the longest.

Desperate and running from a gang who'd chased him for several blocks after catching him walking alone near Fulton Street Bridge, he'd happened upon the open gates and hid among the headstones. The gang, for all their bravery, had refused to enter the graveyard in the dark. The groundskeeper had been on his way to close the gate and had witnessed the whole thing.

While not actually telling him he was welcome to stay, the caretaker knew he was there and hadn't told him to leave. He'd simply closed the gate for the night and proceeded along his way. Tobias had returned to the graveyard every evening since. One by one, he'd collected other orphans from the street and brought them to the safety of his "home." Except for Paddy; that kid had just shown up one day. And, like a stray dog who had nowhere else to go, Tobias had allowed him to stay. He'd even taught the boy how to dip pockets, and how did he show his gratitude? By trying to take over his space the second he had a chance, and him being just a kid. The boy was no more than six years old. Tobias didn't know if or when he'd be back, but that didn't matter. What mattered was that until he made up his mind to stay away, he was still the boss. And as such, it would be his decision who slept in his spot.

He smiled and clapped Slim on the shoulder. "It will be you who sleeps in my place tonight. And you may remain there until my return."

The boys seemed to accept his decision. Even Paddy bent and retrieved his hat without another word. Slim wasted no time moving his belongings to the area Tobias normally occupied. As he passed through the iron gates, he wondered if the true occupant of the space was equally pleased. He wouldn't mind if boys wanted to sleep on his grave; it would have to be lonely under all that dirt. It would be like someone living on the floor above him. He wondered if he would be able to listen in on their conversations. He pondered that thought as he cautiously made his way back to Ludlow Street. By the time he arrived, he'd decided he would work to earn enough money to have one of those buildings they buried people in. At least then, if anyone wanted to share his space, they wouldn't have to sleep on the ground, nor would they have to worry if it rained. He wondered if they would allow him to buy the building early and live there while he was still alive so he could truly get his money's worth and not fall victim to a pauper's burial, the fate most feared by every kid he knew.

Tobias walked into the tenement building as if he belonged and took the steps two at a time. The fourth-floor hallway was empty when he arrived. Dimly lit, it did little to welcome him to his new home. He thought about sleeping just outside the doorway to the apartment but wasn't ready to answer questions if anyone came out and wanted to know what he was doing there. *How could he give answers when he didn't know what had compelled him to come?* Instead, he went to the corner near the stairwell and used the pillowcase with his second set of clothing to rest his head. The walls were thin, the doors thinner, allowing the conversation to drift into the hallway. A baby's wails pierced the air. Soon a woman's voice carried a song that seemed vaguely familiar, and the baby quieted. His heart ached as he listened to children laughing with abandon.

What did they have to be so merry about? Try as he might, he couldn't tell to which apartment the voices belonged. He pondered about the happenings behind the closed door where mother and daughter remained just out of sight and wondered even more why he cared. While the mother was quite striking, he knew it was the girl by her side that pulled at him. Ridiculous, as the girl was nothing more than a child. A young child at that. Maybe it was the piano music; then again, he'd heard piano music before. They played it all the time in joints all over town, dives with women whose attire left little to the imagination. So what was it about the little girl that pulled at him in a way nothing ever had? Something about her made him want to protect her, and that was what he was here to do. What he was supposed to protect her from he hadn't a clue.

As the evening wore on, the voices lessened; the only sounds coughs of disease-filled lungs that echoed through the walls. Just as he was drifting off to sleep, the sound of breaking glass filled the silence. A man's voice bellowed his displeasure. Tobias bolted upright, waiting for the screams he knew would follow.

The screams never came.

He woke sometime later when the door to the stairwell opened and two men stepped inside the hallway. He drifted back to sleep when the men continued to their apartment without paying him any mind. As the night continued, his dreams held laughter with reminders of his family. His sister singing the song that had earlier quieted the baby's cries. A door opened, and Ezra came in, carrying a bucket filled with water. The water sloshed on the floor, and his father's voice boomed his disapproval. His mother's screams filled the darkness. As the screams tormented the depths of his soul, piano music drifted in through the darkness, pulling at him, beckoning him to follow. Tobias turned towards the window and followed the music into the light. He knew in that moment that no matter how dark the skies around him, the little girl with the dancing fingers would help him see the light of a better day.

Tobias woke with tears streaming down his cheeks. It was as if the dream had answered the question as to why he was there, and it was in that moment he knew he would do anything to protect the little girl who had pulled him from the darkness.

***

Linda was sitting with her arms crossed when Cindy finished her section of the journal. "I guess we know when and why Tobias became obsessed with your grandmother."

"I feel bad for the kid," Cindy said, caressing the stack of papers in front of her. "His life could have been so much different. Why didn't he just tell that couple in the apartment the truth?"

"Because he was too tainted. You read it yourself; he'd already told the truth, and all it got him was heartache. I used to spend the summers with my grams and granddaddy in Kentucky. Granddaddy was not a fan of strays. One summer, there was this mangy old dog that showed up out of nowhere. I was a kid, so I liked all animals, but your granddaddy wanted no part of that dog. He'd yell at it and chase it off with a stick."

"I've not heard this story before. What happened to the dog?" Cindy asked.

"After a week of sneaking around and stealing scraps Grams threw out for the cats, he finally ran off, and we never saw him again."

No wonder Linda hadn't shared the story before. It was depressing. "Thanks for sharing."

Linda laughed. "Tobias kind of reminds me of that dog. The boy is a survivor, doing everything in his power to eke by. He's smart too. He knows he will never get ahead without an education, so he found a way to get one."

Cindy sighed. "I wish some of the students I have were as eager to learn. Tobias is, what? Nine now? Can you imagine a nine-year-old in today's world spending even one night in a cemetery? Much less living there."

Linda raised her eyes. "Maybe you should suggest that as a field trip. Do it around Halloween to make it even more interesting."

Cindy stood and reached toward the ceiling in an exaggerated stretch. "Sure, I'll make sure to bring that up to the school board. Right after I reach tenure."

Chapter Fifteen

Cindy pulled the towels from the dryer, dropping them into the basket in a jumbled clump. She switched the sheets to the dryer and took the basket of towels to the kitchen table to fold. She'd just finished folding the first towel when Linda came into the room, eyed the folded towel, and grimaced.

"You didn't get that from me."

"No, I bought them last summer," Cindy said, retrieving another towel.

Linda reached for the towel. "I'm not talking about the towel; I'm talking about your inability to fold them properly."

Cindy relinquished the towel with a sigh and watched as Linda placed the two ends together folded it lengthwise, then repeated the process. The folded towel was then turned and folded three additional times. When her mother sat the towel next to the one Cindy had folded, the difference was obvious. Linda's towel, an exact carbon of the one Cindy folded, was decidedly smaller. "How come I never noticed the difference before?"

Linda shrugged. "Because you're always busy taking towels out of the closet, not trying to put them in. Your way takes up double the space."

"And you wait until now to show me. Tell me it's something you just learned."

"Not hardly. Mildred showed me how to fold them."

"And all this time, I could have had fancy folded towels," Cindy teased. "Hey, I thought you said she wasn't nice to you."

Linda laughed. "She wasn't trying to be nice; she was letting me know something else I did that displeased her."

Cindy bit at her bottom lip. "Kinda like you just did to me?"

A frown fleeted across Linda's face. "Are you trying to say I have become my mother-in-law?"

"Well, you did take issue with the way I was peeling potatoes last night."

"That was because you were removing half of the potato with the skin." Linda stopped mid-fold. "I am Mildred incarnate!"

Cindy laughed. "You're not that bad."

"But I do get on your nerves, don't I?" Linda asked.

Cindy took a towel and folded it to match the one her mother had done. "No, you just have your own way of doing things."

"Yeah, Mildred's way," Linda groaned. She nodded towards the towel in Cindy's hand. "Hey, that's not bad."

"You seem surprised. I wouldn't be much of a teacher if I couldn't take direction."

Linda picked up the last towel and began folding it. "Do you ever regret asking me to come live with you?"

Cindy stopped to choose her words. "The only thing I regret is that you didn't have more time to spend with Dad."

Linda sighed. "Paul and I were robbed of our golden years."

"That's not entirely true."

Linda placed the towel on the stack. "You don't think your father and I were robbed?"

Cindy knew she could regret what she was about to say but charged ahead anyway. "Of growing old with the one you love, absolutely. But you are in relatively good health for your age and still have plenty of life to live. I have to be honest, I was worried about you for a while, but over the last few weeks, you seem...happier."

"I guess I've found something to take my mind off being alone," Linda said with a sigh.

"But you're not alone; you have me."

"It's not the same. You're kind of sullen. Paul made me laugh."

Cindy felt her eyes bug. "I'm sullen?"

"Yes. It's like you're afraid to laugh. You don't have a social life. You never go out on dates. You kind of tiptoe around the house." A smirk crossed Linda's face. "You're like a little mouse. Maybe you get that from your Uncle Tobias."

Cindy rolled her neck from side to side. Conversations like these usually ended up with her mother complaining about the lack of grandchildren. "I tiptoe because I never know what kind of mood you'll be in. You have been so depressed since Dad died."

"Well, I don't feel depressed now. So no more sulking. Sulking won't land you a man."

"I'm not looking for a man."

"Exactly, and without a man, I won't have any grandchildren."

Dang. She'd walked right into her mother's trap. "Mom, I'm around kids all the time. I'm good."

"Well, at least one of us gets to have our baby fix."

"I teach fourth grade," Cindy snorted. "The kids are nearly teenagers."

Linda scooped up the towels and headed down the hallway. "When you are seventy-two, anyone under thirty is a baby."

Cindy replayed the conversation in her head as she followed her mother down the hall. "Wait, Tobias is my uncle?"

Linda placed the towels in the closet and turned to her. "He's Anastasia's brother. Anastasia is your dad's mom, so I guess, technically, he would be your great-uncle. What's the matter?" Linda asked when Cindy sighed once more.

"I guess it just dawned on me that Grandma Mildred is not really my grandmother."

"Not by blood, but she adopted and raised your father, so by legal definition, she is your grandmother. And, from what I read, she did love you. She wouldn't have left everything to you if she didn't care for you."

"So many questions that'll never be answered. I wish we knew Milena's last name. Maybe if we did, we could learn what happened to her."

"I'm pretty sure she died. What do you say we get back to the journals and find out what young Tobias is up to?"

"I know she died, but it would be nice to know where she was buried. Probably a pauper's grave. The city had plenty of them. Mom?"

"Yes?"

"I'd like to talk about Dad."

Linda hesitated. "What do you want to talk about?"

"Not now. It's just we don't mention him much. I don't want to forget him."

"I thought it would make you sad if I mentioned him."

"And I refrain from mentioning him because I didn't want to see you cry. We live under the same roof, yet it's as if we are on the verge of becoming strangers."

"Sounds to me as if we have a lot to talk about." Linda spread her hands, and Cindy stepped into her mother's arms. It was not lost on Cindy that her mother's embrace had grown stronger.

***

Friday, November 1, 1918

Tobias raced down the stairs, skirting around people heading home after a long day's work. It was later than usual. Mileta and her mother had stopped to pick up groceries but were finally settled in for the night. His routine had changed drastically in the months since pledging to protect the girl. He shadowed the pair by day and practiced his trade in the evenings, once they returned home. As luck would have it, his new schedule still allowed him to visit the apartment on Park Avenue twice during the week, one of those days being Monday, when Mileta would go with her mother to an apartment nearby. Mileta would sit in a chair placed just outside the door, which made it impossible for him to watch her without being seen. He felt at ease with leaving her, as the building had a doorman who watched over the building and a mirror that allowed him to see into the hallway where Mileta waited.

He'd been following the duo for nearly seven months, had mastered the skill, and could easily fade into the shadows, even in the light of day. Since he preferred to stay close to Mileta and her mother, he'd had to give up planning the big score. In turn, he'd learned to settle for skimming pockets on the Friday evening commuter trains. Fridays were when the working man got paid, and a stealthy dipper such as Tobias could skim enough pockets to get him through for weeks to come. It wasn't the big haul he'd once dreamed of, but it was enough, for now. He would ride the trains for a few stops then exit, catching a ride on the next train heading back into the city.

He arrived at Flatbush station just before the Brighton Beach Line arrived to take evening commuters home to Coney Island. Not his favorite line, but he'd do okay as long as he was headed in the other direction long before the train reached Coney Island. The last time he had been there, he and Slim had a run-in with a couple of kids from the Neapolitan Coney Island Gang. While they'd left with only a few bruised knuckles, he'd promised himself he would not return.

He stood on the platform as the train approached and locked his knees as the crowd began pushing their way to a better boarding position. Finding a seat on the train during rush hour was nearly impossible, but not an issue, since Tobias was not looking to sit down. He waited for the train to come to a stop then pushed his way towards the lead car. Once inside, he went to work relieving men and women alike of their hard-earned money. Some dippers preferred watches and jewelry; he preferred cash. He didn't have to share the profit, and with nothing to fence, he was able to stay off the radar of cops and detectives, known better on the streets as bulls. He finished with the first train car and moved to the next, just finishing the second car, when the train stopped and reversed direction. Instantly, the passengers came to life in agitated chatter.

"What's going on?" a lady holding a small infant asked.

"Moron driver missed the turn to Coney Island," a man answered sourly.

"Maybe he should let someone else drive," another man shouted, and the train erupted in laughter.

Tobias smiled at the infant, and the child stared, unimpressed. He lowered his hand to his pocket and leaned to look out the window. Sure enough, the train was moving backward down the track. The once complacent crowd, now upset at being delayed, rumbled angrily. Feeling uncomfortable with the turn of events, Tobias made his way to the next car to see if the occupants were any more settled. As he reached the third car, the train picked up speed and the passengers cheered. Encouraged, he got back to the business at hand. He was in the middle of the third car, standing in the aisle beside a thin man who strategically shielded him from the man beside them. A good thing, because his hand was knuckle deep inside the man's coat pocket.

"The train is going too fast to take the curve at the Franklin Avenue Station," the man next to him yelled, drawing the attention of the man in the seat.

The man in the seat caught him by the arm and yelled, spit flying from his mouth as his eyes filled with rage. "Why you filthy little street urchin. You don't steal from a working man! I'll kill ye with my bare hands a'for I let you steal from my family!"

Before he could respond, the man pulled him into the seat next to him. Tobias tried to break free, but the man's grip held firm.

"You'll stay here next to me until the next stop when I turn you over to the authorities. Killing you is too good. Better for a bugger like you to rot in prison with the other scum," the man said through clenched teeth.

"That'll teach him good," the man standing in the aisle agreed.

Tobias' mind was a blur trying to figure out his next course of action. Better to relax and let the man think him compliant then kick him in the shin and run like the devil the first chance he got. The train jostled side to side and seemed to increase speed when it took the downgrade at Park Station.

"It's too fast!" the man standing next to him shouted.

All of a sudden, the train seemed to rise from the rails and pitch to the side, a monstrous sound coming from the front of the train. The man in the aisle pitched forward, hitting the front of the train car. His eyes dimmed as he slid down the wall, collapsing much like a puppet who'd lost its strings. The lights flickered and the car went dark. The seat Tobias was sitting on broke free, lurching forward and crashing into the seat in front of him. Instantly, his seat was struck from behind, his body ripped from the man's grasp. Tobias hit something hard, and the world around him grew silent.

He woke to muffled screams. It was dark, and his chest felt as if it could not get enough air. *Am I dead? It feels dead.* Loud drums pounded his skull. He turned his head and searing pain joined the drums. Surely he would not feel pain if he were dead. He tried to move his arms, but could only free one. His fingers traced the object that weighted him down. It took a moment to realize he was under a body. The body was not moving, and from the feel of it, he didn't think it would ever move again. He found the face, felt the beard, and instantly pictured the man who'd pulled him into the seat. He tried to push him off, but he didn't budge. The man had been angry before the crash. Was this his way of punishing him from the grave? Screams pierced the air. Closer now, tears sprang from his eyes as he realized the screams belonged to him.

Chapter Sixteen

Screaming, pleading, and ever-growing sounds of despair filled the dark train car. It seemed as though it took forever for help to arrive. When it did, the soft glow of the lanterns had never been more welcome. Tobias tried to call for help, but his head pounded and his throat was scratched dry from previous unanswered calls. He'd welcomed the darkness up until now as he hadn't had to stare into the face of his accuser — the man whose grip in death frightened him more than it had in life.

He listened as the rescue workers went to work freeing passengers and squeezed his eyes shut as a woman's screams echoed within the space. A few moments later, the man's body was lifted, and Tobias sucked in a welcomed breath of air.

"We got a live one here; bring me a lantern," a man's voice shouted. "What's your name, son?"

He tried to answer, but the words wouldn't come. His head hurt something fierce. Someone arrived with a lantern, and he raised a hand to shield the light. Rough hands gripped his and pulled. Tobias screamed and the grip lessened as the light moved closer.

"It's his leg; it's caught between the seats. Hang on, kid; we'll get you out. Damn wooden cars, I can't believe they're still using them in this day and age. You're lucky you weren't in one of the first two cars, kid. Doesn't look to be a single survivor." The man's voice mingled with both anger and pity.

Tobias' thoughts were fuzzy, but he had been in the first

two cars, and only moments before the wreck. He remembered the woman holding the baby, and the way the infant had stared at him with dull unblinking eyes as he relieved its mother of a few coins in her pocket. He'd not felt guilty at the time as there'd been paper money among the coins, which he had refrained from taking. Had mother and child perished as well? They had to, as they were standing in the aisle when he'd left them. The bench moved backward and a wave of nausea hit. Leaning forward, he lost the contents of his stomach. Thankfully, it wasn't much, as he had not had anything since lifting a rolled sausage from a cart for breakfast.

"There, boy, feel better?" a voice asked, and someone helped him up without waiting for an answer. The man placed a hand under his elbow and helped guide him around the debris. It was only then Tobias realized the car was on its side. The man stopped and held the lantern upwards. A second later, a head appeared in the opening.

"Reach your hands up, son, so that I can grip hold," the man ordered.

He did as told and strong hands lifted him through the opening, which turned out to be a window.

"Now aren't you a lucky one," the man said as soon as he breached the opening.

Tobias looked towards the front of the train and grimaced. The flames from what seemed to be hundreds of lanterns created a monstrous glow within the wreckage. He could see bodies intertwined within the wood from the train cars, both littering the tunnel in wayward piles of limbs mixed with kindling. He looked inside the opening and closed his eyes against the screams that continued to fill the air. He heaved once again, yet his stomach was long empty, and the heaves remained dry.

The man placed a hand on Tobias' shoulder. "God must

have a plan for you is all I can say. Are you okay? Can you walk?"

Opening his eyes, Tobias nodded, though in truth had no idea what he was agreeing to. Several women rushed towards them, each moving to his side, helping him skirt around the wreckage. He wondered at the loud hum circling overhead like a swarm of bees, causing the pain in his head to pound even more. *Please make it stop.* They'd no sooner stepped out of the tunnel when he realized the noise was from the mass of onlookers that crowded the opening.

Someone broke through, grabbed his chin, and lifted his face towards the light. "This one belong to any of you?"

"Leave the boy be; he'll tell us his name soon enough," one of the women scolded and slapped the hand free. His head bobbled forward as a bright light flashed behind his eyes.

***

Tobias opened his eyes as something sharp stabbed at his head. He tried to move his hands, but they seemed tied in place. He tried once more then realized his hands were not tied, but being held.

"He's awake," a soft voice announced.

"A good sign." This voice was not so soft but seemingly relieved. "Stay still, boy; you have a gash in the top of your head big enough to let your brains escape. I'm sewing you up now. You're going to have a whopper of a headache, but you'll live. Lucky you are. They sent you out here alone. Were your folks with you?"

"Out where?" a voice nearby asked.

"At the ball field. We set up a triage center. You're lucky; we can treat you here. They are taking the worse cases to the hospitals. Some of the routes are so clogged with people coming to look for missing loved ones, ambulances can't make it through."

"My wife, she'll be worried," the voice said.

"That should do it," the man sewing him up said. "Give him some headache powder for the pain and add his name to the list so his folks can find him."

Instantly, the hands released his arms and freed the strap that was holding his head in place. "What's your name, son?"

"Mouse."

"No, your real name. What do your parents call you?"

He placed a hand beside his head to calm the pain. "Tobias."

The woman smiled. "That's better. Now out with the rest of it."

Tobias squinted against the throb but said nothing.

"Okay," the woman said, trying another tactic. "What are your parents' names?"

If what the doctor said was true, most of the Lower East Side was searching for people. While he thought his father to be dead, he couldn't take any chances. He opened his mouth and gave the only name that felt safe. "Lisowski. My father is dead, but my mother's name is Fannie Lisowski."

"Good, come along, and we'll get you those headache powders. You can wait near the fire while we see about locating your mother."

Of course, they would never locate Mrs. Fannie, but the name should buy him a bit of time for his head to stop pounding. Each step felt as though his head would release from his shoulders. They reached the fire, and the woman motioned for him to sit. He did as told and quickly closed his eyes to stop the nausea that followed.

"Drink this," the woman ordered.

He opened his eyes. The woman was holding out two cups; he reached for the one on the right and missed. She moved the cup to his hand; only then did he realize she only held one.

"You took a bad hit to the head. Things may not be settled for a while. This will help with the pain," she said, releasing the cup. She looked up and frowned. "I hate to leave you, but there are so many others that need my help. Promise me you will wait here until someone comes for you."

He tried to nod and stopped. "I'll stay."

Her lips curved upward and she raced off.

Tobias half watched as the flames danced, sending out the occasional spark. He worried what he'd do if the spark jumped in his direction, wondered if he should scoot back. He closed his eyes, not caring either way.

"Is he dead?"

"He looks dead."

"Don't be ignorant. Dead people don't sit up."

Tobias opened his eyes to a group of boys hovering over him, blinking several times until the group became three.

"I told you he weren't dead." Slim sounded relieved.

Paddy leaned in close. "He don't look much better than dead. Look at all that blood."

"Yeah, that's a lot of blood," Tommy agreed. "You were on the train, huh, Mouse. We heard it all the way to the chapel. Climbed over the fence to come see. Sumptin makes that kind of noise be worth g'tting' a stake in the belly."

"Are you hurt, Mouse?" Paddy's concern seemed genuine.

"Naw, most of this blood ain't mine," Tobias lied.

"It's a good thing. I don't think you'd be livin' if it was all yourn," Tommy said.

"Leave him be," Slim said, shooing Tommy away. "What happened, Mouse?"

Tobias thought for a moment before answering. "Someone said the conductor was driving too fast. The train took the curve like the driver was late for a Thanksgiving feast. It all happened so fast, I saw a man fly through the air and then the lights blinked and everything went dark. When I woke up, I had a dead man sleeping on me."

"Woke up? How could you sleep with all that noise?" Slim asked.

"I didn't know dead men could sleep," Tommy said, scratching his head.

Tobias shrugged. "All I know is a man caught me dipping in his pocket and told me he was going to take me to jail. Next thing I know, I'm waking up and he's on top of me, but he ain't moving. I think his eyes were open staring at me, but I can't be sure 'cause it was dark."

All three boys' eyes grew wide, focusing on the unbelievable.

"You got caught?" Slim whispered.

"Ah, don't be looking at me like that. It wasn't my fault. The train was going too fast, and the whole train was in an uproar. Someone yelled about it, and when he did, the man turned to look. That's when he saw me with my hand on his wallet."

Tommy blew out a slow whistle. "Bet he was mad."

Tobias pictured the hatred in the man's eyes, remembered the weight of the lifeless body as if he was trying to get even in death. He swallowed the bile that rose in his throat. A mistake— his stomach lurched and emptied once again.

"Boy, Mouse, you don't look so good," Paddy said, taking a step back.

"Just a little headache from the crack on the head," Tobias said and tilted his head towards the fire so the boys could see.

"So it is your blood," Paddy said. Apparently, blood trumped vomit as he inched forward to take a closer look. "Would you look at the size of that lump! You got a melon on your melon!"

Tommy moved in for a closer look. "Wowzers, Mouse. Someone done went and sewed your head shut."

Slim cuffed Tommy on the side of the head. "Well, they couldn't let his brains spill out now, could they?"

"Now why'd you go and pound on me? I didn't do nothing wrong. I just ain't never seen anyone with their head sewn up is all."

"I need to get out of here before they take me someplace." Tobias stood. His vision blurred, grew dark, then came back in focus. While he wanted to go and wait in the hallway as he did every night, his gut told him this wasn't a good idea. He would have to find another place to stay until he was well enough to continue. This meant he would have to find someone he could trust to watch over Mileta. Slim would be his first choice; however, the kid couldn't stand still long enough to keep from being seen. Tommy was too simple-minded to stay on task, so that left Paddy. While Tobias wasn't happy with the choice, the alternative would be to leave the girl unprotected.

"Give us a minute, guys," he said, motioning to Paddy, who looked nervous until Tobias reached into his pocket, pulled out a handful of coins, and handed them to the bewildered redhead.

Paddy eyed him suspiciously. "What are these for?"

"I got a job for you."

"What kind of job?"

The boy was right to be suspicious; Tobias had never selected him to do anything. "Nothing that'll get you tossed in jail. I just need you to shadow someone until I get back."

The suspicion turned to confusion. "Where're you going?"

"None of your business. I'll be back when I can. If you don't want the dough, just say so. I'll give the job to one of the other guys," Tobias said, reaching for the coins.

Paddy cupped his fist and placed the coins in his pocket. "I'll take the job, but if you're gone too long, it will cost you more 'n a few coins."

It was just like a dang redhead to try to put the squeeze on him. If his head didn't hurt so badly, he might be compelled to punch the ingrate right in the nose. "You just go where I tell you and shadow the girl until I come back."

A smile played at Paddy's mouth. "Got yourself a girlfriend. That splains a lot."

"She's not my girlfriend, and you'll keep your grubby hands off her as well. I just want you to watch over her and see she's okay."

The smile withered, and Paddy turned serious. "What's so special about this girl?"

Tobias held Paddy's gaze and briefly considered telling him of his dream. The moment passed, and Tobias narrowed his eyes. "You just do your job and see she's safe. You need anything, and you find Slim. The boy's no good at staying in the shadows, but he sure can throw a punch."

***

It took longer to get to Park Avenue than he'd expected. The train wreck had caused a domino effect with people who normally rode the trains seeking alternative transportation. Tobias was forced to ride on the outside of the trolley, hanging on the best he could. A game on most days, dangerous with the current state of his equilibrium. Once, he'd become so dizzy he'd fallen into the street when the car came to a sudden halt. Thankfully, the dizziness passed in time for him to clamor back to his perch on rear of the trolley car. It was well after nine when he slowly ascended the stairs leading to the apartment, head pounding. He reached the door, raised the door knocker three times, and slumped to the floor just as it opened. Felisha dropped to her knees beside him, screaming for Adam to come.

***

It was daylight when he next opened his eyes. He was in the spare room, only instead of sleeping on the floor as he'd done on many intrusive nights, he was lying on the bed. He looked to the window in an attempt to judge the time. As he moved, stabs of pain shot through his head, threatening to claw out his eyes. He closed his eyelids, and the pain ebbed to a dull throb. As the stabbing lessened, he opened his eyes once more.

The room was brighter than he remembered; then again, it might have only seemed as such since it was dark each time he'd snuck his way into the apartment and slept on the floor. The large room had always seemed cold and lonely, but with the sunlight bouncing off the walls, it seemed to welcome him. A small vase of flowers sat next to the bed. Were they for him? They had to be, as he'd never seen them during his previous forays into the room.

A large dresser sat against the wall beside the bed, and a wooden washstand with a brightly colored bowl sat within the base of the stand. It was missing the pitcher that normally accompanied it, and he wondered briefly where it had gone. His stomach rumbled. It was Saturday; from experience, he knew not to expect much by way of food in the house. He was fairly certain he'd been bathed, as he was completely naked and covered with the most comfortable bedding he'd ever had the good grace to sleep within.

The door clicked. He closed his eyes, pretending to be asleep.

Hearing water, he chanced a peek and opened his eyes. Felisha was standing with her back to him, pouring water into a bowl at the end of the bed. At least that solved the case of the missing pitcher. She turned, and he squeezed his eyes closed once more. She moved closer, sat on the edge of the bed beside him, and placed a warm cloth on his forehead.

"What happened to you?" she whispered.

He wanted to answer, but his head ached so, and his thoughts were too jumbled to answer the questions he knew would follow. He was tired, and the darkness beneath his eyes felt too welcoming. When at last he opened his eyes, Felisha was gone, and the sunlight had given way to night once more.

Chapter Seventeen

The train sped along the tracks as if racing away from a disaster, not speeding recklessly into a blind curve. A woman with a baby stood next to him. He could not see the woman's face, but the baby watched him. The infant found its thumb and sucked hungrily, and still the baby's stare was unblinking. Tobias removed the coins with nary a jingle, and yet the baby had heard. Its gaze drifted downward then leveled on Tobias accusingly. Tobias lifted a finger to his lips to silence the child. The baby removed its thumb and screamed for all to hear. The screams turned into shouting as someone yelled the train was going too fast. The train slammed into the car in front of it, the lights went out, and Tobias felt blood ooze down his face. He opened his eyes and stared into the dead eyes of his accuser, and it was his turn to scream. A hand gripped his arm, and he struggled to get free.

"TOBIAS!" the man shouted, calling him by name.

Tobias opened his eyes and stared into Felisha's worried face.

He took a relieved breath as he realized it was all but a dream and not a dead man but Felisha who held his arms.

"Welcome back." The relief in her voice was evident.

He relaxed, and she released her hold on him.

"Where have I been?"

She lifted a cloth from the floor, dipped it in a bowl of water, and placed the cool cloth on his forehead. Water trickled from the cloth and he realized it was water, not blood he'd felt during his dream.

"According to the doctor, you've been walking with the dead," she said, dabbing at the errant water.

Tobias scrunched his face. Sleeping with the dead at the cemetery was one thing, but walking with them? He wasn't sure he liked that. "Doctor?"

The worried look returned. While her clothes appeared neat, he wondered at the dark circles beneath her eyes. He hadn't noticed them during any of his previous visits. "Do you remember what happened before you came to our door?"

Tobias searched his memory. So it wasn't only a dream. He remembered the events leading up to the crash. Best to leave those details out. "I was on a train. It was going too fast and crashed."

Felisha nodded her head. "That's what we figured. It was in the papers the day after you arrived."

The day after he arrived? He'd only been here a day, two at the most.

"You've been here over a week," she said, seeing the confusion on his face.

Over a week? *Mileta.* He sat up on the bed and felt the room spin.

"You need to remain still. I've been so worried. I'm sure your poor mother is beside herself. We thought to get a message to her, but I didn't know where to send it. I checked the papers to see if anyone was looking for you, but didn't find any adverts. You had a major gash in the head. Who sewed you up?" Felisha asked, guiding him back onto the pillow.

He shrugged. "Someone on the ball field."

"The doctor said it was a good thing they did or you would have bled to death before you arrived." Her face turned serious. "Why did you come here, Tobias?"

Because I had nowhere else to go.

Tobias hesitated, building his story in his head. "Water?"

She seemed embarrassed at not having offered and hurried to pour him some from the pitcher beside the bed. She handed him the glass and waited as he drank.

"I didn't want my mom to see me like that. Her in her condition and all," he said once he'd drained the contents.

"Your mom... family, I am sure they are beside themselves with worry over you. Give me your address. I must go to them and tell them you are well."

"No, it's okay. I had a friend send them a message that I'm working and will be coming home when the job is finished."

She didn't seem convinced. "Surely they'll be worried."

"They would be even more so if they knew of my injury. My mother is ill, my father beside himself with worry, and my grandmother does not need another person to look after. Please, I'm sorry I came here. I just didn't know where else to go. I can leave if I've caused you too much worry."

"You will do no such thing. You are welcome to stay here as long as it takes for you to get your strength up. I don't care if it takes months." As she spoke, she tucked the covers around him as if doing so would keep him from leaving.

Tobias sighed. While he would love to spend the winter months in a nice soft bed, he didn't have that luxury. He needed to get back to Mileta. At least he had been able to see her safe for the time being.

"Tobias," Felisha said, bringing him from his musings. "Why were you on the train and how come you were dressed in those clothes when you had all that money in your pocket?"

Tobias had expected this. Someone had to have undressed him and in doing so would certainly found the money he had taken before the train crashed. He lowered his eyes, closing the lids so she could not see his lies. "Because I was a dope. A friend of mine told me of a craps game in Coney Island. Told me if a man had the right kind of dough, they had a chance to really make out. I know it was wrong, but with my dear mother so ill and my papa doing all he can for the family, I wanted to do my part to help. I know it was wrong, Mrs. Wilson. Please don't think poorly of me."

The relief on her face was evident. "Oh, Tobias, I could never think poorly of you. You looked like one of those street urchins that lie and beg upon the street. I knew it must be a simple explanation. But why did you have to wear those clothes? They smelled so bad, I had to throw them in the trash. Where are your real clothes?"

Tobias rubbed at his temples. She was talking about his uptown clothes, which were no doubt buried within the rubble of the train, and now she had gone and thrown away the only clothes he had left. So much for sneaking out once his headache lifted. "Gone."

"What do you mean gone?"

"I had my good clothes with me on the train." He lifted the blanket to confirm what he'd suspected. "I am afraid I am not much better than those urchins on the street. Actually, I'm less than them at the moment. For even though they were but rags, they still have something to call their own."

To his surprise, she burst out laughing.

"I fail to see the humor in my words."

"Listen to you being all dramatic. You put poor little Oliver to shame. Why Mr. Dickens himself would roll over in his grave at the thought of a well-to-do boy such as yourself acting this way. If anyone asks, we'll tell them it's because you hit your head. Seems like a good enough excuse to me," she said with a grin.

He thought about asking who this Oliver was, but then

he would also have to ask about Mr. Dickens and his head was beginning to hurt too much to care. His stomach rumbled.

"Are you hungry?" She pushed from the bed and left the room, closing the door behind her before he could answer.

Of course he was hungry; he hadn't eaten in over a week.

Several moments passed before the door reopened. Tobias watched as Adam came into the room. While the man's face seemed pleasant, there was something about the set of his shoulders that implied the man was not pleased.

"Felisha told me you were awake. How are you feeling?"

"My head still hurts, but not so much as it did."

Adam nodded. "Good. You'll be up and about soon. I'm sure your parents will be happy to see you home."

"I'm sure they will."

Another nod. "Then you'll be leaving soon?"

"Yes, sir. Just as soon as my head stops hurting."

"And you'll be going home?"

Something was wrong. "I will."

"And just where is this home of yours, Mouse? That is what they call you on the street, isn't it, son?"

Tobias looked towards the door.

"Don't worry, your secret is safe with me. For now."

"How'd you find out?"

"You were doing a lot of talking while you were sleeping. Saying things that just didn't add up. Saying names and talking about a building on Ludlow Street. So I went over to check it out. Spoke with one of your friends, Paddy. I think I know why you came here now; you were hurt and needed a friendly face. But what about before? You have been hanging around the house for months? Why?"

Tobias knew Adam was talking about his meeting with

Felisha. He couldn't know about the rest, as he'd been too careful. "I wanted to learn to read."

"Is that all you wanted? Are you sure you weren't trying to worm your way into my wife's good graces so that you could steal from us?"

If I wanted to steal from you, I would have already done so. "No, sir. I wasn't here to steal. I just wanted an education."

"And did you get one?"

"I can read most everything and count some too."

Adam kept his voice low. "Very well. Then as soon as you are well, you will leave this house and never return. My wife is a kind woman. She has sat up with you every night since your arrival and slept very little. She has prayed for your mother and family every night since she first met you and all you have done is lie to her. Why didn't you tell us the truth from the beginning?"

"I couldn't tell you the truth."

"And why not?" Adam hissed.

"Because if I did, you would have both looked at me the way you are looking at me now," Tobias replied. "I could hear it in your voice just the same as now. And I was dressed nice and everything."

The door opened, and Felisha entered the room with a serving tray. "Gracious, don't you two look serious."

Adam smiled and took the tray. "We were just discussing Tobias' clothing. Something he seems to lack these days. I'll tell you what, my dear. You take the money Tobias has and run out and get him something suitable to wear."

Felisha's face furrowed. "I was going to feed him his meal."

"There now, darling. Don't worry yourself about that. Young Tobias is feeling much better; I'm sure he can feed himself, can't you, son?" Adam said, turning to Tobias.

"Oh yes, I am feeling much better. I'm sure I'll be well enough to go home very soon." He watched her smile disappear. "But I shall be here when you return. I can't likely go anywhere until you do anyhow."

"Of course not," Adam interjected. "Why, we couldn't have the boy running around the streets like one of those little street urchins now, could we? What on earth would our friends think, that we just pulled a beggar boy off the street and welcomed him into our home?"

Tobias felt his lip quiver and bit into it to still the movement. There had been moments, before his pledge to Mileta, when he'd considered telling them the truth, but then he remembered Mrs. Fannie and the pain of being sent away without even saying goodbye. The fear of being hurt again stopped him. Boys like him were not meant to be happy. Boys like him were meant to fight for everything that came their way. Any hope he'd imagined of living a normal life was extinguished the second Adam walked into the room and looked at him. He'd seen that look too many times. Looks like that reminded him who he was and where he came from. Tobias might be his birth name, but he was Mouse. Mice didn't live in nice houses or sleep in comfortable beds; mice lived in cracks and holes and stole food from the people inside.

Chapter Eighteen

November 20, 1920

Tobias leaned against the trunk of the tree, waiting for the children to be let into the asylum courtyard. He'd done the same thing for the past three days in hopes of speaking with Paddy or Slim. He'd almost gotten caught the previous day when one of the mistresses had seen him standing by the fence and told him to leave before she saw fit to bring him inside with the others. Today, he'd moved to a different location and pulled his wool cap low over his face, hoping to blend in with the base of the tree. The doors opened, and the children poured out into the brisk November air. The boys ventured into the yard closest to him while the girls were funneled into the right side of the yard, each preferring to stay close to the building. Like him, the boys were each dressed in black knickers that stopped at the knee with black socks tucked underneath. The group whooped and hollered, chasing each other like a group of puppies on reprieve from their mother's watchful eye. One of the boys turned, and Tobias caught a glimpse of brilliant red hair. Tobias waved to get his attention; the boy nearly tripped over his feet in his rush to get to where Tobias was standing.

"Mouse! What are you doing here? How'd you come to find us?" Paddy asked in breathless excitement.

Tobias raised a hand to quiet the boy. "Turn around and pretend to lean against the fence. One of those mistresses see me, and they are going to lock me up in there with you."

Paddy did as was told, and Tobias placed his back to the

fence, lowering to stay within Paddy's shadow.

"How did you find out where they'd taken us?" Paddy repeated.

"I was just rounding the corner when Tommy plowed into me and told me they took you away. He thought they were taking you to jail, but since he said you weren't doing anything when they caught you, I didn't think they'd take you to jail. I talked to the newsie on Fulton Street. He said word was they were taking kids to the asylums to get 'em off the streets. I put the word out and just got the news you were here." It was all a lie, of course. Tobias knew where they had taken the boys, as he had been the one to turn them in. He needed to know more about the asylum that was the closest to St. Paul's Chapel, and how best to find out than to have someone on the inside? He knew if the place were bad, Paddy wouldn't survive on his own, so he paid Slim to go with him to have his back. Of course, he paid enough so that Slim would not let on that Tobias had ratted them out.

"Why'd you care what they'd done with us?"

He didn't really. That was why he hadn't come around until now, even though he'd known where they were for nearly two months. "I just wanted to know how you were getting along. Is the place bad?"

Paddy sighed. "It could be worse. There are some bigger kids that steal food, but only if you don't eat it fast enough. Slim, he's here too. He got into a few scrapes with them, and now they mostly leave us alone. The mistresses don't bother us as long as we behave."

Tobias swallowed and asked the real question. "Do you want out?"

Paddy was quiet so long, Tobias wondered if he'd walked away. "I did, at first. I've been on my own so long, it felt as if I'd been put in a cage like those chickens they sell in the market. But I've made some friends, and we get fed three times a day. I got my own bed too. It's not much, but I don't have to sleep on the ground."

This was what he was hoping to hear. "What about the girls?"

"What about them?" Paddy said, wrinkling his nose.

"Do you get to talk to them?"

"Yeah, sometimes. They keep us apart most times."

"Do they seem happy here?"

"I guess so. What's with all the questions about the girls, Mouse?"

Tobias sighed. The only way he could make sure was to take Paddy into his confidence. "Remember the girl, Mileta?"

"Mileta? Sure I remember."

The affection in Paddy's voice was not lost on Tobias, but right now, he had more important things to worry about. "Her mother is ill. She's been trying to work but is getting worse. I've seen this before. It won't be long before her mother is in the ground and the girl will be on the streets."

"And you want to bring her here?"

"Only if you think it is safe."

"I will make it so myself."

"And how will you do this when they keep boys and girls apart?"

"There is only one girl that makes trouble. I will see what can be done with her. It may take some dough," Paddy mused.

"I can get the dough if that is the only way," Tobias agreed.

"Hey, what are you doing over here?"

Tobias recognized the voice and stood so Slim could see him. "He's talking to me. Got something to say about it?"

Slim laughed. "Mouse! I knew you'd come. Have you

come to bust us out?"

"Are you kidding? Paddy was just telling me how much he likes it here."

Slim feigned shock. "Give a kid a real bed to sleep on and he's a goner for sure."

Tobias studied the boy for a moment. "Are you telling me you don't agree? I can get you out."

One of the mistresses clapped her hands and the children on both sides of the fence started for the door.

"Got to go," Paddy said and started across the lawn. "You get her in; I'll find someone to watch over her when I can't."

Slim looked towards the door and shrugged. "Naw, it ain't so bad. None of the boys mess with me, and I don't miss sleeping on the cold ground. I was never good at dipping pockets anyhow."

Tobias watched as the boy bounced from one foot to the other, impatient to get inside. "Don't you worry about picking pockets, Slim. Your talents lie elsewhere. Now go before you get in trouble. I'll check in on you boys from time to time to see if you need anything."

"Yo, Slim?" Tobias said as the boy walked away. "Paddy said something about a girl that causes trouble in there. Do me a favor and get me some information on her. I'll be around in a day or two to see what you come up with."

"You got it, Mouse," Slim said and took off running to get to the door before it closed.

***

November 24, 1920

Tobias got to the asylum just as the kids trickled into the yard. Slim and Paddy made their way to the fence with another boy who was taller by a head.

"This is Chalkie; he likes to eat chalk," Slim explained. "Tell Mouse what you told me."

The boy eyed Tobias suspiciously. "Slim said you pay for information."

He cast a glance at Slim, who offered a shrug. "You know how it is, Mouse."

He held out a quarter. The boy reached through the fence, and Tobias closed his fist. "Talk first. If you have something to say, you get the dough."

Chalkie pulled his hand back. "Yeah, and who says I can trust you?"

Slim pushed the kid into the fence, and Tobias took hold of his shirt collar. "Spill it now and get the coin or I let my friend here beat it out of you, and you get nada. Either way, you are going to talk. Got it?" He waited until the boy nodded his agreement before releasing him. "Tell me about this girl."

"She's a mean one, that's for certain. She's older, so she gets to help supervise the younger kids. What the mistresses don't know is she smacks some of the kids when they aren't looking. No one will say nothing because they know she will tear them into pieces if they do. Word is she is eager." Chalkie wiggled his eyebrows. "If you get my meaning. Rumor is she came in here to have a baby. Might just be that, a rumor, as I've never seen her with a kid. I guess she may have looked fat at one point, but it's hard to tell under the aprons the girls wear."

Slim elbowed the boy in the ribs. "Tell him what else you told me, Chalkie."

"Dorthia told me the girl sneaks out sometimes. She knows because she went with her once. That's all I got," he said, holding out his hand.

Tobias wasn't sure if it was the cold or the mentioning of this Dorthia girl, but Slim's face turned a deep shade of red.

Maybe there was another reason Slim was in no hurry to leave the asylum. Just as well, because if he could get Mileta in, she would be well-protected. He flipped Chalkie the coin and motioned him away with a flip of the hand.

"This girl, how old is she? What does she look like?" he asked after Chalkie left.

The boys snickered.

"She's sixteen, looks at least eighteen," Slim said, cupping his hands and showing the girl to be well endowed. "She's a real looker, except she has a scar on the side of her right cheek. Word is she got in a fight and someone slashed her."

Tobias felt a small stab in the gut and his mouth went dry. "This girl, does she have a name?"

"She got lots of names," Slim answered, naming a few of the more raunchy ones. When Tobias didn't laugh, he offered the girl's true name. "Her name is Anastasia."

Tobias felt his stomach clench. He knew the scar, but it wasn't from a knife fight. His sister had had it for as long as he could remember. It was such a part of her, he'd never questioned how she had gotten it. Would she even be old enough to have a child? *Of course she would. Girls younger than her have babies all the time.* Using his fingers, he did the math and realized he was now as old as Anastasia the last time he'd seen her. He coughed to cover his shock. His mind went to the last conversation they'd had and how his sister had looked at him with a whimsical look upon her face that he had not understood at the time. *But what if he did catch you?* he'd asked. *I would give him something only girls have to give.*

Tobias backed away from the fence and tore off down the street.

"Where are you going, Mouse?" Slim called as he raced away.

Tobias didn't stop to answer, didn't look back to quell the fear in the boy's voice. He needed to get as far away from the asylum as possible before the boys that looked to him for direction saw the tears that streamed down his cheeks. There had not been a day since his sister's disappearance that Tobias didn't think of her. Not a day he didn't worry what'd become of her. To find out that she was alive was a blessing. To hear the things people said about her a curse. How would he be able to look at her without hearing those vile comments? Moreover, how would he be able to hear those comments without wishing to kill anyone who said them? Slim was his friend. Paddy, while he did not trust the boy with hair to match the devil's fire, the boy had shown himself to be loyal. At least in the way he helped protect Mileta. Tobias' heart pounded with each step. He sniffed to stifle the snot that ran from his nose as freely as the tears rolling down his cheeks. He was on the fourth floor of the tenement building without even stopping to think how he'd gotten there. He made his way to the door of the apartment, raised his hand to knock, and caught himself just before his knuckles hit the wood. He'd been protecting her in the shadows in the two years since he'd first seen her sitting on that piano bench. While he didn't know the reason, he knew he couldn't allow Mileta to learn of his existence. Not yet anyway. If he were going to protect her, he needed help. To accept their help, he would have to betray the only family he had left. In his confusion, it did not occur to him that by leaving him on the street that day, it was she who had betrayed him first.

Chapter Nineteen

December 24, 1920

Tobias hunkered against the building on the opposite side of the street watching the entrance of the asylum, waiting. It was not the first time he'd taken up position in hopes of speaking to her. Besides, it was Christmas Eve. Mileta and her mother had long retired, and he didn't have anything better to do. He'd met with Slim earlier in the day and told the boy to give Anastasia a message. To his surprise, Slim had balked. It was not the first time he'd asked him to give his sister a message. For some reason, Anastasia was not interested in meeting with her long-lost brother, but in the end, the boy was loyal to him and promised to reach out to her.

The wind whipped through the alley, chilling him to the bone. Tobias blew into his hands to warm them and considered leaving. Though the hallways of the tenement building were not comfortable, at least the building offered refuge from the brutal winter wind. On days such as this, he found himself wondering if having his freedom was worth it. He could almost see himself knocking on the door and asking for one of those beds. Comfortable or not, it almost felt worth it. Almost.

Hours passed without as much as a shadow in the windows. He'd just about given up hope when at last he heard the click of the massive door. A cloaked figure stepped out, leaned to pick up a rock, and wedged it in the door jamb to keep it from closing. Something told him this was not the first time the person had done this. The figure moved into the light as if hoping to be seen, then stepped back into the shadows of the building.

Tobias took a breath to steady himself, then rising from his hiding place, stepped into the moonlight. He took sure strides, letting her see he was confident in his approach. It was important for him to show her that while he still used the moniker of Mouse, he was in no way the timid little boy she'd known. She pulled her hood back as he approached to allow him to see her face and the scar that confirmed she was who she professed to be. His breath caught as he took in her face, the scar, and the rich brown eyes staring at him behind thick, unblinking eyelashes. She reached and tucked a strand of dark hair behind her right ear. She looked so much like their mother that it took everything he had not to run to her and beg her for forgiveness, even though he had no clue what he felt he needed to apologize for.

She held her hands out and smiled his mother's smile. The smile disappeared when he stopped just short of her embrace. She pulled a cigarette from her pocket, lit it, inhaled deeply, and blew the smoke out in a slow, steady stream. Their mother loathed when their father smoked. She would have hated that her daughter had taken up his habit. The ugliness of the action brought him back to his senses, and he shook his head when she offered it to him. She took another puff and deliberately blew it in his direction. "Look at you. Little Tobias nearly all grown up. What are you now, ten? Slim told me you are a pretty tough guy these days. If I had known what you'd become, I would've given you a better name than Mouse."

Tobias' stomach clenched at the sound of her voice, which again reminded him so much of their mother, it was difficult to breathe. Oh, what he'd give to reach out to her. When he spoke, his words came out in clouded puffs, showing he did not need to inhale the cigarette to spray his frozen breath into the evening air. "I do okay."

"I'd say you do more than okay if you can convince guys to come into a place like this for you."

Her comment caught Tobias by surprise; he'd told Slim not to tell anyone.

Anastasia laughed. "Don't worry; your little secret is safe with me."

That wasn't the point. "Slim wasn't supposed to tell anyone."

"He didn't tell everyone; he just told me," she said, taking another pull from the cigarette.

"Why would he tell you?" He looked to the building, wondering what else Slim had said.

"Because I asked nicely."

Her words taunted him, and he wanted to run as he had the first time, but instead, he remained in place. "Is it true you are a mother?"

Her eyes sprang wide then narrowed. She took one last puff on the cigarette and flipped it away. "There is a baby, but I'm not its mother. Mothers love their children and I do not have any love left to give. That's why I left when I did."

What was that supposed to mean? "I don't understand."

Anastasia drew in the chilled air and blew out a smoky breath of steam. She shivered and pulled her coat tighter. "It doesn't matter. I'm glad you are out of the house, Tobias. How is Ezra?"

"I don't know," he replied and told her what happened the night he left.

She took it all in without emotion. "You've been on the streets all this time?"

"Most of it."

His comment seemed to impress her. "How do you get by?"

He shrugged. "My sister taught me how to steal apples."

She smiled again, and this time, the smile was genuine. "Well, it's good to know I did something good in this world."

A motor car approached, slowed, and continued on its way.

"I need to get back inside," she said, looking toward the door. "I don't know how you found me, but was good seeing you again."

"Wait," Tobias said as she turned. "I need you to do something for me."

"I figured as much. You want me to be nice to your friend?"

Slim must have said something. How else could she have known? "I do. Her name is Mileta, and if I have my way, she'll be coming here soon. I need you to look out for her until I can find another place for her."

She bit at the corner of her mouth. "I thought you wanted me to be nice to Slim."

Tobias laughed. "Slim don't need me to look out for him. The boy can throw a punch like no one I've ever seen."

"Oh, little Mouse, you still have so much to learn." Anastasia shook her head and reached for the door. "This girl, are you sweet on her?"

Tobias wrinkled his nose. "Of course not; she's just a kid."

"Then why go to all the trouble for her?"

The last thing he wanted was to tell his sister the girl made his heart happy. She'd tell Slim, and all the guys would think he was a sissy baby. He pulled himself straight and pulled his hat low. "You just take care of the girl when she comes, and I'll see to it you have smokes and a bit of dough as well. You're not to tell her about me or even mention my name. You don't hold up your end of the bargain, and I'll make sure the headmistress knows you sneak out at night."

"You would too, wouldn't you? You're not a mouse; you're a little rat," Anastasia hissed.

"I'm your brother. The least I can do is help you uphold your reputation."

"I'm glad I left you. I hate you. I've always hated you all." The ugliness in her tone matched the look that spread over her face.

Tobias opened his mouth to speak, wanting to know what had happened to make her heart so black. Deep down, he preferred not to know. Maybe she was just angry he'd threatened to take away what little freedom she had left, but something told him there was more to her anger. Something he wasn't ready to know.

"You have yourself a Merry Christmas, Anastasia," he finally managed, then tipped his hat and walked away without another word.

***

January 3, 1921

Tobias followed the woman down the stairs and waited until she'd filled her buckets. Her face was drawn and her eyes sank into her head. She coughed and spat something into a cloth. She'd been ill for some time, but it still shocked him how quickly she was declining.

He approached, and he saw the recognition in her eyes. "It's you?"

He'd made his presence known to her over the past two weeks, stepping out from the shadow when he was sure it was only she who was looking. More than once, he'd passed so closely that he had slipped a few dollars into her hand. She seemed to know he didn't want anyone else to know, as she never drew his attention or called after him as he passed. Today, he brought food, just some crackers and cheese, but he thought it was more than she'd had in a few days. While she shared the apartment with others from what he could tell, they didn't offer her any help with food or otherwise.

"Yes." He handed her the bag of food and relieved her of the heavy buckets.

"Who are you?" She coughed and reached for the rag once more.

While he wanted to take her into his confidence, he knew she wouldn't understand. How could she when he didn't fully understand himself? "A friend who knows you're very ill."

Tears sprang to her eyes. "My daughter…I don't know what to do."

He looked away to steady himself. While he was quick to use tears, he was at a loss as to handle those of others. Especially dames. He faced her once more. "The people who live with you wouldn't take her?"

Fear mingled with the tears. "I do not trust them. That is why I do not leave her here whenever I go out. I only leave her long enough to fetch the water."

He started walking, and she followed him up the stairs.

"I worry she will end up on the streets," she said between coughs. "There are already so many there."

He paused at the door to the fourth-floor hallway. "I have found a place for her."

"You? I no understand. What do you want with my daughter?" Her eyes widened. "No, not for your pleasure. She is too young. That is why I don't leave her. I have seen the way the man in there look at her and she but a child."

Tobias shook his head. "No, she will not be with me. I

only wish to see her safe."

"I no understand," she repeated. "Why?"

"Because she reminds me of my sister." *At least the sister I used to know.* "You are to take her to the asylum near St. Paul's Chapel. Do you know the one?"

Her lips quivered as she nodded.

"Take her there when you are ready. But don't wait too long. Understand?"

She doubled over, the cough getting worse as she tired.

"Soon, Milena. You must not wait too long."

Her face filled with questions. "How do you know my name?"

"It does not matter. If you want my help, you must do as I tell you. Take her to the asylum and do not wait. Once she is inside, my friends will see she is safe."

"I am scared," she said and let loose with a new stream of tears.

"I know, but you must do this. It is the only way."

"You will watch over her?"

"I will watch over you both," he promised.

"You are but a boy yet you act of a man. I bet you help your momma, yes?"

No, I was too young to help her when she needed me. He smiled and blinked away the tears that threatened.

"I must go inside. I will tell my daughter of your kindness."

"NO! No," he said, lowering his voice. "If I'm to protect her, she must never know it was me who told you to take her there."

Milena nodded her understanding, placed the bag of food under her arm, and took the buckets he was holding.

Tobias turned the doorknob and stepped back so as not to be seen. He'd done what he could. He just hoped he hadn't acted too late.

***

"I don't understand why Tobias didn't want Mildred to know," Linda said, closing the journal.

"He knew she would hate him for taking her away from her mother," Cindy replied.

"So better to hate her mother? Pretty perceptive for a boy his age."

"I think all he had to do was reach inside. I think on some level, he hated his mother."

"Really, why?"

"Because she didn't protect him."

Linda laughed. "Kind of hard to protect someone when you can't protect yourself."

Cindy rubbed at her temples. "Agreed. Even still, I think Tobias was pissed off that she died."

"You missed your calling."

"I thought you said I'm a good teacher."

"You are, but you would make an even better shrink. Are you good to read some more or do you have a headache?"

"A slight headache, but I think it's stress. I'm getting so caught up in this. I forget this all happened many years ago, and there's nothing I can do for the kid."

"I'm glad Mildred insisted he write the journals," Linda said, gathering the next set and handing one to Cindy.

"So am I, Mom. So am I."

Chapter Twenty

August, 1923

Tobias sat on the stoop across the street from the asylum watching the girls milling around the play yard. Mileta stood in the middle of a group of girls, laughing and stretching her arms wide. Yard time was limited to two hours per day, half that if the weather was poor. With the children on such a rigid schedule, he'd built his day around stopping by to chat with Slim and Paddy to check and see how Mileta was faring.

She'd come a long way since the day her mother left her there. At first, she seemed so sad, he thought she would wilt away. So much, in fact, it took everything he had not to pound on the door and tell them it had all been a terrible mistake. He'd visited daily and watched from afar as she slowly rebounded. Though he could not chance getting near enough to hear her words, he could tell she was happy. At least happy as one could be when they thought their mother no longer loved them. While he wished he could tell her the truth, doing so would serve no purpose, as her mother was long dead. Maybe someday when she no longer needed his protection, he could tell her that her mother had not died alone. That he'd been with her when she took her last breath and given the undertaker his last dollar with a promise of more if he would take care of her. Maybe he would tell her about Mr. Livingston, and how it was through shadowing the man that he had been led to Mileta and her mother. He'd tell how after he'd seen her safely inside the asylum, he'd returned to Livingston and finished the job he'd started. The payoff had been enough to see Milena had a proper burial complete with granite stone. Maybe if she knew these things, she would forgive him. Someday.

***

Tobias hid in the closet staring longingly at the stacks of bills that littered the table. He'd not returned to the trains since the Malbone Street crash but remembered the lesson he'd learned that day. While he had no problem with stealing, he'd go hungry before dipping the pockets of the working class. Thankfully, there were enough silk-lined pockets in the city that he'd not gone hungry.

He'd also gotten pretty good at gambling, sneaking into the cigarette shop so many times, he could shimmy the lock and be inside the back room in mere seconds where he often hid, watched, and learned. And what an education it was. While the guys in the room mostly came to drink and gamble, they also freely discussed business once the ill-gotten booze kicked in. He knew the names of all the regulars. Ferret, a man with dark caterpillar eyebrows that stretched over small, close-knit eyes. Smitty, a bookish man that liked to use big words to show everyone how smart he was. Angel, a younger guy that watched more than he spoke. Ronnie, the wheelman. Solomon, a numbers guy who liked to give statistics on horse races. A man with a cleft chin he knew only as Oscar. Lastly, the one that frightened Tobias the most, a thin man with a scar the length of his face the guys referred to as Johnny the Hit Man. On occasion, a new face would appear. Tonight was one of those nights. The man's name was Big Mike, the reason for the moniker obvious. Big Mike could easily fill two chairs, unfortunately for the single chair that currently supported his weight. Tobias stared at the chair, willing it to collapse, fantasizing that in the confusion he would rush in, grab a stack of dough, and be gone. He'd played the snatch-and-run scene so many times, he'd actually mapped out his getaway, planning multiple routes in case one escape path became blocked. It was a beautiful plan, if not for the fact that the fellows were always packing heat.

The chair creaked as Big Mike leaned back. "Hey, Johnny, run out and get us some chow. Fat man gotta eat."

It would take three Johnnys to match the size of the man called Big Mike. Tobias held his breath, waiting to see how Johnny would react.

"What do I look like? A waiter? Get it yourself. Besides, ain't nothing open at this hour," Johnny replied calmly.

Big Mike settled his chair, pulled out a large pistol and leveled it at Johnny. "You talk to me like that in my neighborhood, and I'd put a bullet in you."

The table grew quiet.

Tobias swallowed as Johnny leaned back in his chair and reached a hand towards his breast pocket. Johnny locked eyes with Big Mike, slowly removed a cigar, and bit off the tip. "Yeah, too bad we aren't in Detroit. I like me a good bloodbath."

Big Mike fanned the pistol around the table. "When I get hungry, I get unhappy. No one in the room gonna like it if I get unhappy. Got it?"

Tobias pushed open the door to the closet and gulped as each man pointed a pistol in his direction. He glanced at the door, debating his next move.

"You'll never make it, kid," Big Mike warned. "Move away from the door."

Not wishing to look like a coward, Tobias pulled himself taller and moved to the center of the room.

Ferret looked toward the now empty closet. "How long

you been there, kid?"

Tobias considered his answer. "Months."

"A wise guy, huh?" Johnny said, pointing his pistol at him. "You better start making sense or your mother is going to bury her son today."

Big Mike looked at Johnny then holstered his pistol. The others followed his lead— everyone but Johnny, who kept his pointed at Tobias. The big man nodded at Johnny. "Johnny here has, shall we say, a very special talent. He never misses. Let that sink in a minute just in case you're still considering running. Never misses. You understand what I'm saying, kid?"

"They call him Johnny the Hit Man. I'm pretty sure I understand why," Tobias answered, then added, "And my mother is dead."

Johnny narrowed his eyes. "Ain't no one here said that name tonight."

Big Mike raised his palm to Johnny then motioned to Tobias. "Take it easy, Johnny. Put your gun down for a bit. Why don't you explain what you're doing here, son? Start with your name."

"My name is Mouse. I come here every night and wait for my chance to steal your money," Mouse said, looking at each man in turn.

Big Mike laughed. "Is that right? And you're planning on stealing the money now, with all of us sitting here?"

"No, sir."

"You say you have been living here for months?"

"I don't live here. I pick the lock and hide in the closet, waiting."

"Okay, tough guy. What stopped you?" Johnny said, pointing the gun again.

"Too many guns," Tobias said, and the men laughed. "The money wouldn't be worth nothing if I'm dead."

"Okay, so you've been waiting, and you decide tonight is the night, so you bust out of the closet and have a change of heart?"

"No, I came out because you said you were hungry," Tobias corrected. "I figured if you were willing to shoot someone for something to eat, then it might be time for me to come out. I wasn't doing nothing but watching anyway. Figured I could run and bring you back something to eat."

"And listening to what we had to say. The kid's a spy, Big Mike. Probably working for one of our rivals. Or the coppers, if he knows our names. Let me off him and be done with it," Johnny said, looking at the big man.

Big Mike laughed. "Johnny, the kid just saved your life, and you want to repay him by taking his?"

"You weren't going to shoot me, and you know it," Johnny grumbled.

"You know that, and I know that, but this here kid didn't know that, did you, kid?"

"No, sir. Where I come from, if someone says they are going to do something, they do it," Tobias replied. "I was just going to get you something to eat."

Big Mike's stomach rumbled in reply. He cupped his right hand and clapped Tobias on the shoulder with the other. "The kid's got stones charging out here like a bull. He's got good eyes; I say we trust him."

Angel laughed. "That's just your stomach talking, Big Mike."

The big man shrugged. "Could be, but a fat man's got to eat. Either I send the kid or one of you schmucks is going to go."

Ferret gave a nod to Johnny. "Unless you're going to go yourself, I vote we send the kid. He don't come back, then the next time you see him, you can off him."

Johnny lowered his pistol and returned it to the holster inside his jacket. "Alright, but he better bring me something too."

"Okay, kid, it's put up or shut up time. Where are you going to find something worth eating at this hour?"

"I know a guy," Tobias said, using the same line everyone in the city had used at least once in their life.

The men all laughed.

"We all know a guy, kid," Big Mike said, shaking his head. "This guy better have something worth eating, or I may change my mind about Johnny here having a chat with you."

Tobias wasn't worried. His guy, Lombardi, had been making pizza in the bakery on Spring Street for years, staying up late at night making them and selling in the grocery the next day. "I'll bring you a pizza pie."

Big Mike looked doubtful. "I don't want dessert. I want a real meal."

"It's not sweet; it has meat and cheese."

"Then why do they call it a pie?" Big Mike's stomach rumbled once more. "Never mind, just bring the pizza, and it better be good."

"You'll like it just fine. Lombardi got the recipe from his mother in Italy."

"Now what, kid?" Big Mike asked when he hesitated.

Tobias swallowed. "I need some dough."

"Like I said," Big Mike laughed, removing his wallet, "the kid's got stones."

Tobias watched as Big Mike pulled out a hundred-dollar bill and held it for him to take.

"You don't need that much; I'll take one of those dollars instead."

The large man took the bill and pressed it into Tobias' palm. "You get enough for everyone and bring me the change."

Tobias pushed the bill deep in his pocket and rushed out the door. He was halfway to Spring Street when he finally slowed and checked his pocket to make sure the bill was still there. What had possessed him to leave the closet? These guys weren't street kids. Not that street kids couldn't be mean, but these guys were the real deal. If Big Mike hadn't been hungry, Johnny would've shot him. Then again, if Big Mike hadn't been hungry, he'd probably still be in the closet. The worst part, he couldn't remember making a conscious decision to come out. It just sort of happened. What would've happened to Mileta and the guys if they'd shot him? It could still happen. What if Big Mike or one of the others decided they didn't like pizza? Would they shoot him for not feeding them properly? He fingered the bill again. Did he have to go back? He had enough to live on for months to come. Maybe even the rest of the year. He was still contemplating when Lombardi answered the door to the bakery. Flour mingled with the man's dark features; he studied Tobias as if trying to guess the reason for the late night visit.

"Mouse, it's late. Whadda you doing here?"

"Gennaro, I need six of your pizza pies," Mouse said, pushing his way into the building.

"I no have extra, gotta biga day tomorrow."

"You've got to help me out, Gennaro. I've got money. I can pay double." He flashed the bill to prove he had the funds.

Lombardi eyed the bill suspiciously. "Mouse, where'd you get that kind of money?"

"There are some guys, and they want to eat."

"Guys have that kind of dough are not the guys you wanna be hanging with, Mouse."

Tell me about it. "Are you going to sell me the pizza pies or not?"

Lombardi sighed and moved to the kitchen. "I can giva you two pizza pies."

"Ah, come on Gennaro, these guys are hungry," Tobias pleaded. "I'm paying double, remember?"

"Okay, three, best I do. I put extra toppings to make'a sure they get full. Maybe some sausage, yes?"

"I don't know; it doesn't sound good."

Lombardi smiled. "Those guys gonna like it jus' fine. Giva me thirty minutes, I giva you three tomato pies that would make my mamma weep they are so good."

***

"Hey, would you look at this. The kid came back," Ferret said, opening the back door.

Tobias placed the pizzas on the counter and handed Big Mike his change. Big Mike pocketed it without counting. True to his word, Gennaro had piled each pie high with sausage and cheese, and the smell permeated the room, mingling with the stench of the cigars.

"Hey, that smells pretty good. How are we supposed to eat it?"

"Pick it up, fold it over, and take a bite," Tobias said, pointing.

"What's that black stuff?"

"Gennaro put sausage on it."

Smitty poked at the pizza. "First you tell us it's a pie and now someone puts breakfast meat on it. If you ask me, the food has an identity crisis."

Big Mike smacked Smitty's hand away, pulled out a slice, and took a bite. "Either eat it or leave it, but keep your filthy fingers out of it. Hey, the kid's right. This stuff's pretty good."

Tobias stepped back as the guys each pulled out slices. His mouth watered as cheese stretched, then broke, dangling from the thick crust. He considered bolting out the door while the men had their guard down—in fact, he'd debated not returning at all—but instead, he remained rooted as the pizza quickly dwindled.

"You're all right, kid. You ever find yourself in Detroit, look me up around Gianetti's Italian Restaurant. Got some guys there I think you'd fit right in with."

Highly unlikely, but Tobias nodded.

"You need a place to sleep; you come here. I'll let Livingston know, and he'll be all right with it as long as stuff don't go missing. Mouse," Big Mike's voice turned serious as Tobias reached for the doorknob, "I ever catch you sneaking and listening in to private conversations again, I'll shoot you myself."

Chapter Twenty-One

Late September 1924

Tobias sat on the stoop across from the asylum, straining to see in the courtyard. It was the third day the doors opened, children spilled out, and he'd failed to find those whom he was looking for. He'd nearly given up when the door opened once again, and Anastasia walked to the center of the yard, clapping her hands for the children to gather. He didn't waste any time getting to the fence, whistling to gain his sister's attention.

She narrowed her eyes and walked to the edge of the fence. "Why, if it isn't my dandy little brother in his fine trousers. Did you come to show me how you're spending all the money you steal?"

He pulled his wallet from his pocket and handed her several bills. "You're mad because I don't wish to dress like a child? Wearing trousers allows me to blend in with the right people."

"Fools, can they not see you are but a child?"

He bristled. "I'm fourteen years old, sister. I've not been a child for a very long time."

"I can't speak with you; the mistresses are waiting for me to collect the children," she hissed.

It had been like this since the day he'd asked her to watch over Mileta. They had only spoken a handful of times since that day, but each time, his sister left no doubt of the anger she felt for him. Why she hated him so, he still hadn't a clue. "I just want to know what is going on. Where are Mileta, Slim, Paddy, and the others?"

Anastasia slid a glance to the children who stood in formation waiting for her. "They're in class. There's no need for you to come back; they're keeping them away from the other kids."

She started to leave, and Tobias grabbed her arm. "What do you mean they are keeping them away? What kind of class?"

"They're teaching them manners, something you would do well to learn. Look at you in your fine clothes. You wear the clothes of a man, and yet you have the manners of an ape." She struggled against his grip. "You think your money can buy you everything. Well, it can't, Mouse. Your friends are leaving. They're going to be sent out on the trains, and you'll never see them again. None of them, not even your precious little Mileta."

Tobias eased his grip. Though he'd planned for all scenarios, he'd not expected this. "The trains? When? Where?"

"I don't know where. Not long. Two, maybe three weeks."

"Why aren't you going?"

She laughed. "In case you haven't noticed, I am no longer a child. I have a job here. And while the trains do take some unmarried women, I am not the kind of woman they want. I wouldn't bend to their ways. They wouldn't take me any more than they would take you. Move along, brother; you're done looking after your friends."

He stared after his sister long after she and the others disappeared within the building. Was Anastasia correct? Had everything been for naught? Even if he purchased a ticket on the same train, they wouldn't allow him to be in the same train car. Any of the kids could be ushered off without his knowledge. Even if he managed to get on the same car, he would have no way of keeping track of them all. He didn't have to; the others would have to fend for themselves. He only needed to keep his eye on Mileta. Anastasia said he had weeks. He would use that time to come up with a plan.

***

Tobias sat watching as Gennaro manipulated the dough. Since first introducing the men at the cigar shop to Lombardi's pizza, he had a standing order of four pizza pies every Friday night. They added two additional pies if Big Mike happened to be in town. Today, Mouse was waiting for six pies.

"Mouse, you no look very happy of late. What it is that troubles you?" Gennaro asked, twirling dough around the tips of his fingers.

"It's nothing," Mouse said on a shrug. Truthfully, it was a very big something, just not anything the pie man could take care of.

"Come on, Mouse. It is me, Gennaro. I no see you like this in a long time. You have good clothes to wear and money in your pocket, yet your face say you no happy. You a young guy. What you got to no be happy about? Is it the guys who I make the pies for? I can give the pies more spice. They be hoping to die, the pies be so spicy."

Tobias laughed. "No, the guys are good."

Gennaro flipped the dough high in the air, caught it, and continued to stretch it thin. "Ya, well, all the same, I no like you sleeping there all the time. You take the pizza to da men, and you come back here tonight. I have a blanket in the back. It is warm with the ovens working so hard. You sleep here, okay?"

He considered objecting, but the truth was, he didn't always enjoy being in the same room with Big Mike and Johnny. It was as if each man felt the need to prove himself when the other was in the room. "Yeah, okay."

"Gennaro?" Tobias said as his friend busied himself placing toppings on the dough. "Have you ever thought about leaving the city?"

"You mean a vacation?"

"No, like for good."

"Na, I like it here jus' fine. People are starting to come to me asking for my pies. I go someplace else, and I hava begin all over. Why? You wanna go someplace else?"

"I'm thinking about it."

"Where would you go you had da chance, Mouse?"

Tobias chose his words carefully. "Well, I got some friends who are going on trains to find new homes. This place they are living is looking to see the kids get new parents to live with. I've been thinking of trying to catch a ride with them. I guess I'd go where the trains take me."

"Ah, I've heard of these trains. You no seem like the type that would go along with dat. You a boy used to doing your own thing."

Gennaro was right; finding a family was not in the cards for him. Sure, he'd play the part, but he'd ditch the do-gooders and find Mileta the first chance he got. But first, he needed to find a way onto the trains. "Yeah, well they're cracking down on kids living on the street. It's just a matter of time before they toss me into one of those asylums. I'd rather take my chances with some do-gooder than spend my life behind a locked fence."

Gennaro studied him for a moment. "You come here tonight. Tomorrow you will meet a friend of mine."

"What kind of friend?"

"You just come back here. And, Mouse, don't you worry. I know a guy."

***

Tobias paced the narrow hallway, wondering at the conversation on the other side of the door. At Gennaro's insistence, he was dressed in what he considered children's clothing. Knickers to the knees with stockings tucked inside. While the clothes were clean, Tobias felt uncomfortable. People looked at him as if he were nothing more than a kid, which in reality he was, but he hadn't dressed the part in years.

The door opened, and Gennaro waved him inside. The room was large with tall ceilings, enormous windows with real fabric coverings, and reminded him briefly of the time he spent with Felisha and Adam. He hadn't thought of the couple in years, and the memory caused his chest to pound. He shook off the feeling and removed his hat as he followed Gennaro to an elderly man in a large wingback chair. The man was staring out the window as if seeing something no one else could see. Gennaro cleared his throat to get the man's attention, and after several seconds, the man tore his eyes from his imagined view and looked Tobias up and down.

"This is boy I was telling you of, Loring. He a good boy and would like to go on the trains. He's a hard worker," Gennaro said, addressing the man.

"What's your name, son?" Loring asked.

"Mouse."

"I didn't ask your street name. What's your real name?"

Instantly, the memory of his original trip on the train came to mind. An image of Mrs. Fannie surfaced, of the men who made him leave, and his mood darkened. "My name is Tobias."

"Where do you live, Tobias?"

"Around."

"Where are your parents?"

"My real parents are dead. I had another mom, but men

like you made me leave her," he replied heatedly.

The man's brow furrowed. "Men like me?"

"Yes, men who sit in fancy chairs and ask a lot of questions." He went on to tell him of the first time he took the trains, of his time with Mrs. Fannie, and what happened that got him sent back to New York.

Loring cast a long look out the window before finally speaking. "That's not how it's supposed to work. The system we have in place is far from perfect, but things should have been handled differently. While I cannot say the committee was wrong in removing you from the home, they should've contacted the agent to see if he could have found you another home."

I didn't want another one. I wanted the one I had. Tobias sighed. This conversation was proving to be unsettling. He'd have to find another way to help Mileta, a way that didn't threaten the defenses he'd put in place. He replaced his hat and turned to leave.

"Wait, Mouse," Gennaro said, blocking his way. He opened his coat, removed a book, and handed it to the man. "Loring, this book was given to me when I first arrived in this country. It was an agent from the Children's Aid Society who gifted it to me, but I think you will recognize the inscription."

Loring opened the book, traced his finger on the inscription, and smiled.

"I was told I merely had to bring this to the CAS and I would find a better home. I no needed it as I was lucky to find my own way. But I give this to my friend Mouse so he too can find a better home. Will you no honor your father's memory and help me to give this boy a better life?"

The man studied Mouse for a good moment before handing him the book, which turned out to be a well-worn Bible. "Read to me the words my father wrote."

Tobias held the book close and read aloud. "A lad who is willing to accept that he needs help will grow into a man who can achieve greatness. I give you this book so that you too may someday find your way. Charles Loring Brace."

Loring nodded. "Very good, son. If you are willing to give the system another chance, I will see we have a place for you. There is a train leaving for Detroit next Tuesday. Be at the train station at nine."

At the mention of Detroit, Tobias smiled. Big Mike had told him if he were ever in the city to look him up at Gianetti's Italian Restaurant. While he didn't know anything about the city, it was good to know he already had a connection there. He handed the book to Brace. "Thank you, sir."

"No, I'd like you to keep it. That is, if Gennaro doesn't mind."

His friend smiled. "Be my pleasure."

"Tobias," Loring said with a nod toward the book. "When you get the time, there are more words inside. Read them. They will help you find your way."

Tobias placed the Bible inside the waistband of his pants; it was the second time someone had given him an inscribed book. This time, he intended to hold on to it.

Chapter Twenty-Two

Tuesday, October 21, 1924

Tobias arrived at the train station well ahead of 9 am. Dressed in schoolboy garb, he fit in with the other children milling about the train station. There were groups of children from various asylums in the clock area of Union Station. He kept his distance, not wishing to make his presence known until he was satisfied that Mileta and his friends were to be part of the group heading west. He'd nearly given up when at last he recognized several kids from the asylum, Paddy and Slim among them. He was just about to get Paddy's attention when the boy whistled, and the mistress cuffed him across the back of the head. Tobias held his breath. A thing such as that could get the boy sent back to the asylum from whence he came. Paddy seemed undeterred, smiling at Mileta like a lovesick puppy.

He stepped into the opening, caught Paddy's attention, and motioned towards the bathroom. He disappeared before Mileta looked in his direction, and waited so long, he wondered if the boy would join him. Just as he'd decided to leave, Paddy and Slim hurried through the door joined by a boy named Slick.

"Hey, Mouse, what are you doing here?" Slim asked the second he saw him.

"The same as you. Getting ready to head out on the trains."

Paddy's face clouded. "How'd you manage that?"

"I have my ways. Funny, you don't seem happy to see

me."

Paddy shrugged. "Just didn't expect to."

"More like you thought you'd have Mileta all to yourself now," Tobias taunted.

Slim stepped between the two boys, stretching his hands to keep them apart. "Paddy didn't mean anything, Mouse; we're all excited to be getting out of the asylum. They're going to find us fine new homes with real folks to take care of us."

"You don't believe that?" Paddy asked when Tobias laughed.

"I don't believe a lot of stuff they say."

"Yeah, well, you better watch yourself, or they'll send you packing. They just sent a kid back for puking. It's a good thing that truck stopped when it did. A minute later, and we all would've puked," Slim said, wrinkling his nose at the memory.

The bathroom door opened. A man stepped inside and went into a stall, closing the door behind him. "You guys help me keep an eye on Mileta. Once we get to Detroit, I'll figure out what to do next."

Slick's eyes grew wide. "How do you know we're going to Detroit? They only told us we are going west."

Slim smiled and jutted a thumb towards Tobias. "Mouse knows everything."

Paddy stepped towards the door. "We have to go before they come looking for us. How are you going to get on the train?"

"I've got my ways. You guys get with your group. I'll be right behind you." He gripped onto Paddy's arm, squeezing tight. "And remember, don't let on that you know me."

He waited several moments before following the boys out, staying just out of sight of the chaperones. Sometime later, Mileta's assembly joined the larger group, and the whole procession made their way to the lower level where the train waited. He held back, watching. He'd just moved in line behind the group when the conductor stepped in front of Mileta, preventing her from boarding. He wanted to laugh at Paddy's pitiful expression on being separated from her. The thing that prevented him from gloating was the knowledge his own expression would match if he were placed in a similar position. Mileta and a handful of others were directed to the next car. Tobias was just about to follow, when the placing agent stopped him.

"You're not one of ours," she said, waving him off.

"Ah, but I am." He pulled the Bible from his waistband and opened it for her to see. "Mr. Brace gave me this book and told me to come here today."

The lady looked at the Bible and laughed. "That would be a good trick if not for the fact that Reverend Brace has been dead for some time."

"Not this Mr. Brace," Tobias said, pointing to the inscription in the book. "His son. Although he's also an old man."

"What's the trouble?" a male agent asked, stepping beside them.

"This boy is trying to sneak onto the train. Said Mr. Brace gave him a Bible."

"Ah, you must be young Tobias. Loring said I should expect you." The man smiled. "You go on, son. I'll explain."

Tobias smiled at the woman and climbed onboard without another word. He stood in the aisle searching for Mileta. Once he found her, he approached the seat directly behind her and pulled a small boy from his seat.

"Find another place to sit, kid; this seat is mine," he whispered and doubled his fist when the boy looked as if he would protest. The kid took off, and Tobias sighed as he sank into the vacant seat. It was the closest he'd been to Mileta since he'd convinced her mother to take her to the asylum nearly three years prior.

He eavesdropped as the man beside her struck up polite conversation, further enjoying listening to her voice as she answered. The train jerked to a start and began creeping from the station. Tobias swallowed his fear. Except the downtown trolleys he'd not been on a train since the night of the crash. As the train picked up speed, a queasiness washed over him. He visualized the train car and knew he hadn't passed a privy on the way to his seat. The car behind might have one, but it was full of kids, so odds were it would be in use. He bolted from his seat, racing towards the forward car in search of the privy, his senses screaming as he did. It was the forward cars that had crumpled during the crash and everything in his being willed him to run the other direction. Lucky for him, the privy was empty as he hurried inside, bent over the hole in the floor, and released the contents of his stomach. He stood watching as the ground raced below his feet, comforted only by the fact the train kept moving.

By the time he returned to his seat, the lady sitting with Mileta was asleep, head pushed to the window with a trickle of drool dripping down her chin. Mileta and the husband spoke in hushed tones so as not to disturb the woman. While the man sounded pleasant enough, there was something about him that made Tobias uneasy. The guy excused himself and moved to the rear car. He followed, watching as the man approached one of the agents that accompanied the children. The woman seemed hesitant at first until the man took out his checkbook. It was then the agent's eyes lit up. Tobias hurried back to his seat, his mind racing. While he didn't know the man, he knew of the world in which he lived. He'd seen enough to know the man was in the process of buying Mileta's release. Tobias waited for the door to open, telling of the man's return to the car, and stood calculating the departure from his seat perfectly so as to bump into him as he neared. As the guy took his seat, Tobias circled back and headed for the front car, rifling through the man's wallet as he did. *Not much in the way of cash. He must keep his bills in the checkbook.* No matter, it wasn't cash Tobias was looking for. Tobias wanted to know where the man lived in the off chance he was unable to stop him from taking Mileta from the train. By the time Tobias headed back to his seat, he knew the man's name was Stewart Shively, and that he and his wife, Sonia, lived in Chicago. With the help of a hat check stub and dry cleaning bill, he knew the general area the man frequented. He also found an invitation listing the couple as guests at an upcoming charity ball for the Chicago Museum. Hopefully, it would be enough.

He opened the door and lingered momentarily on the outside porch between the cars. Taking a deep breath of smoke-filled air, he opened the sliding door to the train car where Mileta was traveling and immediately filled with rage. Shively's hand was resting on Mileta's upper thigh. The man saw him looking and quickly removed his hand. Tobias clenched his fist. However, before he could take a step, a hand clasped his shoulder. He turned, ready to strike out, when the train conductor spoke.

"Easy there, lad, I didn't mean to startle you. Have a seat. I have an announcement to make."

Tobias glared at Shively and took the seat behind Mileta. The stakes had been raised. After what he'd just seen, he'd see to it that Mileta didn't leave with the couple—even if he had to throw the man from the train with his bare hands.

***

The Shivelys wasted no time ushering their newfound

prize from the car the moment the train stopped for an unexpected repair. Desperate, he caught Mileta's attention, willing her to break free and join him, but Shively interceded, whisking her out the front entrance to the cabin. As the trio made their way to the country store, Tobias made a beeline to the group of children traveling with Mileta. He wasted no time with introductions, as he told them of his observations and fears. The boys agreed Stewart Shively had to be reckoned with and offered to help Tobias throw the man from the train. It was a girl by the name of Mary who devised the final plan, one she was sure would sway Mrs. Shively in the opposite direction. As the couple led Mileta back to the train, Tobias' resolve wavered. The way she paused and looked in their direction as if it were they who were betraying her nearly crushed him.

He took his seat behind them, making sure to push his knee into Shively's seat as he did. If nothing else, he wanted to make sure the man knew he was there. Moments later, the seat in front of them exploded in a fury as Mileta somehow managed to get eggs on the woman's newly purchased coat. Tobias doubled over in laughter when the woman asked if Mileta knew how much she paid for the thing and Mileta, in a serious tone, replied nine cents. Obviously, Mileta had never shopped on 5th Avenue. Things settled until Mary arrived sometime later. Once again, Tobias felt sorry for Mileta as Mary innocently told her new custodians that Mileta wet the bed. It was a farce, of course, but one Mileta had not been made privy to. It took a few moments before she caught on, but when she did, he was proud of how well she went with the moment. The ruse worked, and he winked at Mileta as she and Mary rushed back to the rear train car. He thought of following the girls but decided against it, knowing Mileta was in good hands for the remainder of the trip. Pulling his cap over his eyes, Tobias slept.

***

After changing from their traveling gear, the children were ushered into a large, unused room in Michigan's Grand Central Station. The lead agent, Miss Agana, floated around the room as if on a bed of air, telling the onlookers about the Placing Out Program, and how the placements worked. With a few exceptions, the speech was verbatim of the one he'd heard years ago. He looked into the crowd and wondered at the people looking back. They seemed so eager, so full of expectation. An image of Mrs. Fannie floated into his memory, and his mood darkened. He was older now and would not let empty promises fill him with childish hope. He was there for one reason, and that was to keep an eye on Mileta. He moved to position himself so he would not lose sight of her. Miss Agana fielded questions like a pro until the bystanders could take no more, swarming to where the children stood, each eager to be the first to snag a child. Tobias tried to hold his position, but with so many people, it proved difficult. Just as he took a step towards Mileta, a man grabbed him by the arm.

"You look like a strong boy; how would you like to come work in my machine shop?" Tobias pulled his arm free and left without comment.

An older couple approached, looking uncertain. The man took off his hat and addressed Tobias. "We are looking for a boy to inherit our farm. It used to be a fine dairy farm. It's not much anymore, but if you wouldn't mind living in the country, we'll treat you fair."

Tobias wavered for a moment, then saw Mileta being led to the side door by a young, well-to-do-looking couple. He caught a glimpse of bright red hair and smiled. If the couple could convince Paddy to move to the country, he wouldn't have to worry about him interfering with Mileta. "You see that boy with the red hair? His name's Paddy, and he's the boy for you. He is bright, honorable, and you'll like him just fine."

The woman looked uncertain. "I don't know... the boy has red hair."

The man chuckled and ran a hand through his head of snow white hair. "Are you forgetting I too had brilliant red hair when we met?"

The woman blushed. "No, that's what scares me. We're not as young as we once were."

Tobias knew how people felt about redheads. "Paddy's not so bad for a red. All any boy his age wants is someone to be nice to him. You do that, and you'll get along just fine."

The woman considered his words then smiled. "Alright, then."

Tobias watched as the couple made their way to where Paddy stood and sighed as a slow smile spread across Paddy's face. The couple laughed at something Paddy said, and Tobias felt a pang in his stomach. He wondered why good fortune seemed to find some and others had to fight for everything. He was still pondering that as he made his way across the room to the door where they took Mileta. There was a line in the hallway, people waiting to enter a room where they documented the newly formed families. Tobias saw Miss Agana coming and stepped close to the line, pretending to wait with the others. He waited for her to pass then walked up and down the line searching for Mileta. He saw Slim standing next to a tired-looking man with a mustache. The man had broad shoulders and spectacles, which exaggerated his deep-set eyes. Tobias nodded towards the bathroom and entered. A few minutes later, Slim joined him.

"Have you seen Mileta?" Tobias asked the second the door closed.

"She went into the room with a man and a woman a few

moments ago," the boy replied.

Tobias sighed, grateful he hadn't lost sight of her. "The man you're with, he seem okay?"

Slim shrugged. "Alright, I guess. His name's Louis Gianetti. He owns an Italian restaurant. Wants to teach me how to cook. I figure if I learn, I won't go hungry."

Tobias swallowed, feeling a knot forming in the pit of his stomach. Could this be the same Gianetti that Big Mike had spoken of? He smiled, not wanting to let on that he'd heard of the place. "Makes sense to me."

Slim looked to the door. "I better go."

"Yeah, don't want him to think you skipped out on him."

"Speaking of skipping, you aren't going to find you a home, are you, Mouse?"

"Na, I've tried that a couple of times. Kids like me do better on the streets."

"You get hungry, come see me, and I'll fix you some meatballs."

"I'll do that," Tobias replied.

He took a few moments to compose himself before exiting the bathroom. As he came out, Slim called him over.

"She just left." He nodded toward the long corridor and Tobias took off running.

He caught up with them just as they reached the front door. It was raining, and Tobias followed them across the street and watched as Mileta slid into the cab of a motorcar. The woman she was with produced a brightly colored quilt and draped it across Mileta's lap before joining her in the cab. Tobias watched in helpless despair as the door shut, and the car motored away. He swallowed back tears as he retraced his steps, and stood in the hallway watching the crowd, waiting for the right mark. He chose carefully then lifted the man's wallet with ease. Taking the cash, he ditched the leather and proceeded to where the families waited outside the room to have their joining documented. Several anxious hours passed when at last the line had dwindled, and he opened the door and entered the room.

The man looked past him expectantly. "You got folks willing to speak for you?"

"No, sir."

"Pity. Most seemed so eager to adopt today. There are some other children in the viewing room. You will join them, and they'll take you to the next station. You seem strong; I'm sure you'll find a home," the man said, closing the book he'd been writing in.

Tobias took the wad of cash he'd lifted and peeled off several bills. "I'd like to have a look at that book of yours."

The man hesitated. "I can't let you have it."

He peeled off two more bills. "Don't want it. Just want to study it for a moment."

The man reached for the bills. "I guess it wouldn't hurt to let you see it for a moment."

"I guess not," Tobias replied. He turned the book and skimmed the pages, searching for Mileta's name. He saw several of his friends and memorized where they'd been placed, but Mileta was not among the names. "She's not listed."

"Who's not listed?"

"My girl. I looked for her name, and she's not here."

"Maybe she didn't get chosen."

"She did; she was in here early. I saw her. She was one of the first, came with a tall man and woman. The woman had a blue coat."

"Oh sure, John and Helen Daniels. Not to worry; John's a good friend of mine. They're not rich, but they do well enough. They'll do right by the girl."

"Where do they live?"

"Why, I don't know the address."

Tobias narrowed his eyes at the man. "I think you do."

"East Fort Street. I don't know the number," the man said.

"I'll find it. If you're lying, I'll find you." He pushed the book around, left the room, and headed towards the main entrance.

"Tobias!" a woman shouted.

He turned to see Miss Agana hurrying after him. "Where are you going?"

"Home."

She looked confused. "You found a family? Where are they?"

"No, you know I'm not the family type."

"It doesn't have to be like this. I heard what happened during your last placement. We, the system failed you. But if you leave now, you're failing yourself."

Tobias took another step. "I've gotten used to the streets."

"Tobias, please let us help you. Let me help you," she said, inching closer.

He had to give the woman credit; she sounded sincere. "You know, you're not too bad for a do-gooder."

"I can help if you let me."

"Na, you go help the others. They need you more than I do." Tobias took off running, never bothering to look over his shoulder until he'd exited the building. Once outside, he lifted his hand and hailed a cab.

"Where to, kid?" the cabbie asked as he slid onto the seat.

"Gianetti's Italian Restaurant," Tobias said, closing the door.

"This is a joke, right?" the cabbie said, looking in the

mirror.

"Do I look like I'm joking?"

"Na, but you might need glasses. Open your eyes, kid. Gianetti's is across the street."

Tobias looked out the window. Sure enough, the sign on the small brick building showed the place to be Gianetti's Italian Restaurant.

"You sure you don't want me to take you somewhere else, kid?" the cabbie asked when Tobias opened the door. "That place has a bit of a reputation and is not the kind of place for kids."

Tobias pulled a quarter from his pocket and flipped it into the front seat. "Mister, I ain't been a kid in a long time."

Chapter Twenty-Three

Cindy pressed her mother's number and hit send. Linda answered on the third ring. "Hey, Mom, I just left Uncle Frank."

"Did he say anything?" Linda's voice was hopeful.

"Nothing that made any sense. He was talking about being in a tunnel somewhere. Probably from his war days. Reba went on maternity leave early, and he has a new nurse. Her name's Carla. I asked her to let us know if he seems to fixate on anything in particular. I also asked her to call us if he ever seems like he's coherent. I told her it didn't matter what time of day or night, that we could be there in minutes."

"Do you really think he'll be able to tell us anything?"

Cindy sat at the light, contemplating her mother's question. Uncle Frank had been living in the past for years. While they visited him frequently, up until they discovered the journals, neither woman had taken notice of what they'd perceived as ramblings. Now they both eagerly awaited bits of information that would help them build on the journals they were reading. The traffic cleared and Cindy turned right on Sanilac. "I don't know, Mom. It would be great if we could get a few hours of clarity so we could get some answers."

"That it would," Linda agreed.

"Hey, I'm going to swing by the Arches. Do you want anything?"

"Sure. Bring me a number seven."

"With or without tarter?"

"Yes tarter, no cheese," Linda replied.

"You got it. I'll be home in a bit."

Cindy pulled up to the outer speaker and placed her order. Moving forward, she paid and was told to pull forward. As she waited for the order, she contemplated what she'd read in Tobias' journals. Sure the boy had been dealt a tough hand, but a lot of his problems were of his own doing. The last trip on the trains could have gone differently if he'd have let his guard down. How would things have changed if he'd gone home with the restaurant owner? Or the older couple who took in Paddy. No, then Paddy would not have been there to marry her grandmother. Cindy jumped when someone knocked on her car window.

"Sorry, Hun, I didn't mean to scare you," the woman said, handing her the bag. "You have a great rest of your day, Sweetie."

"I should've been paying attention." Cindy laughed. She backed out of the space, waited for traffic to clear, and took a left. She was still rehashing the journals when she walked into the house. "Mom, I can't stop thinking things would have been so much different if Tobias had let himself be adopted again."

Always ready to speak about the journals, Linda stepped right into the conversation. "I'm sure things would have been a lot different. But then where would Mildred be if Tobias hadn't been there to watch over her? We've both read Mildred's journals, so we know what happens, but if Tobias hadn't been there to pick up the pieces…"

Cindy sighed. "I am just so worried about that kid. I was saying my prayers last night and actually included him."

Linda laughed. "To be honest, I did the same thing."

"Really?"

"Yes, I am just getting so attached to him. I keep thinking, *I wish Cindy could adopt this kid.*"

And there it was, the daily reminder that Cindy had yet

to give her mother a grandchild. "You're losing your touch. It's lunchtime and this is the first mention of a grandchild."

Linda took a bite of her sandwich. "So you'd have to add a Happy Meal to your order. What's the big deal?"

Cindy laughed. "There's a lot more to having a kid than just ordering extra fries."

Linda stuck out her tongue. "I'll get me a grandchild if I have to do it myself."

"Don't take this the wrong way, but you need a working uterus to have a child."

Linda swallowed, nearly choking on her sandwich. "Bite your tongue. I'm not planning on having the thing, but I could look into adoption."

Cindy shook her head. "Mom, you are seventy-two years old. They're not going to allow you to adopt a child."

Linda took two fries and dipped them in ketchup. "I'm younger than my age." Linda had a point. Since finding the journals, the spring had returned to her step.

"Mom, I know you want grandchildren, but I see the kids in my class coming from broken homes. I'm just not sure I want to do that to a child."

Linda picked up a fry and pointed it at her. "See right there; you sound just like Tobias."

Cindy felt her eyes grow wide. "How on earth can you compare me to that boy?"

"Because you're both afraid to love. You're thinking about it all wrong. You would not be giving a child a broken home. You're not married, so the home wouldn't be broken. The home would simply be home. Instead of giving a child a broken home, you would be giving a broken child a home."

Cindy finished her lunch without further comment. Why was it her mother could always manage to get under her skin? Not always in a bad way, but in ways that caused her to reevaluate her position on things.

***

Tobias sat at the corner table in Gianetti's Italian Restaurant enjoying a hefty plate of spaghetti and meatballs. With brick walls and white linen tablecloths, the place reminded him of Lombardi's in New York. Many times over the last couple of days, he'd walked into the building, half expecting to see his friend, Gennaro. He looked up from his plate, saw Slim, and nodded for his friend to join him.

"Whatcha got for me?" he asked when Slim approached the table.

Slim slid into the chair next to him and wiped his hands on his apron. "Not much. I asked about Big Mike and people got real quiet. I didn't want to push; it's only been three days. I come in here asking a lot of questions and Louis might send me back."

Tobias nodded his understanding. While he wanted to find Big Mike, he wouldn't allow his friend to risk his placement. He'd find Big Mike, and if he didn't, he would find another way to survive. It had taken two days and multiple trips down East Fort Street, but he'd finally found the house where Mileta was living. After walking the length of the street until his legs ached, he'd been standing on the corner waiting for the trolley when a motor car passed and he recognized the driver as the man who'd taken Mileta home. On outward appearances, it seemed like a nice home. A two-story single-family home on a quiet street. What more could a kid ask for? While he knew where she lived, he still didn't know anything about the family who took her. It was his hope that if he found Big Mike, he'd be able to convince the man to use his resources to get answers.

Tobias took a bite of meatball. "Tell me what you have."

"I went down to the basement to get something from the storeroom. When I was coming back, I ran into a couple of guys. They didn't say anything, just walked by like they owned the place. Well, I know Louis owns the place, so I decided to go back to ask them what they were doing down there. Only they weren't there."

Tobias lowered his fork. "What do you mean they weren't there? Did you see them or not?"

"Sure I did. Only then I didn't," he said with a shrug.

"Are you saying the men were ghosts?"

"No. At least I don't think so. But they disappeared into thin air," Slim said with a shrug.

"When was this?"

"Last night before we closed."

"Did you ask about the men?"

Slim lowered his voice. "You kidding? Louis thinks I'm *pazzo*, he's gonna send me back."

Slim had a point. If Tobias didn't know better, he'd think the boy had been kicked in the head by a mule. "Okay, okay, don't say nothing, but if you see the guys again, follow them to see where they go."

"And if they truly disappear?" Slim's tone suggested he was only half kidding.

"If they disappear, we'll both leave and never come back," Tobias assured him, then losing the smile, added, "Hey, if I don't find Big Mike, I'll need a guy that can get me some information."

"What kind of information?"

"I want to know about the people Mileta is living with."

"Sure, I'll ask around." Slim looked up as Louis appeared in the doorway. "I got to get back to the kitchen. You good, Mouse?"

"Yeah, I'm good." Mouse assured his friend. "Hey, can

I take a look in the basement?"

Slim hesitated then agreed. He removed some dishes from a nearby table and motioned for Tobias to follow. Just before they arrived at the kitchen, Slim showed Tobias the door to the basement.

As Tobias reached the bottom of the stairs, he wondered at the men Slim saw and wondered further where they'd gone. If it had been anyone else, he would've thought them to be pulling his leg, but not Slim. Slim was as straight as they came. If he said the men disappeared, then the men disappeared. But where'd they go? He'd spent too much time in the graveyard to believe in ghosts. Nothing bad had ever happened to him in the graveyard. In his opinion, graveyards were much safer than the streets, where gangs and ruffians preyed on the helpless and weak. But this was a basement, not a graveyard. With limited means of escape, basements gave him the creeps.

The space was dimly lit; however, he could see racks lining one side of the room holding pans, linens, and other supplies. The basement walls were paneled with green wood, and a freestanding brick room stood in the middle of the room. Tobias walked around the side and saw an opening. It was darker on this side; however, looking closer, he was surprised to find the brick room filled with dirt. *Why would they go to the trouble to build a room just to fill it with dirt? Where had the dirt come from in the first place?* He continued to search the place, and except for the strange brick room, saw nothing out of the ordinary. He turned to head up the stairs, when he heard a door click open behind him. Impossible, as he'd just searched the space and knew there weren't any doors. He looked to see two men step out of a space he knew to be a solid wall. Engaged in conversation, the men walked past him without as much as a glance in his direction, continuing to the dark side of the brick room. He waited for the men to reappear and when they didn't, he crept along the front of the brick wall and twisted his head to see what the men were doing. Goosebumps traveled up his arms when he realized he was alone in the basement. He felt along the dark walls for a door handle but found none. He was reconsidering his position on ghosts when he heard voices on the other side of the wall. Pressing himself into the darkness, he watched as the wall opened up, allowing four men to enter the space. The men continued to the far side of the room and stopped in front of the wall. One of the men reached out and knocked three times, waited, then knocked twice more. To his relief, the wall opened, and the men went inside. While he didn't know who the men were or their purpose, he now knew them to be real. Taking a deep breath, Tobias walked to the wall and repeated the knock sequence. Seconds later, the wall opened, and he stepped inside.

Chapter Twenty-Four

The moment he entered the room, he knew he'd stumbled into a speakeasy. The soft glow of light did little to brighten the room. Men, some in suits, others in white shirts with dark-colored ties, sat around the room drinking from clear glasses. All eyes turned in his direction, then lost interest seeing the newcomer merely a boy. The stench of stale cigars and liquor filled the small space. Just below a mirror on the wall behind the bar sat shelves that held bottles of liquid in various hues ranging from clear to deep amber. The bartender nodded in his direction and a boy a few years older than him rushed over to where he stood.

Dressed in trousers and a white shirt, the boy brushed the hair from his eyes and smiled at Tobias' schoolboy apparel. "I ain't seen you in here before. Who sent you?"

He pulled himself taller and squared his shoulders. "I came to see Big Mike."

At the mention of the name, the room grew quiet. The boy's eyes narrowed, and without warning, his fist connected with Tobias' gut. Luckily, the Bible in his waistband took the brunt of the punch. Eyes blazing the boy swung once more, and Tobias ducked out of the way of the second blow. Tobias leveled a punch of his own, sending the boy to the ground with a single punch to the chin. Hearing footsteps, he whirled around, fists at the ready.

"Easy, boy," another boy said, lifting his hands with fingers splayed to show he had no intention of fighting. The boy looked at the kid on the floor and frowned. "You've got some nerve coming in here and pounding one of our best guys. Ain't no one ever knocked Butch out before."

If he's one of your best, you're in trouble. "He started it."

"And you finished it. Come on; I'll buy you a drink." The boy stepped over Butch and slid onto a stool at the bar.

Tobias took a seat next to him, and slowly, the chatter resumed.

"Beer," the boy said when the bartender approached. "And another for my friend here."

"I don't drink," Tobias, waving him off.

The boy cocked his head and blew out a long breath. "You come into our joint asking for someone that's never here, pummel our best guy, and then refuse to drink our liquor. It's hard to come by these days. Some might think that maybe you're some kind of stoolie working for the police. A person could get offed for less."

Tobias met his gaze. "I'm not refusing to drink your liquor. I don't drink any liquor. There's a difference."

A slow smile spread across the boys face. "The name's Mac."

Before Tobias could respond, he looked in the mirror, saw the boy called Butch approaching, and spun around to face him. Still dazed, Butch gave him a wide berth and took the stool on the far side of Mac.

Mac nodded to the bartender to bring another beer and turned his attention back to Tobias. "What's your name, kid, and where'd you learn to throw a punch like that?"

"Name's Mouse. I grew up on the streets, I'm not a kid, and a friend taught me how to fight. He wouldn't be happy I allowed myself to be gut-punched," he said with a quick glance at the ceiling. Slim would have been ready for the punch. Then again, the boy never stood still long enough for anyone to sneak in a punch.

"I've lived here all my life. A person who fights like you would have a reputation. Why ain't I never seen or heard of ya?" Mac asked.

Tobias thought about what Miss Agana said about not telling people you came over on the train, saying if you wanted to fit in, you wouldn't want to be known as one of the train kids. At the moment, Tobias had no intention of fitting in with these boys. "I just got into town. Came in on the trains with a bunch of kids from New York."

"I heard about those trains," Butch said, then placed a hand at his jaw. "Sheesh, Mouse, did you have to hit me so hard?"

The kid aint nothing but a sissy baby. Tobias laughed. "Someone's trying to kill me; I don't check my punches."

"I wasn't trying to kill you. I was just teaching you a lesson about lying," Butch countered.

"Who said I was lying?"

"You did when you asked for Big Mike. Everyone knows he refuses to come down here," Mac said, lowering his glass.

"He doesn't like the rickety stairs and refuses to take the tunnels. The guy's so fat, he's afraid he'll get stuck." Butch laughed.

Tunnels, so that's how the men disappeared. "Yeah, well, he told me if I was ever in Detroit, I should look him up. Said to come here. That he had some fellows he thought I would get along with. I guess you two would be the fellows he was speaking of?"

"We're off to a good start, don't you think?" Mac raised an eyebrow. "Big Mike told you to come to the basement?"

"No, he told me to come to Gianetti's. I just kind of

found this place." He decided not to mention Slim or that the boy had seen the men disappear.

"Big Mike don't take too kindly to guys snooping around," Butch said.

I ever catch you sneaking and listening to private conversation again, I'll shoot you myself. Big Mike's words echoed in his mind. "I wasn't snooping."

"Well, if you want to see Big Mike, you have to go over to The Book Cadillac Hotel on Washington Street. The place doesn't officially open until next month, but Big Mike and a few of the other guys live there. Do you know where that is?"

Tobias shook his head. He'd only been in the city for three days and had yet to venture any further than East Fort Street.

"Give me a few minutes to finish my beer, and I'll take you there myself," Mac said, lifting his glass.

***

It was well after ten when they arrived at the Book Cadillac Hotel. Mac parked the motor car at the curb a block down from the hotel and led Tobias and Butch to the rear entrance of the building. Mac rapped on the door, and it was opened by two burly men in dark suits.

"Hey Mac, who's the kid?" the larger of the two men asked.

"Says he's a friend of Big Mike," Mac replied.

The second man jutted a thumb at Tobias. "You pat him down?"

A dark pink blush crept over Mac's cheeks. "No."

The man moved forward. "Put your hands in the air, kid."

Tobias did as told and the man used his hands to search

for weapons. When the guy got to Tobias' waist, he lifted his shirt, pulled the Bible free, and laughed. "The kid's clean unless he's come to preach a sermon to Big Mike."

He snatched the book, tucking it into the band of his pants as he glared at the guy.

"Big Mike's in the pig," the man said and let them pass.

Tobias followed as they walked down a long hall past several service elevators and into a corner store. It was a small, quiet room, not a place likely to placate the likes of Big Mike. One side of the room held boxes filled with premium cigars, and the other had a display of men's leather wallets. Mac led the way to the far side of the room, slipped behind the counter, and faced one of two doors along the back wall, repeating the knock sequence used for the basement speakeasy. The door opened, revealing a blind pig, which was merely another word for a speakeasy. Music, laughter, and heavy smoke filled the room. He followed Mac and Butch inside the large, brightly lit room filled with round tables and comfortable chairs. Bookshelves lined one wall of the room and Big Mike sat in the corner in a large oversized chair that seemed perfectly made for him. He was surrounded by several men who turned to face him when Big Mike raised his log of an arm in greeting.

"Mouse, good to see you. Did you bring the fat man one of your pizzas?" the large man asked when he neared.

"Not this time," Tobias replied, shaking his head.

"Let me tell you guys; the kid's got stones," Big Mike said, and the men laughed. "Ya know how everyone says they know a guy? This kid... this kid knows a guy who makes pizza pies that would make your own sweet mother weep and yet today he walks in here empty-handed. Whatta you doing in Detroit, kid?"

"I came over on the train," Tobias replied.

"You visiting?"

"I'm staying."

"Where're you staying?"

Tobias felt his face flush. "I've been sleeping at the train station."

A frown crossed Big Mike's face. "No friend of Big Mike's gonna sleep on a bench at the train station. You hear that, Mac? You see to it Mouse gets a place to sleep."

"You got it, Big Mike," Mac said, bobbing his head in agreement.

Big Mike pointed a finger at Butch, calling him closer. As Butch turned, Tobias could see a purple bruise where his fist had connected. He cast a glance to the door, calculating how long it would take him to retreat.

"What happened to your face, kid?" Big Mike asked, pointing to the bruise. "Check it out, Abe. Looks like someone clocked your boy."

Tobias felt a knot in the pit of his stomach where Butch's fist had connected. Abe did not look like a man you'd want to cross.

"It ain't nothing," Butch said, averting his eyes. "Just a misunderstanding is all."

Abe didn't seem convinced. "Do I need to send some fellows to take care of anything?"

Tobias sighed. So much for asking Big Mike for help. Once they discovered he'd decked the kid, they'd send him packing. Might as well get it over with.

Mac caught Tobias' arm as he took a step forward and shot him a look that said "let me handle this." "Like Butch said, it was all a misunderstanding. Butch and Mouse traded punches."

Abe stood, lifted Butch's chin with his index finger, and studied the bruise. "You telling me that little kid got the better of you? He's half your size."

Tobias wanted to tell Abe he was exaggerating but decided to keep his opinion to himself.

Abe turned his attention to Tobias. "You know I can't let this go."

"There's another way," Big Mike said from his chair. "Seems to me we could use the kid in our organization."

Tobias wasn't sure what organization Big Mike was speaking of, but decided to see how things played out.

"You saying bring him into the Purples?" Abe asked over his shoulder.

"Why not?"

"How well do you know the kid? Is he even Jewish?" Abe turned his attention to Tobias. "Are you Jewish?"

Tobias had never been to a church in his life nor could he ever remember hearing his folks speak of such things. He thought about lying, but what if they called him on it? "I don't know."

"You see, the kid's not even Jewish," Abe objected.

"What's your name? Mouse?"

Obviously, Mouse was not the name he was after. "Tobias Alphers," Tobias was just about to add Millett, when he reconsidered and added the name he took from Mrs. Fannie instead. "Lisowski."

Big Mike sighed. "Sounds Jewish to me."

The tension left Abe's shoulders. "Could be Jewish. You interested in joining the Purples, kid?"

Tobias had been on his own for so long, the thought of joining a gang and being told what to do didn't appeal to him. Before he could voice that opinion, Big Mike pulled himself from his chair.

"Let me confer with my young friend for a moment, will you, Abe?"

Abe went to his chair and took a seat without comment.

Big Mike wrapped an arm around Tobias' shoulders and led him to the other side of the room. Once there, he released his hold, huffing as he schooled Tobias in the ways of life in Detroit. "You seemed a bit reluctant back there, so I wanted to make sure you have a clear grasp of your current situation. The boy you decked is Butch. Butch might not look like much to you, but he's a young Purple. To make matters worse for you, the boy's also Abe's protege. Abe Burnstein is the head of the Purple Gang and is not a man you want to cross. You get my meaning, Mouse?"

Another reason to stay clear of the gang. "Listen, Big Mike, I appreciate the offer and all, but I work better by myself. Been doing it for nine years, and so far, things have worked out okay."

"You're not hearing me, Mouse. You say no to Abe, and there won't be a 'by yourself.' There won't even be you. He'll tell the boys to give you a ride home, only you won't be going home. Some poor schmuck gonna find your body in the lake once the ice thaws. I can't make it any more clear than that. Say you'll join the Purples, or they'll take you out. I'll leave the choice to you, but you have to decide before we get to the other side of the room," the big man said and escorted him back across the room the same way.

"Well?" Abe asked when they returned. "You want to join the Purples or do you want the boys to take you home?"

"I'd like to make the Purple Gang my home," Tobias said, covering all bases.

Chapter Twenty-Five

October 31, 1924

"You're a fast study, Mouse," Mac said as Tobias guided the Ford to the curb.

"Nothing to it," Tobias replied and pulled back into traffic. "Where to now?"

"Just drive."

Tobias pushed the clutch and shifted into the next gear. "You've taken me on every road and alleyway in the city for weeks; how am I supposed to know which route you want me to take?"

"You've got it all wrong, Mouse. This is an exercise in trust. You see, by driving around like this, you not only get comfortable with the Ford, you're able to get a feel for the city. A good driver knows what road leads to which alley and how to get where they want to go if the road in front of them becomes blocked."

Tobias gazed at Mac then back to the road. "Blocked by what?"

"People, horses, things. One needs to be prepared for anything in our line of work," Mac said and took a puff from his cigarette.

Tobias gripped the wheel tighter to keep his frustration from showing. Nearly three weeks had passed since he agreed to join the Purples and he'd spent the majority of the time behind the wheel of the Ford. At first, learning to drive was exciting, but spending so much time behind the wheel was wearing on him. He was getting bored. For a gang that was supposed to be ruthless, so far, he had been witness to nothing more than schoolboy pranks. Torching a few buildings, throwing dye on some clothing, all while he sat behind the wheel, ready to speed away if necessary. The worst part, he hadn't been allowed to venture out alone. He was under constant shadow, hadn't seen Mileta, nor had he gotten any closer to finding out how her new family was treating her.

He'd been given a new set of clothes, "new" being a technical term. While the clothes were new to him, they were not new. Hand-me-downs from Mac; they were a size too large and needed a rope at the waist. While he'd ditched the short pants that made him look and feel like a child, he now felt like a bum and part of him was grateful he hadn't seen Mileta. Or at least that she hadn't seen him. If only he could get away for a while, he could find a mark and dip enough to purchase some decent clothes. The more he thought about it, the better the idea sounded.

"You know, Mac, I have a few errands I'd like to do if you're ready to call it a day."

"Abe gave strict orders you're not allowed out of sight until he feels he can trust you," Mac replied.

"There are others joining. Why aren't they here?" Tobias asked heatedly.

Mac laughed. "None of the others clocked Abe's prodigy."

Tobias turned on to East Fort Street and slowed well in advance of Mileta's house. As he drove past the house, he slid his gaze sideways, hoping for a glimpse of the girl. They'd nearly reached the end of the street when Mac spoke.

"We're close to Gianetti's. Want to grab some grub?"

"I guess I could eat something." It took everything he had to keep the excitement he felt from showing. He started in the direction of the Italian restaurant, hoping he would be able to speak with his friend without Mac overhearing their conversation.

Slim was clearing a table when they entered. Tobias caught his eye and gave a slight nod to the back, then turned to Mac. "I have to visit the water closet. Order me some spaghetti and meatballs; I'll be back in a minute."

Mac frowned then gave a nod.

Slim was waiting when Tobias arrived. The boy was even more fidgety than usual and moved around the room as if ants were crawling up his legs. "Where've you been, Mouse? I ain't seen you in weeks."

Tobias sighed. "Long story. You got anything for me?"

Slim stopped moving long enough to pull a piece of paper from his apron. "Yeah, I found a guy to look into the family. John Daniels is a big to-do at Henry Ford. He works in the design department and seems to do all right for himself. He's stopped into a couple of speakeasies but always leaves after only one or two drinks. Helen Daniels doesn't work and seems to spend every minute possible with her new daughter. They go shopping, have their hair done, and just seem to laugh and enjoy being together. From what my guy tells me, Mileta has found herself a good home with people who care for her. Mileta is lucky as far as I can tell."

"You doing okay?" Tobias asked when Slim went back to fidgeting.

"Doing all right. It's a lot of hard work, but I'm not cold, and I can eat whenever I want."

"Sounds all right to me," Tobias agreed.

"Who's the guy you're with? He looks familiar."

"Name's Mac. I better get back out there before he thinks I went out the back door. Oh, and do me a favor. Don't let on that we know each other."

Slim raised an eyebrow. "Embarrassed to introduce me to your friends?"

Tobias clapped Slim on the shoulder and looked him in the eye. "You're my friend, Slim; Mac is just someone I know. More importantly, he is someone you don't need to know."

Slim stilled. "Are you in a jam, Mouse?"

Tobias thought about telling his friend of the mess he'd gotten into but worried about the consequences. The last thing Big Mike had told him was if anyone ever asked about the Purples, he was to play dumb. The large man's face had grown serious before adding, *No matter who asks, never admit to being a Purple.*

"No need to worry about me. I've got everything covered," Tobias said, plastering on a fake smile. "Tell your guy we're good. There's no need to follow anyone, but tell him to let you know if he hears anything that may be important. I'll be in touch when I can."

Tobias held the door for Slim then waited a moment longer before exiting the water closet.

"I thought you'd skipped," Mac said when Tobias joined him at the table.

"What and leave your fine company?" he said, skimming the menu.

"What took so long?"

Tobias looked over the menu. "I was in the water closet; do you really want the details?"

Mac shook his head. "I'll pass."

Slim arrived seconds later, placing the deep bowls piled high with pasta on the table. "You fellows need anything else?"

"We're good," Mac said, waving him away.

Tobias let out an easy breath when Slim left without further comment. Mac's gaze followed Slim around the room as his friend moved from table to table, checking on the customers and filling water glasses. Tobias stuck a fork in a meatball, lifted it to his mouth, and took a bite. "I like their meatballs; they have just enough spice."

"They'll do," Mac said, taking a bite. "That boy came out of the water closet just before you."

Tobias stopped chewing. "What about it?"

"Did he say anything to you?"

Tobias laughed. "I don't talk much when I'm in the privy."

"All the same, I think I'd like to have a word with him," Mac replied.

"What's your deal, Mac? Why are you so interested in the guy?"

"No deal, just always looking for new guys."

"Leave the boy alone, Mac. He can't stand still for more than two seconds. What would you have him do?" Tobias said, watching Slim carry plates into the kitchen.

Mac leaned forward in his chair and lowered his voice. "You got a lotta nerve, Mouse. The way you act… I'm working for you and not the other way around."

Tobias leaned in, keeping his voice equally low. "Let's get something straight, Mac. I may be in this, but I don't work for you or anyone else. Working means getting paid and I ain't had any dough in my pocket in weeks."

Mac settled back in his chair. "You sound mighty ungrateful. I've given you a place to live, and you're not going hungry. Whatsa matter, Mouse, don't you like sharing a apartment with me and Butch?"

Actually, he didn't mind that part. While they shared an apartment, Tobias had his own bed and a dresser to himself. Not that he had any clothes to put in it, but if he ever had a chance to find a mark, he could remedy that. "Na, that part is fine, but you're keeping a lid on me like you don't trust me. Besides, not having any dough in my pocket, well, that takes a toll on a man."

Mac finished the last of his pasta and pushed his plate away. "A man. Phooey. You ain't nothing but a train kid. I heard Big Mike talking. Before you came here, you were living on the streets like a street rat. I bet it was your own sweet mother that kicked you out. You keep talking about dough. What would you do if you had any?"

Tobias slammed his fork into the table so hard, the tines pierced the cloth and stood upright a fraction of an inch from Mac's hand. "You ever mention my mother again, and I'll stick that fork in your eye. Yes, I lived on the streets. But I worked them and always had plenty of dough in my pockets. Plenty. I dressed as good as any of the men on Fifth Avenue. I could take their money from their pockets and still had enough time for them to wish me a good day as they strolled by. As for what I would do with the dough, I'd buy me some clothes that fit and a hat that doesn't smell like the sweat ring around your backside."

Mac swallowed and pulled his hand from the table. He reached into his pocket and tossed some coins on the table. "Well, if it was new clothes you wanted, you should have just said so. Let's go."

***

Dressed in clothes that fit, Tobias felt content for the first time since arriving in Detroit. He yawned and glanced at his new watch, a gold timepiece he'd lifted from a mark on Woodward Avenue a few blocks down from where they now sat. Butch, Mac, and several others that had been introduced to him as members of the Sugar House Gang sat at the next table enjoying the company of a redheaded broad Butch had met at the bar several hours earlier. Tobias yawned once more. Mac rose from his chair and joined him at his table.

"Get used to it, Mouse. When we get people in from New York or Chicago, we have to keep 'em company." Mac gave a slow nod to the table he'd just left. "They still consider themselves members of the Sugar House Gang, but they're Purples. We merged a while back, but there are still some holdouts that still use the old name. The man sitting next to Butch is Henry Sherman. He came in from New York a few weeks ago to lay low until things cooled. Word on the street is he and his brother took out Shorty Miller in New York."

"Who are the other guys?" Tobias inquired.

"Don't know their names; they are with the Oakland Avenue Bunch. Hey, keep your head down. The guy who just sat at the next table is Hard Luck Bill. He's small time, but it looks like he's loaded. When the guy gets zozzled, he tends to cause trouble."

Tobias looked at his watch. "Sheesh, it's almost six am. Don't these guys ever go to bed?"

Mac chuckled. "Not when there are places like this that have the coppers in their pocket allowing the liquor to run free."

Tobias took a sip of his ginger ale. "What's the good of Prohibition if people can drink anywhere they please?"

"The purpose of Prohibition is to line the pockets of the Purples." Mac traced two fingers over the sleeve of Tobias' new shirt. "Not everyone has hands as gifted as yours, Mouse. Seriously, I thought you were kidding, but the way you lifted those wallets, the guys never knew they'd been robbed."

Before Tobias could answer, chaos struck. The man known as Hard Luck Bill said something about the redhead's hat, Butch said something off-color about Bill's mother, and insults mounted, profanity readily drowning out the band. Butch stood, pulled a pistol, and fired several rounds, sending most inhabitants in the club diving for cover.

"Time to get the boys out of here," Mac said and rushed over to where Butch and the boys stood. "Put 'em away, boys, before they haul the lot of you to jail."

Just as Butch lowered his gun, a man in a suit arrived with several burly men flashing pistols of their own. Mac raised his hands, fingers splayed. "The guys didn't mean any harm, just a bit too much drink for the kids."

Butch glared at Mac over being called a kid but remained quiet, allowing Mac to defuse the situation. The man, who turned out to be the owner of the club, jutted his thumb to the door. "Go home, all of you."

"Babies need to go to bed," Hard Luck Bill snorted.

"You too," the owner said, motioning to Bill's table. Before Bill or his tablemates could protest, the bouncers leveled their pistols at them.

Tobias stayed with Mac, who doled out cash to smooth things over with the owner. Just as he opened the door to leave, the streets exploded in gunfire. Mac pulled him from the doorway, both boys diving to the floor as the glass from the windows rained down upon them. The whole incident was over in seconds. The only sounds that remained were the panic-filled voices from bystanders unlucky enough to have been hit by errant bullets. Tobias reluctantly followed as Mac dusted the shards from his suit and hurried out the door. They reached the sidewalk just in time to see two of the Sugar House Gang help the redhead into a cab and speed off. A horn blared, and Butch pulled up to the curb, running the tire onto the sidewalk as he pulled to a stop. The passenger door opened, and sirens pierced the air as both he and Mac scrambled into the car, Tobias hurling himself into the back seat.

"Where's Henry?" Mac asked as Butch pulled from the curb.

"The fool took off running. He ran one way, and the Oakland bunch ran the other way." Butch said, spinning the car around. "I'll make a pass and see if we can find him."

"Stop," Mac shouted just as Butch started to turn onto Temple Street.

Butch slammed on the brakes, and the boys watched as a lone patrolman held Henry at gunpoint.

Butch turned to Mac. "Want me to take him out?"

For a brief second, Tobias wondered if Butch was talking about Henry or the cop.

"Na, we'll get word to Abe. He'll open his pockets wide enough to make sure no one puts Henry at the scene. Let's get out of here before the heat arrives."

***

Cindy sat her laptop and the book she was holding on the kitchen table. "It's all true."

Linda reached for the dishrag and dried her hands. "What's all true?"

"All of it." Cindy spooled up her laptop as her mother joined her at the table. "It took me a bit to find Gianetti's Italian Restaurant, but I found a YouTube video talking about a bar in Detroit called Tommy's Bar. I'd been googling the Purple Gang, and at first, I just thought I'd gotten sidetracked. Then I found several more articles talking about the tunnels under the bar. I'd just chided myself for swaying from course when I found another article. I almost clicked the laptop closed when I saw the name."

"What name?" Linda asked, looking over her shoulder.

"Louis Gianetti."

"Gianetti, that was the name of the Italian restaurant," Linda said, taking a seat next to her.

"Exactly. While the article does not mention the restaurant by name, it does say the original building was once an Italian restaurant. The article talks about finding tunnels, and are you ready for this? They found a brick room in the middle of the basement. Do you know what was in the room?"

"Dirt," Linda answered hesitantly.

"That's right. The article went on to say that the dirt was probably the dirt from digging the tunnel. That's not all." Cindy reached for the purple book she'd brought in, one of several books on the Purple Gang she'd purchased after reading her grandmother's journals. "So since Tobias gave us names, I googled those too. While I haven't found Big Mike, Mac, or Butch, I did find Abe Burnstein. Do you know where I found him?"

A wide smile spread across Linda's face. "Living at the Book Cadillac Hotel?"

Cindy nodded. "I googled Henry Sherman but didn't find the one I was looking for. So I started thumbing through the books I'd bought."

"Don't tell me you actually found something?"

"Not only did I find something, but this guy wrote all about the club incident, saying that Hard Luck Bill didn't make it, but that they let Henry go because there were no witnesses. I guess Mac was right about Abe having a lot of pull." Cindy opened the book to the page she'd marked and slid it in front of her mother, watching her mother's expression as she read.

Linda gasped. "It even mentions the redheaded woman. Says here she got shot in the leg."

"I'm not sure how far down you read, but the book says this was the beginning. I guess once the gang tasted blood, they wanted more. Mom, if you ask me, this vindicates everything in the journal."

"Animals are like that. My dad once had a dog that used

to chase the chickens around just for fun. One day, he caught one. After that, we had to keep him chained up because he wouldn't stop killing the chickens. Just think, we get to read all of this first hand. Aren't we the lucky ones?!" Linda closed the book Cindy gave her and snickered. "At least we know the writer took the time to research the book."

"I found something else." Cindy brought up another tab. "Check this out. According to the article, the train crash happened just as Tobias said. There were ninety-three people killed and at least a hundred more injured. After reading the article, I think it is a miracle that boy wasn't killed."

Linda leaned in and looked at the pictures on the screen. "Maybe Mrs. Fannie's right. Maybe that boy is a ghost."

"How about we see what kind of trouble young Tobias finds his way into next?" Cindy said, closing her computer.

Chapter Twenty-Six

November 11th, 1924

The wind whipped off Lake Huron, sending chills racing along Tobias' spine. He buttoned the top button of his jacket and pulled his cap lower to thwart the icy chill. Butch, Mac, Crazy Mooch and Pete-the-driver, two boys from the Sugar House Gang, stood hands in pockets as if oblivious to the biting wind flowing off the great lake.

Pete, a short, stocky fellow, looked like someone who knew his way around the streets. Mooch, on the other hand, was dressed in dress slacks and a shirt so thin, Tobias wondered how he was not freezing to death. Give the man a suit coat, and he would look like someone he would view as a mark and follow until he had the chance to relieve him of his wallet. Given his attire, Tobias wondered how he'd come by the name of Crazy Mooch.

Getting to the rendezvous spot had taken the better part of the day driving up the rutted dirt road along the lakeshore. They'd stopped for an evening meal at the Cadillac Hotel in Lexington, took their time eating, and arrived in the small town of Harbor Beach well after midnight. Stopping just before reaching the city limits, they'd pulled off onto a well-worn path that led to a hidden cove. The guys stood close to the tree line near the edge of the rocky cove, waiting to retrieve a boatload of illegal liquor due to be brought over from the western shores of Canada. Although the skies had appeared menacing most of the drive, they were clear at the moment, allowing the full moon to reflect off the massive lake. The light from the moon danced off the waves created by the wind and illuminated the area for all to see. Not good, given the secret mission at hand. To be safe, they'd backed both the car and truck into a stand of trees to keep them out of sight.

The hum of an engine roared in the distance, and all eyes focused on the lake. The engine sputtered then stopped altogether as the craft to which it was attached began a slow glide towards the shore.

The question of Crazy Mooch's name became clear when the man giggled and raised the submachine gun he was holding.

"What's with the heat?" Tobias asked when the others pulled pistols from their waistbands.

"Lenny didn't give the signal. He's supposed to flash a light before he kills the engine," Pete whispered. "Now Mooch will have some fun with the guy."

The gang moved forward, guns at the ready, Tobias followed halfheartedly, wondering what he was expected to do if trouble arose.

A slender man in a dark coat jumped from the boat as it drifted to the shore. Rope in hand, he pulled the craft closer then stooped to tie the line around a large boulder. Mooch crept close and placed the barrel of the large gun to the back of the man's head, swearing and demanding his name.

"Sheesh, Mooch, you scared the devil out of me. What's your deal anyway?" The man rose and turned to face Crazy Mooch, his expression never wavering as his gaze took in the rest of the men, most of which had pistols pointed in his direction.

Mooch lowered his gun, and the others followed his lead. "My deal is you forgot to use the signal again. We have rules in place for a reason. You keep this up and I become complacent. I do that, then I get me and my boys killed. You've been warned enough, Lenny. Next time, I'm just gonna shoot you and be done with it. Got it?"

"Yeah, yeah, I hear ya. I don't see what the big deal is. We've got a full moon. It's not like you couldn't see me coming," the guy replied. "Besides, I get dead, and you'll have to find another source to get your whiskey. Capone's not going to be happy if he doesn't get his shipment. Now, you want the stuff or not?"

Tobias leaned close to whisper in Mac's ear. "Is he talking about Al Capone?"

"The one and only. Al has a soft spot for Old Log Cabin. We cut the stuff we sell locally, but Al gets the good stuff," Mac answered, keeping his voice low.

Tobias looked to the others and realized he was the only one that appeared surprised by the information. He leaned in once more. "Next time, I want a gun."

"What's the new guy's problem?" Mooch asked loud enough for all to hear.

Mac raised his hands to soothe Mooch. "No problem. It's just that Mouse here doesn't like being the only one out here without a gun."

"You know how to use one?" Mooch asked, fiddling with the pistol.

"Sure I do," Tobias lied.

Mooch grinned, tossed him the handgun, then pointed towards the dirt path. "Good, you go up the bend in the path. Anyone turns down that path, use the gun. Anyone coming down will be looking to either arrest us or kill us and take the booze. Don't wait, don't ask questions. Just yell loud enough for us to hear and shoot. Got it?"

Tobias nodded.

"Okay, Pete, get the truck. We got us some whiskey to

unload," Mooch said, jabbing his thumb towards the boat.

Tobias felt the weight of the pistol in his hand as Mooch and the others waded into the icy water to begin unloading the whiskey. He was still standing in the same spot when Pete backed the truck to the water's edge.

"Yo, Mouse," Pete said when he exited the truck. "Get up that path and keep a lookout. By the time anyone gets this close, they're gonna nab the lot of us."

Tobias climbed the slight incline at a snail's pace, jerking every time a tree creaked. It wasn't being alone that frightened him; he'd been alone most of his life. But being alone in the city is much different than being alone in the country. There were wild animals in the country, and who knew what creatures lived in these parts. They'd passed so many trees driving up the shoreline that he'd wondered what kind of people would choose to live in this kind of wilderness. Heathens, most likely. And bears. Woods this thick would have to have bears. He'd read about bears and how they would maul a person to death. And raccoons, wild dogs, and other creatures to infect you with rabies and claw your eyes out just because they could. The path in front of him disappeared then returned. He looked up to see the clouds were beginning to roll in, taking turns covering the moon and making the dark road appear even more menacing. He gripped the pistol with both hands as he walked to the head of the path. Once there, he stood in the middle of the worn path, straining to hear above the roar of the wind. He thought of the couple who'd approached him at the train station and wondered how Paddy was faring. He didn't like the kid much, but he hoped he was happy with his placement. Tobias was happy he'd declined their offer; he belonged in the city. He liked seeing people, and most of all, he liked the tall buildings, which helped to absorb the brunt of the wind.

He heard the rumble of an engine and hunkered low to

keep from being seen. The car slowed, turned towards him, then swung wide, speeding off in the direction from which it came. Tobias blew out a slow, calming breath of white air.

Seconds later, the quiet night erupted as gunfire filled the air. Without thinking, Tobias gripped the pistol and ran down the path towards the shots. He could hear shouting, and as he neared the rocky beach, the darkness exploded in a stream of rapid fire. Seconds later, the clouds parted and the night was silent once more. In the glow of the moonlight, Tobias saw a second boat in the harbor. Apparently, the threat had not come from the road as Mooch had thought it would. He saw a body, moved closer, and saw it was Pete lying face down on the rocky shore. Tobias couldn't see any movement on the second boat, which remained adrift several feet from the shore.

"Finish getting the crates in the truck before the cops show up," Mooch shouted above the wind. He turned to Tobias, "Stop pointing that gun at me and help them get the whiskey in the truck."

Tobias looked down, stunned to find he had his pistol pointed directly at Crazy Mooch. He quickly tucked it into his waistband and ran to help load the final crates into the back of the truck. When they finished, Butch helped Mooch load Pete into the delivery boat. Mooch climbed in after him, and Butch and two of the others pushed the boat from the shore. As soon as the boat neared, Mooch and Lenny tossed Pete's lifeless body into the second boat. Crazy Mooch jumped in after him as the delivery boat sped away. Mooch fiddled with the steering wheel, blasted several holes in the bottom, started the engine, and jumped from the vessel as it raced towards the open lake. Mooch's teeth were chattering when the guys helped him into the back of the truck.

"You're driving the truck," Mac said with a nod to Tobias. "I'll ride with you and Butch will take the car."

Tobias wanted to argue the point that he'd never driven a truck before but instead climbed into the cab and started the truck. Mac joined him in the cab and pulled a shotgun from behind the seat.

"It's just like the car, only bigger. Now get going," Mac shouted.

Tobias pushed on the clutch and eased the truck into gear, slowly heading up the narrow path.

Mac placed a hand on top of his knee, pressing on the gas. "I don't know if you know this, but you are driving a truck full of illegal liquor. If you get caught, they'll send you to prison. Now drive!"

Tobias had no intention of going to prison, so he pressed on the gas and took the turn onto M-25 so fast, he thought the truck would tip over. He'd driven about a mile when he looked in the mirror and saw a flashing light coming up fast behind them. He looked over at Mac. "We got a problem."

"Slow down," Mac said, glancing out the window.

"You said…"

Mac cut him off. "Just do it!"

Tobias slowed. Just as the police car neared, gunfire erupted from the back of the truck. The car swerved then raced to the left in the direction of Lake Huron.

"You can slow down," Mac said, lowering his gun. "It's a small town; there'd only be one cop on duty this time of night."

Tobias loosened his grip on the steering wheel. "What happened back there?"

"Smugglers, most likely. It wasn't anyone important. Meaning, not someone who came specifically to hit us. Probably someone heard the boat and wanted to get a taste of the profit."

Tobias glanced at Mac. "How can you be so sure?"

"Because they only had a few rifles. Anyone coming at us would have had more men, and it would have been a bloodbath. As it was, we only lost Pete."

"Why put him on the boat? Why not bring him back for a proper burial?"

"Getting caught with whiskey is one thing, get caught with whiskey and a dead body, and we'd never see daylight again."

"So his body will be found with the others?"

"Not if we are lucky. If things go right, the boat will run out of gas and sink to the bottom of the lake before anyone finds it."

"So that's what Mooch was shooting at."

Mac laughed. "What'd you think he was shooting at?"

"I guess I thought he was finishing the guys off."

Another laugh. "Crazy Mooch blasted them with the submachine gun; there was nothing to finish. Any more questions?"

"Yeah, why have me drive? You know I've never driven a truck before."

"We needed the guns in the hands of the people who knew how to use them."

"How'd you know I haven't fired a gun?"

"Because if you knew anything about guns, you'd have checked to make sure the gun was loaded. Mooch emptied the thing right in front of you before he tossed it to you. Be glad he did, or he'd have shot you dead the second you pointed it at him." Mac settled into his seat. "I'm going to take a snooze. Just keep following Butch and wake me if you need anything."

Tobias stared out the window in disbelief. What if a bear had ventured out of the woods and he'd needed to protect himself? Or, even worse, what if the car had decided to turn down the path instead of leaving? The more he thought of what could have gone wrong, the more irritated he became.

"Oh, and just to let you know, things will be different in a couple of months," Mac said sleepily.

"Different how?"

"Once the lake freezes over, you get to drive across the ice and pick up the booze straight from the source," Mac replied, pulling his hat low.

Chapter Twenty-Seven

November 20th, 1924

"I'm beginning to think you're pulling my leg," Mac said, shaking his head.

Tobias started to return the pistol to his waistband, felt the heat of the barrel, and reconsidered. "It pays to have a good teacher. Hey, if I'm going to carry this thing, I'm going to need a holster. After I shoot, it's too hot to put in my pants."

Mac raised an eyebrow. "Planning on doing a lot of shooting, are you?"

Tobias shrugged and started back for the car. "Seems like every time I get with you guys, someone gets shot."

Mac placed a hand on Tobias' shoulder, and he turned, fists at the ready.

Mac raised his hands. "Whoa, Mouse, it's me."

Tobias lowered his fists. "Just don't like being touched is all."

Mac turned and walked to the car. He waited for Tobias to pull onto the road before continuing. "Listen, have you wondered why you've gotten all this freedom of late?"

Actually, he had. He'd had freedom to do as he pleased for weeks and he enjoyed it. Once, he'd even followed Mileta and her mother to the theater, sitting a few rows behind as they watched a picture show. It was as if the invisible handcuffs he'd been wearing had been removed. "I guess I've noticed."

"Yeah, well, I heard Butch talking to Abe, and he's the one that got you cut loose."

That bit of news came as a surprise. Tobias was sure Butch didn't care for him all that much.

"He's not your friend," Mac warned as if reading his mind. "The guy's got it out for you. I heard him tell Abe that if you get out of line, he'd have some of the guys leak to the cops that it was you that killed that guy at the nightclub."

"I wasn't even carrying a gun," Tobias said, pounding his hand on the steering wheel. "You were with me the whole time."

"You know that, and I know that, but the cops are still looking for someone to pin it on. You get even one person mentions your name in the same sentence, and the cops won't ever let up on you."

"I thought you and Butch are friends. What's in it for you?" Tobias asked.

"Butch ain't got any friends. If Abe told him to take me out, he'd do it and never ask why. You, on the other hand, I think you'd at least give me time to get out of town. I see something in you, Mouse. You're levelheaded but can bring the heat when it's needed. People like you do all right in the world. It won't be long before you are doing more than just driving the car. Just thought you should know." Mac glanced out the window. "Besides, when you get to the top, I'd like to be your go-to guy."

Tobias thought about that for a moment. While he didn't mind driving, it wasn't something he saw himself doing forever. "And what if you get to the top first?"

Mac sighed. "I won't. I don't have what it takes. I'm more of a rationalizer."

Tobias laughed. "You're a big talker. I don't even know what that word means."

"It means I'm a smoother. When things get crazy, I can calm the situation, make people think before things get worse."

Tobias had seen Mac do that on more than one occasion. "I can see that. I can see something else as well."

"Oh yeah, what's that?"

"That you are capable of making decisions to benefit yourself."

"Like what?"

"This for one. You've managed to convince me that Butch is out to get me. Now I have to find a way to get Butch out of the picture. If anyone's hands get dirty, it will be mine, and that moves you up the ladder."

"Probably but not likely. You're too smart to make mistakes. What's the other thing?" Mac asked.

"Other thing?"

"When a person starts a sentence with 'this for one,' it usually means there is a number two. What is it?"

"Two is making me drive the truck when it was all I could do to see over the steering wheel," Tobias answered without taking his eyes off the road. "I'm sure the driver would have gotten a larger sentence than those who were merely along for the ride."

Mac smiled. "Like I said, Mouse, you're one smart kid."

Mouse thought about telling him the same thing he'd told the cab driver. But coming from someone only a few years older, being called a kid didn't sound so bad.

***

November 27th, 1924

"Tell me again why we have to wear these rags?" Butch said, pulling on the blue coat.

"Because you don't know what you're doing. If you get caught, just shrug out of the coat and run," Tobias answered.

"And the clothes? What's the purpose of the rags?"

Tobias sighed. He hadn't expected Butch to put up such a fight. "Listen, Butch, if you don't want to learn how to pinch pockets, just say the word."

"Yeah, Butch, you're welcome to stay here," Mac said, coming into the room carrying two identical coats. He handed one to Tobias and gave a hint of a smile. "You're looking pretty snazzy, Mouse."

With the exception of being too large, Tobias' clothes were not too worn. "We all look like most of the folks we'll see today. I'll be getting closer to the mark, so I need to fit in. Remember to leave everything here. Carry nothing that will help identify you. If they grab the coat, relax your arms and slip free. The cops will be left holding the coat."

Tobias stepped back and nodded to Mac. Time to let the smoother do his thing.

Mac looked at each of them and opened his palms. "Today's Michigan's first Thanksgiving Parade. The streets will be filled with people. Abe said you can't move at the Book Cadillac, it's so crammed. The streets are going to be crawling with people and there are plenty of cops to keep them safe. Remember, if you do happen to be caught, use the fake names I gave you. Anyone don't come home, and I'll send Abe to get you out. Now, let's go have some fun."

***

They arrived well in advance of the parade starting, and the streets were already packed full of people of all ages, everyone vying for the best spot to see the parade. Tobias moved through the streets, easily lifting wallets from unsuspecting marks and passing the wallets off to Mac as soon as he'd moved away. Butch followed several feet behind, keeping an eye out for anyone who discovered the ruse. They'd been at it for hours, when Butch voiced his objection.

"You guys are having all the fun. I want to collect some dough."

Tobias smiled. He'd been waiting for this and Butch had not disappointed him. "Whatcha say, Mac? Want to hang back and let Butch have a go at it?"

Mac kept his emotions in check. "Yeah, I guess I can keep lookout for a bit."

The sound of a marching band filled the air, announcing the start of the parade. Tobias started moving again, knowing Butch would be eager to follow. He found his mark, dipped the pocket with ease, and passed the wallet to Butch. They continued with the routine for several moments, Tobias lifting the wallet and Butch shoving the leather into his pockets. By his calculation, Butch's pockets should be nearly full. A good thing, as the band was nearing. Tobias scanned the area and found a flatfoot leaning next to a building watching the crowd. He turned, handed Butch another wallet, and gave a slight nod to Mac, who disappeared into the crowd. He moved a few feet closer to the cop, making sure to keep a line of people between them. He passed off another wallet, and the second Butch looked away, Tobias decked him, sending him to the ground in a crumpled heap.

"Thief!" Tobias yelled loud enough to be heard over the band.

Hearing the commotion, the cop hurried over to see what was amiss. He leaned over Butch, who was out cold, and then narrowed his eyes at Tobias. "What's going on here?"

"I was watching the parade with my family, and this guy stole my father's wallet. I didn't want any trouble. I just wanted my father's wallet back. I saw him steal another one and told him if he gave me the one that belonged to my father, I wouldn't tell about the others. He must not have liked that because he

Shameless

punched me in the gut." Tobias pushed a few tears from his eyes, amazed that he could still make that happen after all these years. He let his lip quiver and rubbed his stomach for good measure.

A crowd was beginning to gather.

Tobias pointed to a man in a derby hat whose pocket he'd just emptied. "You, sir. Check your pocket. I told him to give it back, and that's when he punched me. I had no choice but to defend myself."

"Of course you didn't," another man agreed. "I'd of done the same myself if I'd of seen it."

The man with the missing wallet leaned down and opened Butch's coat. "Why the bloody thief has a whole coat full of wallets."

Butch's eyes fluttered open.

Tobias waited for the cop to bend to help Butch up and made his escape, pushing through the crowd to find Mac waiting near the building where the cop had once stood. Mac rushed to greet him.

"Sheesh, Mouse, I thought you killed the guy. You need to show me how to throw a punch like that."

Tobias thought of Slim and smiled. "Na, my friend's the real teacher. I just throw them when I need them."

"A friend here? We could use someone like that," Mac replied.

Tobias pulled a low-slung hat from his pocket and placed it on his head then removed the coat. "Let's move down the street."

"Why are you ditching the coat?" Mac asked when Tobias tossed it across a trash can.

"The cop got a good look at me. If he's searching for me, he'll probably be looking for a kid wearing a blue coat."

Mac glanced at the coat he had on. "Want me to ditch

mine?"

"Only if you have extra pockets to carry what I gave you. Not to worry, we don't look anything alike. You just remember that half of that is mine." Tobias glanced at Mac. "You know what to tell Abe?"

"Sure, I'm telling him we were at the parade running a scam when Butch disappeared."

Tobias nodded. It was a good plan. If Abe decided to check the jail, he'd be looking for Butch, not Stan Kavieff, the name Butch was instructed to give if he were caught. "As long as Butch sticks to the plan and gives the phony name, everything will go as planned. He had enough loot and wallets on him to be sent up for a long time. You did what I told you, didn't you?"

"Sure did. I went around the back of the building and took all the money from the wallets, and tossed the wallets into the trash."

"Good, now if you get snatched, they won't have anything to pin on you. No law against carrying a lot of dough." Tobias paused, staring open-mouthed into the street. "Check out the stilt man."

"Boy, that guy would be easy to topple," Mac whispered in Tobias' ear.

Tobias knew he shouldn't do it. Not when he'd already drawn so much attention to himself, but he was feeling invincible at the moment. He raced into the street and hit the man with both hands, sending him sprawling to the ground. The stilted man looked so stunned, Tobias placed his hands on his hips and roared with laughter. A whistle blew in the distance. Tobias looked up just in time to see two flatfoots racing in his direction. Tobias laughed and took off in the opposite direction. As he neared the sidewalk, he saw her, and saw the recognition in her eyes.

Mileta.

He slowed, embarrassed she had seen his moment of juvenile foolishness. He wanted to stop, to explain that he didn't act like this, but knew he hadn't the time. Instead, he winked at her and hurried along his way. He ran to the edge of the building and hid waiting for the flatfoots to tire of searching for him. He hadn't expected to see Mileta. More importantly, he hadn't expected her to see him. Now that she had, he retraced his steps, determined to find her and ask how she'd been. He was searching the crowd, trying to remember where she'd been standing, when he saw her in the distance. She was facing the other direction, but he'd followed her enough to know for certain it was she. He was just about to go to her, when Mac stepped out in front of her. Dressed in rags, Mac looked menacing, and he was smiling at Mileta as if he intended to do her harm. Mac took a step in her direction and Tobias was there in an instant, pulling Mileta aside.

"Leave the girl alone, Mac." Tobias' voice was low and threatening.

The taller boy sized Tobias up. "And if I don't?"

"You saw what I did to Butch."

Mac sighed and moved back. "What's she to you anyhow? You sweet on a baby?"

Tobias raised his fist a bit higher and squared his shoulders, causing the boy to take another step back.

"She's none of your concern. Just let it be known this girl is under my protection. Anyone messes with her…" Tobias opened his right hand and extended his index finger slowly, sliding it across his throat. "Get the message?"

"Loud and clear, Mouse. Loud and clear." Mac left without another word.

"You okay there, kid?" he asked once Mac left.

Mileta squared her shoulders. "I'm not a kid. Or a

baby."

He looked at the box she was holding and laughed. "Says the girl with the candy."

Mileta reached into the box and pulled out a tuft of white. "Have you ever tasted this?"

He took it from her and sniffed the fluff. "It doesn't smell like much."

She nodded at his hand. "Just try it."

He shoved the entire piece into his mouth, and it instantly disappeared. "Ha. It's gone."

Her face brightened. "It's marvelous, is it not?"

"Not bad, kid…Mileta," he said, calling her by name.

She shook her head. "They, my new parents, call me Mildred."

Instantly, his mood shifted. "Damn do-gooders. How bad is it? I can get you out if you'd like."

Her eyes grew wide. "Oh, no. It is not like that. My mother and father are very nice. They treat me extremely well. My father gave me a dime for this cotton candy."

You paid a dime for something you can't sink your teeth into? "You paid a whole dime for stuff that disappears before you can even chew it?"

Mildred glared at him. "I did, and I'd do it again, thank you very much. You liked it too. Why all the fuss?"

He shook his head. "You really are a baby. You get plucked up by a rich family who tosses money at you, and you see nothing wrong with them changing your name. What kind of name is Mildred anyway?"

"It's my name, and I like it just fine." Her voice was cold as the air he breathed.

"It doesn't fit you."

"My father sometimes calls me Millie," she said more softly.

"Millie." He rather liked that. "That's not bad, kind of a mixture of your old and new name."

She looked at his clothes, and for the first time, he regretted dressing down.

"What about you?"

He pulled himself taller. "What about me?"

"How are you getting along with your new parents?"

He spat on the sidewalk, biding himself time to come up with a story. The last thing he wanted was for her to learn that he ran with a gang. "Parents? Not for boys like me. The man who took me threatened to send me back the next day. I waited until he went to sleep and I took off. Dang do-gooders. Who needs them anyway?"

Her eyes showed her worry. "You took off? Where do you live? How do you eat?"

"These streets don't have nothing on The Five Points," he said, referring to the streets of New York. "A man knows where to look, he gets by all right. I've made a few friends, so I manage well enough. As a matter of fact, it's time for me to move on. Places to go, people to see; speaking of which, you had better get back before you are missed."

He slipped into the crowd and stopped. He couldn't leave her this way. Rejoining her, he took her hand and turned her in the opposite direction. "You're heading the wrong way. Your parents are over there."

She smiled and pushed the box of cotton candy into his hand.

"What's this for?" he asked, taking the box.

"It's Thanksgiving. My mother and father said we are supposed to give thanks for our blessings. I just wanted you to have something to be thankful for."

"Millie, I know you are being taken care of; that is enough for me." He needed to go before he let on that he knew where she lived and that he'd been keeping an eye on her.

"What?" she asked when he smiled.

"I'll see you around, kid." He took a bit of cotton candy and thrust the box into her hands. He waited just out of view until he was sure she'd been reunited with her parents then went in search of Mac.

"What was that all about?" Mac asked when Tobias joined him.

"You're asking me? You were the one scaring the girl."

"I wouldn't have hurt the girl. You know me, I was just having a little fun."

"Yeah, well, I promised the girl's mother I'd look out for her. I mean it, Mac, that girl is not to be touched. Not today, not ever," Tobias said firmly.

Mac held his hands out. "Got it, Mouse."

"Where's your coat," Tobias asked, changing the subject.

"The cops were making me nervous, so I hid the dough in my sock and ditched the coat. Dumb thing to do too. I'm freezing. Abe has invited us all to Thanksgiving meal with all the fixings at the Book Cadillac. What say we go change and get us something to eat?"

Tobias looked in the direction of where he'd last seen Mileta. While he wished he could speak with her again, he knew this wasn't the place or time. Besides, he'd never had a real Thanksgiving meal before. He looked at Mac. "What are fixings?"

Mac shrugged. "I don't know, but Abe smiled when he told me."

Chapter Twenty-Eight

Dressed in tailored trousers and button-down shirts complete with ties, Tobias and Mac entered the Book Cadillac Hotel through the front door and made their way to the private dining room, where Abe was to hold Thanksgiving dinner. They were early. Multiple tables sat end to end to produce the effect of a single table, which would seat a hundred people. Waiters busied themselves spreading white linen tablecloths along with plates, utensils, and water goblets. Tobias looked around the expansive room in awe, noticing the curved ceiling, arched windows that stretched nearly from the ceiling to floor, and brilliant crystal chandeliers that sparkled when he moved his head. He'd never in his whole life seen anything so magnificent.

"Pretty amazing room, huh, Mouse?" Mac said, following his gaze.

He shrugged. "It's okay,"

"Let's hope the food looks half as good."

"I don't care how it looks as long as it tastes good," Tobias said when his stomach growled.

"Dinner isn't for a couple hours. Let's go see if we can find something to hold us over."

He followed Mac from the room towards the kitchen. As they passed the service elevator, the doors opened, and Tobias looked to see Big Mike and two of his goons pressed inside the small space. A big man to begin with, Big Mike looked even larger decked out in a pinstripe suit with white cap sleeves and a matching white-brimmed hat.

The service elevators were meant for the hotel staff and deliveries, but Big Mike preferred them, as they deposited him closer to his room. The men standing next to Big Mike each breathed a sigh of relief when Big Mike stepped out and eagerly followed him from the confined space.

"Yo, boys, glad to see you here. We're going to have a dinner fit for a king. Abe tells me they are making fifteen birds. Can you imagine that? Fifteen! What kinda oven ya think they got that can cook that many birds? All I know is the fat man gonna get full today." Big Mike laughed and elbowed one of the guys who'd exited the elevator with him. "I'm gonna eat so much, you two are probably going to have to carry me back to my room. Where're you boys off to anyway?"

"To the kitchen to find a bite to eat before the meal," Mac answered.

Big Mike's eyes went wide. "A meal before the meal? Oh, fat man likes that. I think we should make that a daily thing. I'm coming with you in case they give you a hard time. Lead the way, boys."

***

After a bit of negotiation and a few bills slid into the greedy palm of one of the wait staff, the group had procured some freshly baked rolls, soft butter, and a plate of cheese and fruit. They were sitting in a small meeting room chatting and biding their time before dinner when Abe walked in decked out in a tailored white suit and black tie. He looked around the room then focused his attention on Mac.

"Where's Butch? He was supposed to do a job for me today."

Mac's face remained stoic. "I was hoping he was with you, Abe."

Abe's brow wrinkled. "I ain't seen the kid all day. Why'd you think he'd be here?"

"Because he's not with us," Mac said with a nod to Tobias.

Abe glanced around the room. "When was the last time you saw him?'

"A few hours ago at the parade. He was with me and Mouse hustling the crowd. One minute he was there, the next he just disappeared."

"Whatta ya mean he disappeared?" Abe's voice was showing his concern. "What kind of hustle were you pulling?"

"Mouse there was dipping pockets. He passed some leather off to me, and then Butch, well, he seemed upset. Said he wanted his cut. Since we were all gonna share, it didn't make no mind to me, so I backed off to let Mouse hand them off to Butch. You tell him the rest, Mouse." Mac said with a nod to Tobias.

Tobias looked at Mac. This was not what they'd discussed. Mac was supposed to do all the talking since he had Abe's trust. Coming from Mac, the story would not appear as suspicious. It was no secret that Abe remained wary of him. How could he not when Butch kept filling Abe's head with doubt? Tobias remained calm as he turned his attention to the head man.

"Butch followed as I passed him the loot. Big scores from the feel of the leathers. We'd been walking for some time, so his pockets had to be full. Then, after picking a wallet, I reached to hand Butch the leather, and he was gone."

"And where were you when all this was going on?" Abe asked, turning to Mac.

"I was behind a few spaces. The crowd was heavy. The band was playing right next to us. I only took my eyes off of him for a moment, and then when I looked back, he was nowhere to be seen."

"You said there was a lot of loot?" Big Mike said, looking at Tobias.

"I'd handed him lots of leathers from high-class marks."

Big Mike chuckled. "Sounds like your boy gave them the slip so he could keep the dough for himself."

Abe didn't look convinced. "Did you look for him?"

This time, it was Mac who spoke. "Course we did. Whatcha think, that we'd just leave him out there? *We* didn't do the leaving; it was Butch. Beings he didn't come here, maybe Big Mike is right."

"Probably in an opium den somewhere smoking all the dough. He had me drop him at one just the other night," Tobias said, taking a chance then wondering if he'd crossed the line when everyone turned to look at him. Opium dens were as prevalent in Detroit as they'd been in New York. He'd been in one once while living in New York City. The Chinamen that ran them didn't pay any mind to who came in as long as the person had the money to pay. Still, Abe had rules and one of the rules was that while liquor was okay, his young Purples were to stay away from the opium dens.

Abe moved across the room and sat in a large chair under a window. "Mac, you ever know of Butch to go into one of the dens?"

Tobias held his breath, hoping Mac would play along. Doing so could be dangerous, if on the off chance Butch was able to beat the rap.

"Yeah," Mac said after a long pause. "He told me not to tell. Said he'd make up something on me, and went so far as to say he would cut out my tongue if I did. The guy is always doing that, threatening to make up something on someone when it's always Butch that's doing the stuff. If he says he has something on a person, you can be sure he's the one that's doing it. He

244

keeps a lot of things from you, Abe. He skims money from you to pay for his visits."

And there it was, the seed of doubt. Without being here to defend himself, the seed would grow until anything that had seemed amiss over the years would now be blamed on a boy so loyal, he would've done anything to stay in his boss's good graces. Tobias almost felt sorry for Butch. Almost.

"Maybe the cops nabbed him," Big Mike offered.

"Don't be ridiculous. How could the cops nab him without anyone seeing him?" Abe countered.

Tobias caught Mac's eye and gave the slightest of nods. The ruse appeared to be working.

Abe threw the glass he'd been holding against the wall. "Mac, you and Mouse go check the police station. If he's in there, give me a call, and I'll send someone to get him out."

Tobias caught Mac's eye once more. Apparently, the idea was not so ridiculous after all. He grabbed another roll, slathered it with butter, and followed Mac from the room.

"Don't look so deflated," Mac said once they were out of earshot. "I think Abe bought it."

"Then why send us to look for him?" Tobias asked between bites.

"What kind of boss would he be if he didn't? Seriously, the guy would rather think of his guy behind bars than to consider that he betrayed him. That was a good add, by the way. Even if Butch makes his way back, Abe will never fully trust him. Honestly, knowing Abe, if Butch shows up, he'll have someone take him for a ride, poor shmuck. Mouse," Mac said as Tobias pulled his keys from his pocket. "Remind me never to cross you."

Tobias looked over the top of the car at Mac. "If I have to remind you of that, then we already have a problem."

***

While the man didn't go as far as to say so, Abe didn't seem surprised when Tobias and Mac showed up for Thanksgiving dinner alone. The loss didn't appear to affect anyone's appetite. Although once, when biting into his first helping of turkey, Tobias wondered what kind of holiday meal Butch was having. His concern waned as his stomach filled. After all, the guy had brought it all on himself. Tobias reached for another helping of cranberries, just one of the many "fixings" the former street kid was enjoying for the first time.

"Yo, Mouse, you keep eating like that, and you're going to be as big as the fat man," Big Mike said, leaning across the table and spiking his fork into another slice of turkey.

"Why don't you just take the whole platter," Abe called from his place at the head of the table.

"Don't you worry about this bird. I know you have more where this came from," Mike said, taking a second slice.

"Hey, Mouse," Abe said loud enough to be heard over all the chatter. "Stand up for a moment."

Tobias looked over at Big Mike, who smiled and motioned for him to do as told. Rising, he realized the conversation around the table had quieted, everyone looking in his direction.

Abe stood and tapped his fork to his glass, drawing the attention back to himself.

"I want to welcome Mouse here to our inner circle. While he's new to some of you, he's been working with Big Mike for several years. In our line of work, we never know who we can trust, but Big Mike has a lot of faith in this kid. I have a lot of faith in Big Mike, so today, we welcome Mouse as a full member of the Purples." Abe lifted the glass to his lips, and everyone at the table followed suit.

Tobias was just about to return to his seat, when Abe continued, "Now that Mouse is a full Purple I want it to be known that he's taking Butch's place."

Wait. What? Tobias swallowed his surprise.

After several seconds of stunned silence, the onlookers lifted another toast in his direction — everyone except Big Mike, who stared daggers at Abe. Abe smiled, lifting his glass to Big Mike before returning to his seat. Tobias wasn't sure what had just happened, but the look on Big Mike's face showed he wasn't happy.

"Do you have any idea what this means?" Mac said as soon as they were alone.

"That he picked me over others who've been here longer, you included," Tobias answered.

"Don't you worry about that," Mac said with a flick of his hand. "I already told you, I'm not cut out for the job. What it means is you are now untouchable. Nobody will mess with you."

Tobias cocked his head at Mac. "Just what is it that makes me untouchable?"

"You're kidding, right?"

"I'm dead serious. What about what just happened makes me untouchable?"

"Because you are under Abe's protection. A person would have to be crazy to mess with you."

Tobias stopped walking and turned towards Mac. "You're saying I'm untouchable because I'm Abe's guy? You do realize I'm taking Butch's place, don't you?"

"Of course I do..." Understanding crossed over Mac's face. "I was so focused on getting Butch out of the way, I forgot he was untouchable."

Tobias took a step closer to Mac. "You'd better not forget that you're in this just as deep as I am. You ever utter a word of this to anyone, and I'll take you out myself."

Mac swallowed and nodded his understanding.

"And, Mac," Tobias said, handing him the keys, "from now on, you're driving."

Chapter Twenty-Nine

January 9, 1925

Tobias rolled the dice and smiled when his numbers appeared again. He glanced at his watch, collected his winnings, and sighed. People tended to get irritated when not given a chance to recoup their loss.

"Yo, Mouse, it's not like you to quit so early," Joe Burnstein called out when Tobias folded his winnings and slid the cash into his pants pocket.

"Abe's expecting me," Tobias said by way of excuse, knowing that Joe would not go against his brother. He gave a nod to a nearby blackjack table. "Time to go, Mac."

Mac folded his cards and turned to Joe. "You need a lift?"

Joe blew out a puff of smoke and waved Mac off. "Na, I'm going to hang around for a while in case Ray needs anything."

Ray Bishop, the owner of the new gambling den at 2439 Milwaukee Avenue, snorted. "More like Joe thinks he has a chance at winning now that Mouse is leaving."

"You open a gambling den, you have to expect someone will want to take your money," Joe said and moved to the chair Tobias vacated seconds before. "Yo, Mouse, you tell that brother of mine the next time you're ahead you ain't leaving. Got it?"

"I'll tell him," Tobias promised.

Mac brushed the snow from the windshield and slid

into the driver's seat. Starting the Ford, he blew into his hands to warm them. "Book Cadillac?"

"No, head over to Third Street," Tobias instructed. "Don't pull in front; park on the street near the church."

Mac glanced in his direction. "A little late for pasta, don't you think?"

"We're not going to Gianetti's. Abe wants us to pick up a guy named Eldon. Only Eldon don't know we're coming. I'm going to see if he's downstairs."

"Since when are we working for Legs?" Mac grumbled, speaking of Joseph Laman, a man known on the streets as Legs because his limbs did not fit the rest of his body. Legs' gang specialized in kidnapping wealthy Detroit racketeers and gamblers. He'd send out men to kidnap the victim and sit on them in the castle—code for an apartment or house—until a ransom was paid.

"I guess his guys had another date. Abe needs this done now, so we're tasked to do it. Hopefully, the guy is still at the blind pig. If not, we'll have to pick him up at his house. If that's the case, we'll need help."

Mac raised an eyebrow but didn't ask any further questions.

"Kill the lights, but keep the motor running. I'm going to have a look around," Tobias said once they arrived. He entered through the back tunnel entrance, did the coded knock on the door, and waited. Several seconds later, a heavyset man Tobias hadn't seen before opened the door.

"Where's your pass, kid?" the guy asked, blocking his way.

"I don't have a pass. Name's Mouse. I work for Abe. The guys inside will vouch for me," Tobias said, looking past the man.

The bouncer crossed his arms. "I don't care who you

are; no one comes in without a pass."

While Tobias knew the man at the door was just doing his job, he was wasting precious time. Abe wanted the guy picked up before sunrise. "Listen, man, I know you don't know who I am, but if you just let me in—"

The man uncrossed his arms and lunged towards him. Tobias moved to the side and felled him with one punch. He smiled, remembering when Slim taught him the move. He'd just stepped over the downed man when a soft-spoken ex-boxer known on the streets as Knuckles stuck his head through the open the door. Knuckles looked to see if he was alone then moved to let him in.

"Mouse, you keep taking guys out like that, and you're gonna have to change your name," Knuckles teased.

"You see this guy tonight?" Tobias asked, holding up a photo.

"He's been in a few times this week. Name's Eldon. I ain't seen him tonight. He trouble?"

"Not for you. If anyone asks, I never showed you this picture," Tobias said, pocketing the photo.

Knuckles' face turned blank. "What picture?"

Tobias smiled. "Good man. Hey, when you have time, I have a guy I want you to meet. He moves fast and is good with his hands."

"You know I'm not in the game anymore."

"Yeah, I know, but this kid could use some pointers. Like I say, he's good," Tobias said, stepping over the guy once more.

"How good?" Knuckles asked.

Tobias nodded towards the floor. "Taught me everything I know."

"Where to now?" Mac asked when he returned alone.

Tobias hesitated for a moment, knowing Mac was not

going to like the answer. "Head over to 12th Street. We need to pick up Mooch."

Mac slammed his palm on the steering wheel. "Why don't we just drive to the police station and turn ourselves in?"

Tobias understood his friend's frustration. Nothing ever turned out good when Crazy Mooch was involved. "We need Mooch's skills to get inside. Our guy's family is out of town until tomorrow morning. That's why we have to grab him tonight. It's supposed to be a simple grab and go. We'll only have the guy a few hours until some of Legs' men are free."

***

At Mooch's insistence, they'd taken his sedan and left Mac's coupe in an empty parking lot on 12th Street. It was just after three when they reached the Victorian house that had been converted into apartments. The trio climbed the stairs to the third-floor apartment, and Mooch instantly went to work on the lock.

"Piece of cake," he whispered as the door clicked open.

"Whacha doing, mister?"

Tobias turned to see a frail boy standing at the top of the stairwell. The kid looked to be around ten, what little clothing he wore hanging in tattered shreds. He realized the boy must have been hiding in the dark halls, probably sleeping until he heard a creak from the stairs and came to investigate. For a moment, the boy reminded him of the child he used to be.

Mooch smiled and turned towards the boy. "I'll stay with the kid while you get your guy."

"It's better if he stays outside," Mac whispered when Tobias hesitated.

Tobias pulled his pistol and silently made his way into the apartment. They found Eldon in the rear bedroom sleeping with his back to the door. Tobias crept into the room, holstered his pistol, and yanked a pillowcase from his waistband. Moving quickly, he pulled the case over Eldon's head and pushed his knee in the guy's back before the man had a chance to react. He leaned back as Mac reached in and tied a rope around Eldon's hands.

Tobias scrambled from the bed, bringing Eldon to his feet. "We're going for a little ride. Make a noise, and it will be a one-way trip. Nod once if you understand."

Eldon nodded.

"Good, now start walking," Tobias said firmly. Once in the hall, Tobias searched for Mooch. When he didn't see him, he looked over his shoulder and lowered his voice. "I got this; go find him."

Mac raced down the stairs without a word.

Tobias grabbed Eldon's arm and led him towards the stairs. "Take the stairs one at a time. Try anything funny, and you'll get to the bottom a lot faster than I do. Got it?"

Eldon mumbled something that sounded agreeable and took a step. Tobias kept a grip on his arm to help him descend the stairs. When they reached the main floor, Mac was waiting, his face ghostly white. Tobias nodded towards the door, and the two of them helped Eldon into the back seat of the sedan.

"We got trouble," Mac said, easing the door shut.

Tobias almost hated to ask. "I'm listening."

"Mooch took care of the boy."

Tobias' throat went dry. "What do you mean took care of?'

"The kid was lying at the base of the stairs when I got there. Crazy Mooch was standing over him giggling like a little girl. Said the kid saw our faces and we couldn't have any loose ends."

Tobias fought back the bile that threatened. "Where's

Mooch now?"

"He took the kid out back."

Tobias started for the house, and Mac stopped him. "You can't help the kid. Let's get Eldon out of here and then we'll deal with Mooch."

Tobias relented and walked back to the car. When he spoke, his voice was eerily calm. "Ride up front. I'm going to sit in the back with Eldon. When Mooch gets back, remind him not to use our names. Tell him to take us to get the coupe. Once you get inside, don't talk above a whisper. I don't want Eldon to be able to identify our voices. Oh, when we get to 12th Street, make sure to leave the door open when you get out."

"Done," Mac replied without asking questions.

Tobias started the sedan, turned on the heat, and slid into the backseat. Shutting the door, he leaned in to whisper in Eldon's ear, "I don't want to hear a single sound from you. Keep your mouth shut and you'll make it home to see your family. Nod once to let me know you understand."

Eldon nodded.

"It's beginning to snow. That will help to cover the body," Mooch said, sliding into the driver's seat.

Eldon squirmed in his seat, and Tobias elbowed him in the gut as a reminder. Mooch pulled the shifter down, and the car lunged forward.

He leaned forward and kept his voice low. "What happened with the kid?"

"Kid fall down go boom." Mooch giggled.

Tobias worked to steady his breathing. "Why?"

Mooch glanced over his shoulder. "Kid would have talked."

"The kid was skin and bones. Most likely living on the street. A few coins and he'd of been on his way."

Mooch giggled once more. "My point exactly. No need

to hand out dough to some stupid kid no one will ever miss. I don't see what the big deal is. No one cares about street kids."

Tobias sat back in his seat without another word. The streets were mostly empty, and it didn't take long before Mooch pulled alongside Mac's coupe. Mac jumped out of the sedan, leaving his door open as Tobias instructed. He hurried to the back, opened the passenger door, and pulled Eldon from the seat.

Mooch leaned over to pull the door closed, but his fingers wouldn't reach. Disgusted, he opened the driver door, walked around the front of the car, and slammed the door shut as Tobias exited on the other side.

"You want me to follow you? I can help you keep an eye on the guy until the rest of the boys come," Mooch said, rounding the car and keeping his head lowered against the heavy snow. He looked up when Tobias failed to answer, his eyes growing wide when he saw the gun in Tobias' hand.

"No, I think we're done with you," he said, raising his weapon. "And, Mooch, just so you know, I care about the street kids."

A single shot rang out, echoing off the nearby buildings for all to hear. Tobias remained rooted in place, watching as the snow covered Mooch in a blanket of white.

"I'll get rid of the body." Mac said, breaking the trance.

"No!" Tobias lowered his voice. "Take his dough so it looks like a robbery. Then leave him in the snow just like he left that kid."

***

Though Legs' guys were later than expected, they'd had an easy time of things. Eldon was so frightened, he'd sat in the chair not uttering a sound. Mac pulled the coupe into the parking lot at the Book Cadillac and motioned to several autos parked in the spots reserved for Abe's crew.

"Looks like most of the gang's here. Want me to keep going?"

Tobias knew what he was implying. From the looks of things, Abe had found out about Crazy Mooch and had brought in a welcoming committee. They'd walk in, Abe would tell them they needed to go for a ride, and somewhere along the route, things would get messy. Tobias let out a slow breath. It had been a long day. Each time he'd closed his eyes, he'd seen Mooch's face. He didn't regret his decision—he'd do it again—but that didn't take away the guilt of having taken a life. His only regret, he didn't have the guts to return to the house and see the kid got a decent burial. "Na, I gotta face things sooner or later. Might as well be sooner. Don't worry; I'll make sure they know this isn't on you."

"I knew what you were going to do. I could've stopped you," Mac said, pulling up next to the building.

Not a chance.

Tobias thought to argue the point but decided against it. He had more important things that needed tending. "You know the kid at Gianetti's?"

Mac nodded. "You mean the one that moves like he's in a sparring ring? I thought you said you didn't know the kid."

"Actually, I believe what I said was you don't need to know the kid. Anyhow, if things go bad here, I want you to go to him. Give him the dough that's in my dresser and tell him he needs to look after Mileta."

Mac's brow creased. "That's the girl with the candy?"

"It is. I promised her mother I'd look out for her."

"You said that before. Why not have me do it?"

"She knows my friend. She'll trust him." Tobias wanted to add that he trusted Slim not to take advantage of her but decided against it. "Will you do that for me, Mac?"

Mac smiled. "Yeah, Mouse. I'll see it's taken care of. And don't worry; I'll make sure everyone knows the girl's not to be touched."

***

The meeting room was abuzz when they entered, men and boys milling around like a room full of agitated hornets whose nest had been disturbed. Abe was in the corner of the room standing next to Big Mike. Tobias pulled himself straight and walked to where he was standing.

"We've been waiting for you." Abe's tone left no doubt he was just as agitated as the others. "I expected you back hours ago."

"Our relief was late," Mac said before he could answer.

Abe ignored the comment, keeping his eyes focused on Tobias. "Some of the guys are going to take a drive. You're going to go with them."

Tobias was glad Abe had singled him out. The fact that he'd not mentioned Mac told him someone must have seen what went down and ratted him out. A blessing really, as he wouldn't have to convince Abe to leave Mac out of it. Now to get it over with before Abe decided to include his friend in the deal. He looked Abe in the eye to let him know he was not afraid. "I'm ready."

Abe whistled and nodded towards the door. Half the men in the room hurried to shrug into long outer coats; strange, as Tobias didn't realize Crazy Mooch had so many friends. He gave a slight nod to Mac as he followed the group out of the door.

No one took hold of him to ensure he made it into an automobile. Surprisingly, except for telling him he could ride in the back, no one paid him any mind at all. Tobias slid into the backseat and immediately found himself flanked by two other men. It was only when the men pulled their pistols to check the chamber that he realized nobody had bothered to relieve him of his. He knew he'd gained Abe's trust, since the man chose him to replace Butch, but surely someone should have checked to see if he was armed, which he was. He reached into his coat and pulled out his piece, expecting the men sitting on either side to wrestle it from him. When no one did, he opened the cylinder and gave it a spin, once again surprised when nothing happened. He dumped the bullets into his hand, shook them, and reloaded his pistol. Something wasn't right. While he'd never been taken for a ride before, he was fairly certain this was not the way it was done.

"So how is this going to play out?" he asked, stifling a yawn.

The guy next to him laughed. "You hear that? Mouse here is bored."

"Not bored; it's just been a long night," Tobias corrected.

The guy doing the driving shook his head. "Na, you don't get to play like you're the only one tired. Ain't none of us gotten any sleep since the shooting."

Tobias swallowed. They'd known all that time, and yet, he was still alive.

"Listen, kid, we know it's past your bedtime but try not to shoot anybody. Abe doesn't want these guys shot. He just wants us to lean on them a bit. Wants to make sure they know this kind of thing is unacceptable in Detroit."

Now he was really confused. "Help me out here, guys. I didn't get a chance to get the facts from Abe."

"Ray Bishop and Art Wilson were killed last night," the driver said over his shoulder.

"That's right," the guy sitting beside him chimed in. "Joe said it went down right after you and Mac left the club. Some of the St. Louis boys came in through the second-floor skylight and shot up the place. Ol' Ray got in a few shots of his own before they nailed him. Abe wanted us to wait for you so you can see how we handle situations like this. You are to hang back so the guys can't get a good look at you. You do what we tell you, you hear? Anything happens to you and Abe won't like it so good."

Tobias didn't know whether to laugh or cry. In the end, he decided just to be relieved, at least for the moment.

Chapter Thirty

October 15, 1926

Tobias sat on the steps of the Fort Street Presbyterian Church waiting for Slim to join him. It'd been a while since they spoke and he wanted to check in to see how his friend was faring. He heard voices and looked to see Slim and Gianetti in a heated conversation at the back of the restaurant. Slim moved in his normal back and forth steps, hands low to his side. Gianetti spoke in a thick Italian accent. His hands were moving so fast, it looked as if the two were in a sparring ring. Slim said something to Gianetti, and the man threw up his hands and went back inside. Slim looked towards the door as if contemplating going after the man then shook his head and turned towards the church instead.

"Trouble?" Tobias asked when Slim joined him on the stoop.

"The man's up to his ears in debt, and yet he won't let me help him," Slim said, shaking his head.

"How'd you propose to help him?" Tobias asked.

Slim shrugged. "I told him I could go to work with you."

Not happening.

"The man barely tolerates me in his establishment. Why'd you think he'd want you to work with me?"

"It's not you, it's what you represent," Slim replied.

"And yet he has a blind pig in his basement."

"You've got it all wrong. He doesn't have a problem with that. Heck, sometimes he's downstairs more than he's in the kitchen. That's where his money goes."

The fact that the man gambled didn't surprise Tobias. Word on the street was that Gianetti had been talking to several of the heavy money men looking for a loan. "Then what's his problem?"

"He knows I knew you before, in New York." Slim shrugged his shoulders. "It reminds him that I'm not his true son."

Tobias could see where that might bother the man. Then again, maybe it was a little of both. Maybe the man didn't want his "son" to end up like him. "Has he offered to adopt you?"

"Not officially, but he calls me 'son.'"

"And the fight just now?"

Slim looked towards the brown brick building. "Not a fight, just a father looking out for his son."

"I wouldn't let you."

Slim turned his attention to Tobias. "Wouldn't let me what?"

"Work with me."

"You didn't have a problem with me working with you in the city."

He knew Slim was referring to the time before the trains. "That was different. You worked for me."

Slim looked puzzled. "What's the difference?"

Tobias swallowed. "I'm not working for myself, Slim. The guys I work for are into a lot of stuff."

"I've been downstairs. I know about the gambling and drinking," Slim countered.

Though no one was near, Tobias lowered his voice. "That doesn't begin to cover it. These guys kidnap people. They cut off body parts and send them in nice little packages to get people to pay the ransom."

Slim leaned forward. "And if they don't pay?"

"Then they kill them," Tobias said, meeting his stare.

Slim fidgeted from side to side. "You work for them. Have you ever killed anyone?"

The fidgeting grew worse when Tobias didn't answer.

They sat in silence for several moments before Slim ventured to say what they both knew to be true. "So you're in the Purple Gang."

Tobias didn't answer.

His friend continued. "Word on the street is if you're in with the Purples, you are never to tell anyone. Word is if you admit to being a Purple, they take you for a ride and you never come back."

Tobias gave the slightest of nods and Slim blinked his understanding.

After a few moments of silence, Tobias turned towards his friend. "I have someone I want you to meet. He used to be a boxer. Pretty good too. Name's Knuckles. I told him about you."

"You did?"

"Yeah, I told him you showed me how to throw a punch and asked if he'd give you some pointers. That's if you're interested."

"Sure I am."

"Okay, I'll introduce you under one condition. Just boxing. Anything else and you have to clear it through me."

Slim laughed. "You know I'm older than you, right?"

Tobias turned to him, "I know you're not a kid. You're my friend, the only person I can really count on."

Slim's lip quivered.

"Don't you go all baby on me," Tobias warned.

"Mouse, I've got something to tell you."

Tobias took in a slow breath. Nothing good ever started

with "I've got something to tell you." "Go on, then."

"I got a letter from Anastasia."

Anastasia. He hadn't thought about his sister in years. "Why would Anastasia send you a letter?"

"We were kind of close before I got sent out."

Tobias exhaled. "How close?"

"We're friends."

"That's not what I asked."

Slim stilled for the first time since he sat down. "I guess about as close as two people can be."

Tobias turned and stared.

"You're not gonna say anything?"

Tobias leaned back against the stoop. "Sheesh, Slim, here I've been trying to protect you from the hornets, and you've been lying with the honey bees."

"She told me you're her brother," Slim replied.

Tobias remembered the venom with which his sister last spoke to him and the anger in her eyes. "I don't have any family."

"Did you know she had a son?"

"Is he yours?" Tobias asked coldly.

"No, and I don't know who the father is. Anna didn't like to speak about it."

Anna. The name pulled at his heart. He'd called her that so many times. Back then, she smiled when he spoke to her. "Anna?"

"It's what she asked me to call her. Anyway, about the kid, his name's Franky and he's six."

"Why are you telling me this?"

"Cause she asked me to. Said the kid went out on the trains last month. I guess a letter from the placing agent came in and it said he'd been placed in Chicago. She asked me to give you this." Slim handed him a folded envelope. "She told me not to read it. I didn't."

Tobias held the envelope in his hand, struggling with whether to read it or tear it up. In the end, he shoved it into his pocket without a word.

"You told me you went to Chicago a few months ago. You didn't say why, but now that I know about… well, I guess I figure you'll go again, someday. I thought that if you did, you could maybe check on the boy."

"Why would I do that?" Tobias asked.

"I figure it wouldn't hurt to look in on him, beings he's your family."

"Yeah, well, I don't have any plans to go to Chicago."

Slim pushed off from the stoop and started across the yard. After a few steps, he paused.

"Forget something?" Tobias asked tersely.

"We grew up on the streets. That kid grew up in the asylum. If things aren't good, I'm not sure he'd know how to handle it. Besides, wouldn't it have been nice if someone would've cared enough to check on us?" Slim turned and walked away without waiting for a reply.

Tobias waited until Slim went inside before pulling the envelope from his pocket. He flipped it several times, debating whether to open it. In the end, curiosity won out. He broke the seal and pulled out the single page.

My Dearest Tobias,

I hope this letter finds you well. I'm writing to tell you of your nephew, Franky. You asked about him before, but I was filled with hate at that time and could not speak of him. The mistresses told me it would be best if I did not tell him I was his mother. While he doesn't know me, I've watched him grow and made sure he was well taken care of. That is until now. He was sent away on the trains without my knowledge. Maybe it was for the best, as if not for the trains, the boy would spend his whole childhood behind these walls. I guess I have some goodness left inside as I do so worry about him.

Slim wrote and told me you have been to Chicago. That is where Franky is now. Please, dear brother, if you ever find yourself there again, could you find it in your heart to go to him and see to it he is well?

With all my love,

A.

He turned the paper over and found the boy's full name along with a Chicago address. Turning the paper once more, he studied the letter. He didn't recognize his sister's handwriting, probably because he'd never actually seen it before. He remembered the last time they'd spoke. It was as if he were talking to a stranger, a stranger that wanted to scratch his eyes out. He remembered the way she looked at him and the laugh that still haunted his dreams. An icy chill rushed over him as he crumpled the paper and flung it to the ground. He was almost to the car when he reconsidered and retraced his steps to reclaim the letter. Pressing out the creases best he could, he put the letter in his pocket for safekeeping.

***

October 24, 1926

"Keep the change," Tobias said, flipping the shoeshine boy a quarter. He looked at his freshly polished shoes and smiled. Between the shoes and the new pinstripe suit he had on, he'd be able to go anywhere in the hotel without raising an eye. He caught his image in the lobby glass and pulled himself taller. He hadn't felt this good since he'd purchased his first set of clothes in New York. He smiled, remembering. Though only six at the time, he'd felt as important as any man walking down Park Avenue that day. He thought about the man with the tape measure, Kramer. He'd never forget the name or the way the man had looked at him as if afraid he'd catch something. He shook off the memory. He was only a boy then. That life didn't exist anymore. Now tailors smiled when he entered. Welcomed him into their shop with open arms, happy to relieve him of his money. He adjusted his jacket and ran a hand through his freshly trimmed hair. At sixteen, he was a man. A man few dared to cross.

The hotel lobby was a bustle of activity. With several restaurants to choose from, townsfolk often came to eat their evening meals. Several of the nearby theaters were having evening shows, lending to the increased crowd size. The lobby doors opened, and a new rush of people entered. Tobias gave a passing glance and felt his mouth drop open. Standing in the center of the lobby, gathering their bearings, stood Mileta and her parents. Her hair was shorter, edgier as a single curl twisted from underneath a stylish hat. In a matching mint green dress and heeled boots, she looked much older than her thirteen years. Her eyes were alight as her head tilted upward and she took in the expansive lobby. She smiled, and her face lit up. He realized she looked a great deal like Clara Bow, an actress he'd seen recently in a picture show. The realization startled him, as watching the show, he'd become quite infatuated with the young film star. His hands became clammy, and for the first time, he realized his heart was pounding in his chest. She turned, and he stepped behind the pillar before she saw him. He rubbed his hands on his new suit, chastising himself for acting like a dumb schoolboy getting all goofy-eyed over a girl — a child at that.

He caught the eye of the usher and waved the man over.

"How can I help you, sir?" the man asked, hurrying to his side.

"They're having trouble finding their way. I suggest you

show them to the Venetian Room. Find their waiter and make sure he knows they are my special guests." Tobias handed the man a generous five-dollar tip and nodded to Mileta and her family.

The man bobbled his gratitude. "Yes, sir, as you say, Mouse."

Tobias hurried up the stairs and made his way to the balcony overlooking the Venetian Room. He arrived just as Mileta and her family were seated and stood far enough back so that he could watch without being recognized. His heart warmed as he watched the way Mileta took in the room with childish abandonment. She was happy. He could see it in her face. He sighed. It was all he ever wanted for her. The waiter, a new man he hadn't seen before, approached for the sixth time and Tobias shook his head. He'd wanted the guy to be attentive, not obnoxious. At least his attention seemed to be focused on the mother and not Mileta. Her father got the waiter's attention, said something, and the man's face paled. He wondered for a moment if the man had called him on his actions, but then Tobias saw money being exchanged. In an establishment such as this, he had little doubt of what the man was asking. Detroit had been dry for years unless one knew where to look. While the Book Cadillac was not as dry as it appeared, the liquor was reserved for special guests of Abe Burnstein. Understandable, since Abe was the one who smuggled it in. A request such as this could get them all kicked out of the hotel, or worse, if anyone saw it, especially when accompanied by a bribe.

He raced down the stairs and caught the waiter just as he was entering the kitchen. He pushed the man against the wall. "Where're you going?"

The waiter's gaze shifted back and forth as if looking for help. "Out of my way, boy. I'm going to speak with my manager."

Tobias kept pressure on the man, mostly because he was afraid of what he'd do to the man if he released him. "About what?"

The man bristled. "I assure you what I have to say is none of your concern."

"Did you not get the word that those people are my guests?"

To his credit, the man's face turned white. "You're Mouse?"

Tobias released the man. "You've heard of me."

"Oh yes, sir. I thought you'd be…older."

It wasn't the first time he'd heard that. "I'm plenty old. Now, what seems to be the problem at the table?"

"The man wants some spirits. I told him we uphold the law here, but he was rather insistent." The waiter pulled out the money Mileta's father had given him.

"Put that away," Tobias said, slapping the waiter's hand. "Are you trying to get this place shut down?"

"I was only trying to show you I had no choice. I was going to my manager to ask how to handle it."

"I'll tell you how you're going to handle it. You're going to wait on them as if nothing is amiss. I will take care of the tea."

The waiter's brows went up. "The tea?"

Tobias' patience was running thin. "If you want to keep your job then do your job. And quit hovering over the woman before the man stabs you with his fork. Understand?"

The waiter nodded and went inside the kitchen without another word.

***

It took a few moments for Tobias to gather what he

needed and return to the kitchen to don an apron. While still out of place, he would at least look as if he were part of the management coming to check on a table. Mileta's eyes were closed when he approached the table. A frown creased her brow, and for a moment, he wondered if she were ill.

"Your tea, sir." While he spoke to her father, he kept her in his sight, waiting to see if she recognized him, delighted when she did. Her eyes sprang open the moment he spoke. She opened her mouth to speak, and he gave the slightest head tilt, warning her off.

Her father took a sip of the tea and removed the bill from beneath the goblet. "I must say that was a very good year for tea."

It pained Tobias to take his money. But if he didn't, the man would question his motives. He palmed the bill with the barest of smiles. "If you find yourself in need of a refill, just let your waiter know. He'll know where to find me."

"I would like some more tea, if you please," Mileta said as he moved to leave.

His smile broadened. "I will ask the waiter to bring you some fresh from the kitchen."

She eyed the pitcher in his hand. "And what is wrong with the tea you have?"

Tobias wanted to laugh at her audaciousness. "I'm afraid this tea is rather strong. It would not blend very well with the berries in your glass."

To his delight, Mileta lowered the spoon into the glass, fished out the berries, and shoved them into her mouth, swallowing them whole. Lowering the spoon, she offered him the glass once more. He studied her for a moment before looking to her father for direction.

To both their amazement, the man nodded his approval.

Tobias placed his fingers against the spoon, then

proceeded to fill the glass. When finished, he removed the spoon and handed her the glass. "Try not to spit it out. It would be a shame to waste any."

Mileta lifted the glass, sniffed the contents, and took a taste. Her face turned brilliant red as she downed the contents and thrust the glass in his direction once more.

"That will be enough, young man," her father said, waving him off.

Tobias hurried to the kitchen and stashed the remainder of the liquor. He moved to place the spoon he was holding on the counter, thought better of it, and placed it in his pocket instead. Removing the apron, he made his way to the ladies' lounge, leaning against the wall just outside the door.

She came out of the washroom, saw him standing there, and narrowed her eyes. Ignoring him, she turned as if she intended to return to her seat without a word. He grabbed her by the arm and spun her around.

"You will be so kind as to remove your hand," she said tersely.

He laughed.

"What is so funny?"

"Oh, Mileta, if I didn't know any better, I would say you were born to this crowd. Playing hard to get when your face says otherwise. Look at how you are dressed, all prim and proper."

She struggled to free herself. "If you are going to make fun of me, I have nothing more to say to you."

He released his hold, then straightened the hat on her head. "Don't go getting your feathers ruffled; I'm glad you found a nice home. You clean up well, kid. You remind me of someone."

She stilled, waiting for him to say more. When he didn't, she looked him up and down.

"I could say the same about you… that you clean up nice."

"The suit? Na, it is just a loaner to get me into this establishment." He wasn't sure why he felt the need to lie to her. It wasn't as if he was embarrassed by the fact that he had money. Or was he? Maybe he was afraid she would ask him where he got it from.

Mildred jutted her jaw and narrowed her eyes. "I'm not a kid."

He brushed his hand down her arm, surprised by his boldness. "No, that you are not. You've filled out pretty nice there, Mileta."

She closed her eyes briefly. When she opened them, she looked pained. "I am not Mileta. I left that name behind when I left everything else I know. My friends, my piano. Oh, what I would give to play again. That player should be ashamed of himself butchering the keys like that," she said heatedly.

So that's what's disturbing her. The anger in her voice emboldened him. "Want me to cut off his fingers for you?"

"No, of course not. I just wish someone would give him lessons."

"Why don't you play? Your family is loaded. Can't they buy you a piano?"

"They do not know I play. We do not talk about my past. Mother said it is better that I leave that life behind me. She said the girls in my school would not be nice to me if they knew my background. We invented a story of how we had just moved here." Her brow creased once more. "I have to go; my parents will be worried about me."

Tobias pulled her close, pressing his lips to hers.

The next thing he knew, he was running from the building, racing from the things he wanted to do to her. *What was he thinking, kissing a child?* A man could get shot for that.

As the crisp, fresh air cleared his senses, it dawned on him that for the first time in his memory, he wished to be a boy again.

Chapter Thirty-One

August 2, 1928

Tobias followed Big Mike and four bodyguards into the Lexington Hotel on Michigan Avenue. An antique wood counter spanned the length of the room.

Big Mike studied the lobby with a frown. "You'd think Al could afford better digs. This place is a dump."

The big man was right. It was bad enough the furniture was shabby, but the walls themselves looked as if they could use a fresh coat of paint. While the hotel appeared clean, it was a far cry from the marbled interior and chandeliers in the Book Cadillac. Multiple chairs lined the lobby, several occupied by men reading newspapers. Another man leaned against the far wall. It didn't escape his notice that the man's right arm dangled behind the large potted plant by which he was standing.

"What do you want to bet there's a gun in that man's hand," Tobias whispered.

"I guarantee the men in the chairs are not actually reading those newspapers," one of the bodyguards agreed.

"Just stay loose, guys. Al's expecting us," Big Mike whispered.

As the group made their way to the counter, the thin man standing behind it took in Big Mike's size in a stunned stare. Realizing he'd been gaping, the man closed his mouth.

"May I help you?" he asked once they were near.

"Visitors from Detroit here to see The Big One," Big Mike said between wheezes.

Sherry A. Burton

The man behind the counter appraised them, then picked up the receiver and placed a call. "Tell Mr. Capone his visitors have arrived."

When the man looked to the second-floor mezzanine, Tobias followed his gaze to see six men with tommy guns resting on the open rail. Tobias sighed. It was his first trip to Chicago since receiving his sister's letter, and he was suddenly rethinking asking to come along. Whatever his living conditions, he was fairly certain the kid was far safer than himself at the moment.

The clerk pointed in the direction of the elevator. "Take the cage to the second floor."

"Which room is his?" Big Mike asked when the clerk failed to say.

The clerk raised his eyebrows. "Mr. Capone has the entire second floor. But if you need specifics, you will be going to room 230."

Big Mike huffed his way to the elevator, and his face paled. The cage didn't appear to fare the years any better than the rest of the rundown hotel. The big man glanced at the stairs and sighed before pulling back the metal cage doors. Once inside the space, he waited as two of the four men with them hesitantly stepped inside the cage with him.

"We'll meet you upstairs," Tobias said, pulling the cage closed. He'd been on an elevator with Big Mike once. The jerky ride had been enough to have Tobias claim to be afraid of small enclosed spaces and refusing to take the lifts whenever Big Mike was around.

They were greeted at the top of the stairs by three of Capone's men. Two had their tommy guns leveled at the ground; the third greeted them, hands extended.

"I'm sure you'll understand that Mr. Capone prefers to have his visitors leave their weapons outside the door," the man

274

said, using a tone that left no room for argument.

Tobias and the others handed over their guns and were led to the back side of the elevator to wait for Big Mike. The elevator groaned to a stop, the rear doors opened, and the two men rushed out ahead of Big Mike.

"Remind me to talk to Capone about his choice of residence," Big Mike said when he waddled from the elevator.

"You can have that discussion after you hand over your pistol," the man collecting guns said firmly.

Big Mike hesitated before reaching in his jacket and removing the pistol from his shoulder harness.

The man pinched the pistol with two fingers and handed it off to one of the other guys before leading them down the narrow hall to room 230. Once in front of the room, he twisted the bell to announce their arrival.

"My heavens," Big Mike replied when the door opened a crack.

The door opened to reveal three additional doors. The door to the left was open, revealing a bathroom. The main door appeared to be a large office. Several armed men stood near the far side of the room. The closed door to the right remained a mystery. The man who'd relieved them of their guns ushered them in through the center door to a sun-filled room in great need of a facelift.

An enormous walnut desk sat in front of the large three bay windows. On the north side of the room, a cuckoo clock hung over an ornate hand-carved cabinet. There were several well-worn chairs placed around the room, each resting on a threadbare oriental rug. A quick glance showed the man they'd come to see nowhere in sight.

"Mikey, it's been ages. You've changed a bit from our days in New York; how are you, my friend?"

All eyes turned towards Al Capone, who'd just entered

the room. Though he'd never met him, Tobias had seen enough newspaper clippings to recognize the man. Since the main door remained closed, he thought it a fair assumption he'd entered through the door to the right.

Big Mike's body shook with laughter. "You call me your friend, and yet you take our guns at the door. When did I lose your trust, Alphonse?"

Al's round face slackened, dark eyebrows sinking over deep-set eyes. "These are trying times we live in, my friend. I have to watch my back at every turn, even within the ranks of my deepest circle."

Mike gazed around the room. "Al, you must tell me who you used as a decorator so I can make sure never to hire the man. Seriously, my friend, I know we came here to discuss business, but if you are in dire straits, I can maybe see about giving you a loan."

It was Capone's turn to laugh. "I have many a problem, but money isn't one of them. I've only moved in a few days ago. This is temporary until something opens up on one of the upper floors. It's a little run down, but I like the location."

Big Mike laughed once more. "It doesn't hurt that your mistress lives in the same building."

Al's eyebrows lifted.

"You're right to be concerned. We in Detroit hear many things," Big Mike replied, lowering himself into a chair. "Before we get started, I have a request."

"Name it," Al replied.

"My boy here has some errands in your city. Could you spare one of your cars?" Big Mike waved Tobias closer. "Don't let his age fool you. Mouse here has earned a spot as one of Abe's go-to guys."

Tobias did his best to keep his surprise hidden. While he'd told Mike he had business in Chicago, he'd expected to tend to things after talks concluded. It hadn't occurred to him that he wouldn't be allowed to remain in the room.

Capone instantly pointed to the man standing next to the large desk. Tobias hoped he'd been more successful than the man Al picked at hiding his disappointment.

"I don't doubt the boy's clout, but the city is large, and I'd hate to see him get lost. My guy here would be happy to take your fellow wherever he needs to go. Isn't that right, Joey?"

Joey didn't appear pleased, but he collected his hat without argument and nodded towards the door. Tobias followed, stopping in the hall long enough to collect his pistol, and followed the agile guy down the stairs two at a time.

Joey stopped at a new green Ford Tudor Sedan and pulled out a box of cigarettes. He pushed his hat back, pulled a Lucky from the pack, and lit it. "Where to?"

He took out the crumpled letter and showed him the address.

"It's not that far; you could've taken the trolley," Joey said, looking longingly at the building they'd just left.

"This wasn't my idea," Tobias reminded him.

"Yeah, well, I guess it's my day to babysit," Joey replied.

If it had been said by anyone else, Tobias might have taken offense, but he'd had to sit on enough out-of-towners to know that the guy wasn't referring to his age.

"So what's at this address?" Joey asked, starting the sedan.

"What do you mean?"

Joey shot him a look that said he wasn't in the mood for games. "The fat man said you haven't been to Chicago before. What business you got here?"

Actually, he had been to Chicago, but he decided not to argue the point. "The fat man prefers to be called Big Mike. A friend asked me to check on her son. He's just a small boy, so she asked me to make sure he's okay."

Joey took the last puff from his cigarette and flung it out the window. "Why ain't the kid with his mother?"

An image of Anastasia mocking him came to mind. "You know how it is; some women are not cut out to be mothers."

The answer must have sufficed, as Joey was quiet the remainder of the drive.

Once they were away from the industrial buildings, the street opened up to residential homes. Joey took a turn, and within moments, the pleasant upscale street gave way to a more lived-in neighborhood. "Check the numbers. It shouldn't be much further."

Tobias didn't need to check. He'd looked at that letter many times over the past year. He'd often thought to jump on the train and check on the kid, but something had always come up. The house was the only house on the block that looked out of place. The grass riddled with weeds was in desperate need of being cut. "There it is, right next to the one with the barn roof."

Joey looked at the house in question and raised an eyebrow. "Want me to come with you?"

"Naw, I shouldn't be more than a moment."

Tobias climbed the steps, surprised to see two men in various state of undress sleeping in the shade of the brick porch. Neither man moved when he rapped on the front door. He knocked again before testing the doorknob and finding it unlocked. Pulling his pistol, he stepped inside. The smell of opium invaded his nostrils the second he entered. The front room was empty, as was the kitchen. He pulled back the curtain and glanced in the back yard, overgrown and empty except for a small shed. He let the curtain fall into place before making his way to the stairs. Moving quietly, he made his way to the second floor. Trash and clothing littered the upstairs hallway. The smell of urine mingled with the opium, causing his stomach to lurch. Five wooden doors, two on each side and one at the end, lined the fly-infested hallway. He stood to the side of the first door, turned the handle, and pushed it open. Smoke drifted from the room in an opium haze.

Two women and a man turned to look in his direction then resumed the sex act they'd been involved in. Tobias pulled the door closed and continued without a word. The second and third room mimicked the first, and for a moment, Tobias wondered if he'd been wrong about the address after all. The room at the end of the hallway turned out to be a water closet. The room was filthy but appeared functional, leaving him to wonder why the occupants chose to use the hallway instead. The final door was locked. He put his shoulder against the door in an attempt to open it. When it didn't work, he shoved his foot against the lock. The smell of decay flooded his nostrils, his stomach retched, then emptied, adding to the aroma. He braced himself, hoping he had not just found what he was looking for. The body on the bed did not move. From the degree of the odor, it hadn't moved in some time. The imprint of the blankets seemed too large, but he had to be certain. He took a breath, hurried to the far side of the bed, pulled the blanket from the head with the barrel of his pistol, and stared into the face of death. He'd seen dead bodies before, but this one had been left to fester in the heat, and was covered with the larva of flies.

Tobias ran down the stairs and was almost to the front door when he remembered why he was there. *The shed.* He had to be certain. He walked through the kitchen and opened the door, welcoming the humid summer air.

Reaching the shed, he fiddled with the lock to no avail. He checked the windows and found them covered in newspaper. He was just getting ready to leave when he heard the slightest of whimpers. Hurrying to the front, he fired his pistol to release the lock and opened the door. The shed flooded with light and the boy raised a hand to shield his eyes. Tobias stepped inside, and the boy reached for a screwdriver, wielding it like a knife.

"Come near me again, and I'll kill ya," the kid said through clenched teeth.

Clad only in underwear, the boy's hair was plastered to his face, his thin body glistening with sweat.

Tobias holstered his pistol and lowered into a squat, raising his hands the way he'd seen Mac do when trying to calm a situation. "Easy, boy, I'm a friend. I'm not here to hurt you. Your name is Franky, yes?"

Tears sprang from the kid's eyes as he tossed the screwdriver to the ground and ran into Tobias' arms. Franky was thin, but his grip strong. When at last the boy let go, Tobias saw the bruises that covered most of his tiny frame.

His blood ran cold. "Who did this to you, boy?"

"I don't know their names," Franky said, looking towards the house.

Tobias's jaw tightened. "Do you know faces?"

Franky nodded.

"Show me," he said when the kid hesitated.

Tobias led the way into the house and up the stairs. He placed his hand over his mouth to keep the flies at bay, then breathed through parted lips to keep from gagging on the smell. He opened the first door they came to and waited for Franky to shake his head. He did the same with the two additional doors. The last door was still open. Franky caught his arm before he entered the room.

"That's not him," Franky said, shaking his head.

Tobias pulled the door shut, grateful they wouldn't have to enter. "Where are your clothes, kid?"

The boy pointed to the urine-soaked clothes on the floor.

Setting his jaw once more, Tobias led the way downstairs.

Joey was sitting on the brick porch railing when they exited the house. Pistol in hand, he tilted his head to the two men who'd been sleeping on the porch. "I heard the shot and thought I'd keep these two company until you returned. Everything okay in there?'

Tobias shook his head and moved aside to show Franky, who'd been standing in his shadow.

Joey's jaw twitched as he took in the boy's condition.

Franky stepped outside and pointed at both men.

One of the men licked his lips and elbowed the man at his side. "Look who's come out to play."

Tobias pulled his pistol and fired two rounds. Holstering the gun, he turned his attention to Franky. "You are not to speak of them. You are not to allow them to invade your dreams at night. They are dead and can never hurt you again, understand?"

Franky nodded.

Tobias took the boy's hand and turned his attention to Joey. "I guess we're done here."

Chapter Thirty-Two

July 4, 1929

Tobias and the guys arrived at Point Pelee, Canada early enough to get a coveted spot in the shade. They'd been at the park several hours when John and Helen Daniels arrived.

"She's not with them," Tobias said when the couple exited their Ford alone. He turned to Franky. "I thought you said she'd be here."

Franky's eyes grew wide. It had been his job to shadow Mileta since his arrival in Detroit the previous year. "She was supposed to. I heard her talking about it to her friends."

Tobias nodded to the automobile. "Go make sure she's not sleeping in the backseat."

The boy raced off. The group watched as he not only checked the car but stopped to have a brief conversation with Mileta's parents.

"What was that about? They could have recognized you," Tobias fumed when he returned.

"Don't worry; they were too busy making goo-goo eyes at each other," Franky said, rolling his eyes.

"Well, what did you say?" Tobias pressed.

"I told them I was lonely and asked if they had any kids I could play with." Franky beamed. "The mom looked sad and said she had a daughter, but she wanted to stay at home today."

A guy by the name of Thumbs dropped to the sand laughing. "All this trouble and your girl is home alone. You could've had the broad all to yourself."

Tobias kicked the guy in the gut. "You talk about my girl like that again, and I'll do more than kick you."

Mac wrapped an arm around Tobias' shoulders and guided him away. "Listen, Mouse; it's still plenty early. The parents just got here. Even with the traffic, you have plenty of time to see your girl before her folks get home. The kid's already created an opening. We have plenty of spirits with us; we'll use them to make sure they have a really good time."

Tobias considered this a moment. "You don't mind riding home with the other guys?"

Mac handed Tobias his keys. "Not at all."

"Okay, but keep an eye on Little Man. The kid thinks he's older than he is."

"No surprise. Franky's been imitating you from the second you brought him to Detroit." Mac laughed. "I swear, sometimes, the kid even looks like you."

Tobias shook his head and left without commenting. As far as anyone knew, Tobias had found the kid starving and living on the streets. The city was becoming increasingly volatile, and the last thing he wanted was for anyone to hurt Franky to get to him. For that reason, he'd never bothered to correct that assumption.

***

He parked at the curb three houses down. The last thing he wanted to do was sully Mileta's reputation if he made it into the house. He'd just gotten out of the convertible when the front door to her house opened. He stopped near the tree, staying just out of view so as not to frighten her back inside. She sat on the top step eating her lunch. Oh, how he ached to join her. She fanned herself, lifted her head to confirm she was alone, then raised her dress a few inches, fanning the hem to cool her legs.

It took everything he had not to run to her. Instead, he calmly stepped out from the shadow of the tree.

"You keep that up, and you are going to give the neighbors the wrong impression."

She jumped. "What are you doing here?"

"What? You're not happy to see me?"

"Not when you sneak up on me. How did you know where I live?"

"Doll, I know everything about you," he said, leaning back against the tree and using the endearment he'd heard Mac use to sweet talk the dames on more than one occasion.

"That is impossible."

"You just turned sweet sixteen. I am the only boy you have ever kissed. And you wish I would kiss you again," he said, hoping it was true.

She narrowed her eyes. "I will have you know I've kissed lots of boys."

"You're cute when you lie." He pushed off from the tree.

She stood and reached for the door. "I am not lying. And you stop right there or I will scream for my father."

He tilted his head and decided to play his hand. "You better scream loud enough for him to hear you in Canada."

Her body stiffened. "How did you know they were not at home?"

"I told you, doll; I know everything about you. Relax." He leaned back against the tree. "I just came by to check on you. There's a crazy man on the loose or haven't you heard?"

"The paper said the police had arrested a suspect," she said smugly.

"There's not enough evidence to hold the guy. Not that it matters. They put the bracelets on him to still the fears of the public." Tobias wanted to tell her they'd arrested the wrong man. But if she pressed him on how he knew, he might be tempted to tell her. If he did, he would lose her before he even had a chance.

"He had a bloody knife," she countered.

"No matter. I'm telling you, the coppers will set him free."

"Because you know everything."

"Because I know enough," He had to admit the girl had spirit.

"If you know where I live, why have I not seen you before now?"

His smile faded. "I have my reasons."

"Which are?"

He took off his hat and spun it on his fingers, debating on how to answer without telling of the things he'd been involved in over the years. "Maybe I was waiting for you to grow up."

A blush crept up her face. "And now that I have?"

He stilled the hat. "I plan on courting you."

"Courting me?"

He returned the hat to his head. "Will that be a problem?"

She lowered her eyes. "I would like that very much."

"Very well, I will speak with your father when he returns this afternoon."

A look of disappointment crossed her face. "My father will not allow it."

He glared at her. "And why not?"

"He wishes for me to marry an educated man. He has a friend who has a son. He has been speaking very highly of Robert of late. His family is supposed to come by this weekend for dinner."

Tobias pulled himself taller. "How do you know I am

not an educated man?"

"Robert is going to college."

"Do you like this Robert?" For Robert's sake, he hoped the answer to be no.

She wrinkled her nose. "He sounds like a bore."

Tobias steadied himself. "I will speak with your father this evening. He will agree to allow me to court you."

"You seem so sure of yourself. Do you even have a job?"

He did, just not one he could share with her. "I have enough scratch to take care of the both of us."

"You did not answer my question."

Being on trial was new to him. Usually when he spoke, people eagerly followed his direction. "Listen, doll, where my dough comes from is my business."

"My father will expect more of an answer than that," Mileta countered.

"Let me worry about your father. I have dealt with tougher nuts than him." *If not, I have other ways.*

"Promise me you will not hurt him," she begged.

Had she been able to see through him so easily? "What would make you think I would hurt anyone?"

"Obviously, you do not remember our last conversation."

On the contrary, he'd replayed every moment at least a thousand times. "Actually, I remember it rather well."

"Then you remember offering to cut a man's hands off just because he could not play the piano."

"Just his fingers," he corrected. "His playing was causing you grief. I merely wished to alleviate your pain."

"By inflicting pain on him?"

"By doing whatever necessary to make you smile."

"Why?"

"Why what?"

"Why do you care about me? Even before I met you, you were protecting me. That time on the train…"

She shivered, and he almost ran to her. Instead, he remained rooted in place. "It doesn't matter."

"It does to me," she said softly.

He kicked at the dirt with the toe of his shoe. "Back then, it was different."

"Different how?"

"You were a little kid who was about to go to a very bad place. I was not going to allow that to happen." It was time to go; he was dangerously close to telling her everything.

"I'm not a little kid anymore."

"Don't I know it." He leaned against the tree once more.

She patted the concrete stoop. "Would you like to sit beside me?"

More than anything in the world. "That's not such a good idea."

"Why not?"

"As you just said, you are not a kid anymore. I don't trust myself not to soil your reputation."

She laughed. "You think I could not resist you?"

"I think should I wish to have my way with you that you wouldn't have a choice. I'll return in a few hours to speak with your father. Not to worry, I have ways of getting what I want." It took everything he had to walk away, get into the Ford, and drive away without taking her with him.

***

Tobias had just finished dressing when Mac burst through the door to his bedroom. "What's the deal? You forget how to knock," Tobias chastised.

"It's bad, Mouse. Real bad. I'd of been here sooner, but I needed to make sure."

Tobias took a breath. It wasn't like Mac to get flustered. "Is it Franky? What happened?"

"No, the kid's fine," Mac said breathlessly. "It's your girl's parents; they're dead! Drowned this afternoon over at Point Pelee."

Tobias lowered the comb he'd been using. "Both of them?"

"Yeah, the old man was zozzled. We'd no way of knowing he was heavy into the drink even before they arrived. Dumb palooka ignored the heavy current signs and got caught up in a rip current. The dame jumped in to help him and got sucked up right away. The old man saw her in trouble and, well, by that time, there was no hope for either of them. We tried to help them, but the current was too strong.

"We couldn't get away any sooner; the cops were asking all kinds of questions. It seems like it was the theme of the day as there were two other drownings there today."

"Were the other two drunk as well?"

"I don't know. The cops didn't say. Too bad about the dame; she was a real fine dish." Mac pulled out a pack of Luckys, tapped out a cigarette, and lit it. "What do you want to do, Mouse?"

Tobias' mind was racing. "Do the cops have any clue where they got the drink?"

"If they do, they aren't saying."

"Put an ear to the ground. I want to know what they know. Find me a mark in case we need to give them a chump to take the fall."

"You got it, Mouse. Anything else?"

"I can't bring my girl back here. Find me a place to take

her."

"A motel?"

"No something more permanent. No dives either."

"It might take some time, it being a holiday."

Tobias pulled out some bills and handed them to Mac. "I've seen you in action; you can be extremely persuasive. Use this to help grease the wheels. Have Little Man take my things over. Leave the crate for now. Tell him to make it look like I live there."

Mac blew out a smoke ring and chuckled. "Mouse, everything you own would fit in a hatbox."

"Just do what I said."

"I guess this all works out for you."

"How do you mean?"

"Now that your gal's parents croaked you'll have those gams wrapped around you in no time."

Tobias had Mac against the wall before he could take another breath. His arm pushed against Mac's throat, and the cigarette he'd been smoking was in Tobias' left hand hovering dangerously close to his eyelid. "You're my best friend, Mac. But you ever speak that way about my girl again, and I'll burn a hole right through your eyelid. Got me?"

"Sure, Mouse. I didn't mean any disrespect. I just meant that now you wouldn't have to snuff her old man."

Tobias released his hold on Mac, dropped the butt to the floor, and pressed it out with his shoe. "You just mind your place and keep your kisser shut."

"You got it, Mouse."

Tobias pulled his hat from the hook and started for the door. "On second thought, have Little Man leave the address on the dresser. I'll be back to get my stuff. I want to see the place before I take my girl there."

"Where're you heading?"

"I'm going to see if I can head off the bulls. I'd rather be there when they deliver the news."

Tobias raced down the stairs and jumped into his Model A without opening the door. The engine turned over immediately, and he was off. Anger clawed at him. He hadn't meant to lose his temper with Mac. The guy was his best friend. But Mac had hit a nerve.

Tobias originally planned to kidnap Mileta but was worried about how she would react. Some girls didn't take to being forced to do something against their will. He was fairly sure Mileta would be one of those girls. While he'd told Mac his plan was to snuff out Mileta's father, it was a lie. At least at this point and time. He'd opted instead to play the game, spending the better part of the afternoon trying to figure out how to convince Mileta's father to allow him to court her. His plan was to show up right before they left for the fireworks and wiggle his way to an invite. During the fireworks, he'd slip John a flask of the good stuff. The stuff they saved for Capone. He was then going to make sure that John knew how beneficial it could be to have a guy like him for a son-in-law.

That was what he got for trying to rise to the level of a damn do-gooder. Now the guy was dead, and now he was at risk of losing everything he'd worked for. The last thing he needed was for the bulls to find out it was his crew that was responsible for supplying John and his friends with the drink. The coppers looked the other way on a lot of things, but this happened in Canada. While they had friends there, Tobias wasn't sure who'd caught the case. If the bulls were not on the take and found out Mileta had come over on the trains, they would have no choice but to send her back. He was not about to let that happen.

There was a car sitting in front of the house when he arrived. He pulled in the driveway as if he owned the place and took a moment to steady himself before going inside. What he was about to do needed a cool presence. Anything else would never be convincing.

He saw them through the glass in the door. Mileta sat on the couch sobbing as a man he presumed to be a detective tried unsuccessfully to console her. Tobias was hoping he'd know the detectives, but he'd never seen either man before. Squaring his shoulders, he opened the door and walked inside, trying to appear as natural as possible. It was a bold plan, one that could backfire if Mileta did not go along, but at the moment, it was the only one he could think of.

Sliding into the spot the officer had just vacated, he draped his arm casually across Mileta's shoulder. "What seems to be the problem here, officers, and could someone please tell me why my wife is crying?"

Chapter Thirty-Three

"Are you so shameless that you would prey on my grief?" Mileta screeched the second the detectives left.

He moved to the front window and peeked past the curtain. "Shhhh, keep your voice down. The bulls will hear you."

"The bulls are police detectives. Why did you lie to them? Do you not think they will find out?" she said in a loud whisper.

Not if I have anything to do with it. He glanced out the window once more. "They might if they decide to follow up. By then, we'll be married, and they will not be in a position to do anything about it."

Her eyes grew wide. "Did you not hear what they just said? My mother and father have died. How could you possibly court me now? It would not be proper."

Tobias moved away from the window but kept his voice low. "Mileta, please calm down."

"Stop calling me Mileta; my name is Mildred," she said heatedly.

"I'm sorry, doll. I thought that maybe since your parents no longer had a hold over you that you might want to use your real name."

She whirled on him, eyes blazing. "Mildred is my real name. My parents gave it to me."

He drew in a breath. "Did they formally adopt you, Mildred?"

"They did. We went to court and everything." Her lips trembled.

"That's a good thing. Less likely they will send you back on the trains," he said softly.

Fresh tears sprang from her eyes. "Oh, Tobias, I cannot go to another asylum. Not after all of this."

"Don't you worry about that. I wouldn't dream of letting anyone take you away from me again." He knew he was rushing her, but better to prey on her grief than to lose her completely. If he gave her time to collect her thoughts, she might reconsider. The way things worked, the bulls might never return, but Tobias wasn't about to take any chances. This was his one sure chance to make Mileta his own. He'd been dreaming of this day for years, and here she was free for the taking.

"But how can we stop them?" she asked through her sobs.

"We will get married." *And then you'll be mine.*

"I...I don't know." Her voice was hesitant.

"It's the only way, doll. If you stay here, the bulls will find out, and when they do, they will take you to an asylum. I don't know if it would be here or somewhere else. Either way, you will be locked up. And at your age, if you are lucky enough to find a home again, it could be with someone like those uppity folks on the train. That man had his sights on you, and he was up to no good. We need to go soon." He moved closer and captured a tear with his thumb. "You trust me, don't you?"

"Yes." Her voice trembled.

He couldn't tell if she were more frightened of being sent away or of the prospect of marrying him. Her innocence made him want to make her his. If he weren't in love with her, he would have done just that. But this was Mileta or Mildred, as she preferred to be called, and Mildred was a lady. Sweet and innocent and deserving of someone better than himself. But luckily for him, he was all she had.

"Millie… is it okay if I call you that?"

She nodded.

"I know you are hurting inside. But we have to get hitched right away. You are right; the bulls will find out. When they do, it could mean a lot of trouble. But if you have a manacle on your hand, there won't be anything they can do about it."

"A manacle?"

"A wedding ring. Something big and sparkly." He smiled. "A beautiful girl like you needs a large piece of ice to show she is taken."

Her face turned a lovely shade of pink. "Oh, Tobias, you don't need to spend all of your money on me. I don't need anything expensive."

"Don't you worry your pretty little head. I'm going to take care of you just fine. Now you go on upstairs and pack."

"Pack? Where are we going?"

"I'm taking you to my place. They can't send you away if they can't find you."

"But… I thought you said it would be okay if we get married."

"It will. All the same, I think you and I should lay low for a while. Now, do as I said and go pack. I am going to go pick up a larger machine. My Tin Lizzy looks good, but she doesn't have room for all your stuff. I'll be back in a shake, so be ready." He gave her a nudge towards the stairs. "Millie."

She turned towards him. "Yes?"

"Go through your folks' room. Take anything of value. Cash. Jewelry. Anything you want to remember them by. The stuff belongs to you now. If you don't take it, someone else will. They are gone. They're not going to miss it," he added when she hesitated. "Also, when you pack your bags, pack as if you are never coming back."

He was out the door before she could protest. While he hated to leave her alone, he hoped searching through her parents' things would help to keep her focused. He knew she would have trouble deciding what to take and what to leave behind, but if he could get her settled quick enough, he and some of the guys could return and clean out the house. By sending her to collect what meant the most to her, she'd have enough to keep their memories alive at the off chance someone beat them to it. He hoped that wasn't the case, as he knew she would feel more at peace if she had things around her that reminded her of home.

***

Tobias raced up the stairs, relieved to find Mac waiting inside. He went into his bedroom. It was empty except for a wooden crate. "You found a place, then?"

"Yes, everything's been taken care of."

"We're just getting started," Tobias countered.

"Just tell me how I can help," Mac replied.

"First, I need a truck. I'm heading back to pick up some of Millie's things."

A puzzled look crossed Mac's face. "I thought her name is Mileta."

Tobias rolled his neck. "Her parents didn't like it, so they changed it."

Mac blew out a whistle. "I've heard of people changing the names of dogs, but changing the name your momma gave you, that's cold."

Tobias shook his head. "You don't know the half of it."

"So what else do you need?" Mac asked.

"After I get Millie settled, I want to go back and empty her parents' place. If we don't do it, someone else will. They have a lot of stuff, so find some guys to help."

"Done," Mac said with a nod. "Anything else?"

"Millie and I are going to get married, and we need a church. I want flowers, a dress, and people in the pews smiling and telling her how beautiful she looks." He knew it was a long shot, but he was desperate. Mileta had lost her parents; he needed to find a way to put a smile on her face. She'd been living the good life for years; girls like her wanted their dream wedding.

Mac blinked back his surprise. "I'm on it. When are you two getting hitched?"

"Tomorrow," Tobias replied, leaving out the fact he planned on tying the knot before Mileta had a chance to shake off her grief.

Mac's Adam's apple bobbled, but his face remained stoic. "You're killing me, Mouse. Is there anything else?"

"Actually, there is."

Mac hesitated.

Tobias smiled. "Can you tell me where I live?"

***

July 5, 1929

Tobias stopped in the hallway and turned to Franky. "Sorry, Little Man, this is as far as you go. You won't be able to continue shadowing Mileta if she recognizes you."

Franky placed a bag of rolls on top of the box Tobias held, then reached around to open the door, making sure to stay out of view.

Exhausted from cleaning out her parents' house, the sight of Mileta sitting on the couch brought him up short. He and the guys had worked through the night bringing in every piece of furniture from the house on East Fort Street, silently duplicating the placement right down to the quilt draped across the back of the sofa. For a brief second, it was if he'd walked into her parents' home and she was there waiting for him.

She looked up when she saw him and hurried from the couch to lend a hand. He waved her off, closing the door with his foot.

"You're awake. Are you hungry?" he asked, placing the box on the counter.

"Quite," she answered softly.

"Good. I brought cinnamon rolls from the bakery."

She eyed the box on the counter. "They look heavy."

"They're in a bag in the box."

She opened the box, lifted the bag, and gasped. "Tobias, these are all things from my mother's kitchen."

"They are."

"But why? You took …" She waved a hand towards the living room. "…everything."

"We needed things for the apartment. I thought you would approve."

"I…I am not certain what to think. It feels wrong, taking from them."

"Mileta, Millie," he corrected, "I know this is hard on you, but if we don't take the things, others will. As soon as word gets out that they are dead, people will be crawling all over that house like roaches. Locks will not stop looters from stealing everything in the house."

"How did you get in the house? When did you do all of this? Did you not sleep?"

Tobias shrugged. "I gathered a crew, and we picked everything up last night while you were sleeping."

Her eyes narrowed. "So you did break in and steal these items."

Sherry A. Burton

He was too tired to argue. "I broke in, yes, but I did not steal anything. Your parents are dead, Millie. Therefore, I merely brought these items to their rightful owner. I thought you would be happy to have them. I wanted to make you feel at home. I have money. I could have bought you new things. I was only trying to make you happy."

"What are you doing?" she asked when he reached for the box.

"I'm taking everything back."

She placed a hand on his arm. "Please leave them."

"Are you sure?"

"Yes, I think so."

He released his grip on the box. "I will leave them here for now, but if you change your mind, say the word and I will take everything away. Agreed?"

"Agreed."

He started to speak then closed his mouth.

"What is it?"

"The boys are outside with the rest of the loot... your belongings," he corrected.

She walked to the window and let out a sigh. "Tell them to bring everything in."

He rushed to the window and whistled. "Bring it all up, boys!"

***

He'd just finished changing when Mac came in. His friend looked at the suit and frowned. Tobias looked down. "You don't like it?"

"I wanted to surprise you. How'd you find out?" Mac grumbled.

Not having slept, Tobias was not in the mood for

puzzles. "I don't have time for this. I'm picking up Millie and taking her to the courthouse."

"So you don't know? I found you a church. My uncle's neighbor's niece is getting married tomorrow. The church is already set up with flowers and everything. I rousted up some players to sit in the pews. Told them to wear their Sunday best and you'd give them all a double sawbuck. They should be there by the time you get her there." Mac held up his hand, stepped out of the room, and came back with a long garment bag. "I saw a picture, and the niece looks to be the same size as your girl. For a C-note, her father said you can even use the dress. Just make sure to have it back before morning. One more thing, call it my gift to you. I contacted a friend at the morgue. It took a bit of coaxing, but I thought maybe this would be a nice touch. It belonged to the dame."

He looked at Mac in disbelief. "Remind me to take you out for a steak dinner."

Mac laughed. "I'll hold you to it."

Tobias looked at his watch. "What church?"

"Woodward Avenue Presbyterian Church." Mac winked. "If you want me to snatch up a rabbi, just say the word."

Tobias placed his fedora on his head. "Na, you did good, Mac. My girl will like the Presbyterian Church just fine.

***

"That dress will never do," Tobias said when Mileta came into the room.

Tears brimmed in her eyes. "This is the newest dress I own. I tried to get the wrinkles out…"

"It is not the dress, Millie. It is who the dress was intended for." It was a guess, but she'd told him she was supposed to meet her suiter this weekend, which explained the dress Franky saw her and her mother shopping for.

A deep blush crept up her face, showing his hunch had been correct.

"I told you I know everything about you." He moved across the floor and handed her the garment bag he was holding. "I would like you to wear this if you don't mind."

Her face was a mix of awe and delight as she pulled off the covering, exposing a delicately embroidered white on white chiffon dress. She traced a slender finger over the white heeled shoes that hung over the hanger.

"Oh, Tobias, the dress is beautiful. But how? Where?"

"I have my ways. Do you like it?"

She smiled. "Of course. As I said, it is very beautiful."

"It is but a dress. It is you that will make it look beautiful." He didn't have the heart to tell her it was but a loaner. The last thing he wanted was to ruin the moment.

She started for the bedroom and then paused. "I will be quick."

***

Mileta was quiet during the short drive to the church. While he wanted to ask her thoughts, he refrained from doing so over fear if she voiced them, she would rethink her decision to marry him. He was too close now to have the rug yanked from under him. He pulled the car to the curb and worked to steady his emotions.

Mileta's face went white as she stared at the church. Not that he blamed her, sitting on a slight rise the massive English Gothic church looked rather imposing. "What are we doing here?"

He worked to keep his voice steady. "Why, getting

married, of course."

"Here?"

"Unless you would prefer the courthouse." Hearing the fear in her voice helped to calm him. Seeing others panic always seemed to have the opposite effect on him.

She ran a hand over the white dress. "No."

Tobias opened the door for her and supported her elbow as they walked up the front sidewalk and in through one of the large double doors. The inside of the church proved to be even more ornate. The ceiling was mostly stained glass, soft music from the huge pipe organ floated through the air, and the scent of flowers greeted them as they entered. A large crowd of people turned to stare at them as they approached. Mac had outdone himself this time.

Mileta halted. "Who are all of these people?"

"Friends who have come to see us wed. You look beautiful, and since your father cannot be here today, I will walk you all the way," he whispered, then pointed to the front pew to the guys who'd helped him unload the truck. "See, you recognize the guys from earlier."

"I cannot…" She started to pull away, and he tightened his hold.

"You must, Millie. It is the only way I can keep you safe," he replied, urging her forward.

Her hands trembled as she listened to the preacher's words. After an eternity, the preacher paused and asked for the wedding rings. Tobias pulled the ring Mac gave him from his pocket and placed it on her finger. Her face paled the instant she recognized her mother's wedding ring. He held firm as she attempted to pull her hand away. He'd come too far to lose her now.

Nonplussed, the preacher asked her for Tobias' ring. A boy stepped up and handed her a single band. She relaxed slightly, slipping the band onto his hand. The preacher met Tobias' gaze as he pronounced them husband and wife. It was done. His heart pounded in his chest as he pressed his lips to hers. *At long last, she is mine.*

"I love you, Mildred Lisowski," he said pulling her close. "I fell in love with you long before we met, and I will love you until the day I die."

***

"I guess we know how he got the wedding ring," Cindy said, closing the journal. She sat it on the read pile and traced a finger on the one remaining journal.

"I think he would've pulled out his gun and forced her to marry him if she didn't go through with it," Linda mused.

Cindy left the journal on the table and leaned back on the couch. "Sadly, I agree. He may not have killed them, but he truly used her parents' death to his advantage."

Linda sighed. "I wish he'd written more about Franky."

"It wasn't his story to tell," Cindy said, looking at the stack of wooden boxes they'd brought from the attic.

"That's right, I remember seeing Franky's name on one of them."

"Grandma Mildred said the journals belong to the children who rode the trains. While Franky did not ride with their group, he did ride the train."

A smile crept over her mother's face. "I guess we'll learn more about Slim. Wait, I remember seeing a box with Anastasia's name. I knew his sister was hiding something. I'm sure that girl has a story to tell."

"It should be interesting," Cindy agreed.

"He doesn't realize it, but he and his sister were cut from the same cloth. Both know how to manipulate to get what they want."

Cindy tucked her hair behind her ear. "Manipulation or survival?"

"Probably a bit of both," Linda said, picking up Tobias' final journal.

Chapter Thirty-Four

February 14, 1931

Tobias walked into the Book Cadillac barber shop and handed Big Mike a cigar. He was meeting Mac for a job but wanted to give the guys a chance to congratulate him on the new baby.

"There's the man of the hour," Abe shouted from his chair. "How's the little mother?"

"Millie's doing fine. A little surprised that the baby came early is all," he answered.

"How's the little one? A girl, then? What'd you name her?" Abe continued.

"Yes, a beautiful little girl, I named her Fannie Mileta, after both my mother and her mother," Tobias said, puffing his chest.

"We should change the boy's name to Rooster. Look at him strutting around the room." Big Mike brought the cigar to his nose and sniffed. "Better stop wasting money on these things. You're a family man now. You need to watch your back; these are troubled times."

Abe laughed. "Are you kidding? Mouse is untouchable. The biggest hit in the nation and not a mention of the kid's name. He just slips into his little mouse hole with nary a squeak."

Tobias turned to hide his embarrassment. Abe was right; he'd been involved in the St. Valentine's Day massacre and not one mention of his name. Some of the guys joked that he was invisible, some even going so far as calling him Ghost. That one had gotten to him. While happy he hadn't been caught up in things, he'd heard a couple of guys speculate that the reason the cops hadn't picked him up was because he was feeding them information. So far that theory hadn't made its way to Abe's ears. Of course, it wasn't true, but Tobias was well aware of how things grew once the seed was planted.

"Yo, Mouse," Abe called to get his attention. "Next time you do the deed, make sure the kid is a boy. The way the coppers are picking up our guys, we're going to need some new blood in the gang."

Tobias managed a smile. "Not sure it's up to me, but I'll see what I can do."

Big Mike laughed, his whole body shaking. "Can you imagine a whole new generation of mice? With us here to guide them from the beginning, the kids would be unstoppable."

Tobias turned away once more. He'd been thrilled when he saw the baby was a girl. If he had his way, all their children would be girls. He'd see they went to the best schools, dressed in frilly dresses, and when the time came, he'd make sure their suitors were college men with no ties to any gang. That was one thing he and Mileta's father had in common. Mileta was not stupid. She knew he didn't make his living like most men; she just didn't know the extent of what he was into. She'd stopped asking questions shortly after they were married when she'd gone too far, and he'd slapped her. Tensions were high in the city, the streets abuzz with rumors that the cops were about to arrest people involved with the massacre. She was mad because he'd left her alone a few days and he'd snapped. He'd regretted it the second it happened, but the damage was done, and while she said she loved him, she seemed wary of him at times. He'd made a promise to himself he would get the kids out of this life before they were old enough to get pulled in. While Franky was not his son, and so far the boy was only working for him, he was already forming a plan to get him out.

The telephone rang as Mac walked into the room.

"Calls for Mouse or Mac," the barber said, laying the receiver on the phone.

"I got it," Mac said. His friend's jaw twitched as he listened to the caller. He slammed down the receiver and motioned towards Tobias. "We got to go."

"Problem?" Abe asked, folding the paper he had across his lap.

Mac looked at Tobias and hesitated. Setting his jaw, he filled them in. "That was Hugh, one of the kids Mouse has looking after his girl. There's trouble."

"I'll send some more guys," Abe shouted as they ran from the shop.

***

Tobias and Mac ran into the building, guns at the ready. Ignoring the elevator, they raced up the stairs to the third floor. The second they entered the third-floor hallway, they were met by a group of kids set for battle. Not seeing any threat, the men holstered their guns.

"We scared them away," a boy by the name of Hugh said before they could even ask. "The guys wanted to hurt Mrs. Millie, but we scared them real bad. She's a mighty bit scared, but we stopped 'em."

"Hugh scared them," one of the boys corrected. "He told them you were a Purple. One of the men didn't care, but the other guy got plenty scared. He told them you were coming and bringing the gang and they left."

Tobias looked at Mac. "Abe said he was sending people. Find out what these boys know, then take the guys and find them. When you snatch them up, send someone to come get me."

Mac nodded and led the boys to the edge of the stairs. All but Franky, who stopped when Tobias took hold of his arm.

Franky's eyes grew moist, and his ears turned red. "I'm sorry, Mouse, I didn't mean to let you down. I tried to stop them from hurting Mrs. Millie, but the guy was too big. He knocked me into the wall, and I don't remember nothin' after that."

"You did good, Little Man," Tobias said and released his arm.

He expected to find her in a heap. Instead, she stood in the center of the room, umbrella in hand, braced for battle. It was then he knew she'd changed. No longer the girl he'd forced into matrimony, she was a woman. A mother ready to fight to the death to protect her child. Even though she burst into tears the second she saw him, he'd never been more proud than the moment he walked into the room. He collected her in his arms, held her as she sobbed, and whispered as his words brushed against her hair. "I'm here."

She pulled away, and his pride grew into fury as he took in the bruising on her arms and the purple just beginning to settle around her eye.

Their eyes met, the look on her face one of utter terror. It took a moment for him to realize the look was aimed at him. Then he remembered what was said in the hallway and knew Mileta was no longer seeing him. Everything she'd ever read about the Purples stood in front of her this very moment. The monster that was her husband. She took a step back. He panicked and pulled her into his arms, gripping tight as she struggled to get free. He knew he should release her but was afraid she would run away. Surely this was not the way everything he'd worked for would end, with her hating him. He didn't know when she'd stop resisting. Only that his arms ached from holding her so tight. He lessened his hold then released her altogether when it looked as if she'd stay.

"I am scared." Her words came out in a whisper.

"Those men will never hurt you again," he promised.

"That is not all I am afraid of. I know about you. About the Purple Gang. How could you be a part of something like that? According to the papers, the Purple Gang is the worst gang in the city. They even say those men are murderers. How can you be a part of that?"

"I was with them before we married. It was the only way I could survive on the streets."

Anger flashed in her eyes once more. "And now?"

"And now, I have you and Fannie. You do not realize how bad things have gotten since the recession started. Men who were once friends would slit each other's throat if it meant putting food on the table. I've seen it done — proud men standing in line for hours just to get a cup of soup or slice of bread. People, and I'm not just talking about street kids, whole families living in crates, boxes, and alleyways. You haven't been hungry in years, Millie. You don't have to beg or steal. And you don't have to leave our child with strangers while you go off to whatever factory job you can find and work your fingers to the bone simply to bring a few coins home at the end of the day. I've never asked you to work, and never will. But I will not have you judging me for doing what I have to do to put food on our table. Not when most of the country goes to bed hungry each night. I will do whatever it takes, and I mean whatever it takes to keep my family safe," he said heatedly.

"Don't you hurt those boys!" she said when he glanced towards the door.

"They shouldn't have told you."

"They did not tell me. They told the men who had just threatened to…"

He reached for her, and she waved him off. "I think maybe this is all my fault. The men were in the hallway making such a racket; they woke Fannie. She has not been sleeping, and I am just so tired. I nursed her until she finally fell back to sleep. Then they started again, and I was afraid she would hear them, so I rushed out of the apartment to ask them to be quiet. I did not realize that in my haste, I had forgotten to close my blouse. The men thought I was—well, you are a man, you know what they must have thought. If their actions were my punishment, then so be it, but when they threatened to take Fannie, God help me, I wanted them punished. I was glad you are who you are because I knew you would punish them. Now I worry that my anger makes me no different than you."

He moved forward, and this time, she welcomed his embrace. "But you are different, Millie. That's what made me fall in love with you. You have been through so much in life, but you never let it beat you. You are good. You are kind. You are everything that I am not."

"But I hate those men and want to make sure I never have to worry about them harming our daughter."

He remembered her standing in the center of the room prepared to die to protect her child. Their child. "Did I forget to mention that as of five days ago, you are also a mother? It is a mother's job to protect her young. I once saw a woman shoot a guy who was trying to take her baby away. I've seen a mother rat attack a dog ten times her size to protect her young. It's what moms do. I hate to tell you this, Mildred, but you are normal."

This seemed to appease her. "What will become of those men?"

He kissed her lightly on the lips. "You leave those two to me."

"You are going to kill them, then?"

I would kill them a hundred times if I could. "I'm going

to make sure our daughter can sleep safely in her crib at night."

"By killing them."

He released his hold on her and walked to the window to see if Mac had returned.

"I will not tell you what you wish to hear. I saw the way you looked at me when I first entered. I could not bear it if I saw that look every time I looked into your eyes. Just know that most of my life, I have lived with a single purpose: to do whatever is necessary to keep you safe. I would gladly go to my grave if I thought it was the only way to protect you. That is how much I love you, Mileta."

"I will promise never to ask you about your life again if you make me a promise in return. I would like you to make a journal of your life for me. I am doing the same thing. I've been writing them for years. You may read it if you wish. Write it for me, so that one day I will truly know the man I married."

He considered refusing her request, wanting to protect her from the evils he'd committed. "I will do as you ask under one condition."

"Which is?"

"You promise not to read my journals until after I die."

"And if I die before you?"

Then I will die with you. "Then you will go to your grave knowing only that I have loved you. It is a gamble, but then again, I am a gambling man."

She smiled. "I will agree to your terms. Wait, there is another matter I would like to discuss."

"I'm listening."

"About those boys."

"No harm will come to them. You have my word."

"I want more than that. The boys follow me. I have seen them before, but now I know it is not merely for their entertainment."

"They follow you to keep you safe. I will not order them to stop, and that's not up for debate." Especially not after what had just happened.

"I am not asking you to. It is just if they are going to be my guardians, I want you to see to it they are properly dressed. It is the middle of winter, and one of the boys has his toes hanging out of his shoes. They do not have to look like dandies; their shoes don't even have to be new. Come to think of it, it would be best if they are not; something like that could get them killed in this neighborhood. I just want them to be warm. Oh, and one more thing,"

It was easy to see she was enjoying this. "Oh, do tell."

"I am going to make each of them a quilt to keep them warm. So I will need some fabric. Nothing too pretty, of course."

"Of course." Now that she thought herself in charge it would only be a matter of time before she had them in the house, feeding them like puppies she'd picked up along the street. "I'll see it is delivered tomorrow. Is that soon enough?"

"It will do. The one little boy, Franky, got injured while trying to protect me."

Tobias frowned. "The boy is tough. He stayed there when Rabbit ran?"

"He did. I think he would have taken a bullet if it had come to that. And, to be clear, Rabbit ran to get help."

They were interrupted by a knock on the door.

"We've got them," Mac said when Tobias opened the door.

Tobias worked to keep the anger out of his voice. "Tell me."

"Two guys, James and Lyle, out-of-towners. Just arrived in town. Supposed to take up with someone in town, but don't think that happened yet," Mac told him.

"Do we know what gang?"

"They're not saying."

Whoever it was would have to be dealt with. Later. For now, he would see to it that James and Lyle didn't connect with any gang. Ever. He shut the door without a word and walked to where Mileta stood.

"I need to go out for a while. Will you be all right?" he asked, his anger building with each passing second.

"I will." She blinked and winced against the pain.

He kissed her eye and laid his hand against the side of her face. When he spoke, he made sure his words were not misunderstood. "If anyone ever asks, the only thing you know about the Purple Gang is what you've read in the papers. I am not nor will I ever be a member of the Purple Gang. It is important that you remember that, Mildred."

She nodded.

The look in her eye when she nodded gripped at his heart. He hated to scare her, but it was the only way he could continue to keep her safe.

***

June 30, 1931

Tobias pulled to the curb in front of their apartment building after a particularly difficult day. The city was heating up, bought cops weren't staying bought, and the east side and west side continued a tug-o-war to see who was going to gain control. While he still felt safe on Hastings Street, he wasn't sure how long he'd be able to keep his family safe. He'd pondered leaving the city altogether and taking Mileta and the baby someplace warm. He'd heard good things about Florida. Maybe they could move there, and he could actually get a job. Something respectable. Mileta could have morning tea with her friends. Instantly, his mind went to Felisha sitting around the grand apartment in New York City smiling and gossiping. The image switched, and it was Mileta, sitting with her new circle of friends, little Fannie playing on the floor by her feet. Mileta looked in his direction and smiled. It was a true smile, and the image gripped his heart. It had been ages since he'd seen her smile like that. Except for talking to the baby, she rarely smiled at all anymore. He looked towards the orange brick building, singling out the third-floor window that was their home. Why not leave? He had money stashed away for an emergency. Even if he didn't get a respectable job right away, he was more than capable of keeping his family fed. A sense of calmness washed over him as he hurried inside. Not wishing to waste a moment, he ran up the stairs. They could buy new furniture when they got to where they were going, so it shouldn't take long to pack. He'd have to say goodbye to Mac and Slim; he could do both on the way out of town. Maybe he wouldn't have to say goodbye; maybe they would agree to go with them. They could start their own gang. No, not a gang, a respectable business.

He paused at the top of the stairs to catch his breath. The last thing he wanted was to rush in and scare Mileta or the baby. He smiled and felt as if a weight had been lifted from his shoulders. Recovered, he opened the door to the apartment ready to tell Mileta of his brilliant plan.

She was on the couch when he entered, face pale as a waning moon. She clutched the baby in her arms, and for a moment, he thought to fuss at her for holding the child too tight. Something about her face made him reconsider. He dropped his hat on the counter and slowly approached.

"What is it?" he asked when she failed to speak.

Mileta raised her head to show tear-stained cheeks. "Our baby, she is dead."

Tobias sank to his knees as a sea of tears washed away

his dreams of a new life. When at last his sobbing stopped, he raised his eyes to his wife. "How?"

Mileta lips trembled as she spoke. "She just went to sleep and never woke up."

He raised his fist and pounded it into the sofa in desperation. When his pain didn't ebb, he continued. His job was to come up with solutions. There was no one to squeeze. Not a soul to kill. How was he supposed to deal with this? He'd never felt so helpless in his life.

"We shall give her a grand funeral and buy her the biggest stone," he said, thinking of the money he had set aside.

"No, Tobias. Please, I just couldn't bear to think of her lying in the ground all by herself. I wish to put her with my mother."

At first, he thought she meant taking the child back to New York.

"We can bury her tonight." She looked up, her face resigned. "You know people, do you think you could get her a wee coffin?"

He rose and kissed Mileta on top of her head. Stooping lower, he did the same to his daughter. "I'll see that she has a proper burial."

"No," Mileta said, shaking her head. "Leave her here with me. I'll go with you tonight."

"Millie, you can't. If we get caught, they'll arrest us."

She narrowed her eyes. "You will find a way to keep me safe. You always have."

He nodded. "I'll go see to things. I'll be back as soon as I can."

***

Working under the light of a small lantern, Tobias lifted

the final shovel of dirt and lowered it to the side of Mileta's mother's grave. He lifted the lid of the small wooden casket and turned to Mileta. "It's time."

Mileta lifted the blanket and kissed Fannie on the cheek before handing the bundle to him. Tobias kissed the baby's forehead, gently lowered her into the box, and closed the lid.

"Would you like to say anything?" he asked.

Mileta stood and placed a hand on her parents' headstone. "I know you aren't my true mother, but whenever I think of my daughter, I will picture her safe within her grandmother's arms."

"Aren't you going to say anything?" Mileta asked when Tobias raised the shovel once more.

He shook his head. "She knows what's in my heart."

It only took a couple of moments to cover the tiny grave. When he'd finished, he took Mileta's elbow and led her towards the cars, where Mac and a few of the guys waited, watching them from afar.

"It's a beautiful full moon tonight," Mileta said softly.

Tobias lifted his gaze to the sliver of moon too slight to even cast a shadow and nodded his agreement. Somehow it proved easier to leave under the guise of a full moon than picturing their tiny daughter sleeping in the darkness.

Chapter Thirty-Five

November 30, 1933

Tobias looked about as he exited the train. With a few exceptions, the town of Noblesville, Indiana looked much the same now as it did when he'd first arrived eighteen years ago. One difference, he'd gotten on and left the train of his own accord. Okay, maybe he'd left town to keep from answering questions. Butch was back on the streets. So far, Abe had refused to believe his story, but the seed had been planted. Tobias needed some time to think about what that meant for the future. He'd put on a good suit and boarded the train in hopes of finding Fannie still among the living.

He found the house without asking for directions, smiling when he saw the covered porch. The house was smaller than he remembered; then again, he'd been but a boy. He reached for the doorknob, then reconsidering, he rang the bell and waited.

He didn't have to wait long. The door opened, and a man looked at him in question.

He glanced at the number on the house. "Sorry, I must have the wrong address."

"Who you looking for, boy?"

Tobias resisted a smile. No one had called him that in ages. "I thought this was the Lisowski residence."

The man's expression soured. "Fannie? Why, that woman hasn't lived here in years."

"Do you know where I can find her?"

The man's brow creased. "I bought the house about eight years ago. She said she was going to live above the corner drug store. Far as I know, she's still there."

"Appreciate the help," he replied.

"Need directions?" the man inquired.

"No, sir, I saw it when I got off the train," Tobias answered and left without further discussion.

Seven minutes later, he found himself knocking on the door once more. The door opened, and she was there. Older and a few pounds heavier, he'd have recognized her anywhere. Unfortunately, it took her a little longer.

"What do you want?" she asked, opening the door.

"Don't you recognize me, Mom?" Tobias asked, taking off his hat.

Fannie's eyes misted over. "My boy. You came back to me. I didn't think I would ever see you again."

She held out her arms, and he stepped into her embrace with a sigh.

"I have your book," she said, releasing him. She crossed the room, opened the top drawer of the dresser, and reached under her undergarments. "I put it under my unmentionables. Figured if anyone broke in, they'd see the size and be too scared to take a look inside."

He cocked his head to the side. "You kept it all these years?"

She handed it to him. He read the cover and smiled.

Tom Sawyer. He hadn't been able to read at the time. He opened it to see the signature. "That train ride seems so long ago."

"You seemed rather partial to the book. I'm surprised you left it here when you ran off." Her voice held an edge.

Ran off? Tobias jerked his head up. "What do you mean ran off?"

"That's what they told me."

Tobias fought to remain calm. "I didn't run off; they sent me back."

Her eyes flew open. "They who?"

He looked to the window. "Probably the same ones who told you I ran off. I wanted to stay. Begged them to let me, but they told me you were too sick to take care of me."

Tears welled in her eyes. "I knew it. Deep down, I knew you wouldn't have left if you'd had another choice."

"You seem, different somehow. Calmer."

She looked around, though they were the only two in the room. "Laudanum. Not to worry, the druggist meters it."

"How often do you go see the doctor?" Tobias asked.

Fannie laughed. "I haven't been out of this room in years."

He looked around the small space, appalled. "Why on earth not?"

"Oh, quit your worrying. I have a water closet, and Earl, the druggist, sees I get enough to eat. It's my legs. While I could probably make it down the stairs, I don't think they would bring me back up." She laughed. "Lord knows there's nobody in town going to carry me."

So much for his plan. He'd imagined her differently and thought to bring Franky to live here. He imagined she would have been good for the kid, but not now.

"Tell me, son," she said, placing a hand on his.

"Tell you what?"

She laughed once more. This time, it sounded more like a cackle. "Are you forgetting that I can see into your heart?"

He closed his eyes briefly. "If that were truly the case, you would never have opened the door."

Her face turned serious. "Just because you have done terrible things does not mean your heart is ugly."

He didn't respond.

"I see the bulge under your coat. The sorrow in your eyes is not just from seeing your mother in dire straits. Now, you either trust me enough to tell me of your troubles or leave."

He pulled himself from the chair, pacing the room as he spoke. Once he started talking, he couldn't seem to stop. So much had happened in his life since last seeing her. He told of the train wreck, of being sent on the trains, again. He told of his life in Detroit and how he'd been pulled into the Purples. He told of rescuing Franky and how he'd not allowed the kid to cry. He told her of his first kill, his part in the St. Valentine's Day Massacre, and of his most recent tie-in with the Collingswood killings. He told her how each time he'd walked away without anyone knowing of his involvement. He stopped pacing and met her eye, wondering if she would remember the time she'd clapped her hands together and declared him invisible. "People say I'm some kind of ghost."

"Is that why you are here?" She chuckled.

"Partly." In truth, both he and Mileta had been in a downhill spiral since losing their daughter. His plan of leaving town never evolved, and he'd found himself even deeper ensconced within the Purples. He'd allowed Franky to move into the apartment to keep a closer eye on Mileta and found himself staying away longer and longer. He told himself he kept his distance to protect her, but in truth, he didn't know how to deal with the sadness in her eyes. As he grew more desperate, he longed to hear his mother's voice. While not his true mother, she was the closest thing he had.

"Do you really believe I put a spell on you?"

So she did remember. "It's the only explanation that makes any sense."

"Did you ever think maybe it was your own good fortune keeping you safe?"

He thought of Mileta and the sadness in her eyes. He'd been able to protect her from everyone but himself. "I'm tired of being invisible. I don't want to be so cold; I cannot feel the hurt I cause others."

Fannie raised her arms and brought her palms together, her arms wiggling in the wake. "There; it is done."

It was the same simple movement she'd done so many years ago. Same as then, he didn't feel any different.

Her eyes misted over. "You'll go now."

"I will. I have to go back to Detroit." He bent and kissed her on the top of her head and picked up the book, thinking Mileta would enjoy hearing the story about when it had been given to him.

"To your wife?"

Tobias felt a chill race up his arms. He'd told the woman everything except about Mileta. "You really are magic."

She shook her head. "No, just taking a lucky guess. Maybe someday you'll bring her to meet your mother?"

"Maybe someday I will." Tobias stopped when he reached the bottom of the stairs. He went around the front of the building and stepped into the drugstore. The druggist looked up when he entered, and Tobias recognized him as one of the men who'd been in the room when they sent him back. While the man had aged, there was no doubt it was the same man.

"Can I help you?" It was easy to see the man had no clue who he was.

"Do you have a boarding house in town? Or a hospital with a place that looks after people?"

"We have both. You don't look ill. If you're thinking of staying, the boarding house may be a better fit. Sarah has a nice place with lots of room. She charges five dollars a week, including meals."

Tobias pulled out a large wad of bills. "Give this to

Sarah, and tell her to take good care of my mother. I want her to have a ground-floor room so she can go outside and sit on the porch when the weather is nice. Tell her if my mother needs anything, anything at all, she is to contact Big Mike at the Book Cadillac Hotel in Detroit. He'll know how to find me."

"Well, what's your mother's name?" the man behind the counter asked, accepting the bills.

"Fannie, Fannie Lisowski," Tobias replied.

The man blinked his surprise. "You're the boy from the train. I felt awful when they sent you away. Poor Fannie was beside herself. I guess that's why I took her in after she sold the house. She didn't have anywhere else to go, and I had a room. Guess it was my way of making peace with the man upstairs."

"I appreciate everything you've done for my mother." Tobias put his money clip away, making certain to open his jacket wide enough to expose his gun. "That was your choice. Your actions are between you and your maker. You're free of your obligations. Just make sure you don't hold on to any of that money."

"No, sir, I would never even consider it," the man replied.

***

The train jogged along at full speed as he made his way towards the dining car. He'd just stepped into the next car when he met a man in the aisle. Deep in thought, he almost missed the bump as the train swayed along the tracks. To anyone else, it would appear the man had been forced off balance, but Tobias was not a normal mark. He took hold of the man's arm, and the guy muttered his apology.

"Give it back," Tobias demanded.

"Why, I assure you I have no idea of what you are

speaking," the man stammered.

He slid his hand into his suitcoat just to be sure his wallet was indeed missing. Without warning, the pickpocket pulled out a small blade. Tobias opened his jacket, revealing his pistol, and the man sprinted off in the opposite direction. He left his pistol in place, chasing after the guy, meaning to retrieve his wallet and perhaps school the man on pickpocketing etiquette. The man was standing on the outer porch of the train trying unsuccessfully to pry the door open when he grabbed him by the collar and spun him around. The thief's hand came up, slicing Tobias across the upper arm. He slammed his fist into the man's gut then retrieved his wallet. Satisfied, he'd just turned to leave, when the fellow attacked, slamming him against the back of the train car. Infuriated, Tobias took hold of the man and tossed him from the moving train.

***

Mac was waiting at the train station when he arrived. He took one look at Tobias's bloodstained suitcoat and raised his eyebrows. "Rough day?"

"I guess I looked like an easy mark."

"How's the other guy?" Mac asked.

Tobias smiled. "He decided to depart early."

Mac pointed at the arm. "Want to get it looked at?"

"Na, it's just a little nick," he said, shrugging it off. "How are things here?"

Mac frowned. "Word on the street is Butch's been gabbing to the bulls. Claims he has information that can send you up for a long time. He's been in the joint, so unless someone is feeding him information, it's all baloney."

"Okay, so we snatch the guy up and find out what he has. If he has nothing, we let him go; if he squeals, we find out who he's been talking to," Tobias replied.

"Abe doesn't want you involved in this."

Tobias hesitated. "Abe believes him?"

"I don't think so. Abe's just worried they could be watching Butch. If the bulls know you have it in for Butch, then how better to catch you than shadow Butch until you show up to confront him?"

Tobias nodded. "It's what I'd do."

"It's what we all would do," Mac agreed. "You coming back to my place?"

He sighed. He'd planned on going home. He hoped to tell Mileta of his mother and make plans to take her to meet the woman he'd cared enough to name their daughter after. "Yeah, I better lay low for a bit."

***

December 4, 1933

Tobias sat looking at the letters Slim had dropped off in his absence. Letters from his sister that chatted merrily as if they'd been corresponding for years. She seemed happy to hear from him, even though he'd never written her a single word. She had a son. He thought of Franky and wondered what the boy would think if he knew his mother had kept this one. *Little Man's better off without her.* He tossed the letters next to the crate with the others. He picked up the newspaper clipping and read it once more. WE RODE THE TRAIN. I AM LOOKING FOR MY BROTHERS AND SISTERS. PLEASE CONTACT PADDY JONES BOX 132 SANDUSKY MICHIGAN 48471

So Paddy rears his obnoxious red head yet again. Looking for his brothers and sisters, a ploy to be sure. He wants to find Mileta and take her away. He looked for a date on the clipping but saw none. He tossed the clipping to the floor and sighed. Shaking his head, he leaned and picked it up, wincing as the dull throb in his arm turned to a shooting ache. He placed a hand on the bandage and felt the heat that radiated from beneath the wrap. Heat that warmed his entire body. He cursed the man that cut him and not for the first time was glad he'd tossed him from the train. There were codes people followed. Robbers used guns and blades to get people to hand over their money. Pickers dipped pockets and left them high and dry. The two were totally different trades. The man that did this to him gave pickpockets a bad name. He placed the newspaper clipping beside the letters and looked at the stack of journals on the desk. He'd kept his promise and written about his life. He'd told all his secrets; well, almost all. While he'd mentioned both the St. Valentine's Day Massacre and the one at Collingwood, he had neglected to go into details. Nothing she could imagine would be as grave as what truly happened. If it were details she wished for, there were plenty of newspapers ready to fill her in. While he would admit to taking part, he would not let her see the evil through his eyes.

***

Tobias rolled onto his side, the pain instantly pulling him from his sleep. His sheets were soaked, and for a moment, he thought he'd wet himself. Pulling himself from the bed, he went into the washroom to splash water on his face.

"You're not doing so hot," he said to his image in the mirror. He pulled the bandage down and cried out against the pain. It was then he saw the red streaks. Closing his eyes, he shook his head, smiling at the irony. It wasn't often a dead man could exact revenge, but the man he'd thrown from the train had killed him as certain as he'd been killed.

Chapter Thirty-Six

December 6, 1933 2 am.

If not for his feverish state, he would have known something was wrong the moment he walked into the apartment. As it was, the only thing on his mind was climbing under the covers to be near the woman he loved. He tried unsuccessfully to climb into bed without waking her.

"You are burning up!"

"And you are freezing." His teeth chattered as he spoke.

"The landlord turned off the heat," she said, pulling the quilt closer. "He said if I do not pay the rent we owe by the end of the week, he will turn off the electricity as well."

He could tell by the tone of her voice she was angry at him. He'd stayed away too long, and she had every right to be. "I will grab another quilt."

She took hold of his good arm. "There are no other quilts. Except for my birth quilt, which I gave to Franky to use. It is so threadbare, I am not sure how much good it is doing him."

Franky coughed and moaned in his sleep.

Tobias pulled himself from the bed. He couldn't let the boy freeze to death because of his neglect. He would be gone soon, and Mileta would need Franky's pickpocketing skills if she were to survive.

"Where are you going?" she asked when he crawled out of bed.

He scooped Franky off the floor, placed him in the bed

beside Mileta, and climbed back in himself. "How much do you owe?"

"Two and a half months. I sold my quilts in October but didn't get enough to cover the full month."

He tried unsuccessfully to control his anger. "You sold all your quilts and could not pay a month's rent? Who did you sell them to?"

"Mr. Simpson on the corner. Do not go down there. You are in enough trouble. Were you able to find protection?"

No, but he wouldn't need any now.

"It is all my fault; I should not have gone into the hallway."

Tobias sighed. Not for the first time, he regretted telling her he'd been involved in Collingwood. While he didn't share the details, he'd told her of his involvement, hoping it would take her mind off Fannie's death. He'd also used it as an excuse for staying away more and more. "Millie, we have been over this too many times. You did nothing wrong. Louie, Sammy, and I are the ones who took care of those guys. How could we know they were connected with Chicago? It was just poor dumb luck they picked our building…"

She turned to face him in the dark, "It was not poor dumb luck. I've heard the rumors, Tobias. I know Chicago suspects the Purples of being in on the St. Valentine's Day Massacre. Those men were here looking for you."

"Then why run when they could have taken off with you?" Because they weren't looking for her or him. And contrary to what he'd told her, the incident was not connected to St. Valentine's Day.

"Maybe they went to get help, or maybe they were afraid of the kids."

Franky moaned, pulling them from their discussion.

He'd nearly drifted off to sleep when she spoke once

more.

"Why are you home?"

"What? A man cannot return to his home?"

"It's over." He started to tell her he was going to die when she spoke once more. "Prohibition? Yes, I heard. Someone shouted it down the hallway. Another lady used colorful language, telling him to shut up and that was that. I guess it does not matter in a city where liquor can be found even during the dry season."

He kissed her on the forehead. "Yes, but now they will not need to go elsewhere. Everything has changed. Not just Prohibition, everything."

"I don't understand."

"The city, the life we had, the friends I had when I first got here; we've had a great run, but it is over."

"I...I don't understand what you are saying."

"I've tried my best to keep you safe. But I am afraid I won't be here to protect you. No matter; I'm poison to you." His arm throbbed and he grew weary.

"I will not allow you to leave me. Look what I've become in the three months since you've been in hiding." Franky mumbled in his sleep, and she lowered her voice. "I send a child out to steal so that we can have food. Do you know what they would do to him if they caught him?"

He would have laughed if he weren't so ill. "Franky just turned twelve. He is not a child. And you are not making him do anything he wouldn't be doing anyway. At least now you are giving him a purpose."

"You make it sound as if stealing for me is a good thing."

"Mildred, if not for you, the boy would be sleeping on the streets, or worse." It was the first time he could remember calling her by that name.

"What could be worse than sleeping on the streets?"

"Things have changed, affiliations have changed. I have seen things…done things that I never thought I would do." Was he repeating himself? He couldn't recall. All he wanted at the moment was to go to sleep.

***

She was sleeping when he woke. He slipped out of bed as carefully as he could so not to wake her or Franky. He'd nearly reached the front door when Franky stopped him.

"Where are you going?"

Tobias didn't turn around.

"When will you be back? I do what I can, but I'm just a kid you know? Mrs. Millie, she needs you here."

Shaking and chilled, Tobias turned towards the boy. "I'm going to talk to the super. I've got enough to pay the rent and get the heat turned back on. While I'm doing that, can you run and get something for breakfast?"

"Sure I can," Franky said, pulling himself taller.

"Franky, I know you think you are a kid, but when I'm not around, you need to take care of things. I've taught you how to pick pockets without getting caught. There are a lot of bad people out there, and you're the only one I can trust to see that she's okay, understand?"

"Sure, Mouse, I understand," Franky replied.

"Good kid. Now you run out and get what we need. I'll do what I have to do and see you back here shortly."

Franky pulled on his coat. Tobias waited until Franky was out of view before leaving. If the boy knew how weak he was, he'd never leave his side. The super answered after the second knock. He didn't give the man a chance to speak.

"Open your mouth," he said, pointing his pistol at the

man's head. The man did as told, and Tobias shoved a roll of bills into his mouth.

The super reached to remove them, and Tobias stopped him.

"Do you know who I am?"

The man nodded his head.

"Good. Do you know who my friends are?"

This time, the answer was no.

"I'm with the Purples. Now we are not supposed to tell anyone, but now you know. I'm going to let my friends know you know. What this means is if you mess with my family again, my friends will come see you. When they do, they will take you for a little ride. Only they will forget where you live and never bring you home. Blink twice if you understand."

"Good," Tobias said when the man blinked his understanding. "Now I'm going to run a little errand. See how bad I'm shaking? When I get home, I expect my apartment to be nice and toasty. Will that be a problem?"

The man shook his head.

Tobias wasn't sure how he made it to Mac's apartment to pick up the crate. But he did. He pulled the top drawer from the dresser and removed a large envelope of cash reserved for an emergency escape. He placed the cash on the bed. He moved to the desk and pulled out the journal he'd been writing in.

Mac, remind me to listen the next time you suggest I see a doctor. I guess I knew I should have gone a few days ago. If so, maybe things would be different. I guess I knew if I'd gone, they would have taken my arm and, well, I guess I just wasn't ready for that. Not that I'm ready for this.

Please see that my wife gets out of town. There is enough dough for her and Little Man to go anywhere they choose. I want you to send some guys to the house and scare her into leaving. It's the only way she will agree to leave, and there will

Shameless

be nothing left for her when I am gone.

I don't want my wife to have to see me into the ground. Have some of the guys lay me to rest beside my baby girl and I will be a happy man. I wish I could have said goodbye.

Your friend,

Mouse

Tobias tore off the paper and placed it under the cash. Lifting the pencil, he turned back to the journal.

My Dearest Mileta,

This will be my final entry. As my body weakens, I have but one thought, and that is to return to you. From the moment I saw you, I knew my lot in life was to keep you safe. While I managed to keep you from harm, in the end, it was I who was your greatest threat. My lifestyle that threatened to destroy you. I am sorry for the pain I have caused. I know I should not tell you this, but if I had it to do all over again, I cannot say I would not do exactly as I have done. Having you in my life is the one thing that kept me from an even greater darkness. The one thing that stopped me from even greater atrocities. As I put my last thoughts on paper, I realize I am the greatest thief of all time. Because in my quest to keep you safe, I managed to steal your smile.

My time is near; I am returning to you so that you will know me to truly be dead.

Yours forever,

Tobias

***

Cindy closed the journal and wiped away her tears. She knew from reading her grandmother's journal how Tobias had died, but reading his words didn't make it easier. She turned to Linda. "You okay, Mom?"

331

"I knew he was going to die, but it still hurt reading his final words," Linda said, echoing her thoughts.

Cindy hugged the journal to her chest. "I agree. I got so caught up in the story, I expected to read about his death again. I guess since he was doing the writing, he couldn't very well write his demise."

"I think it was time for him to go. The way things were going, he would have taken her down with him."

Cindy placed the journal on the finished pile. "What say we take a break before we open the next box?"

"I think that's a good idea," Linda agreed. "We can begin again in the morning."

Cindy smiled, knowing her mother was right. Finding the journals was a gold mine, and just like the fortune hunters of the past, one could not simply walk away from a treasure trove.

Author's Note

There have been many books and articles written on the Placing Out Program. Some depict the program in a good light, others do not. In this book, Tobias has issues with the committee members during his first placement in Indiana. I want to note that while the town of Noblesville, Indiana is real, the placement and committee members used are fictional. The issues Tobias faced were written for entertainment purposes only. While some of the committees may have had their own agenda, the majority of the committee members were affluent members of the community in which they lived.

The committee members were selected by a placing agent from the Children's Aid Society. Each person on the committee was selected because they lived in the community and knew the folks that lived there. They were city officials, clergymen, doctors, lawyers, bankers, and other prominent businessmen who had knowledge of the way the residents lived their lives, if they went to church, paid their bills on time, how they ran their farms.

It was the mission of all agencies to find good homes with people of strong moral values. Did the committees get it wrong at times? How could they not? No one really knows what goes on behind closed doors. We all know a home can have a Norman Rockwell feel on the outside with wicked injustices going on inside. Some of the children ended up in great homes with loving families and others ended up being used as nothing more than labor. While some of the children were worse off than before they rode the orphan trains, most of the children were better off than if they would have remained in the city. Estimates show that eighty-seven percent of the placements during the seventy-five-year run turned out well.

Credits

My husband, and the keeper of my heart. Thank you for helping me remain calm in a not so calm world and for allowing me to bounce ideas off of you until the pathway clears.

My daughter, Brandy, who assists with postings, plus odds and ends. Thank you for helping me in the writing chair.

My family, who continues to help spread the word about my writings. I thank you.

Laura Prevost, thank you for these amazing covers, outstanding promotional art, and for being a friend.

To my editor, Beth, who gently nudges me forward when I resist cutting my favorite lines. Thank you.

To my beta/proofreaders, thank you for your eagle eyes and for being a part of my team.

To my fans, who are taking this journey with me, thank you for your continued support.

To Murdoc, my rambunctious standard poodle, if not for your persistent desire to go outside, I may never leave the writing chair.

Lastly, to my mother, who is finally at peace after a valiant battle with breast cancer. I miss you.

If you enjoyed this book, please take a moment and leave a review on one or more of these review platforms: Amazon, Barnes & Noble, Goodreads, Bookbub, and please help spread the word.

Coming December 2019, *Anastasia's Story.*

About the Author

Sherry A. Burton was born in Kentucky and married a Navy man at the age of eighteen. She and her husband have three children and seven grandchildren. They live in Michigan with their three cats and Standard poodle. She enjoys traveling to lectures and signing events, where she shares her books and speaks about the Orphan Trains.

CPSIA information can be obtained
at www.ICGtesting.com
Printed in the USA
FFHW011052240819
54431299-60119FF